**Streetwise stories from the
Private Eye Writers of America . . .**

Discover why Lombard Street is called the crookedest
street in the world when detective Nick Polo spies crime
through the eyes of a voyeur in **Jerry Kennealy**'s
"Carole on Lombard."

Get street-smart with Lupe Solano as she investigates the
seedy side of Miami's South Beach club scene in
"Washington Avenue" by **Carolina Garcia-Aguilera**.

Take the high road with dauntless detectives Trace and
Chico as they fly to London for a mysterious visit to the
late great Sherlock's home in **Warren Murphy**'s
"Highly Irregular on Baker Street."

**. . . and eleven more tales of wrong turns
and dead ends.**

The
PRIVATE EYE WRITERS OF AMERICA
presents

MYSTERY STREET

The 20th Anniversary PWA Anthology

Edited by
Robert J. Randisi

A SIGNET BOOK

SIGNET
Published by New American Library, a division of
Penguin Putnam Inc., 375 Hudson Street, New York, New York 10014, U.S.A.
Penguin Books Ltd, 27 Wrights Lane, London W8 5TZ, England
Penguin Books Australia Ltd, Ringwood, Victoria, Australia
Penguin Books Canada Ltd, 10 Alcorn Avenue, Toronto, Ontario, Canada M4V 3B2
Penguin Books (N.Z.) Ltd, 182–190 Wairau Road, Auckland 10, New Zealand

Penguin Books Ltd, Registered Offices:
Harmondsworth, Middlesex, England

First published by Signet, an imprint of New American Library,
a division of Penguin Putnam Inc.

First Printing, October 2001
10 9 8 7 6 5 4 3 2 1

CONTENTS

HOUSE PARTY
An Introduction to *Mystery Street*

by *Robert Crais*

There's this famous Gary Larson cartoon, the one with hawks and falcons and eagles perched in a tree, all of these birds sporting Ray-Ban shades and don't-bore-me 'tudes, the caption beneath the illustration reading: Birds of prey know they're cool.

Private-eye writers know they're cool, too, and for some very good reasons. People like our stuff. I offer as proof of the P.I.'s popularity (aka "coolness") Dashiell Hammett, Ross Macdonald, Mickey Spillane, Sue Grafton, Sara Paretsky, Walter Mosley, Robert B. Parker, and James Lee Burke, along with many others across a broad span of time—each of these authors having huge, blow-off-the-barn-door best-sellers spanning era, gender, and ethnicity. Clearly, a lot of readers think that private-eye fiction is cool, too.

Fictional private investigators are not some clichéd monolithic image: Humphrey Bogart in a snap-brim hat, cigarette dangling from his lip. By turns, fictional private investigators are as diverse as the people who create them: They are funny and morose, thoughtful and physical and many times both, violent and peaceful, dopers and clean, ethnically and geographically diverse, women and men, Christian and Jew, and, in a couple of cases, minors. The modern P.I. is a product of his or her times, reflecting, as does all vital fiction, the personal and real-world concerns of the men and women who create them. These differences make for a satisfying richness, but, if there is a unifying factor in all of this, some single element that explains the enduring popularity of the field, it is that of a character—a human being—who seeks some measure of order or truth or justice, often pitted against the far greater forces of an uncaring or hostile society. In short, the P.I. believes in *something*: some personal code of honor, some ethic of behavior, or—at the very least—some clear focus on the purpose at hand. These days, belief in anything seems rare. And, thinking about it, maybe it always has been rare.

Still, for all of this popularity and coolness, we who practice the art of P.I. fiction are a small and disreputable band, often seen as outsiders (think of the rude cousin who drinks too much and wears a loud Hawaiian shirt) to the larger family of mystery writers (mannered ladies in big hats and pipe-sucking gentlemen who retire to the drawing room for port). For the guys and the gals in the loud shirts, the Private Eye Writers of America is our gang, our family, our home. When you knock on the door, they might not like you much, but they're going to let you in.

Robert J. Randisi (himself a disreputable sort, given to drink, gambling, and questionable women) founded the PWA in 1981. It exists not only to honor the form and the practitioners of the art, but also to promote the well-being of our little corner of the universe. To do this, the PWA presents the Shamus Award to recognize excellence in the field, publishes a newsletter, holds an annual luncheon at the World Mystery Convention, and other neat stuff. The engine behind all these fine events is the aforementioned Mr. Randisi, a veritable one-man nuclear power plant of energy and ideas. But, in truth, the organization has grown beyond any one person. I know that Mr. Randisi would want it that way. It is all of us who write this stuff, and PWA will continue so long as readers want glimpses into the criminal underbelly of this world and the men and women—some good, some not—who work its shadows.

Now, in 2001, PWA has been in business for twenty years. No small feat, the way groups, organizations, and multibillion-dollar dot-coms appear and vanish overnight. Twenty years is a long time, baby, and we deserve a party.

So this book is our celebration, a birthday present to ourselves, and to *you*. It is also a doorway into our home, which we now open. Kick back. Enjoy. Welcome.

Let's rock the house.

NEW GUY ON THE BLOCK
A KEN SLIGO STORY

by Jack Bludis

**The Street: East Baltimore Street,
Baltimore, Maryland**

Jack Bludis is not a familiar name in this or any other genre, but that doesn't mean he hasn't written a ton of stories already. This one just happens to be his first P.I. story under his real name. And it's probably best introduced by the author himself:

The 400 block of East Baltimore Street, traditionally known as "the Block," isn't what it used to be, but there was a time when it was one of the hottest centers of vice on the East Coast. . . .

With a sure hand and a keen eye, Jack Bludis takes us back to that time.

"**B**ail bonds, tattoos, rubber goods, and hot dogs," said the fancy lettered sign in the front window of Sammy's Place. Inside there was a lot more, including the pervading aroma of hamburgers, fried onions, and the old grease that went along with them.

I had no idea which of Sammy's many enterprises netted him the most cash, but I suspected it was the bail bonds. I had just started as a private investigator, and for the last month, he had been calling me in to locate some of his bond skips. He already had his strong-arm guys to bring them in.

Sammy, short and overweight, leaned back in the swivel chair behind the desk at the rear of his establishment. Even from there he had a good view of the foot traffic on Baltimore's infamous Block with its strip joints, dirty-book stores, and penny arcades. He chewed the stub of his cigar, with dark-brown spit sloshing around in his mouth. Miraculously, he kept it from dripping down to his Hawaiian shirt.

"Get him out of here!" Sammy yelled past my ear.

I turned to see a blond-haired drunk in a rumpled suit stumble to the counter. He looked straight up at me, and the short-order cook made a sudden transition to bouncer. He ushered him out the front door, tumbling him to the sidewalk. He came back wiping his hands on his filthy apron as if the drunk had contaminated him.

"This one's murder." Sammy said, regaining my attention. "But you're a smart guy. It's worth a hundred bucks for you to find him."

In 1946, a hundred bucks was a lot of money, and just short of what I was getting for a full week's advance as a private investigator. Sammy gave me fifty on the other cases. I located all three skips in less than two days, but they were pretty easy: just punk kids who showed up at their mothers' houses.

He gave me a quick thumbnail of the story, and I commented, "I thought it was an unwritten law. If you find a guy in bed with your wife and you kill them—you're in the clear. Right?"

"Not if he tells his people he was gonna catch 'em at it. The 'unwritten law' only counts when it's a surprise."

"Oh." At thirty-one, I was learning something new every day, especially after being out of circulation with the war in Europe. The only thing I knew for sure was that I had a living to make, and catching wayward husbands and wives and looking for people and things seemed a better way to do it than working at my brother's butcher stall in the Lexington Market.

"Who said he was going to catch them?" I said.

"Ask the cops." He shrugged and told me that Vincent was a partner with Bennie Traveler in a strip joint called the Wannasea. It was pronounced, "Wanna see ya."

"This one sounds a little tough for me. Maybe I'll pass." I didn't like getting mixed up with murder.

"If you don't do this one, you can forget any more work from me. Maybe you can even forget being a private dick."

Owning any business on the Block implied influence with organized crime. I thought about ignoring his threat and taking my chances, but I didn't want to test him. Besides, I had no other jobs, and I needed the hundred bucks.

"OK," I said. "You got a picture?"

"I knew you was smart." Sammy reached into his top middle drawer and pulled out a glossy photo of some guy in a tux.

"Looks like a singer," I said.

"He was, before the war. Name's Chip Vincent. His face is kind of messed up now, but you'll recognize him. Here's everything I got on him."

Sammy turned over the eight-by-ten photo, and while he printed out some information in rough block letters on the back, I remembered that the double homicide happened just before my first job with Sammy.

"He doesn't live far from the club," I said, looking at the address. "Is that where he caught his wife?"

"That's it. If you get him by Sunday, I'll give you fifty extra."

"That's only a couple of days."

"If you want the bonus, you'll have him in."

I wanted the bonus.

Night people are easier to catch in the daytime, but you have to talk to their friends and associates first, and that's usually in the evening. I stopped up at the Central Branch of the Pratt Library to check the newspapers for the past month. I picked up some new detail and verified what I remembered about the case. Then I went home and took a long nap.

When I came back to the Block, it was nine-thirty. The war was over almost a year, but the street was still crowded with sailors out of Bainbridge and soldiers out of Meade and Hollibird. Some of them were mustering out, and some new ones were in training to replace the guys who hadn't come home yet.

Bouncers, who doubled as barkers, stood in front of most of the clubs shouting out their individual and sometimes raunchy versions of "Girl, girls, girls."

One barker grabbed my sleeve, but I brushed him off. The rest just shouted out their pitch. Some gestured toward the glossy photos behind the club windows, which usually showed women with pasties over their breasts and long, slit skirts that showed the full length of a leg. A staggering red-head stopped in front of me and asked if I wanted a good time.

"I'm having a good time," I said, and I walked around her.

I had managed to catch a wad of gum on the sole of my shoe, and I ground it off onto the curb in front of the blue-mirrored facade of the Wannasea. I glanced at the hand-printed sign that was pasted at the bottom of the wartime poster of Uncle Sam pointing. "Yes. We want to see *you!*" it said.

Like most of the clubs on the Block, they had live music—piano, bass, and drums. On the runway behind the horseshoe bar was a slightly overweight cutie stripping out of something that once upon a time had looked like an evening gown.

I slid up on one of the tall stools and ordered a bottle of National Bohemian Beer. There were six other guys at the bar, along with four women, but nobody at the tables. I wasn't there a minute when a tiny, straw-haired blonde slithered between me and the stool to my right and rubbed her breasts against my arm.

"Ah'm Charlene. You want some company?" she said. She dragged out the words in the thick accent of West—by God—Virginia.

"No, thanks. I'm looking for an old army buddy, name of Chip Vincent."

"You know Chip?" She was still trying to be casual, but she glanced over at the gray-haired bartender when I mentioned his name.

"We were together at the Bulge," I said. The papers said he had been decorated during the European campaign, and just about everybody was involved at the Bulge in one way or another, so I took a guess.

"He ain't been around for a while, but maybe I could keep you happy while you're lookin'."

"Maybe so," I said. "You know him?"

"Sure." The game was to keep me occupied while the bartender made her a drink and put it on my tab. I kept an eye on him, making sure it wasn't the twenty-dollar bottle of champagne he was working on. When the guy put together a phony mixed drink, I figured I'd put it on Sammy's expenses. He might balk, but Charles "Chip" Vincent had skipped on big bail, and Sammy stood to lose a lot of money if somebody didn't track him down.

"How is he?" I said.

She waited until the bartender put up a glass of ginger ale with ice and a cherry. She stirred her drink while he stepped away. "He's good . . . I guess."

"Is it true what they say?"

She spoke very quietly. "He didn't kill no wife."

"Why do the cops think so?"

"I ain't gonna talk about that." She looked toward the bartender.

"Is that Traveler?"

"Sure is. And if I was to tell him what you're askin', you'd be in all kinds of trouble."

"Is that so?"

She took a deep breath. "Now if you was to buy me a bottle of champagne, we might could go into one of them dark corners."

"I don't want to know that bad." I knew she worked for a percentage on the phony champagne, but I had an uneasy feeling about being there.

"Okay," she said, but I could tell that she wanted to talk as much as I wanted to listen.

I tasted the Boh from the bottle and looked straight ahead.

"You really one of his old army buddies?"

"Why would I say it if I wasn't?"

"Chip needs help," Charlene said. She held the glass to her lips so Traveler couldn't see her talking.

"Where is he?" I said, feeling like a traitor.

"Don't know," she said.

"You do tricks?"

Her face flushed so red, it showed through her makeup. "Uh, no. But . . . uh . . . I date."

"Good. What time do you get off?"

"If I don't get called by the boss, I'm usually on the street by two o'clock and thirty minutes."

"Maybe I'll stop back," I said.

The way I figured it, the management had already made me as no good in one way or another, and the chances of me talking to her again in the Wannasea were pretty remote. While I was thinking about it, and with me not so much as glancing at him, Traveler put up a bottle of champagne with a glass for the lady.

I peeled off a ten-dollar bill, dropped it to the bar, and started to walk away.

"Hey, pal. You gotta pay for the champagne!"

"There's enough for the drinks and tips for both of you. Put the champagne on the next sucker."

"Hey!" Charlene called, pretending indignation.

When I reached the front door, the barker-bouncer blocked my way. He was half a head shorter than me but at least that much wider. If I knew the routine, he was carrying at least a blackjack. I was carrying a .38, but neither one of us would use it unless the other showed first.

"Where you goin', pal?"

"You don't want trouble from me," I said, looking straight at him.

"I don't?"

"No."

Somebody behind me caught his attention. Then he said, "OK," and let me slide.

I glanced over my shoulder twice as I strolled up to the Gayette Burlesque Theater. Lili St. Cyr was making one of her few appearances in Baltimore, and I figured it was a good way to kill time. After a couple of preliminary acts, barkers came through the audience selling eight-by-ten glossies of the star, along with "dirty" magazines and "dirty story books," as they called them, but they were only risqué. The real dirty stuff was sold from under the counters in the bookstores and magazine stalls. Sammy even sold some of it, especially the nude glossies wrapped in cellophane.

Lili St. Cyr did a kind of reverse strip by getting out of a bathtub and getting dressed. She did it in such a way that it was far more exciting than the strippers who made that final little move of slipping their G-string to their thigh, and going naked below the waist. It was the only time I ever saw Miss St. Cyr, but it was also one of the few strips I actually remember. Even now it's like a picture going through my head.

After the show, I made it a point to stay away from Sammy's. At two a.m., I sat near the window in a different hot-dog joint drinking some coffee and watching the front door of the Wannasea. I saw my own reflection inside the window, but I also saw the blond guy who had been thrown out of Sammy's this morning. He had cleaned up, and he was nursing coffee at the bar.

At about two-twenty Charlene, in a yellow dress and a red cotton coat, stepped onto the sidewalk. She looked around, confused for a moment. Then she walked east on Baltimore Street. A half block later, a guy wearing a sports jacket grabbed her by the arm. Any woman, whether whore, lady, or schoolgirl, was fair game on the Block at that time of the morning.

"Ah don't think so, honey. Not tonight," she said.

"Come on," he said. "Twenty bucks."

"Sweetheart!" I said.

"Hi!" she said, as if the word were all H's, and she beamed a smile at me.

The guy in the jacket looked at me. His eyes were glazed over, but he thought he knew trouble when he saw it. "I didn't know this was your, uh . . ."

"My girlfriend, right. I'm here now."

"Oh," the guy said, and he stumbled away.

"You want to go get some breakfast?" I said.

"Y'mind if we get a cab?"

Charlene said nothing until the cab stopped at a place just west of downtown that was alleged to be a tavern owned by Babe Ruth's father. The waitress brought us our coffee before Charlene even looked up at me.

"He didn't kill her, you know."

"You told me that."

"They want him dead."

"Who wants him dead?"

"Traveler. If Chip does time up to Greenmount Avenue, he gets it all."

What Charlene called "Greenmount Avenue" was the location of the State Penitentiary and the City Jail, just a few blocks north of downtown.

I nodded and looked down into my black coffee. I recalled the old saying about not looking a gift horse in the mouth, but I also remembered the one about being wary of Greeks bearing gifts.

"Why are you telling me this?"

"'Cause I don't want nothin' to happen to him." Her speech had a cute lilt. I'm a sucker for those southern girls, or maybe it's mountain girls. I can hardly tell them apart.

"You in love with him?"

She didn't answer. Then she went back to another subject. "Why you lookin' for him?"

"For his own protection." It was only half a lie, because

if what she said was true, he was probably in more danger on the street than uptown. "Where is he?"

"You're working for Sammy, ain't you?"

Apparently, my expression had given something away, because her eyes widened. "You are a rotten bastard. Do you know that?"

I knew it.

She pushed back from the table and started for the door.

"Hey," I called, but she kept walking.

I left two dollars and started after her, but by the time I reached the sidewalk, the same red, white, and blue taxi was pulling away from the curb with her in it.

I knew from my friend Detective Vyto Kastel that there were seven individuals who, in one way or another, had an interest in every business on the Block. Either they owned it, were part owner, or accepted a fee from the owner for protection against everyone, including the vice cops. Traveler, who I had heard of in other regards, might be one of them, so I called Vyto at home. Friend that he was, he gave me no crap, even at three in the morning.

"He's slime," Vyto said, referring to Traveler, "but he ain't that far up the ladder."

We had been together on the streets of the Central District before the war. Vyto got wounded early and came back to become a detective. I was back six months after V-J Day. By that time all the police jobs were filled, and I was on a waiting list.

"I thought Chip was a singer?"

"Yeah, he was a good singer too, but one thing led to another and before you know it, he was breaking skulls and working into a partnership with Traveler."

"Skull breakers don't usually get married, do they?"

"He was still a singer when that happened."

"Is the State's Attorney going to push for murder one?"

"Maybe two counts of aggravated manslaughter. He killed them both, you know."

"He caught 'em in bed."

"He knew they were going to be there."

"That's what Sammy says."

"Talk about slime," he said.

"What did you find in his house?"

"Not a thing except the bodies, the suspect, and some clothes he didn't wear the night of the murder."

"Papers said you had the gun?"

"He threw it out the window and into the river."

"How'd you know that?"

"Anonymous tip."

"Middle-of-the-night tip? Interesting."

"Somebody walking along on the other side of the water saw him toss it. The bullets are from the same gun. Looks like a GI souvenir. We got everything we needed. The house ain't even a crime scene anymore."

"Was he mixed up in anything?"

"How do you mean?"

"Prostitution? Gambling?"

"You know the Block. Who's not mixed up with one or the other?"

"You got me there." I thanked him and hung up.

Kastel telling me that Vincent's place was no longer a crime scene was like an invitation to take a look. The two-story brick row house on Front Street was a few blocks away from the Wannasea. It backed up onto the Jones Falls River, a narrow waterway that was little more than a sluice for garbage.

I was uneasy as I approached the house, but not about what was inside. A vague thought in the back of my head told me there was something else I should be aware of. I reached across the single marble step and knocked on the door. I looked both ways on the street, but all I saw was an old lady sweeping a sidewalk two blocks away. No one answered the third knock, and it was easy to get in. A head breaker should have better locks.

I eased into the living room, which showed a dim blue through the paper window blinds. The dining room and kitchen on the other side of the enclosed stairs glowed almost gold from the back blinds, putting a shine on the linoleum-covered floors.

If he had shot them in bed, the murder scene would be on the second floor. So I climbed the narrow stairs, stepping lightly where I thought the steps would be nailed to the supports. I reached the landing and looked both ways. There was nothing in the tiny front room except a vanity dresser with a large mirror and a chair. A double bed would have made it impossible to move in there. The shades in the long bedroom at the back of the house were up, and everything was bright.

Somebody had taken the sheets from the bed, but there were bullet holes in the mattress, along with two bloodstains about the size of basketballs. The rest of the blood was smeared in streaks. There was a crucifix on the wall over the bed.

Apparently, Chip Vincent had come to the top of the stairs, taken three or four quiet steps, and let them have it up close, blam, blam, blam. How many blams, I didn't know, but I wasn't looking for evidence of murder. The cops already had what they needed.

I crossed the room and looked out the back windows.

Somebody could easily throw a gun into the river from there.

"Who the hell are you?" said someone behind me.

I turned and recognized Vincent from the glossy. He wasn't as pretty as in the photo, and he wasn't as young either. His right cheek had been crushed at one time or another, and he seemed almost sightless in that eye. He was pointing a revolver at me.

"I'm working for Sammy. I've been trying to find you." It was what I planned to say all along, but not under these circumstances.

"That son of a bitch would sell his grandmother," Vincent said.

I had no doubt about that, but what I said was, "Do you want to come in with me?"

"Hell, no! You told me who you're working for, but you didn't tell me who you are."

"Oh," I started to reach for my wallet.

"No, no!" He waved the revolver.

From the light coming through the back windows, I saw that he had no shells in the cylinder of his gun, but I kept my hands up as a matter of deceit.

"Name's Ken Sligo. I'm a private investigator, and pretty new at it. I just got back from Europe."

"Ain't that a coincidence? Me too."

"So your wife was one of those bad girls?"

"Yeah, but I didn't kill her *or* the guy."

"Everybody says so."

"Everybody says so because I found them. I called the cops too. And first thing they did was lock me up."

"They found your gun in the river."

"Not my gun."

"So why did you skip?"

"People follow you, and you start to get suspicious, especially after they take a couple of shots at you. That's all I needed to run for cover."

"Look, Vincent. I've got no beef with you. If you didn't kill your wife, that's fine, because it probably means you won't kill me. But I'm getting paid to do a job. So why don't we—"

"That bastard Sammy. He gets me out on bail; then he sets me up."

"You know the rules. You skip, and Sammy comes after you. You can't blame the guy. He put up good money, and he don't want to lose it." It was argument for argument's sake, because I had some other ideas that were just about to be verified.

Behind him, someone peeked around the wall from the stairway. It was exactly who I thought it might be, the blond guy who had been thrown from Sammy's yesterday. He was carrying a sawed-off shotgun, and I could see by the angry look that he intended to use it.

"Look out!" I shouted.

The blond guy thought I was warning him, and he looked behind him. I lunged past Vincent and pushed the double-barreled shotgun up and away, and it blasted off, slamming the wall with shot and scattering plaster onto the mattress along with the splintered crucifix.

If Vincent got killed here in front of me, I would be the major witness to the bounty hunter's argument of self-defense, and I wasn't going to let that happen.

With his empty revolver, Vincent swung his arm in our direction. He could only be going for a kind of self-orchestrated suicide, I thought as I twisted the shotgun in the blond guy's arms and wrestled him to the floor.

"You've been set up," I said.

"No crap!" Vincent said, and the shotgun blasted off again, this time under the bed, with shot pinging at the springs and bouncing all over the linoleum. The blond guy reached under his coat, but when he saw Vincent's revolver point-blank at his nose, he slipped his hand away and let his arm slump to the floor.

I went up on my knees and looked up at Vincent. "Let me take you in."

"Get his gun," Vincent said.

I reached inside the blond guy's coat and pulled the automatic from his shoulder holster.

"You're working for Sammy, aren't you?" I said.

"You dumb bastard," the blond guy said, but I didn't think so.

"There are no shells in your gun," I said to Vincent, as I rose to my feet.

The blond guy tried to get up, but I put my foot on his chest and aimed the .45 at his face.

"Sammy'll get you for this," he said.

"Sammy might fire me, but he won't get me."

Sammy had been setting me up to be his witness in the death of Chip Vincent from the first time he hired me. That was why he gave me the easy jobs right after Vincent was arrested, and it was why he insisted that I take this one. He didn't need me to find anybody. His strong-arms knew as much about finding skips as I did. Sammy had just eased me along, waiting to use me for his big kill.

"You looked at me a little too close in Sammy's," I said to the blond guy. "And you followed me too close. It took me till now to figure out why."

I glanced over at Vincent. "I'll take you in. You'll get a much better shake."

"You got the gun with bullets," Vincent said, and he smiled. "But make damn sure you take me to the cops."

"Sammy set you up. Traveler wanted the whole business for himself, right?"

"He wanted my half. He don't even own half anymore. It's in hock to Sammy, and he can't make it up."

I took the .38 from Vincent. I broke it, verified there were no shells, and slipped it into my jacket pocket. He tied the blond guy to the springs of the bed with his shoestrings, and we left the house. We knew he'd break free before the cops came back, but it kept him out of our way for a while.

"You gonna keep his .45?" Vincent said, as we walked the three blocks to the Central Police Station. I had a gun in both pockets and another on my hip.

"Not if he's got a permit," I said.

"Fat chance."

That's what I thought.

The cops took a while, but they finally got Traveler and the blond guy in a murder-for-hire scheme. Vincent's wife was Traveler's girlfriend and she was two-timing both of them with one of Traveler's creditors.

Chip Vincent was exonerated, but for whatever reason, they couldn't put Sammy in jail. A lot of people knew he was in on it, but there was no proof. All I had was a hunch that the blond guy had come into Sammy's that first morning to get a look at me, but hunches didn't fly in court even in those days. Maybe Sammy just paid the right people. He even gave me a bonus for the quick track. I might be wrong about his involvement, but I didn't think so.

I still work the Block now and then, because wayward husbands often make the trip there. I don't work for Sammy anymore though, and he's still slime.

SHOOT-OUT ON SUNSET
A NATHAN HELLER STORY

by *Max Allan Collins*

**Street: Sunset Boulevard,
Los Angeles, California**

For the past sixteen years or so Max Allan Collins has been
chronicling the cases of Nathan Heller, Chicago ex-cop
turned P.I. Over the course of ten books, Collins has been
nominated for the Best Novel Shamus countless times and
has won twice. He has taken Heller from the 30's up to—in
this story—1949, taken his detective agency from a one-man
operation to a multipersonnel agency with offices in Chicago
and L.A. And along the way, Heller has encountered gangsters and cops from Al Capone and Frank Nitti to Eliott Ness.

In this story, Nate finds himself involved with Mickey
Cohen in—as usual—an incident based on actual fact. Many
of the names in these books and stories have been changed
to protect the innocent and not-so-innocent, but as long as
you see the names Nathan Heller and Max Allan Collins, you
know you're in for a hell of—or Heller of—a time.

The Sunset Strip—the center of Hollywood's nightlife—
lay near the heart of Los Angeles, or would have if L.A.
had a heart. I'm not waxing poetic, either: Postwar L.A.
(circa late summer 1949) sprawled over some 452 square
miles, but isolated strips of land within the city limits were

nonetheless not part of the city. Sunset Boulevard itself ran from downtown to the ocean, around twenty-five miles; west on Sunset, toward Beverly Hills—roughly a mile and a half, from Crescent Heights Boulevard to Doheny Drive— the Strip threaded through an unincorporated area surrounded by (but not officially part of) the City of Angels.

Prime nightspots like the Trocadero, Ciro's, the Mocambo, and the Crescendo shared the glittering Strip with smaller, hipper clubs and hideaway restaurants like Slapsy Maxie's, the Little New Yorker, and the Band Box. Seediness and glamour intermingled, grit met glitz, as screen legends, power brokers, and gangsters converged in West Hollywood for a free-spirited, no-holds-barred good time.

The L.A. police couldn't even make an arrest on the Strip, which was under the jurisdiction of County Sheriff Eugene Biscailuz, who cheerfully ignored both the city's cops and its ordinances. Not that the L.A. coppers would have made any more arrests than the sheriff's deputies: the vice squad was well known to operate chiefly as a shakedown racket. A mighty bookmaking operation was centered on the Sunset Strip, and juice was paid to both the county sheriff and the city vice squad. This seemed unfair to Mickey Cohen.

The diminutive, dapper, vaguely simian Cohen was a former Ben "Bugsy" Siegel associate, who had built his bookie empire on the bodies of his competitors. Rivals with such colorful names as Maxie Shaman, Benny "the Meatball" Gambino, and Tony Trombino were just a few of the violently deceased gangsters who had unwillingly made way for Mickey; and the Godfather of Southern California—Jack Dragna—could only grin and bear it and put up with Cohen's bloody empire building. Cohen had the blessing of the east coast Combination—Luciano, Meyer Lanksy, the late Siegel's crowd—and old-time Prohibition-era mob boss Dragna didn't like it. A West Coast mob war had been brewing for years.

I knew Cohen from Chicago, where in the late 30's he was strictly a small-time gambler and general-purpose hoodlum. Our paths had crossed several times since—never in a nasty way—and I rather liked the street-smart, stupid-looking Mick. He was nothing if not colorful: owned dozens of suits, wore monogrammed silk shirts and made-to-order shoes, drove a $15,000 custom-built blue Caddy, lived with his pretty little wife in a $150,000 home in classy Brentwood, and suffered a cleanliness fetish that had him washing his hands more than Lady MacBeth.

A fixture of the Sunset Strip, Mick strutted through clubs spreading dough around like advertising leaflets. One of his primary hangouts was Sherry's, a cocktail lounge-slash-restaurant, a favorite film-colony rendezvous, whose nondescript brick exterior was offset by an ornate interior.

My business partner, Fred Rubinski, was co-owner of Sherry's. Fireplug Fred—who resembled a slightly better-looking Edward G. Robinson—was an ex-Chicago cop who had moved out here before the war to open a detective agency. We'd known each other in Chicago, both veterans of the pickpocket detail, and I too had left the Windy City PD to go private, only I hadn't gone west, young man.

At least, not until after the war. The A-1 Detective Agency—of which I, Nathan Heller, was president—had (over the course of a decade and change) grown from a one-man, hole-in-the-wall affair over a deli on Van Buren to a suite of offices in the Monadnock Building rife with operatives, secretaries, and clients. Expansion seemed the thing, and I convinced my old pal Fred to throw in with me. So, starting in late '46, the Los Angeles branch operated out of the Bradbury Building at Third and Broadway, with Fred—now vice president of the A-1—in charge, while I of course kept the Chicago offices going.

Only it seemed, more and more, I was spending time in California. My wife was an actress, and she had moved out here with our infant son after the marriage went quickly south. The divorce wasn't final yet, and in my weaker moments, I still had hopes of patching things up, and was looking at finding an apartment or small house to rent, so I could divide my time between L.A. and Chicago. In July of '49, however, I was in a bungalow at the Beverly Hills Hotel, for whom the A-1 handled occasional security matters, an arrangement which included the perk of free lodgings.

Like Cohen, Fred Rubinski attempted to make up for his homeliness with natty attire, such as the blue suit with gray pinstripes and the gray-and-white silk tie he wore as he sat behind his desk in his Bradbury Building office, a poolcue Havana shifting from corner to corner of his thick lips.

"Just do it as a favor to me, Nate," Fred said.

I was seated across from him, in the client chair, ankle on a knee. "You don't do jobs for Cohen—why should I?"

Fred patted the air with his palms; blue cigar smoke swirled around him like a wreath. "You don't have to do a job for him—just hear him out. He's a good customer at Sherry's, and I don't wanna cross him."

"You also don't want to do jobs for him."

A window air conditioner was chugging; hot day. Fred and I had to speak up over it.

"I use the excuse that I'm too well known out here," my partner said. "Also, the Mickster and me are already considered to be cronies, 'cause of Sherry's. He knows the cops would use that as an excuse to come down on me, hard, if suddenly I was on Mickey Cohen's retainer."

"But you're not asking me to do this job."

"No. Absolutely not. Hell, I don't even know what it is."

"You can guess."

"Well . . . I suppose you know he's been kind of a clay pigeon lately. Several attempts on his life, probably by Dragna's people . . . Mick probably wants a bodyguard."

"I don't do that kind of work anymore. Anyway, what about those Seven Dwarfs of his?"

That was how Cohen's inner circle of lieutenants/strong-arms were known—Neddie Herbert, Davy Ogul, Frank Niccoli, Johnny Stompanato, Al Snyder, Jimmy Rist, and the late Hooky Rothman, who about a year ago had got his face shot off when guys with shotguns came barging right into Cohen's clothing shop. I liked my face right where it was.

"Maybe it's not a bodyguard job," Fred said with a shrug. "Maybe he wants you for something else."

I shifted in the chair. "Fred, I'm trying to distance myself from these mobsters. My connections with the Outfit back home, I'm still trying to live down—it's not good for the A-1."

"Tell him! Just don't insult the man . . . don't piss him off."

I got up, smoothing out my suit. "Fred, I was raised right. I hardly ever insult homicidal gangsters."

"You've killed a few, though."

"Yeah," I said from the doorway, "but I didn't insult them."

The haberdashery known poshly as Michael's was a two-story brick building in the midst of boutiques and nighteries at 8804 Sunset Boulevard. I was wearing a tan tropical worsted sportcoat and brown summer slacks, with a rust-colored tie and two-tone Florsheims, an ensemble that had chewed up a hundred bucks in Marshall Field's men's department and spit out pocket change. But the going rates inside this plush shop made me look like a piker.

Within the highly polished walnut walls, a few ties lay on a central glass counter, sporting silky sheens and twenty-five buck price tags. A rack of sportshirts ran seventy-five per, a stack of dress shirts ran in the hundred range. A luxurious brown robe on a headless manikin—a memorial to Hooky Rothman?—cost a mere two hundred bucks, and the sportcoats went for two hundred up, the suits three to four. Labels boasted: "Tailored Exclusively for Mickey Cohen."

A mousy little clerk—a legit-looking joker with a wispy mustache, wearing around five C's worth of this stuff—looked at me as if a hobo had wandered into the shop.

"May I help you?" he asked, stuffing more condescension into four words than I would have thought humanly possible.

"Tell your boss Nate Heller's here," I said casually, as I poked around at the merchandise.

This was not a front for a bookmaking joint: Cohen really did run a high-end clothing store; but he also supervised his other, bigger business—which was extracting protection money from bookmakers, reportedly $250 per week per phone—out of here, as well. Something in my manner told the effete clerk that I was part of the backroom business, and his patronizing manner disappeared.

His whispered-into-a-phone conversation included my name, and soon he was politely ushering me to the rear of the store, opening a steel-plated door, and gesturing me into a walnut-paneled, expensively appointed office.

Mayer Harris Cohen—impeccably attired in a double-breasted light-gray suit, with a gray-and-green paisley silk tie—sat behind a massive mahogany desk whose glass-topped surface bore three phones, a small clock with pen-

and-pencil holder, a vase with cut flowers, a notepad, and no other sign of work. Looming over him was an ornately framed hand-colored photograph of FDR at his own desk, cigarette holder at a jaunty angle.

Standing on either side, like Brillcreamed bookends, were two of Cohen's dark-eyed Dwarfs: Johnny Stompanato, a matinee-idol handsome hood who I knew a little; and hook-nosed Frank Niccoli, who I knew even less. They were as well dressed as their boss.

"Thanks for droppin' by, Nate," Cohen said affably, not rising. His thinning black hair was combed close to his egg-shaped skull; with his broad forehead, blunt nose, and pugnacious chin, the pint-sized gangster resembled a bull terrier.

"Pleasure, Mickey," I said, hat in my hands.

Cohen's dark eyes flashed from bodyguard to bodyguard. "Fellas, some privacy?"

The two nodded at their boss, but each stopped—one at a time—to acknowledge me as they headed to a side door to an adjacent room (not into the shop).

"Semper fi, mac," Stompanato said, flashing his movie-star choppers. He always said this to me, since we were both ex-Marines.

"Semper fi," I said.

Niccoli stopped in front of me and smiled, but it seemed forced. "No hard feelings, Heller."

"About what?"

"You know. No hard feelings. It was over between us, anyway."

"Frank, I don't know what you're talking about."

His hard, pockmarked puss puckered into an expression that, accompanied by a dismissive wave, implied "no big deal."

When the bodyguards were gone, Cohen gestured for me to sit on the couch against the wall, opposite his desk. He rose to his full five-six and went to a console radio against the wall and switched it on. Frankie Laine was singing "Mule Train" . . . loud. Then Cohen trundled over and sat next to me, saying quietly, barely audible with the blaring radio going, "You can take Frankie at his word."

At first I thought he was talking about Frankie Laine, then I realized he meant Niccoli.

"Mick," I said, whispering back, not knowing why but following his lead, "I don't know what the hell he's talking about."

Cohen's eyes were wide—he almost always had a startled-deer look. "You're dating Didi Davis, right?"

Didi was a starlet I was seeing, casually; I might have been trying to patch up my marriage, but I wasn't denying myself the simple pleasures.

"Yeah, I met her a couple weeks ago at Sherry's."

"Well, Nate, she used to be Frankie's girl."

Cohen smelled like a barber shop got out of hand—reeking heavily of talcum powder and cologne, which did nothing to cover his perpetual five o'clock shadow.

"I didn't know that, Mick. She didn't say anything. . . ."

A whip cracked on the radio as "Mule Train" wound down.

Cohen shrugged. "It's over. She got tired of gettin' slapped around, I guess. Anyway, if Frankie says he don't hold no grudge, he don't hold no grudge."

"Well, that's just peachy." I hated it when girls forgot to mention their last boyfriend was a hoodlum.

Vaughn Monroe was singing "Ghost Riders in the Sky" on the radio—in full nasal throttle. And we were still whispering.

Cohen shifted his weight. "Listen, you and me, we never had no problems, right?"

"Right."

"And you know your partner, Fred and me, we're pals."

"Sure."

"So I figured I'd throw some work your way."

"Like what, Mick?"

He was sitting sideways on the couch, to look at me better; his hands were on his knees. "I'm gettin' squeezed by a pair of vice cops—Delbert Potts and Rudy Johnson, fuckers' names. They been tryin' to sell me recordings."

"Frankie Laine? Vaughn Monroe?"

"Very funny. These pricks got wire recordings of me, they say, business transactions, me and who-knows-who discussing various illegalities . . . I ain't heard anything yet. But they're trying to shake me down for twenty G's—this goes well past the taste they're gettin' already from my business."

Now I understood why he was whispering, and why the radio was blasting.

"We're not talking protection," I said, "but straight blackmail."

"On the nose. I want two things, Heller—I want my home and my office, whadyacallit, checked for bugs . . ."

"Swept."

"Huh?"

"Swept for bugs. That's what it's called, Mick."

"Yeah, well, that's what I want—part of what I want. I also want to put in my own wiretaps and bugs and get those two greedy bastards on my recordings of them shakin' me down."

"Good idea—create a standoff."

He twitched a smile, apparently pleased by my approval. "You up for doing that?"

"It's not my speciality, Mick—but I can recommend somebody. Guy named Vaus, Jim Vaus. Calls himself an 'electronics engineering consultant.' He's in Hollywood."

The dark eyes tightened but retained their deer-in-the-headlights quality. "You've used this guy?"

"Yeah . . . well, Fred has. But what's important is, the cops use him, too."

"They don't have their own guy?"

"Naw. They don't have anybody like that on staff—they're a backward bunch. Jim's strictly freelance. Hell, he may be the guy who bugged you for the cops."

"But can he be trusted?"

"If you pay him better than the LAPD—which won't be hard—you'll have a friend for life."

"How you wanna handle this, Nate? Through your office, or will this, what's-his-name, Vaus, kick back a little to you guys, or—"

"This is just a referral, Mick, just a favor . . . I think I got one of his cards. . . ."

I dug the card out of my wallet and gave it to Cohen, whose big brown eyes were dancing with sugarplums.

"This is great, Nate!"

I felt relieved, like I'd dodged a bullet. I had helped Cohen without having to take him on as a client.

So I said, "Glad to have been of service," and began to get up, only Cohen stopped me with a small but firm hand on my forearm.

Bing Crosby was singing "Dear Hearts and Gentle People" on the radio—casual and easygoing and loud as hell.

"What's the rush, Nate? I got more business to talk."

Sitting back down, I just smiled and shrugged and waited for the pitch.

It was a fastball: "I need you should bodyguard me."

"Jesus, Mick, with guys like Stompanato and Niccoli around? What the hell would you need me for?"

He was shaking his head; he had a glazed expression. "These vice cops, they got friends in the sheriff's office. My boys been gettin' rousted regularly—me, too. Half the time when we leave this place, we get shoved up against the wall and checked for concealed weapons."

"Oh. Is that what happened to Happy Meltzer?"

"On the nose again! Trumped-up gun charge. And these vice cops are behind it—and maybe Jack Dragna, who's in bed with the sheriff's department. Dragna would like nothin' better than to get me outa the picture, without makin' our mutual friends back east sore."

"Hell, Mick, how do you see me figuring in this?"

"You're a private detective, licensed for bodyguard work. Licensed to carry a weapon! Shit, man, I need somebody armed standin' at my side, to keep me from gettin' my ass shot off! Just a month ago, somebody took a blast at me with a shotgun, and then we found a bomb under my house, and . . ."

He rattled on, as I thought about his former bodyguard, Hooky Rothman, getting his face shot off in that posh shop just beyond the metal-lined door.

"I got friends in the attorney general's office," he was saying, "and they tell me they got an inside tip that there's a contract out on yours truly—there's supposed to be two triggers in from somewhere on the east coast to do the job. I need somebody with a gun next to me."

"Mickey," I said, "I have to decline. With all due respect."

"You're not makin' me happy, Nate."

"I'm sorry. I'm in no position to help out. First off, I don't live out here, not full-time, anyway. Second, I have a reputation of mob connections that I'm trying to live down."

"You're disappointing me. . . ."

"I'm trying to get my branch office established out here, and you and Fred being friends—you hanging out at Sherry's—that's as far as our relationship, personal or professional, can go."

He thought about that. Then he nodded and shrugged. "I ain't gonna twist your arm . . . two grand a week, just for the next two weeks?"

That might have been tempting, if Cohen hadn't already narrowly escaped half-a-dozen hit attempts.

"You say you got friends in the attorney general's office?" I asked.

"Yeah. Fred Howser and me are like this." He held up his right hand, forefinger and middle finger crossed.

If the attorney general himself was on Cohen's pad, then those wire recordings the vice cops had might implicate Howser. . . .

"Mick, ask Howser to assign one of his men to you as a bodyguard."

"A cop?"

"Who better? He'll be armed, he'll be protecting a citizen, and anyway, a cop to a hoodlum is like garlic to a vampire. Those triggers'll probably steer clear, long as a state investigator is at your side."

Cohen was thinking that over; then he began to nod.

"Not a bad idea," he said. "Not a bad idea at all."

I stood. "No consulting fee, Mick. Let's stay friends—and not do business together."

He snorted a laugh, stood, and went over and shut off the radio, cutting off Mel Torme singing "Careless Hands."

Then he walked me to the steel-lined door and—when I extended my hand—shook with me.

As I was leaving, I heard him in the private bathroom off his office, tap running, as he washed up—removing my germs.

I had a couple stops to make, unrelated to the Cohen appointment, so it was late afternoon when I made it back to the Beverly Hills Hotel. Entering my bungalow—nothing fancy, just a marble fireplace, private patio, and furnishings no more plush than the palace at Versailles—I heard something . . . someone . . . in the bedroom. Rustling around in there.

My nine-millimeter was in my suitcase, and my suitcase was in the bedroom. And I was just about to exit, to find a hotel dick or maybe call a cop, when my trained detective's nose sniffed a clue, and I walked across the living room and pushed the door open.

Didi Davis gasped; she was wearing glittery earrings—just glittery earrings, and the Chanel Number Five I'd nosed—and was poised, pulling back the covers, apparently about to climb into bed. She looked like a French maid who forgot her costume.

"I wanted to surprise you," she said. She was a lovely brunette, rather tall—maybe five-nine—with a willowy figure that would have seemed skinny if not for pert breasts and an impertinent dimpled behind. She was tanned all over. Her hair was up. It wasn't alone.

"I thought you were working at Republic today," I said, undoing my tie.

She crawled under the covers, and the sheets made inviting, crinkly sounds. "Early wrap . . . I tipped a bellboy to let me in."

Soon I was under covers, equally naked, leaning on a pillow. "You know, I run with kind of a rough crowd—surprises like this can backfire."

"I just wanted to do something sweet for you," she said.

And she proceeded to do something sweet for me.

Half an hour later, still in the bedroom, we were getting dressed when I brought up the rough crowd she ran with.

"Why didn't you mention you used to date Frank Niccoli?"

She was fastening a nylon to her garter belt, long, lovely leg stretched out as if daring me to be mad at her. "I don't know—Nate, you and I met at Sherry's after all. You hang around with those kind of people. What's the difference?"

"The difference is, suppose he's a jealous type. Niccoli isn't your average ex-beau—he's a goddamn thug. Is it true he smacked you around?"

She was putting on her other nylon, fastening it, smoothing it; this kind of thing could get boring in an hour or two. "That's why I walked out on him. I warned him, and he said he wouldn't do it again, and then a week later, he did it again."

"Has he bothered you? Confronted you in public? Called you on the phone?"

"No. It's over. He knows it, and I know it . . . now you know it. Okay, Nate? Do I ask you questions about your ex-wife?"

Didi didn't know my wife wasn't officially my ex yet, nor that I was still hoping to rekindle those flames. She thought I was a great guy, unaware that I was a heel who would never marry another actress but would gladly sleep with one.

"Let's drop it," I said.

"What a wonderful idea." She stood, easing her slip down over her nyloned legs, and was shimmying into her casual light-blue dress when the doorbell rang. Staying in a bungalow at the Beverly Hills, incidentally, was the only time I can recall a hotel room having a doorbell.

"I'm not expecting company," I told her, "but stay in here, would you? And keep mum?"

"I need to put my makeup on—"

The bell rang again—pretty damn insistent.

I got my nine-millimeter out of the suitcase, stuffed it in my waistband, and slipped on my sport jacket to cover it. "Just sit down—there's some magazines by the bed. We don't need to advertise."

She saw the common sense of that and nodded. No alarm had registered in her eyes at the sight of the weapon; but then, she'd been Niccoli's girl, hadn't she?

I shut her in there and went to answer the door.

I'd barely cracked the thing open when the two guys came barging in, the first one in brushing past me, the second slamming the door.

I hadn't even had a chance to say "Hey!" when the badge in the wallet was thrust in my face.

"Lieutenant Delbert Potts," he said, putting the wallet away. He was right on top of me, and his breath was terrible: it smelled like anchovies taste. "L.A. vice squad. This is my partner, Sergeant Rudy Johnson."

Potts was a heavy-set character in an off-the-rack brown suit that looked slept in; hatless, he had greasy, reddish-blond hair, and his drink-reddened face had a rubbery softness. His eyes were bloodshot, his nose as misshapen as a blob of putty somebody had stuck there carelessly, his lips thick and plump and vaguely obscene.

Johnson was thin and dark—both his features and his physique—and his navy suit looked tailored. He wore a black snap-brim that had set him back a few bucks.

"Fancy digs, Mr. Heller," Potts said, prowling the place, his thick-lipped smile conveying disgust. He had a slurry voice—he reminded me of a loathsome Arthur Godfrey, if that wasn't redundant.

"I do some work for the hotel," I said. "They treat me right when I'm out here."

"You goin' back to Chicago soon?" Johnson asked, right next to me. He had a reedy voice, and his eyes seemed sleepy unless you noticed the sharpness under the half lids.

"Not right away."

I'd never met this pair, yet they knew my name and knew I was from Chicago. And they hadn't taken me up on my offer to sit down.

"You might reconsider," Potts said. He was over at the wet bar, checking out the brands.

"Help yourself," I said.

"We're on duty," Johnson said.

"Fellas—what's this about?"

Potts wandered back over to me and thumped me on the chest with a thick finger. "You stopped by Mickey Cohen's today."

"That's right. He wanted me to do a job for him—I turned him down."

The bloodshot eyes tightened. "You turned him down? Are you sure?"

"I have a real good memory, Lieutenant. I remember damn near everything that happened to me, all day."

"Funny." That awful breath was warm in my face—fishy smell. "You wouldn't kid a kidder, would you?"

Backing away, I said, "Fellas—make your point."

Potts kept moving in on me, his breath in my face, like a foul furnace, his finger thumping at my chest. "You and your partner . . . Rubinski . . . you shouldn't be so thick with that little kike."

"Which little kike?"

Johnson said, "Mickey Cohen."

I looked from one to the other. "I already told you guys—I turned him down. I'm not working for him."

Potts asked, "What job did he want you for?"

"That's confidential."

He swung his fist into my belly. I did not see it coming, nor did I expect a slob like him to have such power. I dropped to my knees and thought about puking on the oriental carpet. I also thought about the gun in my waistband.

Slowly, I got to my feet. And when I did, the nine-millimeter was in my hand.

"Get the fuck out of my room," I said.

Both men backed away, alarm widening their seen-it-all eyes. Potts blurted, "You can be arrested for—"

"This is licensed, and you clowns barged into my room and committed assault on me."

Potts had his hands up; he seemed nervous, but he might have been faking, while he looked for an opening. "I shouldn'ta swung on ya. I apologize—now, put the piece away."

"No." I motioned toward the door with the Browning. "You're about to go, gents, but first—here's everything you need to know: I'm not working for Cohen, and neither is Fred."

The two exchanged glances, Johnson shaking his head.

"Why don't you put that away," Potts said, with a want-some-candy-little-girl smile, "and we'll talk."

"We have talked. Leave."

I pressed forward and the two backed up—toward the door.

"You better be tellin' the truth," Potts said, anger swimming in his rheumy eyes.

I opened the door for them. "What the hell have you been eating, Potts? Your breath smells like hell."

The cop's blotchy face reddened, but his partner let out a single sharp laugh. "Sardine sandwiches—it's all he eats on stakeouts."

That tiny moment of humanity between Johnson and me ended the interview; then they were out the door, and I shut and night-latched it. I watched them through the window as they moved through the hotel's garden-like grounds, Potts taking the lead, clearly pissed off, the flowering shrubs around him doing nothing to soothe him.

In the bedroom, Didi was stretched out on the bed, on her back, head to one side, fast asleep.

I sat next to her, on the edge of the bed, and this woke her with a start. "What? Oh . . . I must've dropped off. What was that about, anyway?"

"The Welcome Wagon," I said. "Come on, let's get an early supper."

And I took her to the Polo Lounge, where she chattered on and on about the picture she was working (with Roy Rogers and Dale Evans) and I said not much. I was thinking about those two bent cops, and how I'd pulled a gun on them.

No retaliation followed my encounter with the two vice-squad boys. They had made their point, and I mine. But I did take some precautionary measures: For two days I tailed the bastards and (with my Speed Graphic, the divorce dick's best friend) got two rolls of film on them receiving payoffs, frequently in the parking lot of their favorite coffee shop, Googie's, on Sunset at Crescent Heights.

I had no intention of using these for blackmail purposes—I just wanted some ammunition, other than the nine-millimeter variety, with which to deal with these bent sons of bitches. On the other hand, I had taken to wearing my shoulder-holstered Browning, in case things got interesting.

And for over a week, things weren't interesting—things were nicely dull. I had run into Cohen at Sherry's several times and he was friendly—and always in the company of a rugged-looking, ruggedly handsome investigator from the attorney general's office, sandy-haired Harry Cooper . . . which rhymed with Gary Cooper, who the dick was just as tall as.

Mick had taken my advice—he now had an armed bodyguard, courtesy of the state of California. His retinue of a Dwarf or two also accompanied him, of course, just minus any artillery. Once or twice, Niccoli had been with him—he'd just smiled and nodded at me (and Didi), polite, no hard feelings.

On Tuesday night, July 19, I took Didi to see *Annie Get Your Gun* at the Greek Theater; Gertrude Niesen had just opened in the show, and she and it were terrific. Then we had a late supper at Ciro's and hit a few jazz clubs. We wound up, as we inevitably did, at Sherry's for pastries and coffee.

Fred greeted us as we came in and joined us in a booth. Didi—who looked stunning in a low-cut, spangly silver gown, her brunette hair piled high—and I were on one side, Fred on the other. A piano tinkling Cole Porter fought with clanking plates and after-theater chatter.

I ordered us up a half slice of cheesecake for Didi (who was watching her figure—she wasn't alone), a Napoleon for me, and coffee for both of us. Fred just sat there with his hands folded prayerfully, shaking his head.

"Gettin' too old for this," he said, his pouchy puss even pouchier than usual, a condition his natty navy suit and red silk tie couldn't make up for.

"What are you doing playing host in the middle of the night?" I asked him. "You're an owner, for Christ's sake! Seems like lately, every time I come in here in the wee hours, you're hovering around like a mother hen."

"You're not wrong, Nate. Mickey's been comin' in almost every night, and with that contract hanging over his head, I feel like . . . for the protection of my customers . . . I gotta keep an eye on things."

"Is he here tonight?"

"Didn't you see him, holding court over there?"

Over in the far corner of the modern, brightly lighted restaurant—where business was actually a little slow tonight—a lively Cohen was indeed seated at a large round table with Cooper, Johnny Stompanato, Frank Niccoli, and another of the Dwarfs, Neddie Herbert. Also with the little gangster were several reporters from the *Times* and Florabel Muir and her husband, Denny. Florabel, a moderately attractive redhead in her late forties, was a Hollywood columnist for the New York *Daily News*.

Our order arrived, and Fred slid out of the booth, saying, "I better circulate."

"Fred—what, you think somebody's gonna open up with a chopper in here? This isn't a New Jersey clam house."

"I know . . . I'm just a nervous old woman."

Fred wandered off, and Didi and I nibbled at our desserts; we were dragging a little—it was after three.

"You okay?" I asked her.

"What?"

"You seem a little edgy."

"Really? Why would I be?"

"Having Niccoli sitting over there."

"No. That's over."

"What did you see in that guy, anyway?"

She shrugged. "He was nice, at first. I heard he had friends in pictures."

"You're already under contract. What do you need—"

"Nate, are we going to argue?"

I smiled, shook my head. "No. It's just . . . guys like Niccoli make me nervous."

"But he's been very nice to both of us."

"That's what makes me nervous."

Our mistake was using the restrooms: they were in back, and to use them, we'd had to pass near Cohen and his table. That's how we got invited to join the party—the two *Times* reporters had taken off, and chairs were available.

I sat next to Florabel, with Niccoli right next to me; Didi was beside Cooper, the state investigator, who sneaked occasional looks down Didi's cleavage. Couldn't blame him and, anyway, detectives are always gathering information.

Florabel had also seen *Annie Get Your Gun*, and Cohen had caught a preview last week.

"That's the best musical to hit L.A. in years," the little gangster said. He was in a snappy gray suit with a blue-and-gray tie.

For maybe five minutes, the man who controlled bookie operations in Los Angeles extolled the virtues of Rodgers and Hammerstein's latest confection.

"Can I quote you in my column?" Florabel asked. She was wearing a cream-colored suit with satin lapels, a classy dame with a hard edge.

"Sure! That musical gets the Mickey Cohen seal of approval."

Everyone laughed, as if it had been witty—me, too. I like my gangsters to be in a good mood.

"Mickey," the columnist said, sitting forward, "who do you think's been trying to kill you?"

"I really haven't the slightest idea. I'm as innocent as the driven snow."

"Yeah, but like Mae West said, you drifted."

He grinned at her—tiny rodent teeth. "Florabel, I love ya like a sister. I can talk to you about things I can't even tell my own wife."

Who was not present, by the way.

"You're in a neutral corner," he was saying, "like a referee. There's nothin' I can do for you, except help you sell papers, and you ain't got no axes to grind with me."

"That's true—so why not tell me what you really think? Is Jack Dragna behind these attempts?"

"Even for you, Florabel, that's one subject on which I ain't gonna spout off. If I knew the killers were in the next room, I wouldn't go public with it."

"Why not?"

"People like me, we settle things in our own way."

She gestured. "How can you sit in an open restaurant, Mick, with people planning to kill you?"

"Nobody's gonna do nothin' as long as you people are around. Even a crazy man wouldn't take a chance shooting where a reporter might get hit . . . or a cop, like Cooper here."

I was just trying to stay out of it, on the sidelines, but this line of reasoning I couldn't let slide. "Mickey," I said, "you really think a shooter's going to ask to see Florabel's press pass?"

Cohen thought that was funny, and almost everybody laughed—except me and Cooper.

Several at the table were nibbling on pastries; Didi and I had some more coffee. At one point, Niccoli got up to use the men's room, and Didi and I exchanged whispered remarks about how cordial he'd been to both of us. Florabel, still looking for a story, started questioning the slender, affable Neddie Herbert, who had survived a recent attempt on his life.

Herbert, who went back twenty years with Cohen, had dark, curly hair, a pleasant-looking, grown-up Dead-End Kid with a Brooklyn accent. He had been waylaid in the wee hours on the sidewalk in front of his apartment house.

"Two guys with .38's emptied their guns at me from the bushes." Herbert was grinning like a college kid recalling a frathouse prank. "Twelve slugs the cops recovered—not one hit me!"

"How is that possible?" Florabel asked.

"Ah, I got a instinct for danger—I didn't even see them two guys, but I sensed 'em right before I heard 'em and I dropped to the sidewalk right before they started shooting. I crawled up onto the stairway, outa range, while their bullets were fallin' all around."

"Punks," Cohen said.

"If they'da had any guts," Herbert said, "they'da reloaded and moved in close to get me—but they weaseled and ran."

Fred came over to the table and after some small talk, said, "It's almost four, folks—near closing time. Mind if I have one of the parking lot attendants fetch your car, Mick?"

"That'd be swell, Fred."

I said, "Fetch mine, too, would you, Fred?"

And as Rubinski headed off to do that, Cohen grabbed the check, fending off a few feeble protests, and everybody gathered their things. This seemed like a good time for Didi and me to make our exit as well.

Sherry's was built up on a slope, so there were a couple steps down from the cashier's counter to an entryway that opened right out to the street. Cohen strutted down and out, through the glass doors, with Neddie Herbert and the six-three Cooper right behind him. Niccoli and Stompanato were lingering inside, buying chewing gum and cigarettes. Florabel and her husband were lagging as well, talking to some woman who I gathered was the Mocambo's press agent.

Then Didi and I were standing on the sidewalk just behind Cohen and his bodyguards, under the Sherry's canopy, out in the fresh, crisp night air . . . actually, early-morning air. The normally busy Strip was all but deserted, only the occasional car gliding by. Just down a ways, the flashing yellow lights of sawhorses marking road construction blinked lazily.

"I love this time of night," Didi said, hugging my arm, as we waited behind Cohen and his retinue for the attendants to bring our cars. "So quiet . . . so still. . . ."

And it was a beautiful night, bright with starlight and neon, palm trees peeking over a low-slung, mission-style building across the way, silhouetted against the sky like a decorative wallpaper pattern. Directly across from us, however, a vacant lot with a Blatz beer billboard and a smaller FOR INFORMATION CONCERNING THIS PROPERTY PLEASE CALL sign did spoil the mood slightly.

Didi—her shoulders and back bare, her silvery gown shimmering with reflected light—was fussing in her little silver purse. "Damn—I'm out of cigarettes."

"I'll go back and get you some," I said.

"Oh, I guess I can wait . . ."

"Don't be silly. What is it you smoke?"

"Chesterfields."

I went back in and up the three or four steps and bought the smokes. Florabel was bending over, picking up all the just-delivered morning editions stacked near the cashier; her husband was still yakking with that dame from the Mocambo. Stompanato was flirting with a pretty waitress; Niccoli was nowhere in sight.

I headed down the short flight of steps and was coming out the glass doors just as Cohen's blue Caddy drew up, and the young, string-tied attendant got out, and the night exploded.

It wasn't thunder, at least not God's variety: This was a twelve-gauge boom accompanied by the cracks of a high-power rifle blasting, a deadly duet echoing across the pavement, shotgun bellow punctuated by the sharp snaps of what might have been an M-1, the sound of which took me back to Guadalcanal. As the fusillade kicked in, I reacted first and best, diving for the sidewalk, yanking at Didi's arm as I pitched past, pulling her down, the glass doors behind me shattering in a discordant song. My sportcoat was buttoned, and it took a couple seconds to get at the nine-millimeter under my shoulder, and during those slow-motion moments, I saw Mickey get clipped, probably by the rifle.

Cohen dropped to one knee, clawing at his right shoulder with his left hand, blood oozing through his fingers, streaming down his expensive suit. Neddie Herbert's back had been to the street—he was turned toward his boss when the salvo began—and a bullet, courtesy of the rifle, blew through him even as shotgun pellets riddled his legs. Herbert—the man who'd just been bragging about his instincts for danger—toppled to the sidewalk, screaming.

The attorney general's dick, Cooper, had his gun out

from under his shoulder when he caught a belly-full of buckshot and tumbled to the cement, yelling, "Shit! Fuck!" Mickey Cohen, on his knees, was saying, I swear to God, "This is a new goddamn suit!"

The rifle snapping over the shotgun blasts continued, as I stayed low and checked Didi, who was shaking in fear, a crumpled, moaning wreck; her bare back was red-pocked from two pellets, which seemed not to have entered her body, probably bouncing off the pavement and nicking her—but she was scared shitless.

Still, I could tell she was okay, and—staying low, using the Caddy as my shield—I fired the nine-millimeter toward that vacant lot, where orange muzzle flashes emanated from below that Blatz billboard. The safety glass of the Caddy's windows spiderwebbed and then burst into tiny particles as the shotgunning continued, and I ducked down, noting that the rifle fire had ceased. Had I nailed one of them?

Then the shotgun stopped, too, and the thunderstorm was over, leaving a legacy of pain and terror. Neddie Herbert was shrieking, yammering about not being able to feel his legs, and Didi was weeping, her long brunette hair come undone, trailing down her face and her back like tendrils. Writhing on the sidewalk like a bug on its back, big, rugged Cooper had his revolver in one hand, waving it around in a punch-drunk manner; his other hand was clutching his bloody stomach, blood bubbling through his fingers.

I moved out from behind the Caddy, stepping out into the street, gun in hand—ready to dive back if I drew any fire.

But none came.

I wanted to run across there and try to catch up with the bastards, but I knew I had to stay put, at least for a while; if those guys had a car, they might pull around and try to finish the job. And since I had a gun—and hadn't been wounded—I had to stand guard.

Now time sped up: I saw the parking lot attendant, who had apparently ducked under the car when the shooting started, scramble out from under and back inside the restaurant, glass crunching under his feet. Niccoli ran out, with Stompanato and Fred Rubinski on his tail. Niccoli got in the Caddy, and Cohen—despite his limp, bloody arm—used his other arm to haul the big, bleeding Cooper up into the backseat. Stompanato helped and climbed in back with the wounded cop.

Fred yelled, "Don't worry, Mick—ambulances are on the way! We'll take care of everybody!"

And the Caddy roared off.

Neddie Herbert couldn't be moved; he was alternately whimpering and screaming, still going on about not being able to move his legs. Some waitresses wrapped checkered tablecloths around the suffering Neddie, while I helped Didi inside; she said she was cold, and I gave her my sport jacket to wear.

Florabel came up to me, her left hand out of sight, behind her; she held out her right palm to show me a flattened deer slug about the size of a half dollar.

"Pretty nasty," she said.

"You get hit, Florabel?"

"Just bruised—where the sun don't shine. Hell, I thought it was fireworks and kids throwing rocks."

"You reporters have such great instincts."

As a waitress tended to Didi, Fred took me aside and said, "Real professional job."

I nodded. "Shotgun to cause chaos, that 30.06 to pinpoint Cohen . . . only they missed."

"You okay, Nate?"

"Yeah—I don't think I even got nicked. Scraped my hands on the sidewalk, is all. Get me a flashlight, Fred."

"What?"

"Sheriff's deputies'll show up pretty soon—I want a look acorss the way before they get here."

Fred understood: The sheriff's office was in Jack Dragna's pocket, so their work might be more cover-up than investigation.

The vacant lot across the street, near the Blatz billboard, was not what I'd expected, and I immediately knew why they'd chosen this spot. Directly off the sidewalk, an embankment fell to a sunken lot, with cement stairs up the slope providing a perfect place for shooters to perch out of sight. No street or even alley back here, either: just the backyards of houses asleep for the night (lights in those houses were blazing now, however). The assassins could sit on the stairs, unseen, and fire up over the sidewalk, from ideal cover.

"Twelve-gauge," Fred commented, pointing to a scattering of spent shells in the grass near the steps.

My flashlight found something else. "What's this?"

Fred bent next to what appeared to be a sandwich—a half-eaten sandwich. . . .

"Christ!" Fred said, lifting the partial slice of white bread. "Who eats this shit?"

An ambulance was screaming; so was Neddie Herbert.

"What shit?" I asked.

Fred shuddered. "It's a fucking sardine sandwich."

The shooting victims were transferred from the emergency room of the nearest hospital to top-notch Queen of Angels, where the head doctor was Cohen's personal physician. An entire wing was roped off for the Cohen party, with a pressroom and listening posts for both the LAPD and the county sheriff's department.

I stayed away. Didi's wounds were only superficial, so she was never admitted, anyway. Cohen called me from the hospital to thank me for my "quick thinking"; all I had done was throw a few shots in the shooters' direction, but maybe that had kept the carnage to a minimum. I don't know.

Neddie Herbert got the best care, but he died anyway, a week later, of uremic poisoning: gunshot wounds in the kidney are a bitch. At that point, Cohen was still in the hospital, but rebounding fast; and the state attorney's man, Cooper, was fighting for his life with a bullet in the liver and internal hemorrhaging from wounds in his intestines.

Fred and I both kept our profiles as low as possible—this kind of publicity for his restaurant and our agency was not exactly what we were looking for.

The night after Neddie Herbert's death in the afternoon, I was waiting in the parking lot of Googie's, the coffee shop at Sunset and Crescent Heights. Googie's was the latest of these atomic-type cafes popping up along the Strip like futuristic mushrooms: a slab of the swooping, red-painted, structural-steel roof rose to jut at an angle toward the street, in an off-balance exclamation point brandishing the neon *Googie's*, and a massive picture window looked out on the Strip as well as the nearby Hollywood hills.

I'd arrived in a blue Ford that belonged to the A-1, but I was standing alongside a burgundy Dodge, an unmarked car used by the two vice cops who made Googie's their home away from home. Tonight I was wasn't taking pictures of their various dealings with bookmakers, madams, fellow crooked cops, or politicians. This was something of a social call.

I'd been here since just before midnight, and we were

into the early morning hours now—in fact, it was after two
a.m. when Lieutenant Delbert Potts and Sergeant Rudy
Johnson strolled out of the brightly illuminated glass-and-
concrete coffee shop into the less illuminated parking lot.
Potts was in another rumpled brown suit—or maybe the
same one—and, again, Johnson was better dressed than his
slob partner, his slender frame well served by a dark-gray
suit worthy of Michael's haberdashery.

Hell, maybe Cohen provided Johnson's wardrobe as part
of the regular payoff—at least till Delbert and Rudy got
greedy and went after twenty grand for the recordings
they'd made of Mickey.

I dropped down into a crouch as they approached,
pleased that no other customers had wandered into the parking lot at the same time as my friends from the vice squad.
Tucked between the Dodge and the car parked next to it, I
was as unseen as Potts and Johnson had been when they'd
crouched on those steps with their shotgun and rifle, waiting
for Mickey.

Potts and Johnson were laughing about something—
maybe Neddie Herbert's death—and the fat one was in the
lead, fishing in his pants pocket for his car keys. He didn't
see me as I rose from the shadows, swinging an underhand
fist that sank six inches into his flabby belly.

Like a matador, I pushed past him while shoving him to
the pavement, where he began puking, and grabbed Johnson
by one lapel and slammed his head into the rear rider's-side
window. He slid down the side of the car and sat, maybe not
unconscious, but good and dazed. Neither one protested—
the puking fat one, or the stunned thin one—as I disarmed
them, pitching their revolvers into the darkness, where they
skittered across the cement like crabs. I checked their ankles
for hideout guns, but they were clean. So to speak.

Potts was still puking when I started kicking the shit out of him. I didn't go overboard: just five or six good ones, cracking two or three ribs. Pretty soon he stopped throwing up and began to cry, wallowing down there between the cars in his own vomit. Johnson was coming around and tried to crawl away, but I yanked him back by the collar and slammed him into the hubcap of the Dodge.

Johnson had blood all over his face and was spitting up a bloody froth, as well as a tooth or two, and he was blubbering like a baby.

Glancing over my shoulder, I saw a couple in their twenties emerging from Googie's; they walked to their car, on the other side of the lot. They were talking and laughing—presumably not about Neddie Herbert's death—and went to their Chevy convertible and rolled out of the lot.

I kicked Potts in the side and shook Johnson by the lapels, just to get their attention, and they wept and groaned and moaned while I gave them my little speech, which I'd been working on in my head while I waited for them in the parking lot.

"Listen to me, you simple fuckers—you can shoot at Mickey Cohen and his Dwarfs all you want. I really do not give a flying shit. But you shot at me and my date, and a copper too, and that pisses me off. Plus, you shot up the front of my partner's restaurant."

Potts tried to say something, but it was unintelligible; "mercy" was in there somewhere. Johnson was whimpering, holding up his blood-smeared hands like this was a stick-up.

"Shut up," I said, "both of you. I don't care what you or Dragna or any gangster or bent fucking cop does out here in Make-believe-ville. I live in Chicago, and I'm going back tomorrow. If you take any steps against me, or Fred Rubinski, or if you put innocent people in the path of your fucking war again, I will talk to my Chicago friends . . . and you will have an accident. Maybe you'll get run down by a milk truck, maybe a safe'll fall on you. Maybe you'll miss a turn off a cliff. My friends are creative."

Through his bloody bubbles, Johnson said, "Okay, Heller . . . okay!"

"By the way, I have photos of you boys taking payoffs from a fine cross-section of L.A.'s sleazy citizenry. Anything happens to me—if I wake up with a goddamn hangnail—those photos go to Jim Richardson at the *Examiner*, with a duplicate batch to Florabel Muir. Got it?"

Nobody said anything. I kicked Potts in the ass, and he yelped, "Got it!"

"Got it, got it, got it!" Johnson said, backing up against the hubcap, patting the air with his palms.

"We're almost done—just one more question. Was Stompanato in on it, or was Niccoli your only tip-off man?"

Johnson coughed, getting blood on his chin. "Ni-Niccoli . . . just Niccoli."

"He wanted you to take out the Davis dame, right? That was part of the deal?"

Johnson nodded. So did Potts, who was on his belly, and to see me had to look over his shoulder, puke rolling down his cheeks like a bad complexion that had started to melt.

Just the sight of them disgusted me, and my hand drifted toward my nine-millimeter in the shoulder holster. "Or fuck . . . maybe I should kill you bastards. . . ."

They both shouted "No!" and Potts began to cry again.

Laughing to myself, I returned to the agency's Ford. These L.A. cops were a bunch of pansies; if this were Chicago, I'd have been dead by now.

* * *

In the aftermath of the shoot-out at Sherry's, various political heads rolled, including Attorney General Fred Howser's, and several trials took place (Cohen acquitted on various charges), as well as a Grand Jury inquiry into police and political corruption. Potts and Johnson were acquitted of corruption charges, and despite much talk in the press of damning wire recordings in the possession of both sides, no such recordings were entered as evidence in any trial, though Cohen's lawyer was murdered on the eve of a trial in which those recordings were supposed to figure.

And the unsuccessful attempts on Cohen's life continued, notably a bombing of his house, which he and his wife and his bull terrier survived without scratches. But no more civilians were put in harm's way, and no repercussions were felt by either Fred Rubinski or myself.

A few months after Mickey Cohen got out of the hospital, his longtime crony Frank Niccoli—who he'd known since Cleveland days—turned up missing. Suspicions that Niccoli might have been a stool pigeon removed by Mickey himself were offset by Cohen losing the $25,000 bail money he'd put up for Niccoli on an unrelated beef.

The next summer, I ran into Cohen at Sherry's—or actually, I was just coming out of Sherry's, a date on my arm. It was another cool, starlit night, around two a.m., the major difference this time being the starlet was a blonde. Mickey and Johnny Stompanato and two more Dwarfs were on their way in. We paused under the canopy.

The rodent grin flashed between five-o'clock-shadowed cheeks. "Nate! Here we are at the scene of the crime—like old times."

"I hope not, Mickey."

"You look good. You look swell."

"That's a nice suit, Mickey."

"Stop by Michael's—I'll fix you up. On the house. Still owe you a favor for whispering in my ear about . . . you know."

"Forget it."

He leaned in, sotto voce. "New girl?"

"Pretty new."

"You hear who Didi Davis is dating these days?"

"No."

"That state's attorney cop—Cooper!"

I smiled. "Hadn't heard that."

"Yeah, he finally got the bullet removed outa his liver, the other day. My doc came up with some new treatment, makes liver cells replace themselves or somethin' . . . all on my tab, of course."

My date tightened her grip on my arm; maybe she recognized Cohen and was nervous about the company I was keeping.

So I said, "Well, Mick, better let you and your boys go on in for your coffee and pastries . . . before somebody starts shooting at us again."

He laughed heartily and even shook hands with me— which meant he would have to go right in and wash up—but first, leaning in close enough for me to whiff his expensive cologne, he said, "Be sure to say hello to Frankie, since you're in the neighborhood."

"What do you mean?"

Actually, I knew he meant Frankie Niccoli, but wasn't getting the rest of his drift. . . .

Cohen nodded down the Strip. "Remember that road construction they was doin', the night we got hit? There's a nice new stretch of concrete there now. You oughta try it out."

And Mickey and his boys went inside.

As for me, my latest starlet at my side, I had the parking

lot attendant fetch my wheels, and soon I was driving right over that fresh patch of pavement, with pleasure.

AUTHOR'S NOTE: I wish to thank my longtime associate, George Hagenauer, for his help researching this fact-based story. Most of the characters appear under their real names; several—notably, Fred Rubinski, Didi Davis, Delbert Potts, and Rudy Johnson—are fictional but have real-life counterparts. Research sources included numerous true-crime magazine articles and the following books: *Death in Paradise* (1998), Tony Blanche and Brad Schreiber; *Headline Happy* (1950), Florabel Muir; *Hoodlums—Los Angeles* (1959), Ted Prager and Larry Craft; *The Last Mafioso* (1981), Ovid DeMaris; *Mickey Cohen: In My Own Words* (1975), as told to John Peer Nugent; *Mickey Cohen: Mobster* (1973); *Sins of the City* (1999), Jim Heimann; *Thicker'n Thieves* (1951), Charles Stoker; and *Why I Quit Syndicated Crime* (1951), Jim Vaus as told to D.C. Haskin.

THE WOODWARD PLAN
AN AMOS WALKER STORY

by *Loren D. Estleman*

**The Street: Woodward Avenue,
Detroit, Michigan**

Loren Estleman's name is very familiar to anyone who reads mysteries and/or westerns. Equally revered and rewarded in both genres, here Estleman and his P.I., Amos Walker, let us in on the Woodward Plan and what it was supposed to mean to the city of Detroit. The most recent Walker book is *A Smile on the Face of the Tiger* (Mysterious Press, 2000).

Emory Freemantle had been with the Detroit Public Library almost as long as the 1950 Wayne County Manual and had spent even less time outside its doors. His job was to wear a uniform and wake up the odd bum when he started drooling on Shakespeare's sonnets. I'd been bribing him for ten years to unlock the back door for me midnights and Sundays when I needed to check a fact in one of the newspapers on microfilm.

I parked next to the white marble Main Branch on Woodward and rapped on the fire door. He'd been waiting for me; a key rattled immediately in the lock on the other side and he swung the door open just wide enough for me to slide in around the edge.

"Thanks for coming, Mr. Walker. I know I haven't any

hold on you. Our account's square." He gripped my hand gently; he was as big as a city bus and didn't need to prove anything by crushing bone. He had skin the color of oiled walnut, faded a little with age, and pale eyes like Christ on the cross.

"You never know when I might want to take out a reference book," I said.

"The librarians hate that. Meanwhile they let a hundred thousand in rare books crawl out through the ductwork. I pulled a guy out of a ventilator just last month." He spoke carefully as he led me through a mile of metal stacks to the little room where he took his breaks. He read a lot when he wasn't rousting drug dealers and book thieves and liked to make himself crazy diagramming the sentences of politicians.

The break room had a Mr. Coffee, a microwave, a camp-sized refrigerator, and a round table covered with magazines, as if there weren't enough to read on three floors. It smelled of strong Colombian and uncensored literature; Emory's little borrowed stack on the counter included *Ulysses* and Harry Potter.

He poured me a cup from the carafe, tossed a handful of coins into a Town Club box on the counter, and sat down at the table opposite me, folding his big hands on the top. "My nephew's in Receiving Hospital, hooked up to a pinball machine. He may come out, or not. He hurt his head."

"Hurt his head on who?"

His grin lacked heat. "I oughtn't forget you're a detective. He wrapped a Porsche around a lightpole four blocks up on Woodward. You might've heard about it."

I nodded. "It had to be a Porsche. A Chevy wouldn't have made Section A."

"Cops called it a carjack. Lester stuck a gun in a guy's face in the parking lot at the Whitney, they said, and took off for Eight Mile Road. City cruiser got in behind him up past Kirby; he had it up to a hundred when he spun out. They don't know if he'll walk again."

"Should've picked a Chevy."

He worked his hands together. Powerful hands, with balloons of scar tissue on the knuckles; they must have given him hell in damp weather. He never got to the Golden Gloves, but he'd sparred with many who had, and one winner. "My sister did as good a job raising him as she could, but she done it alone. There's some juvie stuff on his record, but that was years ago, and he never raised so much as his fists on no one. Jacking that car wasn't his idea."

"Cops didn't pull anyone else out of that wreck. How long since you talked to Lester?"

"They ain't let me in to see him. I seen him a week before the thing. He had him a job installing car stereos, was saving to buy speakers for his Jeep. You can't put speakers the size he wanted in no Porsche."

"A Porsche buys a lot of speakers. I'm not trying to be tough, Emory. Nobody knows anybody."

"You want to see the gun?"

"Cops said he threw it out of the car. They didn't find it, so it went down the sewer."

"Them sewers swallow up a lot of ordnance. You wonder how the shit gets out to the river." He leaned back to snake a hand inside his pants pocket and clattered something onto the table.

I caught it before it bounced over the edge. It was black plastic, about the size of a cigarette case, with a red muzzle. A spring snapped inside when I pulled the trigger. It was made for shooting plastic darts with rubber suction cups on the ends. I chuckled and slid it back his way. He made no move to pick it up.

"You get points for originality, but that's all," I said. "It won't buy you thirty seconds downtown."

"I gave him that toy gun in a box with a set of darts and a target board for his tenth birthday. I never seen it again till Old Willie brought it to me yesterday. You seen Old Willie. Begs his dinner off folks coming out of the Whitney with doggie bags and eats it in Periodicals."

"He the one with the football helmet?"

"No, that's Cap'n Kirk—he gets messages from Jupiter. Old Willie wears a sock cap with a deer on it. He picked up the gun in the parking lot where Lester threw it when he took off in the Porsche."

I retrieved the toy and turned it over. "It wouldn't make a difference to the charge. It's still armed robbery. They put teeth in the law after too many toy-gun users walked on the weapons beef."

"That's 'cause some toys look real to the victims. You think anybody would be fooled by this one? They don't put red tips on real guns."

"It could happen," I said. "If it was dark enough, and the victim was Mr. Magoo."

"They light the lot at the Whitney brighter'n the MGM Grand. But let's go out on a limb and say somebody might mistake this hunk of plastic for the real thing. You think anybody'd mistake Buzz Bernadotte for Mr. Magoo?"

Bernadotte was the owner of the Porsche. A Chevy might have made Section A at that, if it had been carjacked from him; only if it had been a Chevy, it wouldn't have been Buzz Bernadotte. "Richie Rich, maybe," I said. "Not Magoo. You think the carjacking was phony?"

"You're the detective."

I twirled the gun Tom Mix fashion on my finger. "Old Willie sell you the gun or what?"

"It was a gift. I let him curl up in the stacks sometimes when I'm supposed to be sweeping him out the door. He don't cause trouble, and he's afraid of shelters. He got his teeth kicked in once for grinding 'em in his sleep."

"He see anything?"

"I asked, but he went dummy. Half these boys talk to theirselves all the time. The other half wouldn't open their mouths to tell you you're parked on their foot. Guess which half is Willie's."

"You say he hangs out in the Periodicals section?"

"All day every day, except dinnertime, when he's at the Whitney. And today," he added. "Today he didn't show up."

"He ever miss before?"

Freemantle shook his close-shorn head. "Not since I know him. That says something, don't it? I mean if he saw something."

"Not to the law." I put down the toy gun. "It wouldn't be the first time a policyholder mistook his insurance company for an ATM. If that's the case, Lester might do a jolt for fraud, but not armed robbery. He'll take his physical therapy in minimum security, be out in ten months. The gun's cheesy enough to make the cops ask Buzz some hard questions, but it's no good if they can't place it at the scene."

"That's why I didn't go to the cops." The guard got a worn wallet out of his hip pocket and laid five one-hundred-dollar bills side by side on the table between us, dealing solitaire. "That's all I got. I know you get three days up front. I'll write you a check for the rest, if you don't mind hanging on to it till Friday. That's when I get paid."

I picked up one of the bills. "Case dough. I'll be back for the rest when I have something to sell. Give me a description of Old Willie. Maybe he's found a new hat."

*   *   *

Buzz Bernadotte's line stretched back to Detroit's French colonial period. The family had built its fortune on the trade in beaver pelts, invested it in railroads, then automobiles, and more recently in fast food and sports franchises. Since the 1967 race riot, the Bernadottes had been living in Grosse Pointe Farms, where they grow nothing but billionaires, but Buzz's father Alec had been pouring money into a number of restoration projects along Woodward Avenue, Detroit's main street: Theaters, restaurants, and art galleries had begun to appear on sites formerly occupied by crack houses and ladies named Chenille. Alec, Jr.—Buzz to the people who trailed him picking up fifty-dollar bills—made most of his investments in low-slung cars, high-breasted women, and dinners at restaurants like the Whitney, where his tips alone would keep a Democrat in dates for a year. It was one of the few places on Woodward not owned by his father.

I went to the Whitney, but not to see Buzz. It was dinnertime, and rumor had it the best of the local color could be found at that hour in the parking lot.

How this many-spired monument to the bad taste of a lumber baron managed to survive the years of civil unrest, soaring homicides, and mayoral plundering is one for Ellery Queen. It was serving sliced salmon hips smothered in champagne sauce while the rest of the city's nightlife was roasting rats in the vacant lot down the street.

The parking attendant was a good-looking black kid in a burgundy blazer. When he opened my door, I folded a twenty into a slim rectangle and held it between two fingers. I'd started with a ten, then changed my mind when I caught a whiff of clarified butter from inside. "I'm looking for Willie."

He measured out a centimeter of careful smile. One look at my suit and the car it came out of had told him I wasn't dining there. "That's the first time I've heard anyone call it that."

"This one's homeless. Short, black, about sixty, wears a knitted cap like a hunter's with a deer embroidered on it. Begs doggie bags off customers."

"Him, yeah. I shoo him off every night."

"What about tonight?"

"Not yet. He usually shows up about ten."

"Was he here the night of the carjacking?"

"Probably. I had my hands full with the police that night. I'm the one who called them. I saw the whole thing."

"What'd you see?"

His face showed animation for the first time. "After I brought up Buzz's car, he took it to the end of the drive and waited to turn. This guy stepped from behind a pillar waving a piece. Buzz got out with his hands up, and the guy got in and took off."

"You saw the gun?"

"He had something in his fist. I didn't think it was a pocket calculator and neither did Buzz."

"Did you see him ditch it?"

He shook his head. "Cops said he must have thrown it out during the chase."

"The cops know everything," I said. "That's why there's no crime in the city. Willie show up last night?"

"I wasn't in last night."

"Who was?"

"I don't know. I wasn't here, remember?"

"I forgot. People forget things and think they never knew them." I gave him the twenty.

"I'll get my supervisor. He's here every night."

His supervisor had sixty pounds on him and gray hair. He'd witnessed the carjacking too, but he hadn't seen anything the kid hadn't. He thought Old Willie had been hanging around about that time. It cost me another twenty to find out he hadn't seen him since.

I hung around the lot until ten-thirty, smoking cigarettes and watching foreign cars and the odd Cadillac come and go, taking on and unloading well-fed men in Frank Lloyd Wright ties and glittering women. They left carrying filets of Tibetan yak wrapped in swan-shaped foil, and no one came forward to relieve them of the burden. That nailed it for me. Men who hadn't eaten all day didn't miss such opportunities. I cranked my battered old American make out of the corner where the employees parked and paid a call on the Wayne County Morgue.

My contact there was a neat little guy with bright eyes behind windowglass spectacles he thought made him look older. He looked like Mr. Peabody's boy Sherman. He said, "You're going to have to be more specific. This place is a clearinghouse for the homeless, and the *living* population's eighty percent black."

I told him about the knitted cap. "It might not be natural causes. No wood-alcohol poisoning or OD or passing out on the Penn Central tracks?"

His eyes brightened further. "We got a g.s. early this morning. That's gunshot."

"N.s.," I said. "That's no shit. Show me the body."

"Anywhere else, that'd be a euphemism." He put down his carton of chocolate milk and led the way to a drawer.

The naked body was bluish gray, the face shrunken to the skull. He might have spent the last ten thousand years in a crevasse, except for the blue hole just above his left nipple. Bright Eyes scooped the rolled-up paper sack from the foot of the drawer and pulled out a knitted stocking cap, blaze or-

ange the way they wear them in the woods, grimy from con-
stant wear and no laundering. The deer wasn't talking.

"Him, I guess," I said. "Where'd they find him?"

He returned everything to the drawer, shut it, and went
back to his desk to consult his clipboard. "State fairgrounds.
Ditch along Woodward. M.E. says he was moved. He dug
out a twenty-two long. Pro job, or a good amateur who
wanted it to look that way."

"Straight shot. No pun intended. They were waiting for
him on his way to the Whitney, or more likely on his way
back to the library, after ten p.m. when it was quiet. Probably offered him a handout; that's how they got him in front.
Then they rode him up to the first deserted stretch and
dumped him."

"Doesn't say that here. Who's your snitch?"

"Andy Jackson." I poked a twenty into the pocket of his
white coat.

Alec Bernadotte was easier to find than his son; it's often
that way with philanthropists. They like to be seen and have
their pictures taken, shaking hands with crippled children
and giving out big dummy checks loaded with zeroes. It was
a morning reception in the baroque lobby of the Fox Theater
on Woodward; not his project, which was why he didn't hesitate to rest the plastic glass containing his mimosa on the
head of one of the plaster lions flanking the staircase.

I got in line to shake his hand. He was a small-boned man
in his fifties with black, Gallic eyes and a tanned bald head,
a hundred and fifty pounds of nervous energy in a pinstripe
suit measured and cut under the direct supervision of God.
When he stuck out his hand I showed him my ID.

"Amos Walker, Mr. Bernadotte. I need to ask a couple of
questions about the incident at the Whitney."

The practiced twinkle in the black eyes became a stony glint. Two large men in blue suits stepped forward to flank him. They looked just like the lions. He said, "If you're working for the insurance company, you'll have to talk to Buzz. He and I don't communicate these days."

"Not at all?"

The thrum of voices was loud in the cavernous room, but he lowered his a notch. "I'm a venture capitalist, Mr. Walker. Once an investment has revealed itself to be a losing proposition, I stop putting money into it. My son is a junk bond. He's been on his own for months."

"Where can I find him?"

"You might try the DAC. He likes to keep fit. It's the one thing he does that makes sense. He needs to stay in front of his creditors."

I thanked him and started to leave. Turning back, I pulled the toy gun out of my side pocket.

Bernadotte shrank back. The bodyguards went for their shoulder rigs. They were trained for speed and would probably have gotten off a couple of shots after I'd pumped half a clip into the man they were paid to protect. I think one of the lions gasped. Then the bodyguards saw what I was holding and relaxed. Bernadotte's nervous laugh joined theirs, a beat behind. Echoes of it rippled through the crowd in the room.

"Is life that boring?" Bernadotte asked.

"Calculated risk," I said. "I knew you could afford the best and that their reflexes would work just as well both ways. You knew it was a gag, huh?"

"I'm not an idiot. It might as well have a flag sticking out with 'bang' printed on it in big letters."

"Is your son an idiot?"

"Only when it comes to money. He thinks I have my own

printing press. Or thought it, until I cut him off. But he knows a toy gun from the real thing."

I thanked him again and put away the toy. It was worth almost getting shot.

Woodward Avenue was named for Augustus B. Woodward, who in 1807 proposed his "Woodward Plan" for rebuilding Detroit after the great fire burned it to the ground two years earlier. The plan called for a series of great circles after the fashion of Washington, D.C., beginning downtown and radiating out to where Outer Drive now encloses the central city. The building I walked into, on Madison a quarter turn along the great circle off Woodward, stands just about where the Plan petered out and the gridded blocks begin. That's where we lose most of our visitors; they circle the octagonal lots for hours, fingers clamped to the steering wheel and only the ghosts of hope on their faces.

I hadn't visited the Detroit Athletic Club since the old mayor died. The stately Italianate box had gone up in 1915 to give the old auto pioneers a place to hide from their fan base, but it had taken the optimism of a new administration to rescue it from demolition. Now, gentry like the Bernadottes were re-upping in herds, and restorers were uncovering the ornate painted ceilings and scraping the gum off the Pewabic tiles on the floors. I rode a brass elevator up to the gallery overlooking the Olympic-size swimming pool and gazed down on the spot where a pre-Tarzan Johnny Weismuller had trained for the 1924 games.

Buzz wasn't hard to spot. He was the one dripping in a Speedo at the far end, selecting a towel from among the half dozen offered him by a group of young men his age, all of whom dressed as he did in photographs, in loose unbleached cotton and khakis hand-stitched in Manila or someplace equally difficult and expensive to import from, and went to his hairdresser to tame their cowlicks. He was a slender, muscular twenty-two, with his father's Gallic eyes and a five o'clock shadow that was hard to maintain unless you wanted to eliminate it, as I did. It cost him plenty to look as disheveled as Old Willie had for free. I wondered where the money came from.

By the time I descended the stairs to the pool area, Buzz had put on a terrycloth robe and flip-flops and was on his way to the locker room. I showed him the bottom half of my ID folder, containing the honorary sheriff's star. "It's about the Whitney. It'll just take a minute."

"Minutes are what I'm fresh out of," he said. "The Detroit police have my statement. Don't you boys talk to each other?" He started to push past.

I took my other hand out of my pocket and stuck the palm under his nose with the toy gun lying on it. "Minutes aren't the only thing you're fresh out of, Buzz. Who's paying your dues?"

He recognized the item. His eyes seemed to get blacker. That was just the effect of the color leaving his face.

"Buzz, you want me to get security?" This from one of the youths clustered about him. He still had his baby fat.

"No. Meet me in the bar later. Set yourselves up on me."

That cleared the room. Buzz and I stepped through a door into a locker room that was like no other, with a carpet and a little, leather-upholstered sitting area around a big-screen TV and, if you wanted them, a shower and a couple of rows of lockers. We sat down facing each other. He held out a hand. "I'll take a closer look at that popgun."

I smiled and patted my pocket. "It's evidence of nothing if I can't put it in Lester's hand, but I'll hang on to it just the same. Who are you in to and how deep?"

He shook his head. "What's County's interest? My car was stolen in Detroit."

"The badge is a toy, like the gun. I'm private. They hung the wrong rap on Lester, and I'm out to correct it."

"His family." He showed me his orthodontia; his feet had found the shallow end of the pool. "How much for the gun and to forget you ever saw it?"

"Thanks, Buzz. That saved me some time. There was a bare chance you thought the gun was real, silly as that sounds, and didn't set up the carjacking. What's the insurance tag on the Porsche, couple of hundred thousand?"

"Half a million. It's a commemorative model. But you've got nothing. Even if you can enter the toy in evidence, my lawyers will hang up the case for years."

"What lawyers? You can't pay them. You can't even pay for your friends' drinks. Your old man sent you packing. That's why you decided to run a number on your insurance company, to keep up your lifestyle."

He sat back and crossed his arms behind his head. "You're just like the old man, as you call him. You think he's the only source of income in the world."

That puzzled me for a minute. Then it didn't. My contact at the morgue had said Old Willie was a pro job, or made to look like one. I'd hung up on the second choice and hadn't stopped to consider the first.

"Your father said you weren't an idiot, except when it came to money," I said. "He'll be relieved to know you've learned something. Who's Daddy now, and does he speak with an accent or is he one of the new breed?"

The black eyes shifted slightly. "I don't follow."

"Sure you do. You just didn't expect me to. Alec Bernadotte doesn't care anymore if his kid gets in Dutch, but someone else does. Someone who wouldn't hesitate to put a hole in the only witness who saw the carjacking close enough to know it was fake, then run him up to the fairgrounds and dump him."

"What? I don't—"

"The boys in the Combination like long-term investments. They know if they help you out now with cash, it will come back a hundred thousand times over when Bernadotte dies and his only son takes over the family finances. Except all that goes south the minute you draw a conviction for insurance fraud. Any good conservator would freeze you out forever."

His hands came out from behind his head. "I don't know anything about murder. Who?"

"You wouldn't know him. I doubt you ever stopped long enough to throw him a pheasant leg on your way out of the Whitney. He only became important when he could place a silly toy gun in the hand of a kid who wanted some money to buy stereo speakers. That's why he agreed to fake a carjack and stow the Porsche someplace until the policy paid off."

"I thought at first you killed Old Willie yourself," I went on. "Telling your mob friends about him, knowing what they'd do to correct the situation, amounts to the same thing. That's how the judge will see it."

He gripped his knees through terrycloth. Very slowly his hands relaxed. He shook his head. "There's a flaw. If I had this wonderful source of money, why did I decide to hold up the insurance company?"

"You were looking for a buyout. Maybe you didn't like the way they eat with their mouths open. Too bad you couldn't ask your father for advice. He'd have told you an investment is not a loan. A one-time payoff wouldn't satisfy them."

He smiled with some of his old cockiness. "It's all smoke

without—what did you call him? Without Old Willie. You
could have bought that gun at Wal-Mart."

"You forgot Lester. He's staring at hard time, and in a
wheelchair. Your Woodward plan totaled itself against a
lightpole."

"He's in a coma."

"If he wakes up with this same story, without prompting,
everything else falls into place: the gun, the dead bum, your
bottomless bankroll. If I were the prosecutor, I'd spin the
wheel. But you can always hope he doesn't wake up. It'll
help pass the time." I got up and left him there. The place
was beginning to smell like a genuine locker room.

I filled a glass from my private stock in the file drawer
where I never filed anything but my portfolio on whiskey
futures and drank it down at my desk. I was working up
stimulation to dial Emory Freemantle's line at the library.
The case against Buzz wouldn't hold water in a hurricane;
without it, Lester would be wheeling up to a drill press at the
state penitentiary in Jackson until they ran commuter flights
to the moon. By then everyone would have his own robot
private investigator and I'd be living on other people's left-
overs like poor Old Willie.

Deciding that bad news went down a little less bad in person, I got up and reached for the doorknob just as someone
came in. He was quiet; I hadn't heard him in the outer office.

He was built slighter than expected, and fair, with long
lashes most women would sell their bodies for, although if
they had them they'd get a better price. Well, there are blond
Sicilians. He didn't even have to be Sicilian at all, or Italian,
for that matter. All he had to have was a gun, in this case a
.22 target shooter with a silencer.

"Don't waste your time denying you're Walker," he said. "I pulled your picture from a file at the *Free Press*."

I raised my hands without waiting for orders. He liked that. He was young, and not the type to be patient with aging boomers. He patted the usual places, shook the flaps of my suitcoat for telltale weight. The toy gun in my side pocket weighed almost nothing and was too slim to make a bulge.

"I'm disappointed. I thought all you old-time P.I.'s went around loaded for rhino." He gestured with the .22. I backed up and he cocked a leg over a corner of the desk. "I'm waiting for a call," he said. "Then we'll finish."

"I'll guess. Receiving Hospital."

"Maybe a pay phone outside. He might be in a hurry. Maybe not, though, if he rings for the nurse just before he sticks the ice pick in Lester's chest. That'd give him another forty-five minutes." He laughed. It was a boy's laugh, light and completely unclouded.

"Buzz didn't waste any time getting in touch."

"I like Buzz. We got a special interest in Buzz." He liked saying Buzz. "He shouldn't try to think like us, though. Lester installed the sound system in Buzz's Porsche—that's how they met. If the cops felt like digging, they could link them up."

I'd wondered about that. "That the same piece you used on Willie?"

"Willie? Oh, the homeless guy. No, that's in the river. Guns are cheap."

"Almost as cheap as shooters."

He laughed. "I like you. I'm going to regret this, I can see. It may not even be necessary. But why take the chance?"

The telephone rang and I started toward it, as if from habit. He raised the pistol an inch, stopping me, and lifted the receiver. But he didn't make me go back.

"Hello." He listened, watching me through his long, pale lashes. "No Alderdyce here. Wrong number. You're very welcome." He hung up. "You'd think with all this technology—" He stopped when the muzzle touched his temple.

I didn't raise my voice. We were only separated by the length of my right arm. "Your frisking needs work."

His finger whitened on the trigger of the target pistol. I pressed harder. "Twenty-two's big on accuracy," I said. "Lousy stopper. You can hit something vital and I'll still have time to blow your brains out the other side."

"That's not a real gun. That's that toy Lester used." His eyes were mostly white, straining to see it.

"Probably. Then again, guns are cheap."

We were like that for a while. We might have been like that all day, but the telephone rang. It startled him; he jerked the trigger. But I was already slashing down with the arm holding the toy gun. I hit his hand and the bullet went into a baseboard. It's still there. I crossed with my left fist and caught him on the temple, where his brains would have gone out if I'd been loaded for rhino. I reached down and twisted the .22 free as he tipped off the desk.

The air smelled like a struck match and there was some smoke, but the silenced pistol had made no more noise than a drawer slamming shut. The telephone was still ringing. I picked up. "Me, John," I said. "You took a chance. This character might have known there was an Alderdyce with Homicide."

"He caught me off guard," the lieutenant said. "I didn't expect anyone but you to answer your phone. You all right?"

"Peachy. What about Lester?"

"Still asleep. They say he might come out of it. He missed the excitement. Someone ought to tell these bozos a phony doctor's smock is no place to carry an ice pick."

"I didn't think they'd move this fast. Good thing you beefed up the guard."

"We'd have got him anyway." John never gave an inch. "We picked up Buzz an hour ago. A car's on its way to your office. Should I radio them what to expect?"

"Tell them to bring a real gun. This one's ready for the toy box." I laid it on the desk and sat down with the .22 to wait for my visitor to wake up.

WASHINGTON AVENUE
A LUPE SOLANO STORY

by *Carolina Garcia-Aguilera*

**The Street: Washington Avenue,
South Beach, Florida**

Carolina Garcia-Aguilera is one of a handful of "real" P.I.'s
who have made the leap successfully into simply writing
about it. Much of her Cuban lady P.I.'s background and attitudes are definitely Carolina's, but sometimes one wonders
just where Carolina ends and Lupe takes up. And since some
of Lupe's attitudes *are* the author's, one is sometimes afraid
to ask. Here we go along with Lupe as she gives us a tour of
the nightlife along South Beach's Washington Avenue. The
latest novel in the series is *Havana Heat* (Avon, 2000).

One

Tommy MacDonald and I were sitting at a terrace table at
Oceana—one of the outdoor restaurants that line Ocean
Drive on Miami Beach. We were sipping *mojitos* and enjoying the sunset on the horizon. It was a wondrous sight, the
fiery red ball going down over the palm trees and bathing
the wide stretch of sand across from us with a golden orange
glow as it made its final journey into the deep waters of the
Atlantic Ocean.

It was late summer, my favorite season in Miami, when the

town was deserted. Only the bravest Miamians stayed in town during the hellish three months of summer. Locals who could escaped to cooler climates, and the season was too risky for tourists who feared they would lose their vacation deposits if a hurricane hit. For me, it was perfect. I don't believe there's such a thing as too much heat and humidity. Maybe it's my Cuban blood, maybe it's my contrarian nature.

Tommy and I were trying to ignore our discomfort and make the most of the dismal, pathetic breeze that was struggling to break through the ninety-plus-degree, eight-p.m. heat. Our bodies were sticking to the repellent cream-colored canvas that covered our chairs. I was wearing a white linen sleeveless dress, so I was a little cooler than Tommy, who was in his tan poplin suit. I had had the luxury of going home to shower and change after work. Tommy had come straight from a court appearance.

Of the twenty tables on the terrace, only three others were occupied. That was about right for August. Tommy and I sipped our drinks and looked over the menu—although we had eaten at Oceana so often recently we practically knew it by heart.

That night we were at Oceana for a different reason than the food and the ambiance, though. Leonardo—my cousin, office manager, and supervisor of my professional, personal, and spiritual life—had asked me to go there. Manny Mendoza, Leonardo's longtime friend and Oceana's manager, had some sort of problem that he wanted to discuss with me. Apparently the phone wouldn't do, and Manny wanted to see me in person. I had no problem complying with Leonardo's request, since Tommy and I had planned to go out anyway.

Tommy MacDonald was my friend, occasional employer, and sometime lover. He was also the most successful criminal-

defense attorney in Miami—no small accomplishment in a
city full of people who need legal representation for their
criminal matters, and who often have plenty of money to
pay for the best. At any given time an inordinate percentage
of Miami's population is being investigated, is under
scrutiny by a grand jury, is facing indictment, incarceration,
deportation, or is headed straight for the witness protection
program. It's that kind of town.

I had known Tommy for seven years, when he was just a
few years out of law school and I was starting as an investigator. He had been pinch-hitting for one of his partners in a
personal-injury case, and I was the investigator of record. As
soon as I saw him walk into a conference room for a depo-
sition, the run-of-the-mill case turned very interesting—at
least as far as I was concerned. Our relationship, both personal and professional, took off quickly. Aside from our
personal chemistry, we've worked on some of the more interesting criminal cases in the recent history of Dade
County.

Physically we're different as night and day, but we com-
plement each other. Tommy is light-skinned and Irish; I'm
Cuban and olive-colored. At six feet, Tommy is a full foot
taller than me. He's thin in contrast to my voluptuousness,
and he has light-blue eyes and sandy hair to set off my hazel
eyes and waist-length, wavy black hair that I've worn in a
braid since I was a child. For some inexplicable reason I
have freckles on my face, little black dots clustered around
my nose and spreading across my cheeks.

Tommy knew about the subtext to our dinner that night.
Leonardo hadn't shared any details with me, so I didn't have
any idea what was about to happen. It wasn't really possible
to blindside Tommy, though; he was as unflappable as a Zen
master.

"It's getting cooler," Tommy said as he sipped his *mojito*.

I nodded my assent. At least an oversized blue-canvas umbrella was protecting us from the still-scorching sun. And we had a good view of Ocean Drive. South Beach isn't the place for anyone with an inferiority complex about their age or physical appearance. Only the most self-assured can handle the sight of so many seminaked perfect bodies without contemplating suicide or self-mutilation. Tonight's parade included the usual rollerbladers, young men and women, models and wannabe, all dressed in the most minimal of clothing and showing impossibly tanned and taut bodies with body-fat indexes that could be tallied with the fingers of one hand. And there were the designer pets, the exotic dogs and even a couple of birds. South Beach is nothing if not competitive, from the shape of one's body, to the quality of drugs one consumes, to who can get past the velvet ropes at the VIP section of the trendiest clubs.

Tommy and I were into our second *mojito* when Manny Mendoza came outside. He was small and wiry, in his late twenties, dressed in black from head to toe. He seemed nervous when he came over and, in a discreet voice, asked if I had time to speak with him.

"Of course," I said. "Please. Sit with us."

I introduced Tommy and scooted over my chair so that Manny could sit between us, facing the water.

"Ms. Solano—" Manny began.

"Please, call me Lupe."

Manny looked around anxiously, making sure no one was close enough to overhear. I wondered what could be so troubling to the manager of one of South Beach's most successful restaurants. Could it be that supermodels were going to boycott over the fat content of the sushi? Or were the rock stars heading for another place down the road?

Manny lit up a cigarette and tilted his head toward me.

"Young gay men are dying on South Beach," he said in a dramatic whisper. "It's like an epidemic."

Tommy and I looked at each other. Then Tommy voiced what we were both thinking—it was no secret that South Beach was predominantly gay.

"AIDS?" he asked.

Manny shook his head slowly. "No, that's pretty much under control these days," he said. "It's not the death sentence that it used to be. No, I'm talking about GHB."

GHB. I tried to remember what I knew about that particular drug. I thought it was something like Ecstasy and Special K—which gave users a euphoric high and heightened sexual energy.

"People don't usually die from taking GHB," I said.

"That's right—usually." Manny took a deep drag on his smoke. "If it's taken correctly: on its own, and without any alcohol. But something's happening. This stuff is killing people. I'm almost positive it's because they're drinking alcohol with it, but that doesn't make sense. Everyone on South Beach knows not to combine drinks with GHB."

"I haven't heard anything about this," I said.

"Me either," Tommy concurred.

"I asked around," Manny said. "The guys who died were drinking in the clubs. And their deaths seemed like bad GHB reactions. Word gets around, you know."

"I see."

"You wouldn't have read about it in the paper or seen anything on TV," Manny said. "But we've had six deaths over the last two Saturday nights."

I blinked, and Tommy and I sat in stunned silence. Our food arrived just then, but neither of us started eating.

Manny perked up a little, seeming satisfied that we understood the seriousness of what brought us there. He crushed out his cigarette so hard that I thought he might break the glass ashtray on the table. Then he took out another one and lit up.

"The police are keeping quiet," Manny said. "It's really bad for tourism. Labor Day is just a couple of weeks away, and South Beach is booked solid then. Summer's slow, and businesses here need all the money they can make in the fall. A lot of jobs are on the line, and no one wants to endanger that. Six drug-related deaths in two weekends would be a real party pooper, if you know what I mean."

Manny looked at me expectantly. He had made his point. If people were scared to come to South Beach, then people like Manny would be out of their high-paying jobs.

"Me and a couple other restaurant managers have put some money aside to hire you," he explained. "If you'll take the case."

Sure, why not? I was a straight Cuban woman from Coral Gables who was supposed to investigate the drug-related deaths of six gay men on South Beach. It made as much sense as anything did.

Two

Thinking about what Manny Mendoza had told me kept me from sleeping much that night. Around dawn I got tired of tossing and turning. I got up, showered and dressed, and put on my usual work outfit of jeans and a T-shirt.

The drive from my family's home in Cocoplum—an enclave of the tony Coral Gables section of Miami—to my Coconut Grove office took only about fifteen minutes at that early hour. I drove on autopilot and thought about my conversation with Manny. It was going to be hard to investigate the deaths—whether they were accidental or, I had to consider, murders. The authorities were staying silent, so I'd have to be careful to keep a low profile. I hoped that Manny's obvious fervent trust in me was justified. Leonardo had apparently portrayed me to him as the Cuban Sherlock Holmes, with dashes of Agatha Christie and Hercule Poirot thrown into the mix.

I was so preoccupied by the case that I narrowly missed two bicyclists in brilliantly colored latex outfits pedaling north on Main Highway. I also came a little close to two rollerbladers, who cursed me and gave me the finger. So it was going to be *that* kind of morning.

Solano Investigations operated out of a three-bedroom cottage in the heart of the Grove, which Leonardo and I had converted into two offices and a gym. We'd been happily ensconced there for the past seven years. I slowed down and parked my Mercedes in its usual spot under the frangipani tree. Once inside, I went straight to the kitchen and brewed up an extra-strong *café con leche*, then headed for my office. I got out a fresh yellow legal pad.

After a while I heard the outer door to the reception area open, and I called out to my cousin.

"Leo, I need to talk to you," I said. I heard Leo drop his keys on his desk and rummage in the kitchen for his own cup of coffee.

Close as we were, this wasn't going to be an easy conversation. I was dreading it, in fact, but it was necessary if I was going to get anywhere on the GHB case. Leo poked his head in my office door, took one look at my serious expression, and backed out again.

"Just a minute," he said, going back to the kitchen. "I think I'd better make this *café con leche* a double."

I had no problem with Leonardo fortifying himself with

Cuban coffee before our conversation. I could have used another myself. Because in all the years we'd worked together, I'd never really asked Leo a direct question about his personal affairs. I was more than happy to listen whenever he wanted to talk, but I'd never initiated an inquiry into the specific details of his life.

I had my suspicions about his tastes and inclinations, but I never felt that I had the right to intrude. Now, because of Manny Mendoza and the deaths on the Beach, I was going to have to ask some probing questions.

"*Hola*, Lupe," Leo said. He took his steaming mug of coffee to the couch across from my desk and sat down.

I tried not to wince, now that I had a good look at his outfit. Solano Investigations had a pretty loose policy about office attire, but Leonardo sometimes went overboard even by our standards. A couple of years ago, I'd been forced to implement an "eight-ounce" rule: anything he wore had to weigh more than half a pound. I had a postal scale out in the reception area if I ever needed to check.

This morning, Leonardo was pushing the envelope. He was wearing a fluorescent pink tankini over fuchsia bicycle pants. The ensemble was grounded by orange high-tops. I resisted the impulse to put on my sunglasses to cut the glare.

Leo made himself comfortable, then looked at me with an expression of wary apprehension.

"So," he asked slowly. "*Que pasa?*"

"I went to see Manny Mendoza last night at Oceana," I said. Leo nodded and blew on his coffee to cool it. "Do you know what he wanted to talk to me about?"

Leo looked out the window as though suddenly mesmerized by the family of parrots who lived in the avocado tree outside.

"Sort of," he said.

I was willing to bet that Leonardo knew more than he was allowing, but I played along and told him everything. Finally I got to the part where I needed his help.

"Leo, I've been a P.I. here for seven years," I said, trying to find a way to get to the subject I needed to reach.

Leo nodded. "I know," he said. "I've been here the whole time."

"Right." I nodded too vigorously. "I've worked all kinds of cases, criminal and civil. And I've worked cases for gay clients, and cases that had gay components, but I've never—"

I stalled out. Leo's eyes widened.

"I've never worked a case that dealt so centrally with the gay subculture in Miami."

Leonardo's body language changed completely; he had figured out where this conversation was heading. He sat up straight, very much the deer in the headlights. I felt like dashing over there and hugging him, but I told myself that we had to press on.

"If I'm going to help Manny, then I have to understand gay club life on South Beach," I told my cousin. "I need someone I trust who has connections to the clubs to help me out, tell me things that I couldn't possibly know about."

I exhaled deeply. This was exhausting.

"Okay, Lupe, I know what you're asking me—even though you're not coming out and directly asking me." Leo pursed his lips impatiently.

Well, I wanted to say, *coming out* was an interesting choice of words at that particular moment.

"You want me to be the person who tells you about gay life in Miami," he concluded.

"That's right, Leo. That's what I'm asking you." I was relieved the topic was on the table. Without going into details, I had finally found out that Leo was gay. I supposed that everyone in the family knew it, or suspected it, but we had all respected Leo's privacy.

Leo seemed to realize that the worst was over, and that I wasn't asking to delve into his personal life. Suddenly I realized that he and Manny might have had some sort of relationship.

"No problem." Leo smiled, leaned back, and sipped his coffee. "What exactly do you need from me?"

"First, I need to know about the designer drugs that are being taken in the clubs," I said. "I know a little about the drug scene, but not what's going on in South Beach. Specifically GHB."

I didn't want to get into how I knew anything about drugs, and I wasn't going to ask Leo how he might know about the drugs in the gay clubs. Our mutual don't-ask-don't-tell policy was stronger than ever.

"GHB is different from Ecstasy and Special K and Ruffies because it's not a controlled substance," Leo explained.

"What do you mean?"

"Well, that means that anyone can manufacture it—not just trained scientists or chemists," Leo said. "There's even a Web site that tells you how to make GHB."

"Like the sites that tell you how to make a nuclear bomb?" I asked. I shouldn't have been at all surprised.

"Right," Leo said. "GHB is taken in liquid form. It's a clear liquid that people buy in little vials. Depending on how much you take, it can last as long as twenty-four hours—and it's an upper, so that's a day without sleep. And the sexual energy it gives is really awesome."

Leo seemed to catch himself when he saw me looking at him. He took on a more serious expression.

"Anyway—" he said.

"Manny said something about GHB being lethal in combination with alcohol," I said.

"That's right, and that's what I heard happened." Leonardo shook his head, and I could see how deeply he felt the senseless loss of those six men. "They went into a G hole."

"A 'G hole'?" I repeated. Now I really felt out of the loop, having to ask questions like that.

Leonardo looked me over for a moment, as though trying to gauge just how naive and uninformed I really was.

"A G hole is when someone has a bad reaction to GHB." Leo visibly shuddered. "I've seen it happen. Guys get seizures; they vomit. I heard about one guy who went into a G hole and aspirated on his own vomit. And other people are supposed to have choked on their own tongues. It's really nasty."

"What causes this G hole?" I wondered aloud. "I mean, GHB is sold in individual vials, so that's probably pretty effective in keeping people from overdosing."

"It had to be alcohol," Leonardo said. "Everyone knows not to mix GHB with alcohol. It leads to a very bad trip and can kill you."

"But why risk it?" I asked. "These guys took GHB; they knew they were going to get high. Why try to get drunk on top of it, if everyone knows this is the one rule not to break?"

"I'm not sure," Leonardo admitted. "Maybe—"

As Leo spoke, my voice joined his in completing his thought.

"—they didn't know they'd taken GHB."

I got up and started to pace, which always helped me think. Leo was sitting up very straight, watching me.

"What if they thought they were taking something else?" I wondered.

"Remember Ruffies, Lupe?" Leo asked.

"That was the date-rape drug," I said. "Guys were slipping them into girl's drinks, or else telling them they were something a lot weaker."

"It was awful," Leo said. "Guys were prosecuted and sent to jail—and they deserved it."

"What if something similar is going on here?" I stopped pacing when I reached the big picture window. "I'd love to see the autopsy reports on those guys, but I know that's not going to happen. We're not even supposed to know the deaths occurred in the first place."

I walked over to my chair and slumped down heavily. Leonardo seemed lost in thought; I didn't usually involve him so closely in my investigations, and he was giving the moment his undivided attention.

"And what if there were no autopsies conducted?" I said, thinking aloud. "If the authorities are bent on keeping this under wraps, it's possible they kept autopsies from being performed."

"You can't search public records, like in other cases," Leonardo said. "This is like a lot of other things in the gay world: underground."

I paused and considered what Leo had said. He was right. This case was murky, hidden from public view.

And what was hidden was a killer. I was sure of it. If everyone knew that alcohol combined with GHB resulted in a lethal body chemistry, then those six young men didn't know they were consuming GHB. Two and two made four. They had been tricked or manipulated into consuming a deadly cocktail.

I looked up at Leonardo. He had finished his coffee and gotten up from the sofa.

"You're going to have to be creative on this one," he said.

Which was, of course, quite an understatement.

Three

"So how do you decide who to let in and who to keep out?" I asked the burly, balding man sitting across from me. I noticed he was sporting a couple of new tattoos since the last time I'd seen him.

I was drinking a double-latte-extra-espresso-shot at Starbucks on Lincoln Road. Jimmy de la Vega was having a black coffee. Jimmy was a private investigator who'd become a security guard. I knew Jimmy well enough to confide in him, and I'd told him the bare outlines of my new case. It was no surprise that he'd already heard about the deaths.

Jimmy worked for me a few years back, on a contract basis, first as a moving-surveillance specialist and then as a bodyguard when one of my clients needed protection. Jimmy liked being a security guy, and in a couple of years he had set up his own business, which was now one of the most successful in South Florida. We kept in touch and referred clients to one another. If we weren't friends, we stayed friendly.

I knew that the South Beach clubs had security guys stationed at the front door, where they checked ID's. According to Jimmy, there were guards inside as well.

"We don't let anyone inside who looks drunk or stoned on drugs," Jimmy said. "Or anyone who seems like they're looking for trouble. People are there to have a good time.

We're in charge of making sure things don't get weird or heavy."

Jimmy was on the fast track in Miami, and his clients were trendy clubs and stars who needed someone to watch their backs. In spite of the company he was keeping, though, Jimmy was a serious, laid-back family man. Those characteristics were probably why he survived and prospered in such a tough business, while so many others had crashed and burned.

"And you should see the fake ID's," Jimmy said with a chortle. "I have a stack of them back at my office. I mean, I've seen a little five-foot blond kid with hay sticking out of his ears hand me a green card saying his name is Pedro Flores and that he's six-foot-one and lives in the Bronx!"

"Ridiculous," I agreed.

Jimmy's smile turned rueful. "Well, now there's an outfit in Calle Ocho that's selling green cards! Can you believe that? Green cards for ID's so that kids can party. No respect for anything!"

Jimmy was first-generation Cuban-American. For him, the United States could do no wrong. The idea that someone was selling coveted resident alien cards was abhorrent and borderline sacrilegious.

I liked Jimmy, but now I was remembering that his conversation tended to go off on tangents. I tried gently to steer him back to the subject at hand.

"What about the security in the clubs?" I reminded him.

"Right. Security." Jimmy looked faintly embarrassed. "Well, the first step is at the door. If a person looks suspicious, then we pat him down for drugs."

"What kind of drugs are they taking these days?" I asked.

"The usual club drugs," Jimmy said with a shrug. "Ruffies, GHB, Ecstasy, Special K. There's probably even some new ones I don't know about. These bathtub chemists are always trying to come up with the next big thing."

"What do you know about GHB?" I asked. I already knew that GHB—gamma hydroxybutyrate—was sometimes referred to as 'liquid ecstasy' and sometimes mistaken for 'E' in cases of overdoses. It's broken down quickly in the body, which makes it very difficult to recognize through autopsy. And, as Manny and Leonardo had told me, it could be lethal when mixed with alcohol.

"It comes in little vials—like those perfume samples they give out at department stores," Jimmy told me. "Most of the time they take it with cranberry juice. You probably know how nasty it can be when it reacts with alcohol."

"That's my theory for what's going on," I said. "And it doesn't make sense that all six men would make the same stupid mistake in such a short period of time."

"You're saying someone slipped it to them?" Jimmy asked.

"Or else they thought they were taking something else." I paused. "People can drink on Ecstasy, can't they?"

"Yeah." Jimmy rubbed his chin. "Are you saying you think there's a killer working the clubs in South Beach?"

"That's what I'm saying," I said.

Jimmy made a sour face. Part of his job was keeping the peace in the clubs, and I knew he would take this personally.

"You let me know if there's anything I can do to help," he said gravely. "And I mean anything."

"Which clubs do you handle security for?" I asked.

"Almost all the ones on Washington Avenue," Jimmy said. He rattled off the names of ten clubs. I recognized some as exclusively gay, some as mixed. Among the clubs were the three where young men had died.

"Look, Lupe, to be honest with you, this is reflecting badly on me and my company," Jimmy said.

"I understand," I said. I rubbed my eyes, trying to mine a new idea. "What about when you find drugs on someone, Jimmy?"

Jimmy sighed and rolled his eyes. "Listen, this is between you and me," he said. "The club owners say there's a zero-tolerance policy on drug use in the clubs, all right? Well, that's bullshit. If they cracked down too hard on drugs, then people would stop coming to the clubs. A lot of the time when I find drugs on someone, I just tell them to be careful and stay out of trouble that night. Sometimes I confiscate the stuff, but then there's a hassle turning it in to the police."

I thought about this. "So what's the point of patting them down?" I asked.

Jimmy looked at me as though I was a little child. "Appearances, Lupe," he said. "There are some city commissioners who want to shut down the clubs completely. They think the clubs bring the wrong element to Miami Beach."

Jimmy finished off his coffee.

"But South Beach is famous for the clubs," I said. "Take away the clubs and you take away the top industry on the Beach."

I hadn't considered a political/economic angle to this case, but the possibility was too strong to ignore.

"You don't know the whole story," Jimmy said. He looked around to make sure no one was listening, then moved closer to me. His voice lowered to a whisper.

"What do you mean?"

"Whenever there's an overdose or a bad reaction in one of the clubs, our orders are to take the person out back and dump him in the alley," Jimmy told me. "In other words, get him out and get him away. And we're supposed to search him, make sure he doesn't have a matchbook or anything linking him to the club."

"What then?" I asked. "Call an ambulance?"

Jimmy paused, seeming almost sad for an instant. "Police and ambulances get noticed," he said, turning matter-of-fact. "That brings publicity and investigations. Keep things quiet, and the clubs stay in business. If a guy takes too many drugs and dies, well, I guess it wasn't his lucky day."

Even though it was about a hundred degrees outside, I had to suppress a shiver. I couldn't believe that it had come to this. And I didn't like knowing that Jimmy was a part of it.

"You don't agree with this, do you?" I asked him. "Leaving guys in the alley like they were sick dogs?"

Jimmy looked at me long and hard.

"Lupe, someone *did* call the police about the six guys," he said, very slowly. "And that guy isn't surprised that nothing came of it. You know what I'm saying?"

With that, Jimmy got up, said good-bye, and left. I hadn't learned enough to know how to proceed on this case, I realized. And Jimmy didn't know what to tell me. If anything, he was more frustrated than me. It was shaping up to be that kind of case.

Four

After Jimmy left, I finished my latte and walked back to my car, which I had parked on 17th Street. I planned on returning to my office as I turned off the alarm and unlocked the door.

I began weighing the possibilities, and decided that I needed to talk again with Manny Mendoza. Instead of driving back to the Grove by way of Alton Road, I decided to take Washington Avenue, the street that's home to most of the South Beach Clubs. It had been a while since I'd been there, and I wanted to get the lay of the land.

The three clubs were within four blocks of each other—definitely close enough for someone to cover the area on foot in a short period of time. I saw an empty space in front of the Miami Beach Post Office and parked the Mercedes there. From where I was parked, I could see most of the relevant stretch of Washington Avenue.

The blocks weren't very long, and they were jammed with small storefronts—mostly an odd assortment of shops that sold cheap, glittery clothes, along with a few fast-food joints and delicatessens. The outfits in the windows of the clothes shops catered mostly to cross-dressers, from what I could tell. It wasn't exactly a high-rent district. In the cold light of day, the neighborhood looked rundown and in need of a face-lift. By night, though, I knew it was a different story. The place would be pulsing with activity and energy.

The clubs' entrances were marked with small, nondescript signs, looking as though they were almost an afterthought. I assumed this was intended to convey a cachet of exclusivity. If a visitor hadn't known this was the place to find the clubs, they would have been easy to miss. At night it would be easy to find them; usually there were crowds outside on the sidewalks, hoping they would be among the chosen ones allowed entry into the hallowed ground.

I left my motor running to supply me with life-giving air conditioning, and sat there for a good fifteen minutes trying to figure out why someone would murder six young men in such a nasty manner. No answers came to me, no matter how long I stared, so I grabbed my purse from the floor of the car—where I usually kept it to avoid tempting a smash-and-grab artist. I looked up Manny's number at the Oceana from the case file and punched it in.

I was in luck. Despite the early hour, Manny answered on the second ring.

"Any luck?" he asked hopefully.

"We'll see," I said. "Look, I'm parked a couple of blocks away. Is it all right if I come by to talk to you?"

"Sure," Manny said, a note of cautious curiosity in his voice.

I turned off the car, put some quarters in the meter, and crossed Washington Avenue headed toward Ocean Drive. Manny was waiting for me on the Oceana's terrace. He was again dressed all in black, with a cigarette dangling from his lips and a fresh pack clutched in his hand. He was staring out at Ocean Drive and obviously waiting for me.

He called out my name when he saw me, then bounded down the half-dozen steps to street level to greet me. He kissed me on the cheek, surprising me a little, and escorted me back to the table where we'd talked with Tommy a couple of nights before. I declined Manny's offer of a drink and got down to business.

"Manny, you said these guys died from a combination of GHB and alcohol," I said. "You're sure about that?"

We were the only people on the terrace, but Manny leaned close to me and whispered, "Whatever I tell you is confidential?"

"Of course," I said.

"Promise me?" he demanded.

"I promise you."

Manny put out his half-smoked cigarette and took a fresh one out of the pack. As he lit it, I was willing to bet that smokes were one of the primary expenses in his budget. I didn't want to even think about the condition of his lungs.

"I found out about the deaths from my boyfriend," Manny said, his voice almost inaudible. "He's the one who gave me all the inside information. He's worried sick about what happened, and how it's all been kept quiet. He's really afraid of what's going to happen this weekend."

Manny took a long drag on his cigarette. "He's been a mess since this happened," he continued. "He can't eat, can't sleep."

I knew this might be delicate ground, but I had to ask. "Manny, who is your boyfriend?"

Manny flinched back from me. He thought for a moment, wrestling with some unvoiced question.

"All right," he said. "My boyfriend is an officer in the Miami Beach Police Department."

That made sense. It explained how Manny had access to so much information that was being hidden from the public.

"I don't need to know his name," I said, eliciting a look of relief on Manny's face. "But I need to know more details about the deaths."

"Sure, ask away," Manny said. "But I don't have all the answers."

"What about the police investigation?" I asked. Manny nodded slowly; I could tell that he was worried about getting his lover in trouble. "Was there anything to tie the six victims together, any common links that might explain why they were killed?"

"No." Manny smiled without pleasure. "You know, that was the first question I asked. But my boyfriend said that it seems to be random. Six guys over two weekends. Like a serial killer."

Sounded right. But I had no proof of anything.

"So apart from the fact that they were all partying in gay clubs, there's nothing to link them? You're sure about that?"

"That's what Jake told me." A second after he realized what he had said, Manny gasped.

I pretended not to have heard anything. "Were there autopsies conducted?"

"Yes. The results were sealed, but my boyfriend found out that they had mixed GHB with alcohol." Manny paused. "The victims' families were told that their boys had died as a result of drug overdoses."

Manny lit a new cigarette off the burning end of the one he had just finished. "I guess the families didn't ask too many questions," he said. "They were probably embarrassed their sons died in gay nightclubs, high on drugs."

Through a cloud of smoke, Manny looked at me. "You know, Lupe, we may live in a free and easy place here, where anything goes and all kinds of lifestyles are accepted, but that's not the way it is in the rest of the country."

"And that's why the guys come to South Beach," I said.

Manny smiled, glad that I understood what he was telling me. "Because they can be themselves here," he continued. "And not have to put up with any bullshit about who they are and how they lead their lives. A lot of these guys have families who don't want to know anything about their sons' lives—as long as they're in the dark, they don't have to confront the fact that their sons are gay. It's an old story, everyone in denial. And that's how the police got away with giving the families so few details about how these boys died. The families really didn't want to know. And then the police can say that they didn't disclose detailed information out of respect for the families."

I considered what Manny was saying. Keeping the deaths quiet served more than one purpose. The families didn't have to confront too much information about their sons' lifestyles, and the police didn't have to admit that they weren't solving a case that involved the serial murders of six young gay men.

"Is the investigation still ongoing?" I asked. If it was, I had to be very careful. There were strict rules for private investigators in such cases.

"Nothing much is happening right now," Manny said. "The police are hoping that there are no more deaths and that the whole thing just goes away. Starting a high-profile investigation right now would kill tourism. It would be nothing but bad publicity. There might be a few ghouls—like those tourists who have their pictures taken on the spot where Gianni Versace was murdered—but most people would be scared off."

I knew what Manny was talking about. On more than one occasion I had seen tourists milling around the wrought-iron gates outside the Versace home, trying to get close to the cordoned-off area where the designer had been shot and killed in broad daylight. It was gruesome.

Manny shook his head with a touch of disgust. "The police figure there'll always be deaths from bad drugs on South Beach and that this situation is really no different," he said. "They're playing the whole thing down."

"But your boyfriend doesn't agree," I said. "And that's why he thought of the idea of hiring a private investigator."

Manny nodded. "You got it," he said.

"And you knew about me through Leonardo," I said, almost adding the word *relationship* but stopping short.

"Leonardo always bragged about what a great detective you were, Lupe." Manny smiled. "He said that if anyone was going to find out what happened to those six guys, it was going to be you."

I felt myself blushing at the compliment. I was a little

surprised to hear that Leonardo had spoken so highly of me to his friend.

A few customers were starting to arrive; they were looking around expectantly for a maitre d' to show them to a table. It was clear that things were going to get busy soon, so I stood up to leave.

Before I did, though, I had one question for Manny.

"If it had been six straight men who had been killed, does your boyfriend think the police would have handled the situation differently?"

Manny's silence told me everything I needed to know.

Five

After I left Manny, I decided to check out the alleys behind the clubs, which run parallel between Collins Drive and Washington Avenue, so I could have a look at where Jimmy had told me the bodies of the young men were dragged out and left.

Each club was about half a block wide and occupied the space from Washington Avenue to the alley directly behind it. I began walking the alley behind the Neptune, the most northern club. The back door was unmarked steel secured by three prominent deadbolts. There were no markers to indicate where the door led. There were trash cans outside the back door and there was no one in the alley at that time of early afternoon, unless I wanted to count the mangy cats who were pawing through the garbage.

The smell in the alley was almost overwhelming and grew stronger the longer I stood there. It smelled like rotten fruit, animal waste, vomit, and other fluids that I didn't much want to contemplate. The heat was baking it all to the point at which I felt like gagging.

Looking around, I was filled with sadness for those six young men who had been unceremoniously dumped back there like so much refuse. And if what Manny had told me was true, nothing much was being done to investigate the deaths. If I had access to active police sources, I might have had leads to follow and facts to pursue, but for now I had little more than instinct.

The alley behind the Neptune was yielding no secrets, so I moved on to the next one. The Zenith was also in the middle of its block, with a dumpster next to the back door. It smelled a little better back there—a little. The Zenith's back door was also protected by big deadbolts, along with a sign next to the doorknob warning that the area was protected by twenty-four-hour surveillance. I looked around for a camera but didn't find one, not even a phony one to frighten away amateur thieves. As far as I could tell, the sign was nothing more than a bluff.

The third club, the Majestic, was on a street corner a block away from the Zenith. Unlike the other two clubs, its back door opened onto a side street. That meant, in order to dump a body, someone would have to carry it around the corner in full view of passersby. That wouldn't be easy, with the door in plain sight. I knew that South Beach was crawling with police on a Saturday night. They were out in force, setting up road blocks and stopping drivers who might be impaired. Washington Avenue was typically well patrolled, with cops busting underage drinkers and arresting anyone who got drunk and disorderly.

South Beach came alive after dark. Most clubs didn't even open until eleven at night and closed around five in the morning. And then the after-hours places opened, from five to eight o'clock, sometimes even until ten. So whoever carried the bodies out of the Majestic would have had little opportunity to wait for the crowds on the street to thin out.

I decided to drive back to the office without making any more detours. I had something that I wanted to look into.

Back at Solano Investigations, I went straight to my office and turned on the computer at my desk. Leonardo had left for the day, probably heading home before going clubbing that night. I waited for my computer to boot up and banished from my thoughts what he might be wearing for such an evening.

I was pretty much computer illiterate, but I was able to find a few drug-related Web sites. I struck out on the first two, but the last one confirmed my suspicions about GHB.

I was almost sure the guys who died didn't know they were taking GHB. The last Web site I visited said that it was possible to boil down GHB to a point at which it cooled, became a powder, and then resembled Special K—which could be taken with alcohol without any deadly consequences. What if someone substituted GHB for the victims' powdered Special K without their knowing about it, or sold them GHB while saying it was Special K?

And how could that be done? However it happened, the killer had gotten away with it. The question was: Would the killer be satisfied with taking six lives, or would there be more to come?

I sat and stared at the parrots outside my window. If they knew the answer, they sure weren't saying. I was going to have to come up with an individual who would have the opportunity to commit the murders. And in the clubs in South Beach, that might be anyone. I knew that when someone went clubbing on South Beach, the pattern was often to start off at one club and visit two or three others before the night was finished. So the killer—who committed his crimes at three different clubs over the course of two Saturdays—wouldn't have been unusual in moving about from place to place in a relatively short period of time.

I figured I could dismiss club owners as suspects—from what I knew, they tended not to go to clubs other than the ones they owned, and they would have been spotted if they visited the competition. Besides, it didn't make sense that one of them would knock off his or her own customers.

Another possibility would be people who worked at the clubs, maybe a disgruntled employee. But that would be self-destructive. If the clubs were eventually closed as a result of the deaths, then they would be out of work. Plus, why run the risk of going to other clubs to commit the crime? It didn't fit.

Then there were the city commissioners who wanted the clubs shut down on moral grounds. They weren't likely suspects, since they were older and ostensibly straight and would stand out in the clubs. And from the sound of it, they wouldn't be caught dead in such dens of sin.

I looked down at my notes. There was only one place left for me to go. I picked up the phone to call Leonardo. I hoped he would be free that night. I needed an escort for my night of clubbing.

Six

Leonardo and I agreed to go clubbing together in one car; he was going to pick me up at home at midnight. I didn't want him to ring the doorbell and wake everyone up, so I was waiting by the window when he arrived. When he got out of his car, I was pleasantly surprised to see him dressed in conservative clothes—matching black polyester body-hugging pants and shirt, and boots that John Travolta might have sported in *Saturday Night Fever*. I was also in black, satin jeans and a sheer lurex T-shirt. We headed off for South Beach together, looking as if we were headed for a 70's funeral.

Traffic was relatively light at that hour, and we got there in about thirty minutes. Fate blessed us, and we found a parking spot on Collins Avenue, just a couple of blocks from Washington. Instead of going into the first club—Neptune— I took Leonardo's arm and stopped us across the street, in the shadows, where we could watch the entrance.

"What are we looking for?" Leo asked me, staring across the street in a visibly anxious attempt to look calm and relaxed.

"Anything," I said. "We're just watching."

I took my miniature binoculars out of my purse and focused on the Neptune. The first thing I noticed was the fact that, by night, Washington Avenue looked a lot more glamorous and sophisticated than it did by day.

There were about thirty men outside the Neptune, most dressed in blue jeans and white "wife-beater" T-shirts. Two red-velvet ropes cordoned off the in-crowd from the wanna-bes. I knew the first set of ropes was for normal customers, out-of-towners and the like. Even though the club might be empty inside, those poor souls would be made to wait outside for half an hour anyway. The second rope was for VIP clients, who were let in immediately and without a cover charge.

"That's the door-god," Leo said. "The big black guy in the yellow jacket."

Non-VIP patrons were subject to the whims of the "door-god," a big guy with a shaved head, who decided who was let in and who had to wait. Next to him were a few men in dark suits—not particularly nice ones—who were checking ID's. I refocused my binoculars when I saw another man move out of the shadows. It was Jimmy de la Vega.

"Jimmy's here," I said in a low voice. "I sure found him quick."

Jimmy had been dressed pretty conservatively earlier that day at Starbucks, but now he was wearing a tailored Italian-cut black suit that made him look like chief undertaker at a Mafia funeral home. I watched him pat down a couple of customers after they had been given the nod to pass through the velvet rope. Jimmy took them aside by the door, as their final obstacle before they could enter the hallowed halls of the club.

I knew Jimmy's pat-down was for drugs and weapons, although I knew from what he told me that the clubs' drug policies were basically to wink and look the other way. Leonardo leaned back against the wall and sighed. I knew this wasn't his idea of an exciting start to our evening.

I watched Jimmy pat down a couple of young guys. Something seemed strange to me. I couldn't be sure, so I handed over the binoculars to Leonardo.

"Watch Jimmy, over there by the door," I told him.

Leo focused the binoculars. "Oh, yeah. I remember him. Jimmy de la Vega." He paused for a second. "Um, he really seems to be getting into his job."

"You see what I'm seeing?" I asked him.

"I don't know," Leo said. "But when he patted those guys down, it looked almost like he was feeling them up."

I watched Jimmy perform the next pat-down. His hands were all over a young guy in a black T-shirt and jeans. I didn't know, but there seemed something inappropriate about it. Jimmy was a family man, though, married to his high-school sweetheart. I figured I was just overreacting. I saw

Jimmy's hands reach deep into the guy's front shirt pocket and pause for a second. Jimmy said something to him, then clapped him on the shoulder and waved him in.

None of the other security men or the door-god seemed to notice what Jimmy was doing, but then, none of them were paying attention to much of anything outside their direct line of responsibility. I watched the next pat-down. I wasn't sure, but I thought I saw the young man Jimmy was touching react with a flinch of surprise.

"Let's go inside," I said to Leo.

"Finally," my cousin replied.

Leonardo and I darted across Washington Avenue, and approached the club. Jimmy spotted us and waved us over to the VIP rope.

"Lupe!" he said in a welcoming voice. "You should have called ahead, like you said you would."

I recalled saying nothing of the kind, but I smiled at him anyway. "Hey, Jimmy," I said. "You remember Leo?"

Jimmy gave Leo a nod and an awkward smile. Leo blinked in the bright light outside the club, taking Jimmy in.

"We wanted to check out the clubs," I said to Jimmy. "It's been a while since I've been out in South Beach."

Jimmy took two tickets from a stack the door-god was holding in his hand. He handed them both to me.

"Have a good time," he said. "So how are things going on the matter we talked about this morning?"

"Nothing major," I said. "That's why I'm having a look around."

Jimmy nodded. We were holding up the line. Jimmy held up his hand in the "call-me" gesture and waved us in. He began searching the next patron in line.

We reached a window in a tiny vestibule, where our tickets were exchanged for drink vouchers. I saw that, had we not been comped by Jimmy, the charge for coming in would have been twenty dollars each. And that didn't include drinks.

As soon as we stepped inside, the music was too loud to talk over. It was a sort of tribal rock, part electronic, instrumental with no lyrics. It was so dark in the entryway that Leonardo and I had to grope our way upstairs while our eyes were adjusting.

We hadn't even reached the main room yet when my head began to pound to the same beat as the music. I didn't think I was going to last long at the Neptune. If possible, it was even darker upstairs in the main room. I saw clusters of light in the dark as my eyes struggled to focus. The only lights in the place came from strategically placed high-hats on the ceiling.

"God'd get the day!" Leo yelled at me, his mouth close to my ear. The music was far too loud to know what he was saying.

"What?" I yelled back.

"Gunner diss a drake!" he screamed.

"What?"

Then I got it: he was offering to get us some drinks. I gave him the thumbs-up. Leo left me standing against the wall, watching the scene in front of me. The main room was cavernous, filled with young men mostly in their twenties and thirties. Some wore T-shirts, others were bare-chested. Most wore jeans. All looked amazingly toned and physically fit. I noticed that a few had drinks in their hands, although far more common was the sight of water bottles tucked into the jeans' back pockets.

I was the only woman in the whole place, as far as I could tell, but no one looked at me strangely or made me feel unwelcome. I was pretty much ignored, in fact, which was fine with me.

Just about all the men in the room were dancing—some alone, some with partners. The place was freezing cold from air conditioning, but they were all sweating copiously. I hadn't seen any bullets or vials, but I saw on many faces the spaced-out, blissed-out expression of someone on drugs. Those looks—not to mention the excessive sweating and the water bottles—were pretty broad clues to indicate what was going on.

I watched these young, attractive men, swaying to the tribal beat of the music, and couldn't help but wonder what the future held for them, what would follow after the allure of the clubbing lifestyle wore off. But then I told myself that I was sounding like an old lady.

Leo returned with our drinks: a Manhattan for him, and a red wine for me. Both were served in identical plastic cups. I felt as though I were at a frat party. We crossed the room and found a smaller room off the main dance floor, where mercifully there was an empty table by the north wall. Once we were seated, I had a look around at the tables nearest us. Although I spotted some makeup and cleavage, I was still pretty sure that I was the only biological female in the place.

There were three bars in the Neptune. Each one was three deep with young men waiting to buy drinks—bottles of water, it turned out, were as popular as alcoholic beverages.

Because these young men knew better than to mix booze with GHB. They dissolved it in juice to get high. The guys who were drinking hadn't had any GHB.

At least, they'd better hope they hadn't.

We had been there less than fifteen minutes, but I had seen what I needed.

"What do you think?" Leo yelled at me, straining his vocal cords.

"We can skip the next two clubs, Leo," I told him. "I just realized something. I think I have an idea what happened.

"So what'd you think about the Neptune?" Jimmy asked me. He had come to Solano Investigations in the early afternoon the next day, as I'd requested. "You really should have told me you were coming. I could have arranged the real VIP treatment for you and Leo."

"That's all right," I said. "We had a nice time."

Jimmy was back to his regular casual mode of dress, in dark pants and a white, open-necked polo shirt stitched on the shoulder with "de la Vega Security." Unlike me, he looked none the worse for the late hours he was keeping. One night on the Beach, and I was ready for a week off.

I escorted Jimmy from the reception area toward my office. Leonardo was at his desk, looking over a report before sending it out with a bill. He didn't look up from his work, nor did he offer to make coffee for the first time in my memory. Once inside my office, I motioned toward the chair in front of my desk.

"You want to close the door?" Jimmy asked.

"No, I keep no secrets from my cousin."

Jimmy looked over his shoulder, then back at me. His chair was arranged perfectly so that he couldn't look out the open doorway without turning in his seat. I gave him an "are you comfortable?" look, then hit him with it.

"So, Jimmy, tell me something," I said. "Why'd you do it?"

"Do what?" he said, his eyes widening. "What are you talking about?"

I waited a long moment; we stared into each other's eyes, each waiting for the other to break.

"All I want to know is why," I said.

Jimmy looked at me as though I were a lunatic. For an instant, one tiny moment, I doubted myself. But no, it all fit together too well.

"When you patted down customers at the door searching for drugs, you substituted their bullets of Special K with GHB that you had boiled down into a powder," I told him.

"You're crazy," Jimmy said.

But I saw a look in his eyes—a look that told me I was right.

"You had access to GHB—you confiscated it from a few clubgoers," I told him. "And as door security, no one was going to say much if you were rummaging around in their pockets long enough to switch vials. They're carrying an illegal substance, and they're not in a position to complain."

Jimmy shook his head. "I don't have to listen to—"

"You worked security at a few clubs that night, right?" I said. "You had plenty of opportunity to make your mark at three different places."

Jimmy's lip curled into a sneer, but he didn't get up and leave. I knew that he wasn't going to, either.

"You found six guys who had already been drinking," I said. "You got close enough to smell their breath when you were patting them down. Even if they didn't continue drinking that night, the amount of alcohol in their system would make sure they went into a G hole when they took the GHB."

"Maybe you're the one who's been taking junk," Jimmy said, trying to laugh. "It's made you lose your mind."

"As security chief, you had full access to the clubs at any time. No one would suspect you had anything to do with the deaths," I said. "You took them out into the alley and no one suspected a thing. Even at the Majestic, where you had to take a body out in view of people—your clout and position on the Beach probably made people think you were just taking a drunk guy to a taxicab. And then, like you said, you went through the guys' pockets to take away anything that might link them to the clubs. How perfect was that?"

"I guess I'm a real criminal mastermind," Jimmy said sarcastically.

"And, to top it all off, you were the one who called for help," I said. "And you certainly wanted me to think you were cooperating with my investigation."

Jimmy put his hands on the chair arms, as though to leave. "Why would I do something like that, Lupe? Why?"

I walked to the side of my desk and perched on the edge. "Jimmy, I know you," I said. "Something's wrong. I saw you the other night patting down those guys. Leonardo saw it, too. And after he saw you at the club he said you were setting off his 'gaydar.'"

Jimmy sputtered. "He said what?"

"You're in the middle of all this, Jimmy," I said. "And you're giving off signals. Why'd you do it, Jimmy? Please, tell me."

Jimmy amazed me just then by getting up and closing the door. Before he could turn around to face me again, I pressed the open intercom button on my speakerphone.

"Can I really talk to you?" Jimmy asked me. I could see that he had started sweating, and there was a haunted look in his eyes.

"It's just us here," I said. "I want to know how you thought of it, and why. I just want my curiosity satisfied. You know as well as I do that I don't have any fingerprints or witnesses."

Jimmy looked out the window at the parrots, who were squawking and fighting. I could see the wheels spinning. My heart was beating so hard that I was afraid Jimmy would hear it and not speak.

"You're right, Lupe," he said. "I did it. Does that make you happy?"

"No, Jimmy," I said. "It really doesn't."

"It's a goddamned mess," Jimmy said. "And when I found out you were investigating it, I got worried. I didn't know how to handle you, and I was worried it might come to this."

"Why, Jimmy?" I whispered.

"Is my secret safe with you?" Jimmy said, his voice suddenly hoarse.

I nodded.

"I want those clubs closed down," Jimmy said. "I wanted to do something to get the clubs shut down and out of my life."

"But they employ you, Jimmy," I pointed out.

"That's just it," he said. "Don't you see? I have to be there at those damned clubs all the time."

"So?"

Jimmy hung his head down. He was standing in the middle of my office, his arms limp at his sides. I glanced over and saw that the office intercom channel was still open.

"I was beginning to like it too much." Jimmy raised his hands to his eyes and stifled a sob. "All those young, half-naked kids. Sweating and dancing all around me. I was inside those clubs too much, seeing too much. I don't need the temptation, Lupe. I have a family."

I was speechless. Before last night, I would never have considered Jimmy capable of any crime, much less murder. But after talking to Leo about Jimmy's "vibe," as my cousin called it, I began to realize that my old friend Jimmy was in the throes of a sexual conflict.

"What would people say if they found out I liked the boys on the Beach, Lupe?" Jimmy said, his voice breaking.

"I don't know, Jimmy," I told him. "I guess they'd say you were gay. Or bi. Or somewhere in between."

"Don't *say* that," Jimmy hissed. He took a step toward me but stopped, his face constricted with self-loathing.

"There were better ways to eliminate temptation," I said to Jimmy. "There are plenty of other places you could work."

"Thought of that. Doesn't matter," Jimmy said. "As long as the clubs are there, I'm going to want to be there. The only way out for me is to shut down the clubs. And I found a way to make that happen."

Nowhere in Jimmy's worldview was a thought of remorse for his six victims. I was beginning to see that Jimmy was one sick puppy.

"But the cops were keeping it all quiet," I offered.

"I know. I hadn't counted on that happening," Jimmy said with genuine amazement. "Still, sooner or later word's going to get out. Right?"

Jimmy was still in his moment, still thinking he had options. I was chilled to realize that he was contemplating committing more murders.

"Gotta get rid of those clubs," Jimmy said. He looked at me strangely. "Are you with me or against me, Lupe?"

At that, I whistled sharply, a prearranged signal. Jimmy started when the door burst open and a man with a gun shouted at him to hit the floor. It was Miami Homicide Detective Anderson, whom I'd worked with once or twice before.

"Get it on tape?" I asked him.

"No problem," Anderson replied. "That intercom worked perfectly."

Leonardo poked his head around the corner with a look of mixed alarm and satisfaction. The South Beach killer was caught. All the evidence against Jimmy was circumstantial, but the taped confession wouldn't hurt matters.

"You lied to me! *Puta!*" Jimmy shouted in disbelief as he sank to the floor, his fingers instinctively interlacing behind his head. "You said it was just you and me!"

"You need help, Jimmy," I said.

"That's an understatement," Leo said from the doorway.

Detective Anderson started reading Jimmy his Miranda rights. Jimmy's worst fear was about to be realized. Everyone in Miami was going to find out that Jimmy de la Vega, husband of Maria and father of three, had killed six young men because he was tempted by their youth and beauty.

With Detective Anderson on the case, every detail of Jimmy's crimes was going to become public knowledge very quickly. Jimmy had just been outed. In a big way.

CAROLE ON LOMBARD
A NICK POLO STORY

by Jerry Kennealy

**The Street: Lombard Street,
San Francisco, California**

Sometimes when you're doing these anthologies—and you've done as many as I have—you just don't want to strain your brain figuring out what order the stories should appear in. I took the easy route here, and they appear in alphabetical order according to the author's last name. That's why another of the "handful" of P.I.'s who now write it instead of do it appears right after the Garcia-Aguilera story. Jerry Kennealy recently retired after many years of plying his trade as a P.I., but luckily for us he hasn't retired from writing about Nick Polo. This cleverly titled story has much more going for it than that, as you will soon see. The most recent novel by Jerry Kennealy is *The Other Eye* (NAL, 2000).

The eleven-hundred block of Lombard Street. The "crookedest street in the world." Even if you've never visited San Francisco, you've seen it in television commercials or in chase scenes in movies.

There are eight switchbacks on the one-block descent. It looks as if it had been laid out by a drunk who stumbled off a cable car, but actually there's a simple, and greedy, reason for the corkscrew design—this way they were able to build more homes.

We natives shun the area, because tourists flock to it, causing traffic jams, overheated cars, and road-rage confrontations.

My flat is just four blocks away, so I decided to walk. A tour bus was parked at the bottom of the hill on Leavenworth, and a little island of onlookers weighed down with cameras and camcorders were filming the slow-moving traffic negotiating Lombard.

The woman I'd come to see lived on the top of the hill, and turned out to be as twisted as the brick pavement in front of her house.

The call from David Herris had come into my office just before lunchtime. Herris is a successful plaintiff's attorney and throws a good deal of work my way. Usually our conversations are brief and to the point. Find this, do that, in a hurry, and don't spend too much money.

But today Herris was polite, pleasant, gracious. When an attorney starts acting gracious, tighten your buttocks—something long and pointed is headed thataway.

"Nick, I know you don't like taking on private-party cases, but I'm hoping you'll make an exception this time. I have a client, Carole Reed, who wants the services of a private investigator, and naturally I recommended you."

"What's her problem?"

"I don't know, actually. Carole is . . . a bit eccentric. Her husband, Ronald, passed away some fifteen years ago. He left her with something like forty million dollars. And that's back when forty million was really big money. She lives right here in the city, on Lombard Street. Can I tell her that you'll talk to her?"

Forty million was still a lot of money to me. "Sure. Why not?"

"Good, good. And Nick. Do me a favor. Let me know what Carole looks like."

"I thought she was a client of yours, David."

"Oh, she is. She definitely is. But I haven't seen her since her husband kicked off. And I don't know of anyone who has."

Mrs. Reed called within the hour.

"Mr. Polo? This is Carole on Lombard Street. Please come to my home at four o'clock." She gave me the house number, then hung up, without so much as a "good-bye." Just like they do in the movies.

So there I was, at the appointed hour, out of breath from walking up that damn hill, ringing her doorbell.

"Who is it?" a strong, clear, demanding voice asked.

I looked up at the video camera centered over the door and smiled. "Nick Polo, Mrs. Reed."

"Show me some identification."

I freed my private investigator's license from my wallet and held it up to the camera.

"There's no photograph," the clear, demanding voice complained.

I stretched on my tiptoes and held my driver's license up to the camera. "Can you see this?"

I guess she could, because the door buzzed open.

There was a marble-floored entry hall, then a white-carpeted staircase. The walls were painted white to match the carpet. Or vice versa.

I paused at the first landing. A large, spacious room filled with large, spacious furniture and a grand piano, all of it covered with white sheets.

"Keep coming, Mr. Polo. I'm up here."

"Up here" turned out to be the third floor. The second floor was more white walls, white carpeting, and furniture covered with sheets.

Mrs. Reed greeted me with a thin smile and a formal, "How do you do."

She appeared to be in her seventies—tall, full-figured, with pale, alabaster skin and surprisingly few wrinkles. Her hair was red gone gray, and worn short without attention to style. She was wearing a baggy black turtleneck sweater and corduroy slacks. Think of Katherine Hepburn with about twenty-five extra pounds on her bones.

Three sides of the room were floor-to-ceiling windows, some half shuttered. Slitted sunlight shone through the plantation shutters, etching a pattern on the oak floors. Comfortable-looking sofas and chairs with dust skirts and lots of piping were scattered around the room. Unframed watercolors dotted one wall. An easel stood at one end of the room. A computer sat next to the easel, the screen saver splashing in brilliantly colored silence.

There were telescopes spaced around the room. Long ones, fat ones, all on stands. Some had electrical cords attached. A high-backed leather bar stool was parked in front of one of the telescopes.

"Nice to meet you, Mrs. Reed." I extended a hand, but she folded hers quickly and backed away.

"I thank you for coming. This is not easy for me, Mr. Polo. I'm sure you're a fine young man, but I'm just not comfortable around people. It's . . . a social phobia, they say."

I liked the "young man" call. It didn't happen often anymore. "I understand. How can I help you?"

I must have edged closer to her without realizing it, because she backed away quickly, nearly stumbling.

"I'm worried about one of my people," she said. "John. He's missing. I want to be sure he's all right."

"Your people?"

She held out a hand. It looked clean and as freshly scrubbed as a surgeon's. "Yes. I . . . observe my neighbors, Mr. Polo." She smiled shyly. "There's really nothing on the television anymore."

"What's John's last name?"

"I haven't a clue. I don't know any of their real names. I just make up names for them."

"What can you tell me about John?"

She settled down on the arm of one of the chairs. "Well, I would estimate his age at forty. He's quite good-looking, in a swarthy, Mediterranean way. Dark curly hair. Quite tan. He likes to sunbathe in the nude. He has an enormous penis."

I coughed, hoping it would disguise the sound of my jaw hitting the floor.

"John is a bit of an exhibitionist," she explained, then added, "I'm a bit of a voyeur."

"Does he know that you're . . . watching him?"

"Oh, yes. Definitely. He waves to me. He has women over, young women. Prostitutes, I would think from the things that they do. John always leaves the windows open. Come. I'll show you."

She led me over to one of the telescopes.

"Look through there. That's John's place. On Filbert Street."

I bent over and peered through the lens. It was focused on the outdoor patio of the top-floor apartment two blocks away. I could see plastic furniture and several chaise longues.

"His bedroom is to the left," Mrs. Reed said. "The kitchen to your right."

"You said John's missing. Maybe he's away on a trip. Or a vacation."

"No," she said firmly. "I didn't see him doing any packing. Mr. Polo, I'm truly worried. I last saw John two days ago. He had a visitor, a man I've seen there numerous times. He's older than John, heavyset, balding, and has a mustache and old-fashioned sideburns. They got into an argument—on the patio. A very animated argument. They went inside, and I haven't seen John since."

I dipped my eye back to the telescope.

"The man closed the bedroom blinds, Mr. Polo. When I next saw him, he was in the kitchen. Flushing ice cream down the sink."

"Ice cream?"

"Yes. Half-gallon containers. Some kind of chocolate. I couldn't make out the label. John eats a lot of ice cream. And meat. Much too much meat. He barbecues all the time. What bothers me is that the man was wearing gloves. Long green rubber gloves that reached up past his elbow."

I looked at Mrs. Reed. She must have seen the skepticism in my eyes.

"Do you have money problems, Mr. Polo?"

"Just the usual. Rent, food, that kind of thing."

"My problem is that I have too much money. I have no children. No grandchildren. No nieces or nephews. My needs are relatively simple. I hate the thought of dying and leaving it all to the government, but I can't seem to find a charity that I'm comfortable with. All I have are my . . . people. I will pay you five thousand dollars to find out what happened to John. Will you do that for me?"

"Yes. I will. One question, Mrs. Reed. Your other people. Do they know that you're watching them?"

"Heavens, no," she said with a shy grin. "That would spoil the fun."

I didn't have a problem finding "John's" place on Filbert Street. It was the top unit on a four-story condominium. There were no names on the mailboxes. The door to the alleyway was open. There was a string of garbage cans, neatly stenciled with the unit numbers on the lid. I lifted the lid to number four. It was stuffed with leaking butcher-wrapped parcels and cellophane packs of sausages. The sausages were all labeled F&Q Quality Meats. I poked around and found the empty cartons of ice cream. Dreyer's Chocolate.

I opened one of the parcels and found a big hunk of prime rib. Another contained a boned leg of lamb. The meat was soft, but still damp, as if it had been defrosted.

I went back to my office flat, booted up the computer, two-fingered my way into a database, typed in John's address and, for the princely sum of seven dollars, found out that a Lawrence Forest was the owner of "John's" condominium. He had purchased it three years ago. The screen continued to roll, providing me with Forest's Social Security number, his date of birth, his prior addresses, both in New York City, and his telephone number on Filbert Street.

Lawrence Forest and Adam Quill had formed a corporation three years ago. F&Q Quality meats. The firm's address was on Kansas Street.

In the last seven months, five supply firms had filed money liens against F&Q.

I tried the number for Forest's condominium. It rang fifteen times before I hung up.

I looked up the business address in the phone book.

"F and Q," a perky female voice answered.

"Mr. Forest, please."

"He's not in, sir."

"When will he be back?"

"I'm not at liberty to say, sir."

"Is he out of town? I tried his home. There was no answer."

"I'm not at liberty to say, sir."

I took a page from Mrs. Reed's book and hung up without saying good-bye.

F&Q Quality Meats was housed in a shoe box–shaped, one-story, concrete-block building located in an industrial area of the city.

It was surrounded by a barbed-wire-topped chain fence that was laced with fast-food wrappers and Styrofoam coffee cups.

There were dozens of cars in the parking lot. An open space had the notice RESERVED FOR MR. FOREST stenciled on the wall. I slotted my car in Forest's parking spot.

The receptionist, Miss Liberty herself, smiled at me from her desk when I entered the lobby. She was in her twenties, with clear olive skin. Her dark hair was a mass of tangled curls. She looked like Medusa on a bad snake day.

"Is Mr. Quill in?" I asked politely.

"Who shall I say is calling?"

"Nick Polo." I handed her a business card.

Her smooth forehead crinkled when she read the card. "A private investigator. What's it about?"

"I'm not at liberty to say."

She stared at me for a moment, then shrugged her shoulders and picked up a phone. "He'll be with you in a few minutes," she informed me.

I wandered over to the far wall. Interior windows gave a visitor a look into the plant. Men in gray coveralls were lugging sides of beef from a freezer. They were wearing green rubber gloves that reached up past their elbows. They carried the meat through a red, rubber-ribbon curtain and disappeared from sight.

A young man wheeled a tray over to the receptionist's desk. There were sodas, bottles of wine, and an array of hors d'oeuvres on the tray.

He got into a cozy chat with the receptionist, gave me a courtesy smile, then walked away.

"Help yourself," the receptionist said, waving a hand at the food and drink tray.

"One of the perks of the job?" I asked.

"Today it is. We close down for three weeks after tonight." Her forehead did the crinkling thing again. "It's nice, but then again, it's not nice. We all have to take our vacations at the same time."

"What's the reason for that?" I asked, fingering a cracker larded with something pink and gooey.

"To clean the plant. Mr. Quill's a fanatic about it. Every year we have to—"

A bald, big-shouldered man hurried toward the desk. He had a weedy, tobacco-stained mustache and white sideburns that looked like woolly pillow stuffing. The receptionist handed him my business card, then turned and began clicking away at her computer.

"I'm Adam Quill. What can I do for you?"

"I'm looking for Larry Forest. Can't seem to find him."

Quill flicked the card with a fingernail. "You're a private detective?"

"That's right."

"What's your interest in Larry? Who hired you?"

"I'm not at liberty to say, Mr. Quill."

That didn't go over very well with him. He bit down on

his lower lip and scratched between his eyebrows with his thumb.

"I don't know where Larry is. He's on vacation. You can check back in a few weeks."

"I thought the plant didn't close until tonight. Why did Larry take off early?"

Quill poked me in the chest with a finger that was close in size to one of his sausages. "It's none of my business where he is, and I don't see that it's any of yours, either."

He tossed the card in my direction. It fluttered in the air and landed on the floor. I stooped to pick it up. The receptionist gave me a sorrowful look and crinkled her forehead again.

I called Mrs. Reed and filled her in on the investigation.

"I will keep an eye on John's place, Mr. Polo. I'll call as soon as there's any action."

I wondered if keeping an eye on "John's place" took Mrs. Reed away from her other "people" and their "actions."

The phone rang a little after one in the morning.

"It's Carole, on Lombard. He's back. The man with the sideburns."

The night was clear and warm. Unusual for San Francisco, even in October, our best weather month. I parked in the driveway alongside a panel truck with F&Q painted on the side. The back door of the truck was unlocked. I checked. It was empty.

I thumbed the buzzer to Forest's condo four times before there was an answer.

"Who is it?" Adam Quill sounded scared.

I pinched my nostrils with two fingers and said, "Is that

your truck out front? Sorry, but I hit it backing in. It's pretty bad. You better take a look."

I could hear Quill thundering down the interior stairs. He yanked open the door and strode over to his truck. He was wearing coveralls and green rubber gloves.

I slipped into the front door while he was checking the truck and hurried up the steps. The door to Larry Forest's condo was locked. I took a piece of celluloid from my wallet and tried to jimmy the door, but the fit was too tight. It would have taken me twenty minutes to pick the lock. I was debating my next move when the elevator doors hissed open. Adam Quill must have been too tired to use the stairs again.

He caught sight of me, let out a strangled snarl, and started running toward me. Something was glinting in his right hand. A knife. A big knife.

"Listen," I said, "you better—"

Quill wasn't in a listening mood. He raised the knife over his head, a la Anthony Perkins in *Psycho*, and lunged at me. I ducked. The knife dug into Forest's front door.

Quill made a mistake in trying to free the knife. I kicked him once in the shins, once in the groin, and slammed an elbow in the back of his head as he was falling to the ground.

The key to Forest's condo was in Quill's coat pocket. I dragged him inside, unbuttoned his coveralls, removed his tie and belt, and bound his hands and legs before calling the cops.

I went looking for Larry Forest. I found him in the kitchen. The floor was layered with sheets of black plastic, leading from the freezer to the table to the sink.

The freezer was empty, the door propped open by a plastic five-gallon bucket.

The table was also covered with plastic. A battery-operated skill saw sat on the table next to an array of knives.

A naked man lay on the table, on his back, arms akimbo, his head hanging over the edge.

There was a thick gash under his breast bone. A frozen trail of blood ran from the gash down to his groin. He stared up at me with icy blue eyes. His skin was a purply-blue color. If I had flicked his skin, I think it would have pinged.

Carole Reed was right. Even in death, Larry Forest had an enormous penis.

"It was a partner dispute," I explained to Carole Reed the following morning. "The business was going under. My guess is that Adam Quill had some type of insurance that would have paid him off if Larry Forest disappeared. The police are still trying to figure it all out."

"He was going to dismember John, wasn't he? Then dispose of the body parts."

"Yes, I'm sure he was." Actually, I was certain that Adam Quill had been planning to deliver Larry Forest to sausage heaven, but there was no sense in bringing out all the gory details.

She made a clucking sound with her mouth. "What a waste. This is for you, Mr. Polo."

The check was for five thousand dollars. I thanked her and started for the stairs.

She moved to one of the telescopes. "You live over there, don't you, Mr. Polo? On Green Street?"

"Yes, I do."

"A beige building, with a small sun deck? With lots of potted plants?"

"That's right."

She put her eye to the telescope and adjusted the lens. "I can see it from here. Is that your bedroom above the deck?"

THE JUST MISSED BLONDE
A LANE TERRY STORY
by Patricia McFall

The Street: The Pacific Coast Highway, Los Angeles, California

This is not only Patricia McFall's first P.I. short story, it's her first short story, period. She is, however, the author of one novel, *Night Butterfly* (St. Martin's Press, 1992), which was named by *The Los Angeles Times* as one of the ten best crime novels of that year. She is also in charge of New Program Development: Writing & the Arts, University Extended Education, at Cal State Fullerton. After reading this story, I'm hoping she'll start teaching less and writing more. I hope you'll feel the same way.

"You'll have to bleach your hair," Levy said in a tone that didn't invite discussion.

"But that isn't natural," I said. "Can't I—"

"Holes in your ears and nose and God-knows-where-it-doesn't-show aren't natural. Neither's a tattoo on your ankle. Be consistent, Terry."

I hadn't worn a nose ring in over a year, but he was technically correct. I hate it when my boss points out flaws in my logic. They're rare, but he always finds them and tells me. My name is *Lane* Terry, by the way, and his is *Martin* Levy, but we call each other by our last names. We work at

Levy Investigations, located just a block inland from the Pacific Coast Highway in Laguna Beach, California. This time I knew I was beaten, but I tried anyway: "Why?"

"Because you're going undercover, and it needs to be blond. A wig isn't going to do it. You've got to take it seriously. There's risk involved."

"Tell me about it. You ever dye your hair, Levy, what's left of it?"

"Don't be insulting. Anyway, that and blue eyes, got to be blue. Go to an optometrist and get disposables with zero prescription. And the hair. I checked with my wife, and she says to go to her guy Scott at this place." He held up a needlessly rococo business card for a beauty shop with an address in a fancy part of Newport Beach. I read it but didn't reach for it.

Levy read my mind. "Don't worry, we can expense everything. The family says no amount is too much."

"Sounds like our kind of client. What family?"

He hunched over and frowned, which made him look even more like the brooding poet he'd probably have become if he hadn't had to make a living, family to support and all that. I knew he was having a rare pang of conscience. Hey, in this business you can't let excessive scruples rob you of judgment. He'd said it himself, the day he hired me.

I poked his upper arm gently. "What?"

"It involves a certain amount of danger. I consider myself like a father to you, but—"

"But that doesn't stand in the way of you giving me a risky assignment?" I poked him again, only this time it was a punch. "I like that in a father. Okay, give me that card and tell me about the case."

He sighed. "You already know about the case. It's the family of—"

"—Heather Moran," I finished for him, and he nodded

gravely. My stomach constricted. I was going undercover? Some kind of decoy, because blond and blue, I'd look just like her? I shuddered, feeling like a character in a horror story who discovers she's already dead.

Most locals in Laguna Beach knew the case, and since the victim was roughly my age, I had followed what little information made the local paper. A large and hairy apartment manager named Brad Albrecht had come on to Heather Moran, a twenty-three-year-old tenant, but she wasn't interested. After living there about six months, she was murdered. Despite lots of suggestive gossip from the other tenants about how Brad had passed the order blank to Heather early and often, how she'd politely declined—not to mention how his wife had suffered from his attempts at infidelity—the cops and prosecutors hadn't been able to file a case.

It turned out not to be their fault, either. Levy, without further comment, slapped a fat three-ring binder on the cramped, messy computer station that passed for my desk. I was rarely at the office, and when I was, it was usually to deal with databases and such. The black vinyl contained a rather complete version of a homicide cop's murder book, and I knew much better than to ask Levy about how we'd come into possession of the documents inside.

As I read through the police reports and the Orange County District Attorney investigator's internal files, I realized what the authorities had been up against, what the public didn't know. If I'd been sitting in their place, I'm not sure what I could have done when such a likely suspect had a perfect alibi. He'd been helping a guy named Clancy close down a bar called the Sand Trap, where they had just met that evening. So Clancy had no motive to protect Brad Albrecht, right? And Clancy had separately recalled the very same discussion as Albrecht—of women with gapped

front teeth. He'd have made a good witness, too, since he
was a recovering alcoholic testing his resolve while watching the suspect get drunk. The bartender recognized but
didn't know Albrecht, and he knew the time because he
knew he was breaking the law for staying open. He even
told the police he'd served Clancy three plain tonics with
lime over the two and a half hours he was there. Albrecht
had been drinking steadily since he came in at eleven—here
the bartender was again in violation himself for serving an
intoxicated patron, so he was either giving the cops the
straight story to his own disadvantage—or he could be con-
cealing something else.

Clancy and Albrecht had left about 4:30 a.m., way after
the legal closing time of 2:00 a.m. Albrecht staggered off
down PCH—that's short for Pacific Coast Highway, if
you're from someplace else—in the direction of the apartments he managed. Without benefit of defense counsel, he'd
been interviewed by the police, but as he had very little
memory, he couldn't have done much for his own defense.
His was, in fact, one of the shorter statements in the murder
book. By 5:00 a.m., when the body was discovered, everyone agreed that Brad Albrecht was asleep in his bed with his
wife Charlene, who said she hadn't heard him come in and
couldn't say when that would have been.

Interviews of the neighbors also mentioned that Brad Albrecht had a little substance-abuse problem. I set the file
down and wondered how a drunken linebacker-type could
fail to awaken someone he slept in the same bed with when
he came crashing in at approximately the dead of night.
Maybe Charlene Albrecht was the kind of drunkard's wife
who could sleep through an earthquake during a hurricane.
If I'd been married to him, I'd probably have said I heard
him. Maybe perjury is perjury, but so's loyalty. Loyalty, I

mean. But that's only if I knew he couldn't have done it. Maybe Charlene knew better. Maybe she was pissed off enough to hope he went down for the crime. But why would she stick around, if that were true? Of course, the encyclopedia of homicide is full of people whose attachment to each other just can't be understood by any rational person. But who said murder was rational?

I turned the page to the next statement, from Cissy Kirk, a neighbor, saying she was on her way to take her morning run along the beach when she saw the deceased lying on the path just outside the door of Apartment F, which stood wide open. I jumped ahead to the back of the book, to the crime scene photographs in plastic sleeves. The victim lay on her back, feet pointing toward the open door, eyes still open in surprise. Her long blond hair was soaking in a maroon pool of blood. Charlene Albrecht had called 911 when Kirk came and banged on the Albrechts' front door. After the cops heard about Brad's always bothering the deceased, they decided to interview him at length. Once they heard the alibi witnesses, though, there wasn't much to hang on him, even though the public was screaming for revenge as soon as the story hit the paper. His picture in the murder book—he hadn't been charged but had submitted to being photographed—was of a rather handsome baby-faced athlete starting to lose his looks. He was thirty-five years old but already fraying badly, dissipation showing around the eyes.

I flipped through some of the forensic evidence, but it didn't amount to a case either. Blunt-force trauma to the back of the head—one "lucky" blow—the victim falling backward, probably ambushed while in the act of returning to her room. The murder weapon—a four-pound mini-sledge hammer Brad had been using to set in some garden edging just outside Heather's door—seemed like an instrument of opportunity, not premeditation. No prints had been found on it, but Brad used gloves when he gardened. I learned from the autopsy report that the angle of impact was inconclusive as to the height of the killer, and that despite the look of it, most of the bleeding had been internal. The killer could have walked away without much blood on him. And if it was Albrecht, he didn't leave anything more behind than a normal apartment manager could reasonably claim was in the line of business.

The victim's profile wasn't any help to the investigation: no enemies, only heartbroken friends, saddened co-workers at the car dealership where she worked as a finance manager, a devastated family. Exceptional, I thought, for a twenty-three-year-old beauty living alone in a hot-blooded beach town, Heather hadn't had relations with anyone. *Hymen intact*, read the medical report, and I whispered "no way" to myself. Well, things weren't always what they seemed. You could look like a babe but not be one; wasn't I about to prove that? And somehow that made her murder more personal to me, and sadder, that she'd had her life taken before having that first experience, and now she never would.

A year of investigation yielded insufficient evidence to file a case, and the Moran family had turned to Levy Investigations to accomplish—what? That part intrigued me. My boss explained, "You play Heather's ghost. Haunt Brad Albrecht's guilty conscience so he'll slip up, panic, do something. Snoop around and see if you can find anything the cops might have missed. No entrapment, but if you see an opportunity to catch him in anything illegal, take it. The Morans aren't picky about what crime he goes down for. And take another look at that perfect alibi." He assured me that even if Albrecht had killed Heather, he wasn't likely to "go serial." Oh, thanks, boss. No matter what proof Levy might lack at any given moment, he always gave the impression of knowing what he was talking about. This time, though, it wasn't much comfort for the soon-to-be-sitting blond ducky.

Cop-speak describes people startlingly like singles ads. Me, for instance: Lane Terry, a "25-year-old single white female, 5'4", 120, light brown/gray"—the last meaning hair and eye color. My mother always said I just missed blond, but that was about to change, and I didn't much like it. There's a difference between embellishing yourself and altering genetic dictates. But it was part of the job, and now, already as blue-eyed as a Nazi general, I sat down dutifully in Scott's ergonomic stylist's chair in a chaotic corner of the salon. Unfortunately, it had valet parking. I'd left my elderly Honda up the hill and walked back down because I knew it would defeat any poor valet's attempt to restart it. The gas pedal requires a deft touch and a perfect timing with the ignition.

Scott turned out to be a fast worker, with a stick-skinny assistant who talked a lot about needing dates because she didn't want to pay for her own meals. Judging from her anorexic appearance, she didn't seem to be getting many offers.

I told Scott I was going beach-bunny blond but added, "Don't make me look like a slut."

He looked hurt.

"Just a potential slut, okay?" I said, and he brightened.

"So what do you do?" Scott asked, not really interested, setting out chemicals and scissors and razors with the concentration of a terrorist assembling a pipe bomb.

"I'm an actress," I said, kicking myself internally because this would only generate interest and more questions. "But

I'm playing Helen Keller in *The Miracle Worker.* 'Scuse me if I practice," I said, and shut my mouth and eyes. I didn't know if the hint was too blatant, but I didn't want to get into my failed performance artistry, nor my "career" at a community-based theater-with-an-*re,* which had run out along with somebody's grant money. A relic of my drama major, it was a fig leaf of a career anyway, hence the quotation marks. When it ended, I'd moved back home in ignominy, broke. My parents were 60's people with some idealism untouched by time and reality. We didn't own a TV until my junior year in high school, which made me decidedly bookish for my generation, and they tried to instill firmly held values like independence. In other words, they soon encouraged me to leave. You might say they gave me the gentlest, most understanding of shoves. I'd gone to work for Levy on impulse, but stayed because I could keep on acting and get paid better for faking it in the real world—that is, playing roles—than I had on stage.

When he hired me, he was looking for help from someone young enough to look innocent, and I told him that his troubles were over because I was a chameleon.

He'd fixed me with a baleful stare under his bushy eyebrows, which go any direction they damn well please and give him an intimidating exterior. "A chameleon," he said, then, "Oh, I didn't hear you. You're a *comedian.*" His tone said shut up, so I did. Shutting up at certain times is not only a good idea; it can save your life in an investigation, though I didn't know it at the time, and it must have clinched the job.

"You'll serve an apprenticeship, put in time watching and reporting. Lots of hours, not a lot of money, and the work's a whole lot more boring than you'd think."

"I can entertain myself. Are you trying to scare me out of it?"

But he hadn't.

* * *

Heather's furnished single, now altogether too familiar to me from the crime scene photos, wasn't easy for the Albrechts to re-rent, and that worked in my favor. Over and above that, Levy'd made sure the fix was in by having one of our men point out that the place was a murder scene to each potential tenant who came by. Some of them left tire tracks, they were in such a hurry to get out of there. We'd had the place under surveillance all day, and around four, just as I was leaving the salon, I got the call to tell me Charlene had gone out and to go on over.

Miracles do happen, and I pulled up in front of the place on PCH just as a black Jaguar vacated a metered parking space. Everyone in Laguna carries around a bag of quarters, each of which will buy you fifteen minutes of grace from the hypervigilant traffic wardens. I maneuvered into the space, killed the engine, and pulled off my L.A. one-ways to check my reflection in the rearview mirror. I blinked, still a little unaccustomed to the blue contact lenses, but overall, I was amazed at the transformation. I hadn't set out to do it, exactly, but with the long, straight hair, my regular features outlined in the kind of soft-porn makeup any actress knows how to do, I'd become a reincarnation of Heather Moran. It was creeping me out big time, so I put my sunglasses back on, grabbed my keys, and twisted out the driver's side door against the endless flow of summer weekend traffic. It was hot, and I was sweating for several good reasons.

Tile-roofed and probably not up to code, the old Spanish-style apartment building had lots of funky-plaster-and-wrought-iron character, meandering up a hillside blanketed in bougainvillea, ivy, and geraniums. It looked nicer than the cottage in South Laguna I was sharing with a roommate who smoked and didn't do her half of the cleaning, and I considered whether I had the courage, if we got Brad Albrecht put away, to stay there after the Morans stopped picking up the tab.

I hadn't reached a conclusion by the time I knocked on the front door of Apartment B, marked "Manager." The place seemed to be unoccupied. It wouldn't hurt to look around if Brad was also out, so I went on up the garden path, so to speak, to Heather's apartment. The grounds were certainly clean and well tended, the path and plants still wet from a recent watering. That reminded me of a neighbor's statement that he was always watering, using it as an excuse to look into windows.

Apartment F was up near the top of the hill, but I already knew its location from the diagrams of the crime scene. I peeked through a window at the sparse furnishings—a pull-down Murphy bed with built-in bookshelves on one wall, a small, white-painted table and two chairs, tiny refrigerator and microwave. I couldn't tell if there was a television inside and was thinking my new character would certainly require one even though I didn't. As I stretched over, leaning into the windowsill to see the far corner of the room, I remembered that part of the insufficient evidence was that Brad's left-hand fingerprints had been found on just this windowsill, probably to support his weight as he tried to get a better look, the degenerate. But that only showed he'd been looking. Dust on the inside windowsill showed me no one had entered there—but as a manager with a key, why would he? And since the murder happened outside anyway, what did that matter?

The case was full of such differences that made no difference. Like a number of Brad's hairs inside Heather's apartment, but any competent defense attorney would point out the obvious: that the suspect had lots of dark head, facial, and body hair which he shed as freely as any Labrador retriever. The tenant Cissy Kirk had called him Sasquatch behind his back. And though several statements indicated that everyone knew Brad found excuses to skulk around Heather's place, usually running a garden hose to "water the plants," nobody could claim to have witnessed him there last year on the night of June 29 between 11:30 p.m., when Heather hung up the phone for the last time, and 5:00 a.m., when the jogging neighbor spotted the body.

Satisfied at spotting a small TV-VCR combo in the far corner, I pushed off from the windowsill. Something hissed behind me, but before I could look, a man's voice said, "You're Terry, right?" and I just about lost it.

I held my breath and turned around. Looking exactly the way he had in the paper, he stood holding a garden hose in what I took to be a menacing green noose until I blinked and my brain caught again. That was where the hissing sound was coming from. He had a light mist aimed at a hanging fern, not much of a reach for him at six-two with a line-backer's big frame. A defense attorney would have played him as a lovable loser, the kind of jerk who would sign a sin-gles ad "Lonesome Teddy Bear." But this guy looked plenty confident, smirkily so. Maybe getting away with murder did that for you.

From Brad Albrecht's leer when he took in my red V-necked T-shirt powered by my roommate's Wonderbra with liquid inserts, the hip-hugger denim mini, and the platform sandals not exactly made for running from danger, I decided that both Scott and I had gone beyond the potential to the probable-slut level. Hoping the tremble in my arm didn't show, I bought time by riffling my straight blond mane and pulling down my red-framed mirrored shades to show off my newborn baby blues. My voice was a husky monotone:

"Yeah, Terry Lane." I often reversed my first and last names on a case. It created useful confusion if my cover was ever blown, and I always answered to either name.

Now I had to think fast, since the ad hadn't specified which was the vacancy. "The neighbor said this is the apartment you have for rent."

Fortunately, Brad didn't ask which neighbor. He told me to wait, squeezed off the garden hose, dropped it, and disappeared down the path with frightening speed to return with a bunch of keys. "Sorry about the walkway being wet," he said. "The gardener was just here, and we tell him to hose everything down even if it wastes water. My wife hates those blowers, you know. But then he forgets, and I have to do it for him. Can't even tell him to remember since he no speak English." He said the last part with sarcasm, as though speaking English was something any decent person would know how to do. He was grinning, inviting me to share the stupid joke, so Terry Lane smiled back in spite of Lane Terry's inner loathing.

He was a jerk, and no surprise that he had a nasty side—for all I knew, it was his only side. I felt a certain healthy terror wash over me as I imagined him strangling me instead of the keys as he wrestled the old salt-air-corroded lock open. I found myself figuring the chances of fighting him off with only intermediate self-defense skills. But then I empowered myself with the thought that acting experience gave me advanced yelling and screaming skills.

As he showed me the place, I pretended to examine everything carefully while actually watching him from behind the shades, asking questions like were utilities included. But once we were inside, his cocky manner unaccountably evaporated, almost as if he didn't know what to do in the same room with a woman. He just gave grunts for answers, wouldn't even make eye contact. Maybe he was re-living his crime for all I knew, planning to strike again. But objectively, he looked like a big, beefy guy who was inept around girls but, well, normal.

Then I remembered something Levy had stressed: Murderers don't look any different from the rest of us. "For one thing, real-life homicide's usually a situational crime. There's crimes of passion, bar fights from the fatal combination of alcohol and testosterone, and sometimes homicide is just an assault that results in the victim's death. You know, manslaughter. They're not all serial killers with a profile."

I'd considered that a distinction lost on the victim.

That night around eight, I stopped by to drop off the security deposit, and Charlene Albrecht opened the door to Apartment B. Practically hiding behind the sliver of door, she gave me a long, morose stare, and I could well imagine that after what had happened, she hated me on sight. She told me her husband was out, took the cash, and said, "Just a minute. I'll get your keys and a receipt," not inviting me in. I could see from the doorway that everything inside was symmetrical, from the matching ball-shaped fake ivy plants one either side of the fireplace to the two love seats that faced each other, ruffled throw pillows in the same spot on each. Six ceramic ballerinas looked as though they had been glued to the mantelpiece in a row with exactly two inches between them.

Charlene returned and handed me two keys, one for the door and one for the mailbox, and I got a better look. Like me, she'd just missed being blond, but her hair was slicked back and clipped down. As neat as her house, and as severe, she wore a plain white shirt buttoned all the way up, pressed khaki slacks, and deck shoes with white socks. She never smiled. In fact, she seemed downright gloomy—too bad, since she was the kind of person who could be attractive if she'd just loosen up a little.

I decided to act clueless and friendly. "Sure is a beautiful place here. I just know I'm going to love it."

If anything, she looked even more depressed, but I kept going. "Look, in case you'd like to come up and say hi later, I've got a bottle of wine—hope it'll fit in that little fridge."

She just said, "It'll fit," then seemed to hesitate with this needy look on her face, as though she were about to say *be my friend*, but instead she closed the door.

I walked up the path unfolding the receipt, so precisely lettered it was almost calligraphy.

Before long, I got my first visitor, though it wasn't either of the Albrechts. It was Cissy Kirk, the runner who'd found Heather's body. She looked about six feet tall, skinny everywhere, a serious athlete, short hair, no makeup, and large eyes that gave her a melodramatic expression. She wanted me to know her claim to fame right away. Telling me the resemblance between Heather and me was uncanny, she added, "I hope this doesn't make you uncomfortable or anything, but I thought you should know."

"No problem," I lied. We were sitting at the little white table, but I didn't offer her any of the wine, which I was saving, just in case. "So what happened, exactly? Were you close?"

Stretching her long legs out and weaving her fingers at the back of her neck, she warmed to her tale, but she seemed preoccupied with the stud in her pierced tongue, which intermittently undulated like a lava lamp as she told it: "Oh, Heather and I were really close. She was such a sweetheart, really generous. You know, since she worked a lot of evenings, she tended to sleep in. She always let me borrow her newspaper every morning and bring it back before she woke up. What a sweetheart. She said it kept her paper dry, since Brad would be out there watering so early, he'd hit it half the time and leave it all soggy. I'd put it up on the little plant shelf by her door so it stayed dry every day. Even that day." Her wide eyes opened even wider, white all around the brown irises. She lowered her voice to tell a secret. "They kept on delivering it for a couple of weeks, but when it stopped, I called and got my own subscription. So what do you say, Ter? Don't you think he's weird? Everybody thinks he did it, you know, killed her, but they couldn't prove it."

"Do *you* think he did?"

"He kept after her all the time, didn't he? Let me tell you, he wouldn't try that kind of stuff with me. She was just so sweet, she'd let him talk to her instead of slamming the door in his face. That's what I'd do."

I believed her. She was starting to sound like quite a piece of work. Then I had an idea and said, "I like to run sometimes. Maybe I'll join you. What time did you say you go out?"

"Time depends on the season, but I try to make it really early, so I can watch the sun come up. I'm kind of a Druid or something, I don't know. You can if you want, but you'd have to keep up."

"Uh-huh. And you're up and reading the paper before that?"

"Oh, no. Same as back then, I just run down and get it and toss it in my place, then go have my run and get to it when I get back."

"So you and Brad are the early birds?"

"Yeah, but he knows better than to hassle me. Well, early to rise, so I'll be on my way. You want to go tomorrow?"

"No, I guess not. Wouldn't want to slow you down."

She stood in the doorway as though she regretted sounding so athletic as to preclude an opening to friendship. "Well, great meeting you, and welcome to the neighborhood."

I was excited but had to hide it. "Thanks. Come by anytime, Cissy," I said, but was thinking *Hurry up! Go!* Off she went, unaware she'd said something significant, maybe. At least I thought so. If she'd picked up the paper before going out on her sunrise run, then Heather was still alive when the paper was delivered, because otherwise she'd have seen the body then. That pushed the time of death way forward, possibly far enough for Brad to have done it! I had to think it through, not get revved up over nothing before I was sure.

I tried to remember the time line in the murder book, which obviously I didn't have with me. Tomorrow morning first thing I could go over and check, but I was pretty sure there was no mention of any newspaper being delivered. So in the morning I'd compare the alibi time against the time of delivery before the sun rose last year on June 29. Now, everybody agreed that Brad left the Sand Trap at 4:30, and if it took more than about thirty minutes, he was still in the clear. But exactly how long would it have taken him to get home on foot? It meant a long hike up Coast Highway, but at least I could find that out immediately.

The night had cooled a little, so I pulled on a pair of capris and some tennis shoes. It was past nine, and I hated to leave Charlene in the lurch, but I didn't want to bother her just to say I was going out, so I cruised on past. After the trek downtown, foot traffic got pretty heavy, with people crowding the sidewalks even at 9:30, slowing me down and throwing off my timing. Then it took an eternity for the signal to change, where Laguna Canyon Road morphs into Broadway and funnels cars onto PCH. Finally I got across the highway to the beach side, where the Sand Trap was located up the hill and down a side street. My calculations were screwed by all these delays, so I decided to kill a little time until the crowds and traffic thinned out, then try it again on the way back.

And while I waited, I might as well go into the Sand Trap and probe Brad's alibi. I wanted to ask the bartender a few innocent questions about the murder. I could play Blanche Dubois, or Laura in *The Glass Menagerie,* winsome and lonely and helpless. No, that would only remind me of poor fragile Charlene Albrecht. Better: an updated version with enough edge to be believable, something more Sam Shepard. Investigations could make a person cynical, and I was wondering how long it would take me, or if I already were and just didn't realize it.

Another plan foiled: The place was groaning with tourists and locals getting to know each other better, a colorful blur of Aloha shirts and tank tops and T-shirts under the down lights. The bartender would be far too busy to talk. But hey, I had all night. I worked my way through the crowd to an empty seat at the far curve of the long bar, amazed at the unaccustomed number of appreciative glances and comments that Terry Lane and her new hair and her Wonderbra were getting. I wouldn't want to say anything against the male of the species, but how obvious, crude, primal, and immature can you get?

I admit it felt interesting.

Sitting down at the one empty stool wedged between a cooing couple and two guys absorbed in a sports argument, I flagged down the bartender to order a glass of the house red and nursed it while I watched him work. He was about my age, thin but fairly buff, bleached hair at the tips sticking up, wearing a muscle T-shirt with a No Doubt logo. Something jumpy in his manner caught my eye, reminding me of another case I'd worked at a liquor store where a female clerk was cheating the management. This guy was moving fast, so I watched even closer, and it didn't take too long to get his number. He would fill a bunch of drink orders but only ring up, say, four out of five when he put the money in the till. He must have been counting in his head, because now and then, he'd slip himself out a twenty-dollar bill and slide it under the little rubber mat next to the register. It was so smooth, so quick, you'd have missed it if you weren't paying attention.

I estimated him to be skimming at least three hundred and fifty every weekend night, and thought that this must have been why he'd been so helpful to the cops, telling some truth to cover up what he was doing. Didn't want to be too clean and make them suspicious. That answered one question, at least.

Right then someone put his paw on my shoulder and muttered, "Howya doin'?"

I whipped around ready to tell the fool to keep his hands off, only to find myself centimeters from the beefy smirk of Brad Albrecht. His breath smelled like warm beer, and I almost gagged. He'd been in there all along? Damn it, I should have checked the place, just to know, and I hadn't. Not smart. Dumb, in fact—dumb, lazy, unprofessional, and dangerous. The brew had not improved his already marginal personality, but it was my job to help him make a mistake. I had to throttle my fear and regard this as an opportunity to do just that.

He was making it easy, acting as if we were old pals, trying to sound clever but just sounding drunk. "So how'd you fine the cooless place in Laguna so fass, Terry?" he demanded, his words sliding all over each other. "You din fol-

low me, didja? Thass okay, why'n you come and siddown?"
He gestured at a row of dark booths beyond a sea of heads.

I tossed a bill on the counter for the embezzler to find
later, grabbed my wineglass, and got to my feet. Trying to
sound like a party girl, I said, "If you're buying, I'm sitting."

"Aw, you women are always takin' vantage," he whined,
but bulldozed a reasonably straight path through the crowd.
I followed him, thinking this was the part where Jonah got
swallowed whole, and I was just another piece of plankton.

Brad ordered us refills from a passing server, who stared
as though she knew and hated him. I realized she saw me as
the replacement bimbo who looked like Heather, sitting with
her probable murderer. The town would not easily forgive,
and rightly so. After we'd got our drinks, I tried to introduce
several neutral topics. When that didn't work, I asked him to
tell me about himself. That had him going for a while, his
high-school athletic career featuring prominently, followed
by employment with a construction firm. When he ran
down, probably avoiding his more recent notoriety, I figured
he was warmed up enough to introduce the topic of Heather
Moran's murder.

"Brad, why didn't you tell me what happened to the last
person who lived in my apartment?"

He didn't look guilty, only sheepish as he licked beer
foam off his upper lip. "Well, you wouldna rented it."

A simple enough explanation, but not helpful. I had to
press. Trying to sound harmlessly curious, I confided,
"Cissy said one of the cops even thought you might have
had something to do with—"

With speed that approximated a striking rattler, Brad
slammed his beer mug down on the table, breaking off the
handle. The liquid sloshed out, but the glass didn't shatter.
He leaned toward me with the jutting handle still in his grip,

and I started to slide out of the booth, glad I could see the exit through the thinning crowd. He threw down the handle and grabbed my arm to restrain me. "'Scuse me, but I'm sick and tired of hearing about that. Understand?"

I didn't say anything because I was too scared to. My teeth actually chattered inside my attempt at clenched jaws. My legs were vibrating, boneless rubber. I saw my arm pull back from his hand of its own volition, barely avoiding the broken glass handle he was trying to pick up again.

"Hey, bitch—*hear* me?"

Everyone heard him screaming this at me, and the room froze. The bartender, one hand on the phone, waited to see what would happen next. There was an attenuated moment while I could hear glasses clinking, scraps of conversations with the word "Heather," almost blotted out by the pulse thundering in my ears.

Then the door opened and Charlene Albrecht walked in.

She seemed to know where Brad would be and came over to us, looking disappointed. "Please, Brad. Let's go home," she said, all but cringing. He gave her a contemptuous little smile with no remnant of affection. Seeing unhappily married people tear each other up is a special form of torture to the involuntary audience, and I hated to watch these two, as miserable together as any couple could be. She saw I was about to head off elsewhere and said, "No, wait. Let's walk back together."

I didn't want to, but the job required that I keep up the interaction and observation. Besides, I noticed my wobbling watch face at 10:45; I could time the real Brad Albrecht walking home while intoxicated. I got up and followed them to the door, deciding it was smarter to act a bit drunk myself, *non compos mentis*, while sitting with a married man in a bar and all that. No reason to make her feel worse.

On the walk back, we must have made an interesting little trio, Brad working himself up about how Charlene never let him have any fun, her silent as death, me lagging a little bit behind, hoping to be ignored if not forgotten. That failing, I was going to wait for a lull to excuse myself. But when he kept on ranting, I not only felt scared of him but scared for Charlene, who seemed not to realize that he was escalating and might turn on her. I tried to concentrate on the time to control my fear. Cars were still whooshing past on PCH, the lighter traffic increasing the speed, but the sidewalks were pretty well rolled up until the late movie let out. Good, not that much different from 4:30 in the morning. Brad and Charlene walked right past Broadway with the nice big signal and crosswalk, staying on the beach side. He was telling her what was wrong with her was that she wanted everything perfect.

"You shut up!" she screamed at him. He did, stumbling along beside her, matching her furious pace until finally he passed her. Then she just blew, let go of all the devoted-wife stuff she'd had to do for the last year when she must have known he'd done it. A few of her words drifted back to me over the rumble of cars and the muffling roar of nearby waves: "Don't you *dare* turn your back on me—" She shoved him from behind.

He whirled on Charlene and shoved her back with both hands, sending her reeling into me. I tried to help steady her, but she shrugged me off violently, almost ready to take the big man on. That was insane. I decided not to wait, to cross over to the other side as soon as there was a gap in traffic, to call the Laguna cops while I tried to keep the Albrechts in sight. I eased toward the curb, figuring they wouldn't notice.

But suddenly Charlene was running toward me, her face contorted with panic, shouting, "I can't let it happen again!"

She was terrified. In an instant I realized what she was afraid of.

Not Brad, but me.

It was too late to react, to sidestep her as she threw herself against me to push me into the path of an oncoming SUV.

There was a shriek of tires, and the starry sky and asphalt traded places before I came to rest, stunned, against a fender that by some miracle had not hit me head-on. The SUV vibrated and breathed exhaust warmly in my face, alive, still alive. I didn't feel any pain. Not yet.

I remember the cacophony of emergency vehicles responding.

I remember seeing Brad holding Charlene in a firm hug, whether from love or as a restraint I didn't know.

Charlene started confessing to the first uniform on the scene about how Brad had come home drunk, babbling about being in love, falling asleep with Heather's name on his lips, how she'd gone up there in the middle of the night to beg the whore to leave Brad alone, how Heather wouldn't listen and tried to turn her back on her. I wanted to break character to tell her to wait, that she'd just have to start over when the suits got there, then realized I must be delirious. It was over, I was myself again, not playing a role anymore: The broken arm was real, the pain stabbing like ice picks now for real, none of this in the script, all real, all caused by the force of one woman's hatred of another's image.

I had to stay in the hospital long enough to be sure the concussion wasn't serious. Levy came down with two bouquets for me, one from him, the other from the Morans. He said, "They wanted to thank the P.I. who caught their daughter's killer," then added, "if only by accident." I was glad he wasn't treating me any different.

When I got out of the hospital, in the crook of the cast on my arm I carried the flowers to put on Heather Moran's grave. I told her, "I swear to your soul that even if I make my living from deception, now I know it's more than a game, and I will never forget its power. And Heather? I'm going to let my hair grow out. I want to be myself again for a while."

THE PECULIAR EVENTS ON RIVERSIDE DRIVE
A JACK WEST STORY

by *Maan Meyers*

The Street: Riverside Drive, Manhattan, New York

I was amazed at how many writers did not "get" the concept of this anthology. The story had to feature a P.I. and an actual street in an actual city. After I received about a half-a-dozen stories which did not have either a P.I. or a street—or both—this was the first one I saw where the authors actually "got it." That's because husband and wife Martin and Annette Meyers—who write historical mysteries under the pseudonym Maan Meyers—are thoroughly professional writers. So here is the very first story I accepted for *Mystery Street,* which features P.I. Jack West in 1900 New York. As you'll see during the reading, West is the father of a little girl who grew up to be a very famous—and infamous—actress you "Mae" or may not recognize.

Annette's newest book is *Murder Me Know* (The Mysterious Press, 2001), the first in a new series set in the Greenwich Village of the 1920's. Marty's first novel, *Kiss and Kill,* originally published in 1975, was recently reissued in an iUniverse edition. It introduced private eye Patrick Hardy.

*F*rom *Jack West's Casebook: 18th December, 1900.*

The rider was a powerful man, easily two hundred pounds, barrel-chested, all muscle. He had ridden up from Greenwich Village to 42nd Street over city cobble packed with snow. The snow had started early that afternoon and had come down heavily. Gusts of wind blew frozen flakes as sharp as needles into his face. He had come out this night to visit the scene of a crime.

He guided his horse, Sullivan, around the trolley that was stalled in the middle of the Seventh Avenue–42nd Street intersection and dismounted for a smoke alongside Hammerstein's Victoria. The theatre was a marvel, the first of its kind in the underdeveloped neighborhood.

With the butt of his whip he broke the ice in the horse trough near the stage door so Sullivan could drink his fill. He was considering turning back when as suddenly as it had begun, the snowfall slowed, then ceased.

In less than a mile, he had left the city proper. West of Central Park there were a few farms, but their days were numbered if the apartment buildings and private houses along 57th Street were any indication.

His progress was muffled by the dense snow that lay like a thick, lumpy blanket over the whole of the city. Sullivan, his black mount named for the noble John L. Sullivan, was old, but reliable in this kind of weather, more than he could say for public transportation or the motorcar. The snow had closed down the Elevated.

The road called Riverside Drive was hardly discernable and he had seen neither person nor vehicle, and the farther he went, the fewer the houses.

In the light of day, one would be able to see Riverside Park and, beyond it, the Hudson River. But this night, the landscape brought to mind the desolate terrain the Frenchman Jules Verne had described in his book *From the Earth to the Moon.*

Jack West was his name, Battling Jack West in his prize-fighting days. His head, the size of a large muskmelon, seemed to rest on his massive shoulders without an apparent neck. Altogether, he was a formidable being.

One had to look closely—if one dared get that close—to discern the crisscross scars around his hooded eyes. His nose was regal, Romanesque, his ears shells—large shells, but shells. Neither ears nor nose offered evidence that he had once been an awesome, even a menacing, pugilist.

West sat his horse with aplomb, his attire unassuming. Under his wide-brimmed hat, his hair was jet. He wore it short, brushed straight back and flat on his august pate.

Suddenly, reflected in the moonlight, the skeletal struts of a burnt-out mansion rose up, almost human in their white cover, solitary in their guardianship. He had no doubt that he'd reached his destination.

To be certain, he dismounted and kicked the snow from the stone marker at the corner. There it was in carved-out numbers: "89th St." It could as well have said graveyard, for the look of the surroundings.

He tied Sullivan loosely to an almost-hidden hitching post only a few paces from the ruined mansion, gave the creature a reassuring pat on the flank, and took his battery-powered bull's-eye lamp from his saddlebag.

Turning his collar up against the sharp northeast wind, Jack West strode through the snow to the remains of the mansion, noting as he did that he was not the first to do so this night. A slurred track, perhaps made by someone too weary to walk properly—or someone trying to disguise his trail—led him directly to the wasted manse.

West was not a man to be deterred by the machinations

of either man or nature. He had made his own way in the world, first as a prizefighter—he had once fought the great John L.—then as the proprietor of a hire-and-supply business, hiring out his horses and carriages and sometimes himself as driver.

With the turn of the century, it had become clear to him that the day of the horse-drawn conveyance was rapidly coming to a close. Besides his home in Brooklyn, he owned free and clear the large townhouse on No. 26 Washington Square North, and the carriage house and stable behind it in MacDougal Alley.

McKinley, though a Republican, had turned out to be a fine president. And best of all, Jack West's family in Brooklyn was thriving, and the light of his life, his little Mae, all of seven, was singing and dancing and doing travesty impressions and acrobatics.

She'd already declared she was going on the stage. Well, if that was what she wanted, he would be proud to help her all he could. Why not? She very well might be the next Lillian Russell.

His motto was: Seize opportunity. And if opportunity was unwilling, shake it by the throat until it was.

West had found his "opportunity" in confidential investigations. He'd given it careful thought. His carriage trade had brought him in touch with the gentry, the wealthy and influential citizens of the city. He was ready.

The husk of the mansion was shrouded in darkness despite the sheen of moonlight on the snow. Jack switched on the bull's-eye. A wheelbarrow stood in a ditch at an odd angle, protected under a horizontal thrust just inside the yawning space that must have been an elegant entrance hall. In the barrow were assorted pieces of debris, charred wood, scraps of cloth, and the like, in particular, chunks of marble that could have come from either floor or hearth.

From the sounds beyond, Jack imagined the visitor to be one of the many wretched scavengers who lived in flimsy shacks all through these parts. Soon enough, because of the subway line being dug, this area of spotty development would be swarming with builders.

Jack West jiggled the wheelbarrow. His light caught a glint within the detritus. Reaching down, he plucked a twisted piece of metal from under a broken ceramic tile. He turned his find over under the light. It was a flame-damaged tin frame. The backing dissolved into crumbling ash in his hand.

The remnant of the photograph was another story. Gently, he blew some of the accumulated soot from the fragile paper. On it was the almost complete image of an exquisite child.

"Here, gimme that, it's mine," a voice wailed out of the wind.

The astonishing specter confronting Jack was just that: a woman, a banshee in flapping rags, face contorted, waving a rusty sword. He knew her. Crazy Kate Callahan.

Shielding the frame behind his back, Jack said mildly, "Doing a bit of scavenging, are you, Kate?"

She took his measure with crafty eyes, prepared to run, then stopped, eased closer. "You ain't no copper."

"No."

"Then watcha doing here?"

"I'm trying to help a friend."

"By filching what is rightfully mine?"

"By finding out what happened to the people who lived here."

The hag's laugh was thin and wild. Caught in the wind, it

whipped around him. "They think Kate don't know? Kate knows." Her eyes were two hot pieces of coal in a ghastly mask.

She was mad, but sometimes madness had clarity. "What does Kate know?" he asked as he would a child.

She made as if to turn away, then came at him swinging the sword. Jack easily avoided her attack, but was thwarted by a depression in the floor. Stumbling, he lost his balance, dropping his lamp and the blackened frame.

Kate darted over and scooped not one but two prizes from the snow. She reeled out onto the all-but-indiscernible road and, cackling her triumph, was gone.

Jack gave a mirthless chuckle. Wrestling a horse and carriage around town didn't seem so bad on nights like this. After all his day's work, except for the light from the silver December moon, he was completely in the dark.

It had begun that very afternoon, before the snowstorm. Miss Lillian Russell had sent for him, the request written on rose-scented paper. "A confidential matter," the note had said.

Lillian Russell's home was a brownstone situated among other similar dwellings on West 77th Street near West End Avenue, which had begun to take on the airs and elegance of Fifth Avenue.

A bare block west, bordering on the Hudson River, was Riverside Drive and Riverside Park. One block east was Broadway, with its many shops, hotels, and restaurants, and its lush island of greenery dividing uptown and downtown traffic.

Bridget, Miss Russell's housekeeper, took West's hat and showed him to the parlor, where a robust fire burned in the marble-mantled hearth. It was a grand room with a carved and rosetted ceiling.

The furnishings were in the latest fashion—large pieces in dark wood, spacious divans, an upright piano, a rosewood-and-brass table that held an array of snuff boxes and a collection of souvenir spoons under a glass dome.

On one wall a beveled mirror ran from floor to ceiling. Ruby-velvet draperies covered the tall windows, and soft electric light came from an extensive chandelier of multi-colored glass globes. The beautiful fixture gave the appearance of a giant flower against the high ceiling.

He was gazing at the light fixture when Miss Russell opened the double doors and stepped into the room, Albert, her Pekingese, under her arm.

"I see you are admiring my beautiful chandelier," she said. "It arrived from France only a week ago, a gift from Jim." She set Albert down, and the Pekingese immediately took to sniffing at Jack West's boots.

Jim was Jim Brady, known as Diamond Jim for his passion for decking himself and his pal, Lillian Russell, in diamonds and other gems. Brady had, on occasion, retained Jack West for certain confidential investigative matters.

"It's like nothing I've ever seen," West said, tearing his eyes from the chandelier and taking the small, plump hand Miss Russell offered.

She was a fine-looking woman in her stylish yellow bicycling costume. Its fitted bodice and leg-of-mutton sleeves were designed to show off her tiny waist and full bosom and hips. She wore boots of supple mahogany leather. A perky yellow hat sat on her golden curls.

Though Jack knew her to be past forty, no spring chicken, Lillian Russell looked like a lass of twenty.

She waved him to a chair. "So kind of you to come."

"Honored," he said. The chair was broad-bottomed and sturdy, good for the likes of him—and Jim Brady, of course, who was a man of considerable girth.

No sooner had Miss Russell settled herself on the sofa, but the Pekingese jumped up and made himself at home in her lap. "I trust your wife is well. And your daughter. Mary Jane, isn't it?"

"Both fine. Mary Jane—she's seven—we call her Mae now. Took her to see *Fiddle-dee-dee*. You are her idol. She's singing and dancing all of your songs."

The actress smiled. *Fiddle-dee-dee* was doing well, second only to *Floradora*, the biggest hit of the season. *Fiddle-dee-dee* was a Weber and Fields show and one of their best. "So you have a budding star, do you, Jack? Well, it's not a bad life. I hope she'll be as lucky as I've been."

West waited. He was patient. Miss Russell would tell him what she wanted of him when the time was right.

She stroked Albert's silky coat. Then, as fleet as a moment, her face took on an unlikely expression: distress. "Do smoke your cigar, Jack," she said. "I've asked Bridget to serve tea, unless you'd like something stronger."

Jack wouldn't have minded whiskey but he said, "Tea's fine." He took a cigar from the case he kept in his inside pocket and bit off the tip, placing it in the dish provided, then lit the cigar with a wooden match.

Miss Russell shook a silver bell and returned it to the table in front of the sofa. When the bell brought no response, the actress called out in her unique voice, "Tea's fine, Bridget." To Jack she said, "A friend of mine . . ." She gazed down at Albert, who licked her hand.

It appeared to Jack that she needed encouragement, so he prompted her with: "Stories starting that way are usually about the person telling them, Miss Russell."

She lifted her eyes; they were full of tears. "Not this time, Jack." With a sigh, she plunged into her story. "A friend, a dear friend—"

Bridget appeared with the tea service on a silver tray and set it down in front of the tearful actress. At her mistress's signal, Bridget served the tea and withdrew. The dainty, patterned china cup practically disappeared in Jack West's meaty mitt.

Miss Russell, abstractedly amused, moved Albert aside and rose, crossed the room to the piano, and returned with a photograph in a mother-of-pearl frame. The girl in the photograph was uncommonly pretty, her smile angelic, her face surrounded by wild ringlets. "Ada Walton. Ada Walton Hopkins. This was taken two years ago. Before she married, Ada was an actress. She was in *Princess Nicotine* with me. The girl was a wonder. She received a standing ovation every performance for her splendid juggling of five apples. Ada had a bright future, but she preferred being Mrs. Phineas Hopkins."

"The steel man?"

"That's the one. One of Jim's partners. They make undercarriages for trains." Taking the photograph from him, she sat down once more on the sofa. "Can you think of anything duller?"

Jack didn't reply. He wouldn't have minded having the kind of money those steel men made.

"Phin didn't want to share Ada with anyone, which is why she gave up the stage. He restored the old Ten Eyck house up on Riverside Drive for her."

"I read about the fire last week. No bodies, correct?"

"Precisely. No one knows what happened to Ada or Phin, though the police say the fire was an accident, that accidents happen, and that Ada and Phin are dead, nothing but ashes, and they have closed the case."

Jack West frowned. Nothing but ashes. He didn't believe that for a moment. There had to be bodies, or at least bones. He chewed his cigar. Yes, this would be something worth pursuing.

"I'm the only one who seems to care," Miss Russell was saying. "Even Jim thinks I should stay out of it, but I can't." She touched her hand to her breast. "I have morbid dreams. I fear that something more terrible even than the fire happened there. My heart tells me that Ada's soul will not rest until her remains are found. I want you to inquire into this for me, Jack West. Will you do that?"

"Of course. You want me to find out what happened to your friend. But what of Mr. Hopkins?"

"He can go to blazes for all I care."

Jack let out an uncharacteristic laugh. "He may have done just that."

In spite of her grief, Russell showed the glimmer of a smile; Battling Jack was not known for his sense of humor. "Why, Mr. West, you've made a joke."

Solemnly, he set his teacup down and knocked the ash from his cigar into the ashtray. "Then again, they might not be dead."

Lillian Russell's distinctive laugh carried a bitter tinge. "Wouldn't that be a joke on me? When the police and the fire volunteers said the bodies had burned up, I believed them."

She rang for Bridget. "Whatever you do, be discreet," she whispered to Jack. "There's more."

Big Jack sighed heavily, "There always is, Miss Russell."

"I believe that Ada's old sweetheart, Bill Kennealy, was back in her life."

"Anything else I should know?"

"Only that Mr. Hopkins is, or was, a widower with two sons."

"And Mrs. Hopkins?"

"No family that I know of."

"Did the sons live in the house with them?"

"No. One is in Pittsburgh learning the steel business, and the other is a physician here in town."

"Who lived in the house? There were servants, of course."

"Oh, yes. The O'Days. Tom and Mary—no, Marie. Ada hired them herself. Phin's previous housekeeper, an elderly woman, just couldn't keep up with their new life. Phin pensioned her off."

"The O'Days?" West asked. "What became of them?"

"I don't know. The fire happened on a Sunday, their day off. They were not in the house. The police spoke with them, but I don't know anything more."

When Jack West left Miss Russell's, he was surprised to see two or more inches of snow covering the ground. It was coming down thick and heavy with no sign of slowing. He took the El down to Eighth Street and walked to his carriage house in MacDougal Alley, where he found Jack Meyers strewing sand and straw across the cobblestones. The two had met five years earlier, when the lad was living on the streets.

"Come upstairs. We have a new client."

Meyers placed the bag of sand inside the door and knocked the snow off his boots. "Miss Russell?"

"And folks tell me you're not smart."

"Who says that about me?" Meyers demanded.

West feinted a left. When his twenty-year-old assistant

covered up, he tapped him lightly with a right on the top of his head. "Just playing with you, boy."

After West relit his cigar, he filled Meyers in on the case. There was silence as they eyed each other.

Meyers spoke first. "The servants, the O'Days."

"Right you are." West was pleased with his assistant. He had a nose for the investigating game. "Finish up the stable chores and we'll call it a night. First thing in the morning, go find these O'Days. Meet me at the house on Riverside Drive at noon."

Jack Meyers was a scrawny young man whose coloring and peasant face identified his origins as Eastern Europe. However, except for a slight foreign cast, he spoke with barely an accent.

When the situation required it, he could work as hard as the next man, but like the Tom Sawyer character from Mr. Mark Twain's books, Meyers was adept at getting other people to do the work for him.

He figured his first stop to be Police Headquarters on Mulberry Street, where the Commissioner's squad that dealt with special cases had an office. And the best thing about a special case was that it might be anything.

Dazzling sunlight glanced off the white-blanketed city and glared in his eyes as he trudged through the snow to Mulberry Street.

The cop in charge of the Commissioner's Special Case Squad, which answered directly to the Commissioner, was Inspector Fingal "Bo" Clancy. The only other permanent member, and the reason Meyers made Mulberry Street his first stop, was Captain John "Dutch" Tonneman, with whom Meyers had a passingly good relationship.

Back in '95, Jack West had put Meyers to work with the

horses. West's only business then was horses and carriages. It was only a year now since West had hung up his investigator shingle and elevated the dark-haired Jewish kid from chief hay tosser and shit shoveler to his assistant investigator.

The two Jacks had gotten involved in a murder case Bo and Dutch were working on. Tonneman had treated Meyers straight from the beginning. Clancy was another story.

Burke, the fat desk sergeant, looked down at him suspiciously. "What you want, boy?"

Meyers's fists clenched. He'd like to take a stick to that one, but he kept it to himself. "Captain Tonneman—"

"He ain't here." Burke raised his voice. "Inspector Clancy, there's a—"

Meyers tore out of there, the raucous laughter of the desk sergeant ringing in his ears.

"Now what?" he muttered, kicking at the snow, snarling and punching at the flying flakes. Who else would know about Tom and Marie O'Day? Who? The newspapers. They liked fires, especially mysterious ones. Sold a lot of papers.

Meyers trudged through the snow for a while, then hopped on a trolley going uptown on Broadway. He got off at 34th Street. The two-storied *Herald* building sat in the triangle running from 34th to 36th Streets, where Sixth Avenue bumped into Broadway.

Tipping his snow-laden cap to the bronze woman, some Greek goddess or other, that lorded over the southern front of the building, Meyers passed the small group of ragged boys, newsies, waiting to pick up the afternoon edition. He knew some of them and they called out "hey" to him as he passed.

Inside, though the presses were on the second floor, the

thundering noise overpowered all other sound. Meyers grimaced. A man could go stone-deaf here.

Slapping his cap against his leg, he strolled past a grizzled old porter snoozing at a table. On the table was a handprinted sign: "Hiram Jones, Corporal, Grand Army of the Republic." Meyers, not sure why the sign was there, left three pennies for the old man and entered the big room.

A drab expanse of desks crowded one against the other under the shuddering electric lamps that hung from chains attached to the ceiling. The air was so thick with smoke that he could barely see the reporters in their hats and green eyeshades, but he could hear the click-clack of the typewriters right through the noise of the presses. All the while the floor trembled and desks shook, and no one paid any mind. No one paid him any mind, either.

Still, it wasn't hard to find Flora Cooper, as she was the only female in the room, and she was off in a corner, typing like a locomotive and smoking like its chimney.

Meyers approached. "Miss Cooper."

Flora Cooper removed her eyeshade and briskly ran her fingers through her honey-colored hair, propelling a pencil that had been nesting there at Meyers. It bounced off his chest and fell to the floor. He picked it up.

"Jack Meyers," she declared, seizing a packet of Richmond Straight Cuts from her untidy desk. She found it wanting, crushed it in her fingers, discovered another packet under some papers, and lit a new from the old that clung to her lips. "What can I do for you?"

Awkwardly, he offered her the pencil. When she waved her hand at the desk, he deposited it there amongst the rest of her debris. "I—"

"Sit. I have to finish this." She banged on the typewriter keys for a few more minutes, plucked the paper from her machine, tearing a corner, then read what she'd written. "Damn," she said. "Where'd you put my pencil?" She found it or one like it, printed some missing words on the page, and yelled, "Copy." A pimple-faced kid limped to her desk. She shoved the paper at him. "Hurry, they're waiting."

They watched the boy move off, a speedy crab.

Since there was nothing available to sit on, Meyers waited, standing.

"What?" she asked.

"That fire up on Riverside Drive last week. The Hopkins mansion."

She leaned back in her chair and blew a smoke ring, eyeing him through slitted lids. "What about it?"

"The Hopkinses ain't been found."

"Burned up in the fire, so they say." She offered him a cigarette. "Sit."

Meyers took a rickety chair from behind a scarred desk and accepted the cigarette. "Yeah, well."

"Jack West working a case here?" Flora asked with a friendly smile.

"Could be," Meyers said, offering a friendly smile back. But he was on to her. He knew she was looking for a wedge into a story.

"So what can I do for you?" But she meant, "What can you do for me?"

"Tom and Marie O'Day—know where they got to?"

"O'Days? Now who would they be?" She could have fooled anyone else, but not Meyers. He knew she knew and she knew he knew she knew.

He smoked the cigarette, taking short, intense puffs. "Miss, you ain't no dummy and you know I ain't neither."

"Okay," she said. "They had a room in a house on 16th Street off First Avenue." She pawed through some of the scraps of paper on her desk. "Here it is. No. 350 East 16th. Rooming house."

"Thank you, miss." Meyers stood, setting his cap squarely on his head.

Flora bounced up. "Hey, hold on a minute. I went to see Tom and Marie O'Day. They were on their day off when the fire happened and they lost everything, which I don't think was much, judging from the run-down place and his clothing. He shed a crocodile tear or two, but I could see he was more upset that they were left without money or position than about the fire and what might have happened to the Hopkinses."

"You saw the missus, too?"

"Actually, no. Marie, his wife, had taken to her bed and was in such a state of collapse—she'd been particularly close to Mrs. Hopkins—that she was unable to talk to anyone." Flora followed Meyers as he worked his way past the desks in the large room.

Near the old soldier's table, Flora stopped him. "Listen here, Jack Meyers, you tell Jack West that I'll be grateful if he keeps me informed."

Flora Cooper waited till Meyers was out the door, then grabbed her coat and hat and went after him.

After sending Meyers on his way, Jack West sat behind his desk mulling his next move. From time to time he glanced out his window. The snow hadn't ceased and didn't look as if it was going to.

The police report would be the logical next step.

He pulled over the telephone, lifted the listening arm from its candlestick receiver, and turned the crank. "Central, I'll be obliged if you'd connect me to Captain Tonneman at Mulberry Street police headquarters."

"Inspector Clancy talking."

"Ah, Inspector," West said. He would have preferred the less explosive Tonneman, but it was information he needed and however he got it was fine. "Jack West here. I've been asked to look into the disappearance of Mr. and Mrs. Phineas Hopkins."

"Oh, yeah? And who asked you?"

West smiled. "My client's name is confidential, Inspector."

"Sure, and so's police business."

"Okay, Inspector. I thank you for your trouble."

"Wait a minute, West. Everyone knows they were burned up in the fire."

"Oh, really? Well, that does it. I'd heard that no remains were found, not even a bone, but I reckon I heard wrong. Thank you, Inspector."

"What kind of game you playing, West? We didn't find any bones, but no one could have lived through that inferno."

"I'll take your word on it, Inspector."

"We closed the case. Who put you up to this, that crazy doctor and his wife?"

"Oh, you mean the son, Dr. Hopkins?"

Bo Clancy snorted. "You know damn well who I mean, West. And I don't want you meddling in police business."

"But you just told me the case is closed, Inspector." Now Jack West knew what his next step would be. He rotated the crank at the base of the telephone. When the sharp bell let Central know that he was through, he set the listening piece back on its hook.

Dr. Howard Hopkins's listing in the City Directory stated that he was on 53rd Street. The address placed his house just off Fifth Avenue.

Jack knew that corner. St. Thomas Episcopal Church

stood there. Along 53rd Street, between Fifth and Sixth, one fine townhouse followed another.

Slow as molasses, the trolley crept uptown through the snow. Impatient, West jumped off as it slowed for a curve and walked.

Dr. Hopkins's townhouse was of more than average width. Spacious stone steps led to a fine oak door with highly polished brass fixtures. Over the door was a leaded-glass half-moon window.

The melodic ring of the door chime was answered by a maid, a young Irish girl, in a neat black uniform with lace collar and cuffs.

"Dr. Hopkins, if you please," West said.

"Are you a patient, sir?"

"No, but it's very important that I see him."

"Dr. Hopkins is out visiting patients, sir."

He stepped inside. "Then perhaps I should wait—"

A door opened and a voice called, "Margaret?"

Margaret bobbed her head, even though the woman talking was not yet visible. "Yes, ma'am."

"Who's there?" The woman appeared at the top of the stairs, her dark hair back from her sharp-featured face and piled atop her head. A broad expanse of woman in voluminous clothing. Holding tight to the banister railing, she moved slowly down the stairs. She was, he saw now, going to have a child.

The detective handed Margaret his hat. "Jack West. Are you Mrs. Hopkins?"

"Yes. My husband is not here. His surgery hours are in the morning."

"I'm not a patient, Mrs. Hopkins. I'm investigating the disappearance of your father-in-law and his wife." West presented his business card.

She drew herself up as best she could, considering her condition, and glanced at his card. Her face showed no expression. "Please follow me." She led him into a small parlor.

"Margaret, I do not wish to be disturbed." The woman closed the door, then turned to West with an odd smile, her forefinger to her lips.

Abruptly, she opened the door, saying sharply, "There's no reason for you to be standing here, Margaret. Go on about your business."

Mrs. Hopkins shut the door again. "They do take some satisfaction in our tragedies. Please be seated, Mr. West. My husband will be visiting his patients the rest of the afternoon. Perhaps I can help you."

"As I said, I'm investigating the disappearance of—"

"I heard what you said. Why do you persist in saying disappearance?" She dabbed her forehead with a small square of silk. "I can tell you, quite unequivocally, that my father-in-law is dead. That woman killed him."

"That woman?"

"My father-in-law was a fine gentleman, a widower, a very wealthy man. She had him so besotted, he couldn't do enough for her—clothing from Paris, jewelry, elegant parties. He even changed his will on her behalf. But he was an old man. He found out soon enough that it was not the life he wanted."

"He told you this?"

"Not in so many words. Believe me, I am telling you more than my husband would because I know she was up to no good. She was just a common actress who put on airs. The fire was an accident, a spark from a poorly installed electric wire, we were told, and they both died."

"But there were no bodies, no bones remaining."

"The police said nothing could have remained because

the fire was so intense." The woman, fanning her face with the silk handkerchief, sighed. She seemed suddenly weary. "You're thinking that I didn't like her because my husband would lose his inheritance, but it wasn't like that. My husband is a wealthy man in his own right from his mother's people. Ada was killing that poor old man; my husband spoke to his father, as his doctor, to caution him. I knew all along she was nothing but a fortune-hunting slut."

Jack got to his feet. "I thank you for your time, Mrs. Hopkins. I hope you don't mind me asking, but is this your first child?"

She smiled suddenly, a lovely smile. "Oh, yes. I am only sorry my sweet babe won't know his grandfather."

Jack Meyers stopped at a saloon near Irving Place for a beer and the free lunch of hard-boiled eggs and corned beef. Afterward, he continued on to No. 350 East 16th Street.

The house was a wooden three-story structure in dire need of paint. The glass on the front door was cracked. When Meyers used the tarnished knocker, it came off in his hand. He stuck it back in place and opened the door. "Hello, inside," he called.

While he waited for a response, Meyers ran the soles of his boots over the scraper and shook the snow from his muffler. He stepped back and looked up at the windows, curtained and blank. He blew his nose. The snow hadn't stopped and didn't look like it was going to. "Hello, up—"

A window opened. "Quit your hollering," the woman shouted, in an accent like she just got off the boat from the Bog. The window slammed shut. A minute later, the slattern appeared in the doorway.

"I ain't got all day." Her voice was a cat's screech. Oily red strands licked out from under the rag she wore on her head, and her face was foul with ashes, as was her once-white apron. Her blue eyes were cockeyed worse than he'd ever seen. "What the hell you want?"

"Can I come in? My name is Meyers. I work for Mr. Jack West, the detective."

She was unimpressed. "So . . . ?"

"Who might you be?"

She rubbed her nose with the back of her hand, stared at the resulting soot and wiped it on her skirt. "Been chimney sweeping. Carrie Dugan's me name." She thrust out her hand. "Use it but don't abuse it."

Meyers shook her surprisingly delicate hand, then wiped his own on the back of his trousers. "I'm looking for the O'Days."

"Ha! Who ain't? They bunked, owing for the room." She beckoned him to enter. "But I'll thank you to wipe your feet."

Once more he used the foot scraper, then brushed the snow from his coat and stepped inside. "When did you last see them?"

"Yesterday," Carrie said, rubbing her nose again. "Said they'd found a new position in Boston. The missus has family there."

"Are you on the telephone?"

"For my lodgers?" she brayed, one eye drifting up, the other down. "What would they be needing the telephone for?"

Meyers handed the woman Jack West's card. "If you see the O'Days or hear anything about them, call Mr. West here at his office in MacDougal Alley." At the sour twist of her lips, he searched his coat for a nickel and flipped it to her. Her quick hands plucked the coin out of the air, the way a frog catches flies, and dropped it in her apron pocket. "There's four-bits more in it for you, if you do."

She scratched her nose with the card. "Sure 'n begorra," she screeched, clapping him on the arm, "If I wouldn't run on me bare feet to Boston meself for fifty cents."

The only change Jack West observed in the terrain of the burnt-out mansion was the missing wheelbarrow and the familiar slurred tracks now leading toward the back of the property. Crazy Kate had probably come back for it as soon as it was light.

He was feeding Sullivan a fourth carrot when the crunch of wheels on snow made him look up. Jack Meyers, sitting on an open wagon, was coming down the hill from West End Avenue. He had that jaunty look in his eye, filled to bursting as always when he'd done something he deemed clever. The clever part was sitting right next to him. Flora Cooper, from the *Herald*.

"I got blueprints!" Meyers shouted when he caught sight of West.

West tipped his hat. "Miss Cooper?"

"Don't trouble yourself about me, Mr. West. I gave Meyers my word I wouldn't put anything to paper until you gave me your okay."

"Whoa, Tessie." Meyers reined the wagon to a halt and jumped down.

"Why the wagon, boy?"

"You didn't expect me to tote the shovels in my arms, did you?"

"Where'd you find these?" West held the stiff paper blueprints open and stared at them.

"Architect on 72nd Street. Miss Cooper had his name and

got the plans, easy as pie." He looked at West sheepishly. "But only if I brought her along."

"I promise I won't get in your way," Flora said, shading her eyes from the brilliant sun.

"I'll thank you then to just sit here on the wagon, Miss Cooper." West motioned to Meyers and they walked to the shell of the house, West studying the blueprints as they went.

"I suggest you consider the servants' entrance under the double staircase," Flora called.

West muttered to Meyers, "Damned if I don't agree."

The detective directed his eyes to the place on the blueprint where the staircases had been, then to where he judged was the corresponding area on the snowy ground.

He had come directly in when he was here last night. How could that be? He'd passed right through the servants' door under the staircase without realizing it and had stood in the pantry itself. That was why Crazy Kate's wheelbarrow seemed to be tilted into a ditch.

Meyers kicked at the snow-covered waste from the fire. Crumbling bricks appeared, at uneven heights. "Would have been here." He settled on his haunches. "One set for going up, one for coming down." He looked up at West, saw him musing, and scrambled to his feet.

Back on the wagon, Flora Cooper was standing, watching, scribbling in her notebook, a cigarette smoldering between her lips.

West retraced his steps of the night before, stopped, and stared at the blueprints again. "See here. Behind where these stairs on the left were. A cellar . . . Give me one of those shovels."

"I'll do it," Meyers said. He scraped the shovel back and forth, exposing three stone steps. Meyers picked up a piece of debris. "Cooking pan." He tossed it over his shoulder, narrowly missing Flora, who unbeknownst to him till that moment, had gotten down from the wagon and joined them.

"You're in the kitchen," Flora said. She peered into the depression they were excavating.

Meyers stopped digging when he heard a metal clunk. "Another pot, probably."

West stuffed the blueprints into his coat pocket and reached down. "Don't believe so," he said, exposing a ring handle in the floor. He pulled, to no avail. He pushed up his sleeves. After Meyers dug at the rubble around the metal ring, West spat on his palms, seized the ring with both hands, and hauled.

Up came the trap door, letting loose the putrid smell of the grave.

"Must be Aaron Burr's old smuggler's den. . . ." Flora puffed urgently on her cigarette, discharging a cloud of smoke. She shone the bull's-eye lantern Meyers had stowed in the wagon down into the hole. "I read about it in Valentine's . . . Oh, my God."

At the bottom of several more steps were two bodies, entirely untouched by the fire.

"What a stink." Meyers stepped back, gasping for fresh air. "You'd think with the cold . . ."

Jack West took the lantern from the reporter and, ducking his head, stepped into the cellar, then came right up and shut the trap door. "Go get the cops," he told Meyers.

"The Hopkinses?" Flora asked, as Meyers took off up the hill.

"Looks like it." West's face was grim.

"They hid out from the fire and died because there was no air." She wrote in her notebook.

"They were dead before the fire," West said. "Cut to ribbons with what looks like a machete."

Flora scribbled, mumbling, ". . . machete, similar to those brought back by soldiers who fought in Cuba, leading investigators to surmise that the killer might have been a Cuban or a veteran."

Pulling the blueprints from his pocket, West stared at them. "You just have to know where to look." Careful where he set his feet, he moved toward the back of the structure. In spite of his caution, he almost tripped over the handle of the wheelbarrow.

"You knew," Flora said with admiration. She followed after him. "What's that?" She wasn't referring to the wheelbarrow, which West had bent down to inspect, but to a bit of color against the gleaming white crust in what must have been the gardens behind the house.

That was how they discovered the remains of Crazy Kate, her head bashed in with a heavy object.

The day was past saving by the time West and Meyers returned to MacDougal Alley.

While Meyers caught up on the stable work, Jack West's task was to sit himself down and write his report for Miss Russell. The case was closed. Ada Hopkins and her husband had been found, victims of a terrible crime. Dr. Hopkins, the son, had identified the bodies. Ada's wedding ring was still on her hand. It would be up to the police now to locate the O'Days, who seemed the most logical suspects. And the O'Days, according to what Meyers had learned, had fled to Boston.

As for Crazy Kate, perhaps she'd been killed because she could identify the O'Days. Or perhaps by another scavenger. Yet, the madwoman had claimed she knew things. . . . .

He never liked writing sad reports, so he procrastinated by polishing his boots.

"Boss?" Meyers's voice came from below. "We got a message here." It was from Miss Russell: "Come at once. Ada is saved."

"Saved?" Meyers said, scratching his head.

"Hitch up Tessie and the brougham and make yourself presentable."

Because a brougham is a closed carriage with the driver sitting outside in front, the two detectives were perforce separated on their journey to Miss Russell's house. Little Jack Meyers drove, while Big Jack West sat inside.

But as usual, Meyers didn't accept his limitations. He yelled to Battling Jack, "If Ada is alive, who's the woman we found?"

Meyers resumed his harangue each time he stopped at a crossroad. "Marie O'Day? She's most likely. . . . . But if Marie, why? And if it is Marie O'Day, dead as a mackerel, who's the man lying beside her? Tom O'Day?" This time Meyers leaned his body over and peered into the carriage. "Or old Mr. Hopkins?"

Tessie whinnied and took off at a fretful gallop along Broadway. When Meyers, a fair hand with horses, had Tessie under control, he resumed his rant. "And if it's Hopkins, what sort of pussyfooting was going on?"

Jack West, who had come to much same conclusion, leaned back, smoking his cigar. The little bugger had become as good at detective work as he was with horses.

Bridget had barely a chance to take West's hat when an agitated Lillian Russell greeted them in the wide entrance hall and ushered them into the parlor. Meyers, his cap still on his head, gawked at the grand room with its sculpted ceiling and glowing chandelier. He did not at first take notice of the other presence in the room.

"I'm so glad you're here," Miss Russell said, her expression a mixture of joy and sorrow.

"At your service," West said, snatching Meyers's cap from his head and stuffing it into the mesmerized lad's jacket pocket. "This is my associate, Jack Meyers." West was well aware of the slight figure resting on the small sofa under a light blanket.

"My dear friend, Ada Walton Hopkins." Lillian Russell was overcome with emotion. "May I present Mr. Jack West and his associate, Mr. Meyers?"

Jack West saw a pale girl in a blue frock. The frock was a match to her eyes, which were now swimming in tears. She dabbed at them daintily with a tiny lace handkerchief. Her red hair was parted in the middle, the curls in a cluster on top of her head. She was strikingly beautiful. Meyers, who'd transferred his gawk to her, obviously agreed.

"Bridget," Miss Russell said. "Whiskey for the gentlemen, sherry for the ladies. No. Whiskey for me, too."

Ada nodded. "Certainly whiskey." She had a sweet, melodious voice.

"Yes, ma'am." Bridget sailed out, a woman on a mission.

Jack West cleared his throat. "Would you care to wait for your libation, Mrs. Hopkins, before you tell us what happened?"

"If you'd be so kind." She closed her eyes.

Bridget served the whiskey and left promptly.

Ada lifted her glass. "Long life!" Her tearful gaze rested on Jack Meyers briefly, then slipped away.

Meyers was overwhelmed. He was surely in love and might have fallen to his knees to tell the lady he would be her slave, and thus embarrass himself and Jack West, were they not interrupted by the arrival of Police Inspector Bo Clancy.

Once Clancy had his whiskey, he pulled over a chair and sat down near Ada Hopkins, taking her delicate hand into his. "Tell us what happened," he said, with an un-Clancy gentleness that did not surprise Jack West. Ada Hopkins had them all enthralled.

"It's a fearful story," Miss Russell said. "When my poor tattered Ada arrived at my door today like a beggar, I thought she would die in my arms. She has been badly used." Tears coursed down Lillian Russell's cheeks, making little trails in her powder.

"How did this happen, Miz Hopkins?"

Ada's hand fluttered to her cheek. "The O'Days. Mr. Hopkins hired them, but they were not to be trusted. Things began to disappear, small things at first. A brooch. Coins. Then larger amounts of cash. Mr. Hopkins spoke harshly to them, gave them a warning. He intended to report them to the police as soon as we found their replacements . . ." Ada stopped and hid her face in her hands. Lillian Russell sat beside her friend and took Ada's frail form in her arms.

"Can you go on, Miz Hopkins? Rest assured we'll catch these villains and you'll have justice. You know that two corpses were found in the cellar and that one is your husband?"

"Yes." Her voice was barely a whisper, yet West heard her across the room. "My poor, dear Phin."

"It was in the late edition of the *Herald*," Lillian Russell said.

"We thought the other was you. Dr. Hopkins, the son, identified both bodies. The dead woman had your ring on her finger."

"Mr. Meyers," Miss Russell said, "Would you mind re-

filling Mrs. Hopkins's glass?" She pointed to the decanter
Bridget had left on the tray.

Mind? Jack Meyers was ecstatic. He took the goblet from
Mrs. Hopkins's hand and poured a healthy dollop of whiskey.
Her fingers grazed his when he returned her glass, and he
stared down at them. Jack West gave a small growl and
brought Meyers back to reality. The younger man stood aside
and watched as Ada continued.

"O'Day himself was vicious. He knew Mr. Hopkins was
no fool. He attacked us in the night. They took my ring."

"How did you escape?" Jack West asked.

She shrugged. Tears reappeared. "I can't recall. The next
thing I knew I was lying half frozen to death in a shack near
the river. I must have run off and wandered around in a
trance."

"The other body . . ." West prompted.

"Marie O'Day," Bo Clancy responded. "Has to be her.
Maybe she got in the way."

"My husband liked to keep large sums in the house.
There was a big cash box under the bed. . . ."

"Ashes, I'm afraid," Clancy said. He got to his feet. "We'll
be notifying all precincts to be on the lookout for this Tom
O'Day. To think, the day after the fire we had the devil in our
hands, and we let him loose. Fooled the lot of us."

"I'm so frightened," Ada said. "What if he comes looking for me?"

"You've nothing to worry about, Miz Hopkins. My guess
is he's bolted. . . ."

"Boston," Meyers said. "Mrs. O'Day had kin there."

Clancy put his hand on Meyers's shoulder. "Now how
would you be knowing that, boy?"

Meyers looked at West, who nodded. "I went to the
rooming house where they was staying."

"Who's they?"

"The O'Days. There was a missus, the landlady told me. And Miss Cooper, she said the same."

"Flora Cooper," Bo exclaimed. "Wouldn't you know she's got her pretty little nose in this. So that's how she came to be at the place of the crime this morning."

Jack West poked young Meyers. The infatuated youth was staring at Ada Hopkins again like a lovesick pup. "Why would he have killed his wife?" West asked.

Ada's voice was very faint. "Another woman?"

Something, he couldn't think rightly what, was giving Jack Meyers pause.

"No more, please," Miss Russell said. "Poor Ada is in a state of collapse."

"Yes, of course, Miss Russell," Bo Clancy said. "Let's go, boys."

Miss Russell took West aside. "Thank you, Jack. Well done. I'll expect your bill."

"Do you have two bits, boss?" Meyers said under his breath, while digging in his own pockets and coming up with nothing.

"What for, boy?"

"An experiment is all."

"Now?"

"Yeah. It's important."

West gave him the quarter; Meyers turned suddenly and flipped the two-bit coin to Ada. Her quick hands plucked it out of the air, a frog catching flies. "Good catch. Hold onto it—it'll get you all the way to Boston barefoot."

The dour Jack West laughed so hard, he popped a vest button. "No applause this time, Madame juggler."

Her face flushed red, Lillian Russell chided, "For shame,

Mr. West. This is no laughing matter. What do you think you're doing, Mr. Meyers?"

Ada Hopkins could have pierced Meyers with her look, but the young man didn't falter. "Sure 'n begorra, you know what I'm talking about, don't you, Miss Ada? Or should we call you Carrie Dugan?"

Jack West never liked delivering bad news, but it was part of the job. He always delivered both good and bad news in person because he owed the truth to his clients. You never knew how a case would turn out when you took it on.

"I can't believe this of my little Ada," Miss Russell said.

Lillian Russell had a big heart, West knew. "She took everyone for a fool," he said.

"It was that sweetheart of hers, Bill Kennealy. His idea from the beginning. She broke down and admitted it. He had her under his spell. The police will understand. You know they've put her in the Tombs."

"I heard, but I daresay she'll have finer accommodations than most. She may not have done the killing, but she was not innocent. And unless they find Kennealy, we'll never know for sure."

"No gentleman would leave his sweetheart in this kind of situation—"

"I don't think a man who's killed three people could be counted as a gentleman, Miss Russell. You see, it was a plot from the beginning. Miss Ada had an elderly, wealthy widower who wanted to marry her. They saw a way to get his money, and they would have gotten it all when old Hopkins died."

"But what about the O'Days?"

"There were no O'Days. Kennealy became Tom O'Day, and he and Miss Ada hired an actress to be Marie. The poor girl needed the job because she had a child. Now the tyke will probably end up on the Orphan Train and have to live in St. Louis or some godawful place like that. Everything was fine until either Ada or Bill got impatient."

"Jack, I have to admit she had me duped. And perhaps if I hadn't brought you into it, she might have succeeded. She was a very good actress, my Ada. Better than even I thought."

"Yes, they might have gotten away with it if my associate, young Meyers, hadn't figured out he'd met Ada before when she was acting the part of the landlady."

"How did he do it? He's hardly more than a lad."

"But a sharp one. Said it was her hands. They were not the hands of a woman accustomed to hard work. And when he refilled her glass here in this room yesterday, he recognized her hands. You might say that this time the lady juggler dropped the ball."

Lillian Russell smiled sadly. "Why, Mr. West, you made another joke."

BEAUBIEN
A Mary Shelley story
by *Deborah Morgan*

**The Street: Beaubien Street,
Detroit, Michigan**

Deborah Morgan introduced her lady P.I., Mary Shelley, in
Lethal Ladies II and again features her here. Morgan's first
mystery novel, *Death Is a Cabaret*, which features antiques
dealer Jeffrey Talbot, was scheduled to appear in October
2001. She is also the editor of the PWA newsletter, *Reflections in a Private Eye*.

As many times as I've walked into Detroit Police Headquarters, it still makes me nervous.

I can't think why. I'm not a criminal. But my heart thuds
like a Ford engine on a cold morning, then gains rpm's and
pounds hell against my ribcage. My nerves beg for a shot of
anything. My senses are never sharper.

You know the feeling. The nervousness causes one of
three reactions at any given time: fear (always visible in one
form or another), cockiness (on the defense and ready to take
on anything and anybody), or innocence (coupled with a de-
termination to prove it by keeping a low profile). Point of
fact: Any one of these emotions will put the cops on red alert.

We're screwed, no matter what.

Today, I opted for low profile. Lieutenant Harold Bittenbinder had asked me to come by for a piece of birthday cake that the department had ordered. Rumor had it Harry was turning fifty-five on Saturday. Since my father never reached that age and Harry doesn't have any daughters, I was honored to be included.

I made it through the metal detector without a peep from either of us. That always surprises me.

Down the hall, just outside the bank of elevators, was a display case containing memorabilia for sale. I wondered how many of the navy blue coffee mugs emblazoned with *Detroit PD* in gold were being unwrapped on the fourth floor by our birthday boy.

By the time I arrived, the party was in full swing. Harry spotted me and made his way through the post-battle confusion of uniforms and smoke, a Polaroid shot in one hand and a mug from the case downstairs in the other. Instinctively, I looked at his desk. Triplets.

If a two-hundred-forty-pound German-American can bubble, Harry was bubbling. "Look at this, Mary!" He shoved a photo of the cake up to my face. It had been designed in the image of a double-nickel speed-limit sign. Catchy.

"Where's the real thing, Harry? I haven't eaten all day."

"You don't wanna see it. It looks like a train wreck."

I was starving, so I took my chances. After surviving two pieces of cake and countless curious stares directed my way, I went back in search of Harry. I hadn't planned ahead, but hoped he was free for dinner. When I found him, he was talking with a young uniformed officer who looked like she'd be more at home on the cover of *Vogue* than in a squad car.

"Lee Khrisopoulis," Harry said, "meet Mary Shelley, a

good friend and a hell of a P.I. Mary, Lee's one of the best
cops we've got."

She awkwardly shifted a cigarette to her left hand and
took my extended right. I noted that her grip was as firm as
my own.

"Harry says you're the best P.I. since Philip Marlowe."

"That's saying a lot, coming from this old man." I
squeezed his arm. "The cake was great, Harry, but I need to
find something more substantial. Can you join me?"

Just then, Harry was hailed from across the room. "Can't.
I'll call you later." He left, and I turned to Lee.

Her smile behind the olive skin was still intact, but her
dark eyes told me something was up. "Meet me. Pegasus.
Fifteen."

I nodded, understanding, and smiled. "A pleasure meeting you, too."

I walked out the front door and onto Beaubien, fed the
meter on the way past my Chevy, then turned the corner and
took in the aromas of skordalia, baklava, and ouzo. If I
worked down here, I'd gain back every pound I'd lost since
my divorce.

The only person I know who can bake better than the
Greeks is my son, Vic. He learned in Michigan's culinary in-
stitute, called the state prison system, from a French-trained
chef who had used his knife to fillet a restaurant owner for
shorting his paycheck.

As I walked, I caught myself hoping that Officer
Khrisopoulis was being melodramatic. Vic was joining me
for the Fourth of July festivities, with a Tigers game and
some cold ones thrown in, and I didn't want to spend my
time playing gumshoe.

When I arrived at the Pegasus, instinct told me to search
out a more secluded table. I ordered a beer and a sampler

plate of appetizers that included spanakopetakia, dolmathes yalantzi, and saganaki. Apparently, I'd bastardized the pronunciations so much that the waitress repeated my order of spinach triangles, stuffed grape leaves, and cheese that's been set on fire in English so I'd know what I was in for.

When Lee arrived by way of the back door, she slid into the chair opposite me and ordered coffee. "I don't have much time, so I'll cut to it. The powers that be want to partner me up with a new cop on the force for a special detail. I'd like to know more about him beforehand."

My brows shot up. "You pulled cloak-and-dagger shit on me for this? Why didn't you have someone at headquarters get you the lowdown? Harry, for instance?"

"No. Even if I weren't a female cop—which I am—it'd be difficult to check out another officer."

"Yeah, for all of us. Do you have any reason not to trust this new cop?"

"Nothing like that. Just trying to watch my back is all." The waitress put our drinks in front of us. Officer Khrisopoulis gulped the steaming liquid and set the cup down with a thud. "No one can know about this. Not even Harry. Got it?"

"I can handle that."

"I'd like a daily report, too. Meet me here at the same time every day and I'll pay you for the extra trouble. Can you handle that, too?"

I said I could. "But I'll warn you. I may not have much to report by tomorrow. Could be a challenge to dig up much on a new cop, working from the outside in."

"Easier than from the inside out." She pulled a cigarette from her pocket, lit it, and took a ragged drag. "The cop's name is Joey Partello. Just over six feet, dark, buff—some would say sexy, if you're into the Italian-lover type."

"Anything distinguishing?"

"That's not distinguishing enough for you?"

"I like my men short and nearsighted. Less competition that way." I waited for a smile. She didn't oblige. "What does he drive?"

"When he's off duty, he drives a dark blue Jimmy, loaded."

"Off duty is when?"

"The harsh, bright light of day."

I nodded.

The waitress showed up with my appetizers, touched a match to the saganaki and yelled *"Opaa!"* Khrisopoulis was gone before the flames died out.

It was getting close to five o'clock, so I made the appetizers serve as dinner, then searched out the pay phone and called my source at the Secretary of State's office. If you're not in Michigan, you probably know it as the DMV. There is the seldom, wonderful occasion when the computers aren't down, and this was one of them. I obtained Officer Partello's address and decided to make a swing-by to check it out.

For the most part, the old Italian neighborhood hadn't changed since FDR was president and Ford was making bomber parts for the war effort. Joey Partello's house looked pretty much like the other clapboard homes that lined the street—for now, anyway. A sign out front boasted TRIPLE A CONSTRUCTION, and on the driveway were stacks of smooth-planed lumber. Sacks of cement formed a barricade in front. Footings had been trenched along the east side of the original structure, about ten feet out; they cornered and continued out of sight around back.

Our Officer Partello was sinking a hefty chunk into a major addition.

I drove to the next block and pulled over to where a plump Italian woman was walking along the edge of the yard, picking tomatoes from vines that formed a frame around the property and hammocking them in a red-stained apron. Anywhere but here and I'd have thought it was blood. Hell, I'd have thought the same thing in an Italian restaurant. In the safety of the neighborhood, though, it was always tomato sauce.

"Nice house," I said by way of introduction.

She glanced up, then went back to picking tomatoes. When she spoke, her accent was as thick as marinara. "We've been here since '42."

I took that to mean she liked the place.

She stopped picking then, and sized me up. "You looking for a house?"

I love it when they make the job this easy. "Yes, ma'am. I thought that was a for-sale sign." I pointed toward Partello's. "Turns out it's a construction outfit advertising what they haven't done yet."

"That's the way of things these days. Joey would like to sell out, but"—she paused to cross herself—"he knows his mother would haunt him from the grave, so he's changing everything he can about the look of the place." She pulled a guilty look, as if she'd spoken out of turn. Apparently in order to absolve herself, she added, "He's paying cash, though. That's a good sign he's sticking with the old ways."

"A tough order nowadays."

"For some, I suppose." She paused, then picked up a small basket of tomatoes and handed it to me. "Go home and make some spaghetti. You're rail thin."

I didn't have the heart to tell her I couldn't cook.

*   *   *

There wasn't much more I could do that night, so I went home and drew a hot bath in the old clawfoot tub I'd rescued from the junk pile that came with the place. After an admirable attempt at becoming a prune, I set my alarm for god-awful early and turned in.

At three minutes after seven the next morning, I was at the intersection of Clinton and Beaubien when Partello pulled the Jimmy out of police parking and headed over to Brush. Tailing the cop was as easy as following a train down a railroad track. He took a left on Madison and nosed the Jimmy in for valet parking at the Detroit Athletic Club. I breezed on by.

The DAC. I knew the place, only because I'd once had a client ask me to meet him there in the Grill Room. With the annual membership fee of thirty-five hundred dollars, I had to wonder if I should trade in my plastic badge for a cop's shield.

While Partello spent the next hour working up a sweat in the comfort of an air-conditioned weight room, I trolled for parking under anything that looked like it might offer some shade. Giving that up, I sat and perspired.

My Corsica's air conditioner blew as hot as Ross Perot and by the time my cop emerged at eight-fifteen, I was mopping up rivulets of sweat that ran between my breasts and down my stomach with a Subway napkin I'd found under the front seat.

The Jimmy took off, and I tailed it until it entered Partello's neighborhood. I figured him to be going home for some sleep. I made my way to the City-County Building, thinking that a peek at some of the cases featuring Partello would give me an idea about how this new little rich cop was getting along with the fine citizens of Detroit.

As I walked past the bronzed, muscular statue of a man known as the Spirit of Detroit, it only served to remind me how much time had passed since I'd been laid.

Public records are a private eye's best friend. According to them, Joey Partello had been on the Motor City's payroll longer than Chrysler had sucked hind tit to Chevrolet. I traced cases back five, ten, twelve, sixteen years—Partello's name was all over the place. It didn't make any sense. I wasn't sure how long Lee Khrisopoulis had been with the force, but she'd have to have her head buried not to know that Partello was a fixture. I knew one thing: Our pre-arranged meeting wasn't soon enough.

I drove to headquarters.

The officer standing guard at the metal detector checked his roster and told me that Khrisopoulis was on days off.

I debated looking in on Harry, but what was I going to say? I was admittedly confused, even a little pissed. But until I knew what this little goose chase was about, Lee Khrisopoulis was my client and I had promised confidentiality. I'd give it, too, at least until the odds showed that I needed to do otherwise.

For the second time in recent history, I called the Secretary of State's office. My source asked if my calls were going to come in threes, like death.

"You never know until that third one hits, do you?"

He didn't have a comeback, so he gave me the information I needed and hung up.

The house looked like a Norman Rockwell painting in a Norman Rockwell neighborhood, light years from the barred windows and graffiti of downtown Detroit. I hurried up the concrete walk that led to the front door, noting that the flower gardens were in need of weeding. I had a sudden image of America's Painter turning in his grave.

I stood head-on in front of the fisheye, figuring that any smart cop would check the peephole before opening the door.

Lee Khrisopoulis didn't disappoint me. She flung the door open and yelled, "What in the hell do you think you're doing?"

"Turn that question around and walk it right back at yourself." I eyed her evenly. "Joey Partello has been on the force nearly as long as Coleman Young was in office. But you knew that already, didn't you?"

She grabbed my arm and pulled me inside. As thoughts of police brutality shot through my mind, she slammed the door, jerked the cigarette from her mouth, and jammed her eye to the peephole.

I'd never seen anyone look more disgusting with a smoke. But I hadn't been sent here from Lung Patrol. "You're paying me for this little game," I started, "so here's your money's worth. He's got some dough. I don't know how he's making it, but I can find that out, too, if it's important to you. Also got a major remodel going on, and he's apparently making enough money to join the crowd at the DAC."

She turned, surprised. "You got all that in twenty-four hours?"

"Hell, don't you know anything about gathering information? I had all that before your first cup of coffee this morning."

"Harry told me you were good," she said matter-of-factly.

"Did Harry put you up to this? Tell him April Fool was three months ago."

"No, Harry doesn't know about this." She took another drag, went for the peephole again, then backed up and fanned smoke as if she was fighting off bees. "I meant it when I said no one else could know about this. I had to be sure you could do a job quickly and without anyone getting suspicious. Besides, I figured my odds were better with you since you're a woman. I thought you would understand."

"The first thing *you* need to understand is that acting like a damn woman will bring six courses of hell down on you. Start acting like a cop."

"You're right." She made a sound that could've passed for either a laugh or a cry. "Of course, if I weren't a woman, I wouldn't be in this damn mess."

"You're giving men way too much credit."

"Possibly, but I have reason to. Do you know what kind of danger you've put me in by coming here? Not to mention yourself."

"Since you seem to be playing some sort of game with me, how the hell am I *supposed* to know? It took me no time to get the scoop on Joey Partello. I sure as hell wasn't going to wait around for our meeting this afternoon. Now, are you going to tell me what this is about, or do I walk?"

"I'm paying you five hundred a day." She turned and glared at me. "That should be enough to make you stick to the game plan."

"I don't play games, Officer." I grabbed for the doorknob.

She stopped me. "You can't leave now."

"Watch me."

"I'm not the one watching." She let go of my arm and nodded toward the door.

It was my turn to check the spy hole. There was a blue

sedan parked up the street, the same one I'd noticed earlier when I'd pulled up.

She started walking. "Come sit down. I'll tell you the whole sordid story."

The officer's home was immaculate, except for an ashtray full of butts on the coffee table. When she started to light up another smoke, I frowned. She paused, then slid it back in the pack. "I didn't smoke before . . . well, before everything. Thought it would calm my nerves, but it probably just shows how much of a wreck I really am, doesn't it?"

"Pretty much."

She nodded. "Have you ever had your privacy violated, Mrs. Shelley?"

"Mary."

"Mary. Your home invaded? Things taken?"

We were seated on the couch, angled toward each other. I shook my head, waited for her to continue.

"It started three months ago. I work the Property Room at headquarters. Items began disappearing. When I reported what was going on, I started getting threats."

"Then someone gained entry to my house, my *home*. It wasn't a B and E, and it didn't look like anything was missing. But I knew someone had been in here." She shuddered slightly, then went on with her story.

"Do you know what it's like to realize that? To walk into a room and *know* that someone had been there? To wonder, Did he sit on that chair? Did he go through my clothing? Did he see his reflection in the bathroom mirror—the mirror I have to look in every day? And the kitchen. Did he put poison in my orange juice? Did he hide something in the cereal box?"

"It almost drove me insane. I ended up throwing out

everything in the house. But I couldn't figure out what he'd been doing here."

"How do you know it was a he?"

"He called, finally. Asked if I'd determined what was missing."

"So he *did* take something."

"Oh, yeah, he took something, all right."

I waited for her to tell me what it was. She didn't offer. "So?" I prodded.

"How in the hell do I say this?" She buried her face in her hands.

"Just say it, Lee. You're not going to shock me."

She looked at me. "Okay. Panties. He stole a pair of panties from the bathroom hamper."

"Panties? Why in the hell would he want—" I stopped. There could only be one explanation, unless he was a pervert. "They have your friend's DNA, right?"

"Yes. Damn it. Partello found out I was having an affair with a married man. Worse than that, actually—a fellow officer. The DNA from the panties can prove it.

"That's why I think he's the one. Partello. The one who was here, the one who's been calling, threatening me, threatening us. And if my friend's wife finds out, well . . . It will kill him if he loses his wife and kids.

"You see, my friend found out about a crooked cop ring. He doesn't have proof yet, but he's getting close—and it looks like Partello is the leader. So, my friend confronted him—I begged him not to, but he really thought he could use the cops' unwritten code of loyalty. Partello just told him that loyalty was a two-way street. Apparently, he started doing some investigating of his own. He threatened to expose us. Leverage, you know.

"Only now, my friend is wondering if he should bust the

ring—for the greater cause. He feels that fewer people will
be hurt in the long run, that it may be worth risking his marriage. It's eating him up."

I waited, taking it all in. When she didn't volunteer any
more information I said, "What do you think?"

"At first, I thought all I wanted was to get the panties
back. Remove the incriminating evidence from the equation.
But now, laying it all out like this." She shrugged. "Nothing
makes me sicker than crooked cops. The police department
is supposed to be made up of people who are willing to serve
and protect. Sounds corny, sometimes, when you boil it
down to that. But I don't want to see the department under
siege from within."

"You're a twenty-first century Beaubien."

"What?"

"Mademoiselle Beaubien?" I watched her face, but noth-
ing registered. "Don't tell me they let you work at 1300
Beaubien without telling you where the name came from.
Chief Pontiac united all the Indian tribes in the Northwest
Territory to lay siege against Fort Detroit."

"When the hell did this happen?"

"Something like three hundred years ago. This young
Frenchwoman named Beaubien—I don't know her first
name—she learned of it and warned the Fort's commander.
Saved the day, as it were. More than that, really. She saved
Detroit.

"You're our Beaubien," I continued, "only you're already
on the inside. You need to dig the department out of this. We
just have to figure out how."

"I don't know about that, but I do know one thing. I don't
want this to hinge on an incriminating pair of panties." She
lit a cigarette, then laughed bitterly. "Sounds like the
damned White House, doesn't it?"

"Just like," I said.

"Well, I can't help that. But I can tell you that I haven't been with my friend since Partello was in my home."

"The property that's missing. What is it?"

For the first time, she looked truly frightened. "Drugs," she said. "Meth, crack, coke, heroin, GHB—tons of marijuana. Drugs. Lots and lots of drugs."

We talked over options, laid some new ground rules that we both could live with, and worked on our strategy.

I asked about the blue sedan.

"One of Partello's boys. Been watching the house, but I haven't caught anyone tailing me while I'm at work. My guess is there are enough cops involved to watch me while I'm on duty." A tremor shook her body. "It's scary, not knowing who to trust."

I told her where I'd parked and asked if my car was blocking hers in the garage.

"No. I'm on the other side."

"Good. I'll leave it here for now." I told her my plan while I made a call from my cell phone. I wasn't sure if I could trust her line not to be tapped.

In twenty minutes, my son was following my instructions to the letter, slowly pulling through the alley behind Lee's house. I darted across the lawn, keeping the house between me and the surveillance goon. On my cue, Vic made a rolling stop and I slipped into the backseat of his beige Plymouth.

The bland set of wheels was the last thing you'd expect someone who looked like Vic to drive. He's got a shaved head, more holes than Dillinger, and he's on the annual Christmas card lists of four tattoo emporiums.

He'd recently begun working for a lawn service so he

was tanned, and his tall, slim physique was quickly showing some muscle definition. He'd be perfect for the job I had in mind.

I asked him to swing by MC Sports on the way home. He frowned, but obliged, and I made a quick run inside while he circled the parking lot so he could keep the air conditioner humming.

Plastic bag in hand, I crawled back into Vic's car and told him to swing by my office. Prometheus Investigations offers about as much leg room as a crop duster, but its location just off Woodward is handy to my downtown haunts.

"You're always wanting to help out, right?" I asked Vic after we'd climbed the stairs to my office.

"Sure," he answered, giving the word an extra syllable with a wary lilt. He lit a Camel as if he knew he was going to need something to steady his nerves.

I handed him the shopping bag. "Here's your costume."

He leaned over a round coffee table the size of a Frisbee, ground out the cigarette in an ashtray with HOLIDAY INN printed in the bottom, and headed for the bathroom.

Plastic crackled on the other side of the bathroom door, then everything was quiet. When Vic spoke, I could barely hear his voice from the other side of the door. He'd uttered a confused-sounding *"What the hell?"* that was followed by more silence.

Then: "No way!"

That I could've heard from Cleveland.

"Mom," he said then with that two-syllable sing-song he'd used as a teenager when he was annoyed with me, "you gotta be *shitting* me."

"You can get in the men's locker room at the DAC a hell of a lot easier than I can. Besides, you pick locks better than I do."

He was still cursing as he walked out of the bathroom, wearing the tennis whites and carrying a racket and a navy duffel bag. "I look like a damn Harvard prep."

"Not yet you don't. Tuck in the shirttail, lose the nose ring—where's the belt I bought?"

Getting the panties was as simple as throwing fifty bucks out the window. There's always someone around to pick it up.

Vic told me how he'd gone about it, how the kid gathering up towels in the locker room had told him he looked ridiculous in that get-up.

Vic paused and gave me a told-you-so smirk. When I didn't say anything, he got back down to business.

He'd agreed with the guy, then cut to the chase and told him it was a front. This excited the kid, so Vic pulled the fifty from his pocket and asked which of the vertical coffins belonged to Partello. The kid spit out the number, took the bill, and offered to stand watch while Vic picked the lock. The red-lace panties were zipped up tight in a plastic evidence bag inside a sneaker.

Sometimes you had to wonder how a crooked cop ever hooked together enough brain cells to pull off a scam.

I arranged a meeting with Harry while Vic paid a few calls to his connections in Detroit's underworld. Don't ask; I don't and I never will. After getting Vic out from under his father's spell, I learned to thank God for every day I have with my son. I can't do much more than that. After all he's been through, my son is in many ways a lot older than I am.

We—Vic and I—reconnoitered at my office and, after an all-clear from Lee, swung by her place and picked up my Corsica. I checked the glove compartment first thing for my Smith & Wesson .22 snub-nose.

We subverted, snaking our way along backroads and through subdivisions in what we determined was a successful job of arriving at my house without being tailed. We had a pizza delivered and waited for nightfall.

Besides the oppressive humidity, another drawback of summer is the challenge of where to hide a gun on you without the benefit of jackets. At least my weapon's small, so I can usually come up with something.

Tonight I opted for a stylish rendition of a fishing vest I'd bought in khaki and dyed black for just such occasions. It's longer than a man's vest and the zip pockets are priceless for stakeouts, bugouts, and my all-too-infrequent campouts. It's made of lightweight cotton with an elastic insert at the middle of the back which provides just enough gathers to camouflage the .22 I had tucked in my waistband.

I was parked down Beaubien, as far away from police headquarters as I could get and still be able to see anything. I'd driven my little pickup—a '56 GMC stepside, ginger metallic—in case Lee's goon was watching for my Chevy, and had let Vic out to walk from my office.

I watched for him now, using the binoculars he'd given me for Christmas. When I saw him climb the steps and go through the doors of 1300, something gripped my chest like a vise and I regretted having ever dragged him into this.

I thought about the conversation I'd had earlier with Harry. I'd persuaded him to trust me on this one, told him that Vic had a great *in,* that he was going to tell the guy in Property to use his cell phone and call the cop ring's street connection to verify that Vic had been sent there to pick up the goods.

"Vic's not in that racket anymore," Harry had said.

"I know that, and you know that. As it turns out, the other guy doesn't know that."

"Hell, Mary, how can you be sure?"

"I guess I can't be, but Vic told me not to ask questions. He just said that the thing he has on this drug dealer is a hell of a lot more dangerous to the guy than a few crooked cops." I closed my eyes, as if that would erase my fears. "Harry, if I knew the things Vic learned under the tutelage of his father and his years in Jackson prison . . . well, it would scare me a damn site more than his trying to buy drugs from a cop while you're hiding in the wings."

Bittenbinder sighed heavily. "What if something goes wrong? If Vic gets hurt—"

"You think I haven't thought of that? If I didn't think Vic could handle it, I'd nix the whole thing right now. But remember, Harry, you have no choice. You can't use a cop on this one. We'll just have to make sure we cover every base.

"You can position yourself so that Vic's covered. Lee will be there, too.

"You know how good Vic is with electronics, right? He's rigged up a recorder in this huge gothic cross he wears on a chain around his neck—"

"We'll modify it," Harry said, "make it a wire and put one of my men at the other end."

"Let's get on it, then," I'd said, glad to see that Harry was back in cop mode.

I knew I wouldn't make it past the metal detector, so I gave Harry a call like we'd planned earlier, and he got me in by way of an old service entrance that most of the newcomers don't know about. He stashed me in a supply closet and told me to stay put until it was all over. I said okay. The lie came easily. But I wasn't about to hang back when my son might be in the crossfire.

I'd learned the layout of police headquarters earlier from Lee, so I knew I wasn't too far from the Property Room. I stepped into the hallway and moved close enough to hear what was going on inside.

"You Rutledge?" It was Vic's voice.

"Who's asking?" Cocky attitude.

I could envision Vic pointing to his T-shirt, which was being used as the code. It had a picture of Curious George lying unconscious on the ground beside an open bottle of ether. "George needs something to wake him up."

"Then I'll need to call the doctor for a prescription." More code.

I could hear the faint, high-pitched beeps as Rutledge punched buttons on a cell phone. "Yeah, Doc. I gotta sick monkey here." A pause, then: "Ether. Yep. That's the one." Another pause. "Okay. Got it." Another beep sounded as he ended the call. "Doc says you're cool. I'll go in back and get the stuff. Anybody comes down here, you play like you're lost, got it?"

"Got it," Vic said.

The time stretched on with the flesh-tingling tension of a Hitchcock film. I considered going in, but thought I heard some sort of movement so I stayed put. More time passed.

The next thing I heard was Vic ask, "What's goin' on?"

"Looks like the doctor is in." That was Rutledge's voice, sarcastic.

There was a shuffling noise. I moved closer to the door. I wanted to peek inside, see how many there were, but decided not to take the chance. Not yet.

"We've got a deal, Rutledge," Vic said. "I gave Doc here

fifty large this afternoon. Now, tell your goon to get the gun off me." Goon. The guy from Lee's house, the blue sedan.

"Trouble down here?" It was Lee's voice. Her coming out of hiding meant only one thing: The deal had turned sour.

"Nothing that a little showdown won't fix." This was a new voice.

"Don't try it, Partello"—Lee's voice—"I've got you covered."

"The only thing you're covering is your boyfriend's ass."

"Wrong, Partello. That would be Bittenbinder covering my ass." I figured the voice had to be Lee's friend. "He's bearing down on you right now."

"You expect me to believe that shit?"

I'm not sure why, but I took that as my cue. Maybe, if I could get in there in time, Partello wouldn't check whether or not Harry was behind him. Maybe the wondering would slow him down. I pulled my gun and walked gingerly through the door.

The only thing that registered when I got in there was the gun pointed at Vic.

Words can't describe what I felt, seeing that gun zeroed in on my son. In that instant, I saw Vic—the infant I had bonded with as only a mother can; the toddler who had come to me when he fell down; the schoolboy who had come to me when he was knocked down; the teenager who had gotten snared into white-collar crime by his own father; the man who had overcome it. I saw all the incarnations that were my son, and I knew that I would kill the man who was holding a gun on him now. I knew I was going to kill Joey Partello.

I forced myself to concentrate. My heart pounded in my ears and I wasn't sure if anyone was talking, but then someone spoke and the pounding subsided. My focus had never been keener. My aim had never been sharper.

The Property Room was set up similar to an old bank, with teller windows framed in by glass partitions and a single door at one end providing access to the back, where the loot was kept. Standing in that doorway was Joey Partello.

In front of Vic, on the other side of the opening, was a young male officer I took for Rutledge, and behind him was another officer—the goon—with a massive forearm across the neck of a very thin man in dark, baggy clothes. Doc—somebody must have brought him along. Behind Vic, and off to the right, was Lee Khrisopoulis. To her right was a uniformed officer—the boyfriend.

"Who's that?" Partello's tone told me he expected me to identify myself. He didn't move his aim away from Vic.

"You don't need to know that," Lee said.

"Shut up, bitch." Partello spoke through gritted teeth.

"Watch your mouth." This was Harry's voice.

Partello swung the gun away from Vic and toward the back, where Harry had been waiting silently.

Partello had made his mistake. As he swiveled, I put a bullet behind his right ear. He fired as he crumpled, squeezing off three rounds before he hit the ground. Everyone opened fire.

Vic lunged to the floor and slid on his stomach toward me as if he was stealing home plate. Rutledge, who had fired at Vic and missed, readjusted and drew a bead on Lee, and the uniformed cop opened a hole in Rutledge's chest, but not before he'd squeezed off a shot. Lee fell.

The goon, who was still holding Doc, swung around to fire on Harry, and Lee's friend capped him before he got off a round. Doc pulled free of the falling man, then rolled himself up in a ball in the corner.

The gunfire stopped.

Vic and I each made sure the other hadn't been hit; then we both went to Lee. Her friend was already there, cradling her in his arms and stroking her face.

Blood was seeping from her chest, but not enough to cause the dark red puddle quickly growing under her.

I looked at the officer inquiringly.

"Ricochet got her in the back."

"Mary?" Raspy little coughs came from Lee's throat.

"Yes, Lee. I'm right here." I grasped her hand.

"That Frenchwoman—Beaubien? Was she injured?"

"No, I don't think so."

"That's good." She coughed some more. "I'm a cop. I'm supposed to be ready to die."

"You're not going to die. Don't you know that?"

Lee looked at the man holding her. She tried to swallow, made a choking noise. When she spoke again, her voice was congested with liquid. "No, I can tell. But it was worth it."

"What was?" I asked.

"Saving the fort."

We left her alone with her friend.

I looked around the room. It had filled with officers. Many I recognized from Harry's birthday party, only now their faces were behind guns.

The paramedics arrived, counted fallen bodies, and called for some backup of their own.

Vic and I picked up Harry around eleven on Sunday and headed to Comerica Park. Crappy name for a baseball stadium, if you ask me. I don't care how many fountains and Ferris wheels they add, it'll never replace Tiger Stadium. Apparently, though, they've got all us die-hard fans by the balls, because we were out in full force, shoving through the wide concrete ramps toward the seats like so many cattle in the chutes.

After Harry and Vic and I had eaten our hot dogs and gotten a second round of brewskies from a vendor in an orange cap with peach fuzz on his face, Harry updated us on what he'd learned so far about the cop ring.

Five officers were involved. The two still alive after last night's shootout decided to stay that way by singing like Joe Valachi.

In spite of our efforts when Vic picked me up in Lee's alley, Goon had figured something out and tailed us. He had Polaroids of both of us on his person when he died.

Harry wrapped up by telling us that Lee Khrisopoulis's funeral would be Wednesday.

We were silent for a while and then Vic asked Harry if he knew the meaning of the word Beaubien.

"No. Do you?"

"Sure. It means 'beautiful and good.' You need to teach that to your cops."

Harry sat quietly and drank his beer.

HIGHLY IRREGULAR ON BAKER STREET
A TRACE STORY
by Warren Murphy

**The Street: Baker Street,
London, England**

Warren Murphy has been to me, at one time or another in my life, mentor, friend, and colleague. He has won many writing awards—including MWA's Edgar—the most recent of which was the PWA Shamus Award for best short story a couple of years ago. I am very pleased to present the first short story in some time to feature his series P.I., Devlin Tracy. The Trace series was at the height of its popularity during the 80's, bringing Warren several of those awards. One hopes that the appearance of a new Trace story might herald the appearance of some new Trace books in the near future.

(In which our redoubtable heroine is advised that she will take a long voyage with a tall, weird man not unknown to her.)

"List' to me, while I tell you . . .
"Of the Spaniard who blighted my life, la-la-la-la.
"List' to me while I tell you . . .
"Of the man who stole my future wife.
" 'Twas at the bullfight where . . ."

"Trace, why are you singing?"

"From the sheer joy of living," Trace said. He was a big man, but even as he spoke, all the electricity in the room seemed to be gathering around the small, beautiful Eurasian woman who was glaring at him across the kitchen counter.

"You're doing it again, aren't you?" she asked. Her name was Chico and she was Trace's partner in a New York City detective agency that would have to have its three best years in a row to rise to the level of abject failure.

"'Doing it again,'" Trace mocked. "Doing what, pray tell, kind lady?"

"You've got something planned. The only time you sing those stupid songs of yours is when you have something planned. Something stupid and hateful that will embarrass me for the rest of my life."

"You know, you have a particularly sour view of the life process," Trace said. He sloshed some liquid from a bottle of vodka into a water glass that held one lonesome ice cube.

"God, I hate you," Chico said.

"Anything in particular?"

"Now that you mention it, yes. I hate your drinking and your womanizing. I hate how you make federal cases out of nothing and ignore big, important things. I hate that you know lyrics to songs that no one else ever heard of. I hate that you're irresponsible, thoughtless, neurotic, and quite nuts."

"Well, nobody's perfect," Trace said cheerily. "Have a drink? Only a small one, though. This bottle was full yesterday and now look at it. Have you been imbibing behind my back?"

"I've promised myself that the only drink I will ever have in my life will be the bottle of cheap champagne I glug down when I'm stomping a mazurka atop your grave." She paused suspiciously. "So what is it that prompts you to explode into what you laughingly call song?"

"I'll tell you later," Trace said.

"Why later?"

"Because the wait will intensify the guilt you are sure to feel. And then you'll feel compelled to make nice with me."

"I have a lyric too," Chico said.

"Oh?"

"Yes. Dream the impossible dream."

Later, they sat on the sofa in their small living room, watching television. Chico had an affinity for true-crime stories, seemingly unending documentaries on how the Salt Lake City police department had solved a crime committed twenty-seven years earlier. She watched these while consuming vast quantities of what Trace called feed—chips and nuts and little ugly green things—none of whose caloric content ever seemed to find its way onto her tight little dancer's body.

The TV shows, however, always brought Trace to the verge of sleep, and whenever Chico left the room, he quickly flipped the TV remote and switched to some nature show, hoping to find footage of whale gang-rape or male lions eating their own cubs. Chimpanzees committing murder on neighborhood macaques was an especial favorite of his, one he had seen a dozen times and still found fascinating.

Chico came back into the room and, without even looking at the TV, hit the remote to return to her crime channel.

She settled back onto the couch and said, "I've been thinking about this. I'm leaving you. I hate you. I hate the ground you vomit on. When I finally walk away from you, I am going to salt the earth between us so nothing else can ever grow there. I hate everything about you. I hate your stupid clothes, your stupid ideas, your stupid schemes for getting rich. I hate those stupid waitresses who seem to find you so irresistible. I hate. I hate. I hate."

"Something I said?"

"Grrrrrrrr."

Trace poured himself another drink. "I guess the surprise I had for you will just go unclaimed," he said.

"On the other hand," Chico said brightly, "I have always believed in the redemption of the subhuman soul. Surprise me."

"This one's really good," Trace said.

"We'll see."

"You're going to love it."

"The jury waits."

"Stay right here," Trace said.

He got up and went into the bedroom. When he returned, he was wearing a hat and he handed Chico an unwrapped red box.

"What is that thing on your head?" she asked.

"That's my surprise," Trace said.

"That you've found something even uglier than what you normally wear?"

"This is a deerstalker cap. Authentic. And there's one just like it in the box. For you. Look and see."

"You think you're taking me deerhunting? Hah! It is to laugh."

"No, dear heart, I am taking you to London. To Baker Street. To the home of the world's first consulting detective, the one and only Sherlock Holmes. These hats are so we fit right in."

Chico opened the box and removed a hat identical to the one Trace wore. She held it gingerly at arm's length as if it were a recently killed skunk.

"Neat, huh?"

Chico just shook her head in wonderment.

"Actually, I've always regarded us as sort of a Holmes and Watson team," Trace said. "Me cleverly using ratiocination and deduction to solve the most complicated and nefarious of schemes, you blustering around brainlessly, hmphing like Nigel Bruce, never quite understanding how I work my detective magic."

"This is all a joke, right? London?"

"No joke. I have it planned."

"And I am supposed to go with you?"

"Of course. What would Holmes be without his faithful Watson to chronicle his exploits? Of course you're coming with me."

"Is this going to be some stupid thing like you've sold me to some Arab sheikh or something?"

"No, you're too old. They're more interested in my waitresses."

"Then why?"

"This is complicated."

"I'll try to struggle along," Chico said.

"Bud Barton. You know, Barton TV, Barton Classic TV, Barton TV Filmworks, Barton . . ."

"I know who he is."

"Right. Anyway, this nitwit has decided to open a theme park, all centered around Sherlock Holmes. As part of it, they're going to make new interactive movies of all the Holmes stories, and don't ask me what interactive means because I don't know. Anyway, he's going to announce all this next week in London. At 221B Baker Street, Holmes's old digs. And he's invited all the beautiful people."

"That explains why they want me there. But why you?"

"Because our old insurance company is going to be one

of the big investors and the company president invited us," Trace said.

"Oh, no."

"What?"

"Oh no, 'cause you're talking about Bob Swenson. He's the only man in the world who drinks more than you do. This will be a nightmare in London. You two will always be drunk."

"Details, details, God, I hate details. The big picture. We're on the guest list. You, me, Bob, Bud Barton, and twenty other moneyed representatives of America's leisure class."

Chico looked at Trace for a few long seconds, making sure he was telling the truth. Then she stepped alongside him and turned him around so he faced a mirror on the wall behind their telephone. Then she put on her own deerstalker cap and they stood there looking at their reflections, tall and short, dark-haired and blond, sober as a monk and drunk as a skunk.

"There we are," Trace said. "The tall, elegant one is Sherlock Holmes. The squat, swarthy thing is my faithful Watson. So what do you say?"

"I say when do we leave," Chico said.

"Yoicks. Yoicks. That means 'oh, joy' in Brit-speak."

"It means no such thing. I'm going to live to regret this lunacy."

"Oh, lighten up. What could go wrong?"

(Our dauntless detectives embark for London, but little do they know that trouble awaits.)

One day a week later, they flew out of New York first-class on the Concorde. Chico had hidden both deerstalker caps in the back of one of her dresser drawers, but since that was the place where she hid everything, Trace had immediately found them and packed them deep in the bottom of one of their suitcases. Next to them, just out of perverse habit, he had packed the small tape recorder which he always wore while working. Simply knowing he had it with him gave him an odd sense of security, even though there would be no work to be done on this trip.

While they waited on the runway, Chico looked around the first-class cabin and asked Trace, "Where are the rest of the beautiful people who are going to this do?"

"Who cares? Bob Swenson will meet us in London and we'll see the rest of them soon enough. It's enough that I'm here with you, fair lady."

After a few minutes, the big jet started bumping down the runway, its engines roaring. Suddenly, the plane bumped as if it had hit a pothole on the runway.

"Holy Mary, Mother of God," Trace said. He leaned forward to one of the flight attendants who had assumed take-off position in a jump seat just ahead of them.

"Tell me," he said, "the pilot ever fly this thing before?"

The pretty young attendant smiled reassuringly. "Hundreds of times. A veteran pilot."

"Yeah. He's real old, right? Hands shaking. Nipping a little brandy from a flask to keep his heart beating. Trying to remember what city he's supposed to be flying to. 'Am I going to Lisbon or London? Or maybe Paris.' Shouldn't you go up there and check and see that he's still conscious?"

"Trace, you promised," Chico said.

"It's all right, miss, a lot of people get nervous on take-off," the attendant said.

"He's not nervous," Chico said. "He's just being a pain in the ass."

Trace was not listening. The plane had started rising from the runway and he covered his eyes with both hands and stuck his thumbs in his ears for good measure.

"Is he like this often?" the flight attendant asked Chico.

"Not often . . . always," Chico said. "He'll be better when he has six or seven drinks."

Trace was humming.

The attendant smiled at Chico and spoke as if Trace did not exist. "See? He's feeling better already."

Chico shook her head. "He's humming 'Nearer My God to Thee.' He knows many songs, most of them stupid, all of them inappropriate."

"Next time," Trace mumbled, "we take the QE2. I don't trust this drunken flyboy." He lifted one hand and peered out at the stewardess. "And if we ever reach land again, don't forget my wings. I want my plastic wings. And I want vodka. Lots of vodka."

He covered his eyes again and Chico sighed. "It's going to be a long flight."

But the flight was uneventful, even if Trace did continuously badger the flight attendants to have the pilot make some kind of announcement over the intercom, so Trace could see if he was slurring his words and thus make some kind of judgment on the pilot's level of drunkenness and the imminence of the plane's destruction. When the pilot did finally speak, well into the flight, he sounded like Chuck Yeager and Trace complained, "He's putting that on, that voice. He's really a little midget Frenchman up there swilling champagne."

They breezed through customs at Heathrow Airport, and a big, boxy cab was waiting to take them to their luxury hotel in the heart of London. The driver said the fare was twenty-five pounds and Trace said, "Do you know the way to Scotland Yard?" and Chico wound up hiring and paying for the cab herself.

At the hotel desk, as they were checking in, a loud voice bellowed from behind them: "Hey, my favorite couple in the world. Chico, are you ready to dump this loser and run away with me?"

She turned toward Bob Swenson, the head of the insurance company that retained their detective firm. "Right now," she said. "This minute. Let's go. You sure your wife won't mind?"

"Aaaaah, you spoil everything," Swenson said and stepped forward to swallow her in a giant bear hug. He was a big, bluff man, as tall as Trace but even thicker through the shoulders and chest. He was wearing a khaki bush jacket, long khaki shorts that reached below his knees, and a pith helmet.

"Doctor Livingstone, I presume," Trace said.

Swenson released Chico and gestured toward his own clothes and said, "When in Rome, you know."

"I hate to be the one to tell you this, but this isn't Rome."

"Who cares? Let's get a drink. Let me get this babe liquored up so I can work my wicked will on her."

"You two bums drink. I'll shop," Chico said.

And so they did until the next night, when Bud Barton's welcome dinner was held in a large private dining room on an upper floor of the hotel. Chico wore a gown she had bought especially for the occasion and Trace even allowed himself to be forced into wearing a shirt with a tie.

When Chico came into the bedroom of their suite, she almost took Trace's breath away. She was always beautiful, but when she wanted to turn it on, she became simply phenomenal.

"I've got an idea," Trace said.

"I know, I know. Let's forget the dinner and roll around on the floor. Not on your life, big guy."

"Cheez, I'm not used to having my open-mouthed adoration treated so cavalierly."

"Anyway, I guess that means I look all right."

"Not bad for an old broad. They'll be sniffing after you all night like a T-bone steak."

"I don't know. These are the beautiful people. Tough competition. I'm nervous, Trace."

"No competition at all," Trace said. He put his arm around her shoulders and squeezed. "The whole world's no competition at all."

He let her go, and she wanted to kiss him very much but instead she said, "Hey, why are you putting that on?"

Trace was hooking his small tape recorder on the back of his belt. A thin wire extended from the recorder, under his shirt, to a golden-frog tie clip that hid the microphone.

"I don't know," Trace said. "I wear a jacket, a tie, I feel undressed without my tape machine. Anyway, who knows? Somebody here says something real stupid and I can sell the tape to the National Enquirer. We'll be rich."

"Good idea. Wear it in good health."

Bob Swenson called for them at their room. He was wearing a tuxedo. When he saw Chico, he said, "Let's let Trace go to dinner. How about you and I stay here and mess up the bedroll?"

"Okay," Chico said. "You want to call your wife up to watch us? Or should I call?"

"Trace, this is one pain-in-the-ass vicious woman."

"Ignore her. She's just crabby 'cause I rejected her. Come on, post time."

*   *   *

They were among the last to enter the private dining room, a large cavern, its walls hung with drapes, and again a testament to Britain's absolute inability—no matter what their state of technological advancement—to operate a simple cooling system. The room was Turkish-bath hot.

Perhaps twenty other people were there, and Trace recognized many of them from seeing their pictures in the tabloid press. Curiously, Bud Barton had decided on a buffet-style dinner, and the two dozen guests were lined up now in a queue leading toward a food-packed table that seemed big enough to ice-skate on.

"God, look at these people," Chico said as she steered Trace toward the foot of the line. Meanwhile, Swenson peeled off and headed for the bar in the far corner of the room.

"Just like you," Trace sniffed. "Being impressed just because you're around a lot of famous rich people. You are a shallow human being."

"It's not that."

"Oh? What is it?"

"Being around the beautiful people makes me realize again how truly insignificant you are." She pointed. "Look . . . isn't that . . ."

"Stop pointing. You're embarrassing me. Yes, it is. The richest man in the world."

"He really does look like a geek." Just then, the young man they were discussing looked back, saw Chico, and smiled at her. "But a nice geek," she said. "He's country, but I could work with somebody like that." She smiled back.

"Gold-digger. Hey, did you ever notice that when you see rich people, really rich people, they're always standing in line to get free food?"

They were in line behind a former United States Senator

and his wife. The senator smiled at Chico; his wife, whose hair looked as if it had been immortalized in epoxy, pulled him forward as the line slowly inched ahead.

"Is that who I think it is?" Chico whispered in Trace's ear. She was looking at a thinnish man with graying hair and a small, well-trimmed gray mustache. He was in the middle of the line in front of the buffet table, a cell phone plastered to his ear.

"Exactly. Our host. Bud Barton, the biggest by-God communications mogul in the world."

"Bill Gates is richer," Chico said.

"He ought to be. Gates is smarter too. But Barton's done all right. He spent ten years in Texas working as a telephone lineman and installer and now he owns all the phone companies. And the TV companies. And the movie studios. Not bad for somebody who hates capitalism and thinks that Fidel Castro is a prince."

"Well, nobody's perfect," Chico said as Bud Barton smiled at her. "If that's him, that must be . . . no, that can't be . . . not his wife."

She was actually gawking at a woman who shuffled mousily along in the food line behind Barton, who seemed to be unaware of her existence.

"That's her. Viet Velma, the pinup girl of America's enemies. Dodged the hangman's rope for treason and here she is. If I were her, I'd be ashamed to leave the house."

"But not for treason, man. Just look at her. She must weigh two hundred pounds."

"Clean living and dirty thinking," Trace said.

"She sells exercise tapes. Nutrition tapes. What happened to all that?" Chico asked.

"She ate the tapes," Trace said.

"She's got more lines in her face than dried mud."

"Who cares?" Trace said. "They're both Communists."

"There are no Communists anymore."

"Just those two," Trace said. He looked around the room. There was a well-known Hollywood couple whose presence probably meant they were going to be featured in Barton's new Sherlock Holmes films. He recognized one of Hollywood's hot new young directors, a bespectacled black man whose films Trace regarded as incoherent, hate-mongering junk. The rest of the crowd must have been investors, quiet-looking, almost faceless men with X-ray wives who seemed quietly intimidated. In the far corner of the room, Trace saw Bob Swenson leaning on the small bar, in animated discussion with the pretty woman bartender. Swenson, he reflected, talked a good game. He would hit on any reasonably presentable woman he encountered—usually at full throat—but so far as Trace knew, it was all chatter and Swenson was rock-faithful to his demure, ladylike wife.

Trace looked back as Chico pulled him along in the food line. She was still watching Bud Barton and his wife, Viet Velma.

"He hates her, you know," Chico said.

"Of course he does. Everybody hates her."

"No, he hates her special. Look. Watch him."

Trace glanced toward Bud Barton. The telephone mogul had stopped talking on his cell phone, but he still held it in his hand. He was keeping up a line of chatter with the two people in the food line ahead of him and the people who were working their way back on the other side of the buffet table. He did not even glance at his wife, who managed to stay two full steps behind him. She was busy putting food on her plate in giant piles—small, slick pieces of chicken, slabs of blood-rare roast beef, thick and slimy potato salad. Whenever she moved closer to Barton, he moved away from her.

It seemed almost an instinctive act, for he did not even glance in her direction, and while he was talking to everyone else around him, he had not a word for her.

"You're right," Trace told Chico. "He'd be happy if she'd just vanish."

"That's what she gets for eating herself up to half a ton," Chico answered, with the cold contempt that slim women always have for fat ones. She smiled again at Barton as he looked in her direction.

"Don't go getting any ideas about him," Trace said. "He may have more money than me, but he doesn't have my charm or wit or natural beauty."

"Trace, I used to have a pet lizard that had more charm and wit and natural beauty than you. Uh-oh, he's coming this way."

"I'm going to smack him in his Soviet mouth."

"Give him a chance. Maybe he wants to give us some money."

"Okay, he gets one chance," Trace said. He reached behind him under his jacket and pressed the "start" button on his hidden tape recorder.

Barton brushed past the former senator and his wife without even acknowledging them, and stopped in front of Chico.

"I don't believe I know you folks," he said. There was a soft Southern accent to his voice. "I'm Bud Barton."

"I'm Devlin Tracy. This is my beloved, Michiko Mangini."

Barton barely glanced at him. "Tracy," he said, then took Chico's hand and raised it to his lips and kissed it. "Miss Mangini."

"We call her Chico," Trace said. "Like in Marx. That's Groucho and Chico, like that, not Karl Marx."

Barton ignored him. "And what brings you here?" he asked Chico.

"We're friends of Bob Swenson," Chico said.

"She carries a gun," Trace said. "Get her mad and she shoots anything that moves."

Barton ignored him some more. "Good old Bob," he told Chico. "His company's a big investor in our little extravaganza. Where is he anyway?"

"Where else?" Trace butted in. "At the bar. We were just going to join him."

Barton finally looked at him with a large, pearly smile. "Why don't you do that, Tracy? And I'll help the little lady here get through this chow line before these parasites gobble up all the grub." Without waiting for an answer, he put his hand on Chico's elbow and walked with her toward the serving table.

"I wasn't hungry anyway," Trace mumbled to no one in particular and walked across the room toward Swenson.

"Jilted, huh?" Swenson said. He handed Trace a drink that he had waiting. "Women are like that, you know?"

"Who cares? Easy come, easy go."

"Oh, good. I thought you were annoyed."

Trace was not paying attention. He was more interested in watching Velma Barton because she had finally finished loading her plate and was now sitting alone at a table, her eyes fixed on Barton and Chico, who were moving away from the food line. Velma was clearly not happy.

Trace noticed a man in a dark suit, leaning against a far wall of the room. He was blond and slim, but there was something hard about him, something that reminded Trace of a piece of wire. His hands were moving in front of him, near his waist, and Trace wondered what he was doing until he realized that the man was surreptitiously cleaning his nails with a knife.

"Who's that over there?" Trace said. "Don't tell me he's a billionaire too?"

Swenson glanced over. "No. Bodyguard, chauffeur, chief cook and bottle washer, I guess, for the Bartons. Every time I see them, he's hanging around. I think he's a cowboy or something. Got a funny name. Mmmmmm . . . Waco. Waco. That's his name."

As Trace watched, Waco seemed finally to notice Velma sitting alone, and he snapped the knife closed and put it in his pocket and walked to her table. Before he sat down alongside her, he touched her shoulder, but she did not react or turn. She kept staring at Barton and Chico, now just a few tables away.

After dinner, the room had settled into a faint buzz of polite, waitful conversation when Barton stood up at his table.

"Well, okay, pardners," he called out. "Time to get this show on the road. First, I want to thank you all for coming here." He smiled slyly. "It's a big hoot for an old telephone installer like me to be here, hosting you rich and famous and beautiful folk. Who'da thunk it?"

He paused as the audience chuckled. Trace said to Swenson, "What a phoney. Does anybody buy this Pappy Yokum crap?"

Barton was talking again. "So we got all these special cabs downstairs waiting for us. And we're going to ride over to the Sherlock Holmes museum. They're opening it special for us. We'll just take a little look around, a little cab tour of London, and then we'll come back here for a press conference and I'll tell them that we're going to build the damnedest, biggest, greatest theme park that anyone has ever seen. And with movies too. Damn, it makes me proud." He paused and winked slyly. "But just keep your eyes on those press guys when we come back. They'll all try to get you to say something bad. Maybe you just say that you love the theme park and you wanted to be involved. And I can answer all their questions." He looked around. "That way you don't have to get all dirtied up talking to them creeps. Got it?"

When no one answered, he chuckled again and said, "We don't need no stinking press." He looked around one last time and got mostly blank looks, except from the Hollywood acting couple who seemed distressed that they might miss an opportunity for personal publicity. But they said nothing, and Barton finally barked, "Then, let's go. Time to boogie."

(Our detective duo finds that the Baker Street of Sherlock Holmes may exist no longer, except as a tourist trap, but some things—namely crime and evil—may just be eternal.)

After a quick stop in his hotel room, Trace met up with Swenson again outside the hotel. A dozen horse-drawn hansom cabs were lined up at curbside and Bud Barton was micromanaging everything, assigning his guests to cabs, helping them in, giving the cab drivers instructions. Chico was standing near him.

Barton saw Trace and Swenson and called out, "Hey, Bob. You two, come on over and take this one." As he walked past Chico, Trace took her arm.

"Come on, darling," he said. "The game is afoot. Or in my case a foot and a half."

"Dream on, white boy," Chico said but let herself be pulled along with him. Trace elbowed Barton aside and helped her up into the hansom's backseat.

"Oh, Chico's going with you?" Barton asked.

"You betcha life, pardner," Trace said.

Barton scowled and spun away as Trace and Swenson got into the cab alongside Chico.

"How neat this all is," Chico said. "When I'm married to a billionaire and become a mogulette, I'm never going to forget you, Trace, for bringing me here."

"Who'd want you?" Trace groused.

"I would," Swenson said.

"You two deserve each other," Trace said. He saw Barton at the next hansom call to Waco, the wiry bodyguard. "Wake, I'm sure you won't mind going with Velma. You two get there, and I'll bring up the rear."

The thin blond man nodded and then helped Barton's wife into the back of the cab. The first step was a high one, and she seemed to have a little trouble managing it. Waco grabbed her arm and helped her into the cab.

Just then, Trace's cab bolted forward and started clip-clopping quickly down the street.

Swenson yelled, "Giddyap. Hiyo Silver, away." He pulled a silver-colored flask from his inside pocket and glugged from it.

"So, how do you like our little billionaire telephone installer?" Trace asked Chico.

"An absolute jerk," Chico said. "Trace, I always thought you were the crudest, least housebroken human being in the world until I met Bud Barton."

"He didn't make a pass at you, did he? I'll punch his little mustache off his little face."

"He wouldn't know how to make a pass. He makes Donald Trump look smooth. What a dork. Do you know we were sitting there at dinner and he made three calls on that stupid cell phone of his?"

"Well, then, what the hell were you talking about for so long?"

"His balance sheet. He seemed to think I would be interested in how poor he started and how rich he is now."

"And you weren't interested?"

Chico smiled and Trace thought again how beautiful she truly was. "If I were interested in wealth, why would I have wasted the best years of my life with you?"

"Just what I always wondered too," Swenson said.

The cab trip through central London was pleasant, although Trace was a little discomfited by driving on the left side of the street while cars went whizzing by on the right. Chico, though, leaned out of the cab, intent on watching the city as it passed.

Baker Street itself was only a few short blocks away from their hotel. Trace was disappointed to find that it could have been any well-kept street in any well-kept small American city. He grumbled as he passed the large dome of a planetarium, then groused when he saw a software shop and a theater given over to playing dismal art films.

They passed an immaculate-looking small hotel, and then a string of one souvenir shop after another.

"Old Sherlock would be spinning in his grave if he saw this street," Trace said.

"I don't know," Chico responded. "Trees, street lamps, they've tried to keep the flavor. Except for all these dopey people wearing those stupid deerstalker caps."

"Why is that?" Swenson asked. "What are those things?"

"They think it makes them look like Sherlock Holmes," Chico explained.

"Well, it doesn't. They just look like fat American tourists. Dopey, dopey."

Chico smiled. "Small things amuse small minds," she said. Trace growled.

Their cab pulled up toward the end of Baker Street, taking its place in the long line of parked hansom cabs. Swenson, Trace, and Chico clambered down and strolled down the street to Number 221B, one of a row of identically neat Victorian buildings. The buildings were fronted with three floors of tannish brick over a white-stone ground floor. Small balconies outside the second floor overlooked Baker Street below. The other hansoms were driverless, and Trace saw a pub across the street where he guessed they were waiting until it was time to take their fares back to the hotel.

"I looked it up," Chico said. "This place really was a lodging house all the way back to 1815. And now it's protected as a historical site. All for a make-believe detective."

Even a long line of hansom cabs on Baker Street must not have been a major curiosity because hardly anyone bothered to look at them, and Trace was struck that there were not any policemen to be seen. Billions of dollars on the hoof inside one building and no cops.

He led Chico into the building, past a sign that said "Museum Closed," then paused in a small alcove. To his right was a souvenir shop.

"Hey, where's Holmes's apartment?" he asked.

"Upstairs," Chico said.

"It's supposed to be on the first floor," he said. "I read that."

"The Brits call the second floor the first floor," she said.

"Well, isn't that stupid."

Up a short flight of stairs, they could hear the buzz of voices, and Trace and Swenson let Chico lead the way. The hall door was opened into a room that Trace had seen in films for most of his life. Most of Barton's dinner guests had already arrived and were milling around the replica of Holmes's study, under the watchful eyes of museum staff members. There were armchairs set neatly in front of the crackling fireplace.

In one corner was an acid-scarred table that served as a chemical bench. A black clay pipe lay on a table, and Trace could see a bag of pipe tobacco in the coal scuttle next to the fireplace. A violin case was propped up in a corner.

"Look, Chico. There's Holmes's hat. His deerstalker cap. Now what do you say?"

"I have no comment to make."

They walked around the small room and into Holmes's bedroom. They looked around at the quaint display, surprised at how small the bed was. On a dresser, they saw an open notebook and a box that seemed to hold face paints. Probably for Holmes's disguises, Trace thought.

Behind them, they heard someone grumble, "Man, this be a lot of crap."

Trace turned into the face of the bespectacled film director.

"I wonder if this is where old Holmesy kept his cocaine stash," the director said.

"Hey, why don't you go to a basketball game or something?" Trace said. "Annoy somebody besides us."

Trace led Chico from the room and they walked upstairs, where they found Dr. Watson's bedroom in the rear of the house. It overlooked a small yard, and Trace saw that a light rain had started to fall.

As they walked back down to Holmes's apartment, they saw Velma Barton walking inside.

"Momma Barton, all by her lonesome," Trace whispered to Chico. "Watch out for the Vietcong."

Back inside the study, they listened to an attendant give a

well-rehearsed recital of the building's history. Trace saw Velma glance at her watch, and then Waco walked into the room too. The shoulders of his suit jacket glistened with droplets of fine rain.

Velma stepped into the center of the room and said, "Ladies and gentlemen." He realized it was the first time he had seen her talk since dinner. Her voice was deep and trained and carried through the room easily.

"Bud will be here any moment," she said, then shrugged with a small smile. "And then we'll leave and get back to the hotel for the press conference. The cabs will be waiting for us back outside. On behalf of Bud and—"

She was interrupted by a loud shout from outside the building, which ripped into the room through the open window.

"Help! Police!"

Other voices followed. "Call an ambulance."

A police whistle shrilled from nearby.

And then another shout. "It's that Barton fellow."

Velma Barton looked around in confusion and fright. The people in the room milled around aimlessly. Chico stepped forward toward Velma, who looked at Chico. Then Chico saw her eyelids fluttering and her eyes rolling back into her head. As the small Eurasian grabbed her, Velma started to slip toward the floor.

Trace pushed through the crowd toward the hallway door. Brushing past Waco, he said, "Wake up, you. Help the lady."

Trace took the seventeen steps in just a couple of jumps and then waited on the top step outside the door. The rain was still not much more than a mist, but a heavy fog had begun to roll in over Baker Street.

The cabs were still lined up, and now some of the uniformed drivers were coming back from the pub across the street.

At the bottom of the steps lay Bud Barton. There was blood seeping from a slash wound in his neck; his eyes, sightless, wide open, were all the proof Trace needed that the man was dead.

Bob Swenson came out of the building too and stood alongside Trace. "Jesus Christ," he said. "This is disgusting."

Trace saw a cell phone in Barton's right hand. It was flipped open, the antenna up. In the street's night darkness, Trace could see the faint green pulse throbbing, showing the telephone was turned on.

Three uniformed bobbies were around Barton's body. Two of them knelt alongside the man, glancing down the street as if awaiting an ambulance that was already too late.

Trace saw one of the policemen reach to take the cell phone from Barton's hand.

"Hey," he called out. All the policemen looked up at him. "Leave that phone alone," Trace shouted. "Don't mess with it. He might have been trying to reach someone. Wait for the detectives."

The bobby looked at Trace with barely disguised annoyance and said coldly, "I was doing just that, sir."

"Could have fooled me."

"And who might you be?" the bobby asked.

"I am a consulting detective," Trace said imperiously.

"Good for you," Swenson whispered to him. He had apparently recovered from the shock of seeing a murdered man because he offered Trace a drink from his flask. This time, Trace took it. Truth was, he did not like dead bodies.

Even if they were Communists.

*   *   *

Chief Inspector Bucket of Scotland Yard was a tall man in a rumpled gray tweed suit. He was balding but his scalp had obviously failed to tell his face, because the lower half of his face was obscured by an aggressive walrus mustache that gave his speech the intonation of someone whispering through weeds.

He had clearly been briefed on his way to the crime scene because his first act was to dispatch a policeman to take Velma back to her hotel. She left quickly with Waco in tow.

Bucket was meticulous and as totally unflappable as if he spent all day every day dealing with American billionaires. He apologized for the inconvenience but insisted upon speaking to each person himself. The interviews were conducted behind the closed door of the Holmes bedroom. They were brief and implacably the same. Everyone had been here in the museum. They had not gone outside since arriving. They were awaiting the arrival of Bud Barton. The first they knew something was wrong was when they heard shouts in the street.

By now, a small gang of press people were gathering outside, and the uniformed bobbies were keeping them back behind hastily erected wooden barricades, to prevent their stomping all over the area where Barton's body had been found.

As Bucket finished speaking to each person, he nodded to another policeman at the door, who led the guests out, apparently through a back exit, to a small paved court where police cars were waiting to take them back to their hotel.

Trace and Chico stayed well back in the room, listening to Inspector Bucket's questions, gleaning what they could from his few comments.

It seemed, they learned, that Barton had been knifed about twenty yards down the block from the entrance to

221B Baker Street. Bloodstains showed that he had staggered or crawled toward the entrance to the building where he was found dead. Nobody had seen anything.

Everyone else had left Holmes's study, and Bucket looked at Trace and then Chico.

"I seem to have saved the prettiest for last," he said to Chico. "And you two are?"

"Michiko Mangini and Devlin Tracy," Chico answered.

"I'm a consulting detective," Trace said.

"Oh, shut up, Trace," Chico said.

"Consulting detective. Yes, I've heard about you from my men outside. You're a regular Sherlock Holmes, aren't you?"

"You've got it, Inspector. And this is my faithful assistant."

Chico looked disgusted. "Dr. Watson?" Bucket asked with a mild smile.

"More like Dr. Frankenstein," Trace said.

"You might get your eyes examined, sir, when we are done here. And are you billionaires also?"

"I don't know. I haven't looked recently."

"I have. We're not," Chico said.

"But I'm the one who stopped that fumble-fingered cop outside from messing up the cell phone evidence," Trace said.

"And what evidence might that be?" Bucket asked.

Trace sighed. It seemed sometimes that he had to do everything. "Barton's cell phone was turned on. I could see the light flashing. I thought with his dying little fingers, he might be trying to call someone. That might be a clue, I thought." He paused. "Was it?"

"I talked to the police laboratory," Bucket said. "Apparently Mr. Barton had dialed the digits 9-2-2."

"And that's the start of a phone number around here, right?" Trace asked.

"No, it isn't," Bucket said. "Around here," he said dryly, "there is one prefix you dial before calling a local number, and another prefix one dials to call long distance. This was neither of those. I suspect that Mister Barton, in his dying moments, perhaps panicky, perhaps just confused, was simply trying to dial 9-1-1—that is the emergency number you Americans call, isn't it?" When Chico nodded, the inspector said, "But I think in his last gasp of life, he pressed the incorrect button and hit 9-2-2 instead."

Chico nodded again, but Trace shook his head.

"Oh?" said Bucket.

"Barton was a phone guy. All his life. Started out installing phones in houses." Trace picked up the black clay pipe from the table by the fireplace.

"And 'phone guys,' as you call them, never make mistakes dialing?"

"I don't know. It's not part of my detecting method to jump to conclusions in the absence of hard evidence." He pointed at Bucket with the stem of the pipe.

"Mind if I write that down?" Bucket said. He took a small pad from his pocket. "It may be useful to me in the course of future investigations."

"Write away," Trace said. Chico rolled her eyes. Trace replaced the pipe and seemed to adjust something in his back pocket. "I wonder what Sherlock Holmes would have done now," he said.

"You do know, don't you, Mr. Tracy, that Sherlock Holmes was a fictitious character, someone made up out of the whole cloth?"

"I know that," Trace said.

"He knows that," Chico said.

"I also know that sometimes fiction tells us more truth than fact."

"My, my, another aphorism for my notebook. It will be delightful in my memoirs." He looked quizzically at Trace. "What is that you're always fidgeting with in your back pocket, sir?" Bucket asked. "It wouldn't be a murder weapon, would it?"

"No."

"Then what?"

Sheepishly, Trace removed from his back pocket the two deerstalker caps.

"Are these what you use in place of calling cards?" Bucket asked. "To let people know you are a consulting detective?" He held the two caps in his hand, examining them.

"She made me buy them," Trace said.

"Liar, liar, pants on fire," Chico said.

"Would you like to wear them while we continue our interview? Would it make you feel more at home here in this saintly residence?"

"No, it's all right," Trace said.

"So do you have any idea of what might have happened here tonight? Who might have been . . . the perp, I think you Americans say."

Chico shook her head.

Trace said, *"Cherchez la femme."*

"Any particular femme we should cherchez?" Bucket asked.

"Well, on general principles, you might start with that traitorous Communist wife of his," Trace said.

"Reasonable. Except she was, of course, upstairs here when Mr. Barton was killed."

"Confederates," Trace said. "Look for a dacoit. Or a lascar. Someone swarthy and untrustworthy. They'll do anything for money. They were always the ones in the Holmes stories."

"Right now, sir, we're more inclined to think of a street crime. A man with a reputation for being . . . what is your word? . . . feisty . . . is mugged on the street by a common criminal. He fights back. He gets stabbed for his trouble. His wallet, you see, was missing."

"You don't know how billionaires live," Trace said.

"And how do they live?"

"They don't carry wallets. They don't need money or credit cards. They have people who do that for them."

"An interesting idea. And worth examining. Do you have any other thoughts for me?"

"No," Trace said. "Not right now. But I'll let you know what I come up with." He tapped his forehead. "Inquiring minds never rest."

"One of my men will take you back to the hotel," Bucket said.

"Soon I hope. Before the bar closes," Trace said. He took Chico's arm and turned toward the doorway.

"Don't forget your caps," Bucket said and tossed them across the room to Trace. "One can't tell the consulting detectives without their deerstalkers." One cap fell to the floor, and when he bent to pick it up, Trace saw a thin smudge of dried tan mud on the highly polished dark wood floor.

"We will see you again," Trace said.

"I certainly hope so."

(Sherlock Holmes may not be alive but the spirit of deduction and analysis lives on forever, as our two heroes now demonstrate.)

* * *

They rode back to the hotel in the rear seat of a police car, driven by a uniformed officer who seemed to think these two weird Americans might be his passport to a Hollywood career. He told jokes, he sang, he asked questions, and when his questions were ignored, he asked more in stubborn good humor.

Trace just looked out the window. The fog had become thicker, and he could barely see past the headlights of the police car.

"Look," Chico said. "Trace, look at that."

He turned and leaned over her to look out the window but saw nothing in the darkened misty street.

"What was it?"

"It was a fox. I saw a fox running across the street."

"Hell, fox. It was a freaking rat," Trace said. "What the hell would a fox be doing in London?"

"Lady's right, sir," piped up the patrolman. "It was a fox. For many years now, there has been some family of foxes living in this area, and sometimes you'll see one of them out at night."

"Sure," Trace said, unconvinced.

"It's true, miss."

"Trace." Chico clutched his arm. "Do you think . . . do you think . . . ? Put on your little deerstalker cap. Please."

"No."

"Please."

Trace pulled the cap over his head. He wore it sideways so he looked like Napoleon.

"That's good," she said. "Do you think that fox is the spirit of Sherlock Holmes? Maybe he's come back to haunt the scene of his great triumphs over evil."

"Oh, for crying out loud," Trace said.

"That's a good one, miss," the policeman said.

"Maybe it was an omen for you," Chico said. "The world's newest, greatest consulting detective. Devlin Tracy. The man in the cap."

Trace looked at her for a long second, then turned away in disgust.

"Everybody's a comedian tonight. You. Inspector Chamberpot. The whole gang. You'll see. I may have to solve this crime, just to make you all feel guilty."

"Yes, sir, that is a good one," the policeman said, laughing.

"Put a jolly cork in it, will you?" Trace said.

As expected, Bob Swenson was in the hotel bar. Even though his hotel room was filled with almost every variety of liquor ever fermented by man, he always opted to drink in hotel bars because, he said, drinking alone "was for losers."

He waved the bartender for a drink for his two new companions, then asked Trace, "So what's new with the investigation?"

"That Scotland Yarder couldn't find a bass drum in a phone booth," Trace said.

"I don't know. I thought he seemed pretty efficient."

"I guess Chico did too. Didn't you?" Trace demanded.

"Well, actually, yes," she said. "I thought he was the second-best detective in the room."

"Thank you, then," Trace said.

"After me, that is," Chico said.

"You're a treacherous little Nipponese," Trace said.

He turned to his drink and sipped at it with the slow deliberateness of a man with a troubled mind.

"You're really taking this badly, aren't you?" Chico said.

"No, it's not that. Barton was a dirtball. Who cares? But think about it. All the mischief he was able to do, it's going to be that much worse when Viet Velma gets her hands on all those billions. Cheez, it's going to be a bloodbath out in the streets. Condoms in kindergarten, assault weapons for criminals, rocket launchers for protestors, more dough for Jesse Jackson. It's the apocalypse, the start of the fall of the Roman Empire. All funded by that brainless fat cow."

"I hadn't thought about that," Swenson said.

"That's why you'll never be anything more than a poor multimillionaire. You lack the ability to focus."

"If I were Velma Barton, I think I could focus on umpty-ump billion dollars," Chico said. She ignored the drink that was sitting in front of her; she never drank, but that never dissuaded Swenson from buying her drinks. Trace drained his glass and picked up hers.

"Timing is everything," Swenson said thickly into his drink.

"What do you mean?" Trace said.

"Mama and Papa Barton. The story is they were going splitsville," Swenson said.

"No," Trace said.

"Absolutely. The story was around. I have it on the very highest authority."

"Who is?"

"My wife. Who never gossips and never makes a mistake. She told me."

Trace looked at Chico, whose face was suddenly bright and animated. "Are you beginning to spot the first faint inklings here of a motive for murder?" he asked.

She nodded and reached under his jacket.

"Not here, you savage," Trace said. "What's gotten into you, girl?"

"Not much recently," Chico said. "I want your tape recorder."

"Why?"

"Because."

"That's good enough for me," Trace said.

"Me too," Swenson added.

Trace unclipped the recorder from the back of his belt and handed it to the pretty Eurasian.

"Thanks," she said. "Later."

Trace and Swenson both watched her go.

"You know, when she finally dumps you, Trace, it's going to be a terrible blow."

"Yeah," Trace agreed. "I don't know how she'll get along."

"Not for her, you beanbag. For you."

"I'll be at the curb waving good-bye. I won't even grieve for a moment," Trace said.

"Good attitude. I'll drink to that," Swenson said.

"You'd drink to anything."

Later, after another round, Trace said, "You know what Chico's doing? She's back in the room, wasting her time, listening to that tape I made and thinking she'll find a clue on there to solve the murder."

"Yeah," Swenson said.

"Delusions of adequacy," Trace said.

"Yeah," Swenson said.

"She thinks she's a real detective," Trace said.

"Yeah."

"But I'm the one who has the hat," Trace said. He pulled a deerstalker cap from his pocket and put it on, screwing it onto his head as if expecting a gale force wind to blow through the bar. "And I've got a real clue."

"Yeah," said Swenson.

He turned and saw what Trace was wearing.

"Take off the hat," he said.

"Doesn't matter," Trace mumbled. "I've still got the clue."

In their room, Chico drew herself a hot bath and made a cup of green tea. She traveled nowhere without tea and a heating coil to boil water, it being her theory that no one outside of Asia knew what tea was supposed to taste like.

She reclined in the large tub and began to play back the sporadic tape that Trace had made of the evening.

She smiled when she heard Trace insulting Bud Barton. The telephone magnate was an awful man. But still, murder was murder.

Trace had kept the tape running while they were getting into the hansoms and she heard Barton's voice, clearly disappointed, when Chico was pulled away by Trace. And then Barton telling someone to go with Velma. "(Something) . . . I'm sure you won't mind going with Velma." Something . . . what was the something? Who was the something? What was Barton saying? She listened again. Waco probably. No. Not quite.

Who was that? She played it again but could not tell anything from the tape.

And here was Trace again: "Momma Barton, all by her lonesome. Watch out for the Viet Cong."

There was a lot of dead air on the tapes. A lot of clicking as Trace had turned the recorder on and off.

And here was Inspector Bucket, explaining how Barton had probably made a mistake while trying to dial 911.

And Trace again arguing. "Barton was a phone guy. All his life."

A phone man. A self-made billionaire who started out installing phones in the hill country of Texas.

She played it again. "A phone guy."

Chico clambered out of the tub and without even bothering to dry herself off walked naked into the main room of their suite. She picked up the telephone and looked at the dial.

Barton had dialed 922.

Nine: the letters W-X-Y on the keypad.

Two: the letters A-B-C.

Could it . . .

Trace opened the door with a key and came into the room.

"Get some clothes on, you wild beast. Suppose I had been sneaking a woman in here. She'd think you were a perv."

"Call Scotland Yard," she said.

"Now, don't get crazy. I'm not going to do anything."

"But we are. Call Inspector Bucket."

"Why?"

"Because when you have exhausted all other possibilities, whatever remains, no matter how improbable, must be the truth. So saith Sherlock. Something like that."

"Well, here's another one from Sherlock. There was mud on the floor at the museum."

Using his handkerchief, Trace unscrewed the bulbs in the lamps along the hotel hallway. When he was done, the corridor was cast in deep shadow. He walked up to a hotel room door and pounded loudly. After a long while, it was pulled open by Waco, still dressed.

"What do you want?" he said. His voice had a cowboy twang.

"I found your knife," Trace said. He pulled a closed knife from his pocket, showed it for a split second in the darkness, then slid it back into his jacket.

"Not mine," Waco said.

"Okay, then I'll just give it to the cops," Trace said. Waco started to close the door, then stopped.

"Where'd you find it?" he said.

"You didn't see me. Right where you got rid of it." He kept his hand in his pocket atop the knife. "Now you and I can talk and maybe you can explain how it'll be worth my while to return your knife. Or I can just go talk to Scotland Yard. I'm sure they'd be interested too."

"You're that detective, aren't you?"

"Well, sometimes. And sometimes I do other things for a living."

"Like blackmail."

"A nasty word," Trace said. "I prefer to call it information suppression."

"And your partner, the pretty nip. What does she call it?"

"She doesn't know anything about this part of the business," Trace said. "You know, women, they don't get it sometimes."

"Some women," Waco said. "Come on in."

Inside the room, Waco sat on the bed and looked at Trace, who stood just inside the closed door.

"So what do you think you know?"

"I know a hard guy works for a rich man and gets a lot closer to the wife than is good for him. I know rich man and wife are headed for the courts. I know hard guy leaves for a museum party with the wife, but she arrives alone. I know hard guy takes to the rich boss with a knife. And then tosses it. And then gets back to the party through the back door but he doesn't notice that it's raining and that his shoes have picked up mud, which he leaves on the museum floor."

Trace saw Waco look down at his shoes.

"You know a lot," Waco said. "And the police. How much do they know?"

"Not a thing," Trace said. "What kind of businessman would I be if I gave away what I know for free?"

Waco grinned and opened the drawer of the end table.

"A live one, maybe," he said.

But before he could pull anything out of the drawer, Trace jumped forward and slammed it shut with his foot, trapping Waco's hand. The thin man screamed in pain, just as the door to the room opened and Inspector Bucket entered, followed by three uniformed policemen and Chico.

As one of the uniformed bobbies pulled Waco to his feet and cuffed his hands behind him, Trace said to Bucket, "Hear enough?"

"More than enough, thank you. This was very good work. By both of you." He nodded back to Chico. "Realizing that when Barton dialed 9-2-2, he was spelling out his nickname for this Waco was a very big development. You are to be commended."

"You know I'm going to say it, don't you?" Chico said to the inspector.

"Don't you dare," Trace said. "It's mine."

"Say what?" Bucket asked.

"It was elementary, Inspector. Elementary," they both said in unison.

"Then I must say it too," Bucket said with a sigh. "You two are certainly the Baker Street Irregulars. I will be very glad when you both leave London. And please, I want my knife back."

Trace handed it over. "It's all yours."

Chico and Trace sat in the first-class cabin of the Concorde, looking at one of the London tabloid newspapers.

"Well, I guess the Sherlock Holmes theme park is shot to hell," she said.

"With Viet Velma in the can for putting Waco up to murder, I guess so," Trace said. "Works for me."

"Me too." Chico put the paper into the back pocket of the seat in front of her.

A flight attendant came up and asked to take their drink order. But first she said, "I love your hats. I really love them."

Both Chico and Trace reached up to touch their deerstalkers.

"We do too," Chico said.

"We wear them whenever we're on a case," Trace said.

"A case?" asked the stewardess.

"Yes. We are consulting detectives," he said.

"Wow."

"Scotland Yard calls us in whenever they have a case they can't handle."

"You two, you're like a regular Sherlock Holmes, aren't you?"

"What gave you your first clue?" Trace said.

MURDER BOULEVARD
A TREVOR OAKS STORY

by Percy Spurlark Parker

The Street: Industrial Road,
Las Vegas, Nevada

Among the many achievements of Percy Parker is the creation of a fictional P.I. called "Randy Sea." Okay, let's put that among the more *dubious* of Percy's achievements. A fixture on the short story scene for many years, Percy creates a new character in this story, working out of his own new home, Las Vegas. His only novel to date is *Good Girls Don't Get Murdered*, published in 1974 and now available through catalogues at a high price. If it is not considered a cult classic, it should be.

One

Nine times out of ten, if you mention Las Vegas, the first thing that comes to anyone's mind is the Strip. It's as it should be. It's the street everybody has heard of, with its mega-hotels and all the glitz. It's what the tourists come to see. Rome, Paris, New York, jousting knights are all within a few blocks of each other. But like in any city, there are a few streets that aren't highlighted in the tourist brochures.

I'm Trevor Oaks. I carry a P.I. ticket, have for about nine years now. It was nearly 2:00 a.m. when I pulled out of the

Treasure Island's parking garage. I'd just wrapped a two-day bodyguard stint for one of the city's frequent high rollers. It was an easy enough gig. Most of the time I just stood around and looked imposing. I'm black, six-four, and usually carry about 240 pounds, so the imposing part wasn't difficult at all.

I cut across Spring Mountain, hooking up with Industrial Road. It's a six-lane asphalt track at that point, sitting between the Strip and I-15. I could've taken the Strip back to my place, but a lot of times I find Industrial quicker.

A half dozen heartbeats and you're on the fringe of the Naked City, so named for the string of nude clubs that sit mostly on the west side of the street. The boundary waffles somewhat depending on the coming and going of different clubs. Day to day, the area keeps Metro busier than any one spot on the Strip. Whatever you want, drugs, women, men, if that's to your liking, can be obtained here. A picked pocket and a good old-fashioned mugging are also on the menu.

I saw her when she first darted out into the street—blond, short skirt, long legs, high heels. She ran like a track star, head up, arms pumping; her heels didn't seem to hinder her at all. I couldn't tell if she was running from anyone or not, I just knew she was on a collision course with my car's front bumper.

I hit the brakes, gripping the steering wheel with both hands, bringing the Towncar to a rocking stop. But it wasn't soon enough. My right fender clipped her with a hollow thud. Damn.

I hit my hazard lights and jumped out, running around to where she sat on the pavement holding her right knee. "Are you all right?"

She just looked up at me, not saying anything at first, then, "I'm . . . I'm okay." She started to get up.

I reached over to help her. She didn't pull away.

"It was really all my fault," she said, brushing herself off. Her hair was a little disheveled, a blond curl puffed up on one side. She was pretty damn close to being drop-dead gorgeous. Her nose was a little off center and her eyes were a mite too small, but these were minor points. She went a little heavy with her makeup, dark eye shadow, deep red lips. She could easily have been one of Naked City's featured dancers. She had the body for it.

"Are you sure you're okay?"

She looked down at herself, flexing her right knee. "Honest, I'm fine. These pantyhose have seen their last days, though."

The car fender or the pavement had done a job on the right leg of her pantyhose. A big swatch of the fine mesh hung to one side, exposing a shapely but badly bruised thigh.

"Looks like I owe you another pair."

A limo swished past us, stirring a current of warm air. Farther down the street, a pair of headlights turned into one of the clubs.

"Forget it. I said it was my fault."

"What were you running from?" It wasn't a question I'd planned to ask, one I'd calculated to present at the right moment. But once it was out, it was a question I knew I had to ask.

"I was late for meeting a friend of mine at the Riviera," she said, but she wasn't looking at me when she said it; she was looking across the street in the direction she'd been running from.

I looked myself. Directly across from us was the parking lot for the Wicked Babes Strip Club. Whatever lights illuminated the parking lot came from the club's marquee. It did a great job of touting the attributes of its dancers, and a piss-ass poor job of keeping the shadows from overlapping in the lot.

I didn't necessarily believe she was lying. Cutting through the back side of the Stardust across the Strip to the Riviera wasn't impossible, but it was a good distance running or walking.

"Wouldn't a taxi have been easier?"

She shrugged. "I need my exercise."

"You sure you don't want to go to the hospital? Sometimes other stuff could pop up later. I'd feel better if a doctor checked you over."

She held up a hand. "No. I'm okay, really," she said, taking a step back.

I heard a car start up and glanced back to the parking lot. A black sedan pulled out onto Industrial heading south. Its windows were rolled up, and I couldn't guess the number of people in it, let alone if it was a man or woman behind the wheel.

"Look, you seem to be a nice guy." She took a couple more steps back from me. "Let's just drop it."

"At least let me take you to the Riv—"

The screech of the tires got my attention first. The sedan that'd pulled out of the lot made a U-turn, heading back toward us. My hazards were still flashing, but I somehow didn't think that was a Good Samaritan coming back to lend a hand.

The sedan's bright lights came on and its engine roared into high gear. I yelled at her to get out of the way, thought for a second about trying to pull her to safety, but I only had time to jump back out of the way myself. The sedan met her head on, flipping her up and over. She hit the windshield, careened off the top of the car, and landed in a tangled mess ten feet away.

Two

"Now let's get this straight," the motorcycle cop said. He'd been the first policeman on the scene. "You clipped her, then another car comes along and finishes the job?"

"Not exactly."

"Oh, yeah. The second car deliberately ran her down."

He was almost as tall as I was, older, heavier in the shoulders, and the red-and-blue flashing lights of the ambulance and patrol cars danced off his burnt-gold helmet. Given my line of work, I've come to know a number of the members of the Metropolitan Police Department. This was a first meeting for the motorcycle cop and myself. It wasn't turning out to be a memorable one.

"What type of car did you say it was?"

"Late-model black four-door Ford or Mercury, tinted windows." I'd only gone over the details about a half-dozen times, including that I'd used my cell phone to dial 911 and that I was a private investigator.

"And you didn't get the car's license number?"

"I couldn't even tell you if they were Nevada plates."

The ambulance and squad cars had attracted a fair-sized crowd, women in various lengths of dresses, men from suits to jeans.

"Could be there's a lot of things you're not telling me."

"I don't know why you've got it in your head that I'm responsible. Take a look at my car. There's no dents or broken glass. I didn't do it."

The cop nodded. "Okay, okay. There was a second car involved. But who's to say she didn't jump out of your car into the path of the other car? Or maybe you two were just standing in the street haggling about price. You got pissed, gave her a push."

"That's not the way it happened."

"Yeah, so you've said."

Looking at it from the cop's angle, he had a plausible theory working, and right now it was my word against a corpse.

"I know people on the force who'll vouch for me."

"Were they here when this happened?"

I gave up. I wasn't going to convince him I was telling the truth, and there was no sense getting uptight about it. There were other people at Metro who would have a say in this matter. And if need be, I had one of the city's top lawyers in my corner.

"Look. Why don't you at least try to find out who she is? I'm guessing she was coming from the Wicked Babes. Why don't you check with the crowd and see if somebody knows her?"

"Telling me my job, Mr. P.I.?"

"Not in the least," I said as calmly as I could.

His mouth crunched up some; then he looked over to the crowd and shouted, "Anybody here from Wicked Babes?"

"Yeah, we are," a woman answered.

She was tall and curvy, long red hair, beauty mark on her left cheek. The split in her ankle-length gown rose to the midpoint of her thigh. The rest of the "we" was a block of granite, with Elvis sideburns, square shoulders, no neck to speak of.

The motorcycle cop shot me a last glance and went over to them. He escorted them to the covered body that still lay in the street. The woman screamed, burying her head into the granite's chest when the cop pulled back the sheet the ambulance boys had thrown over the remains.

Two guys I knew from the detective division showed up then, and things got a little easier for me. I still had to go down to the station and give my statement all over again. I

saw the block of granite there and the woman who'd identified the body. I didn't communicate with them, but I did find
out the woman who'd been killed was Jill Masachowski,
and she had been a stripper at the club. All in all, it took
about another two hours before I finally got back to my
place.

The motorcycle cop had been right about one thing
though. I hadn't told him all there was to tell. I'd rushed to
Jill as the black sedan spun off. She'd managed to whisper
something to me. I say something because I'm still not sure
exactly what she said. That was one of the reasons I hadn't
mentioned it to the cops.

Anyway, as low in volume and as garbled as it was, it
sounded like she said, "Glen Kidd." Which meant exactly
nothing to me. But Glen could've been tin, or pin, or sin.
And Kidd could just as easily have been hid, or rid, or none
of the above.

Three

Besides being a P.I., I also own Miller's Game Room. The
arcade was left to me by a former client. We're located on
the rag-tail part of the Strip north of the Stratosphere and not
quite downtown. We cater mostly to locals, seeing a number
of the same faces week in and week out. My living quarters
are on the second and top floor. I've got a bedroom with a
private bath, another washroom off the kitchen, and the rest
of it is pretty much a big-ass room with furniture. And a big-
screen TV, of course.

I managed about three hours of sleep—strike the word
restful. Consequently, it took a couple heaping cups of black
coffee to get me feeling close to human again. Screwing my
knee up back in my UNLV days not only ended my football

career, but it left me with a permanent limp. Most of the time it's not a bother. I rarely even think about it or limp that much, except on the few cold, damp days we have around here. Then, the knee reminds me it's never going to be quite right.

And there's the times like now, when something's playing on my mind and I'm not sure what I should do. For some reason it seems like all my stress kind of settles in my knee, and I wind up hopping around like the old one-legged man in a kicking contest. Psychosomatic? Sure, but knowing it never seems to help.

A woman had been killed. An inch or two, and I could have been occupying my own slab in the morgue now. Regardless of what the motorcycle cop had intimated, I wasn't a serious suspect. I wasn't worried about anyone trying to pin anything on me. It was the fact that someone had been killed right in front of me, and I hadn't been able to stop it that was getting the better of me. Common sense said to let it lie. Let the cops do their thing. But I was never content watching from the sidelines.

I had the Channel 13 news on. They'd mentioned the hit-and-run a couple times. They hadn't said too much, just that Metro was investigating the hit-and-run death of a local stripper, and that Metro was asking for help through their Secret Witness program. The film clip they showed caught the patrol cars, the ambulance, and a corner of my Towncar. They went from that to the weather, then to a string of commercials.

I was at the sink washing out my coffee cup when one of Vegas's premier used-car dealers came on. The guy has one of the larger dealerships in the Valley Automall. He's used his nine-year-old son on a number of the commercials. They would always end with the son behind the wheel of whatever car they were featuring, and the dad's tag line: "Mackey Glenn Auto Sales. Hurry on down. The kid and I've got the deal you're looking for."

I stared at the TV as if I expected the commercial to repeat itself. Glen Kidd. Had she been trying to tell me something about Mackey Glenn's son? And if so, what?

Call the cops? It might be a good time for it, but suppose I was wrong? Maybe it would be best if I checked it out myself. If I turned up something, then I could go to the cops with something concrete, instead of a bunch of ifs and maybes.

Over the years I've built up a book of addresses and phone numbers of people I've worked with, or may have to contact one day. Mackey Glenn's home address wasn't in the book. My fail-safe source is Greg Hillman, a features writer at the *Review-Journal.* He always balks at the idea of helping at first, but generally he comes through swearing this will be the last time.

I stopped at the Game Room long enough to let Holly Warrington, my one and only full-timer, know I'd be running the streets for a while.

"Take the whole day. You'll just get underfoot anyway."

She'd said it with a wide smile on her dark, high-cheekboned face, but she'd also told me a number of times that she only needed to see me on paydays.

Glenn lived southeast of the airport, in Henderson. It was a golf course community, and his home was on a small rise overlooking the ninth hole. It was a two-story structure with an attached three-car garage. The used-car business had been very good to him.

I handed the maid my business card when she answered the door. Tiny embroidered red diamonds bordered her apron and the sleeves of her gray uniform.

"I'd like to see Mr., or Mrs. Glenn, please. It's about their son."

I threw in the part about their son in hopes of ensuring that one of the Glenns would speak to me. I didn't expect the reaction I got. The maid screamed and ran, disappearing into the house and leaving me at the open door.

I wasn't sure whether I should stay, go in, or turn around and head back to my place. While I was trying to make up my mind, the maid returned, along with Mackey Glenn and three others, two women and a man.

"What's this about my son?" Glenn demanded. He was thinner than he looked in his TV commercials, but his square jaw and sandy hair were the same.

"I witnessed a hit-and-run last night. Woman got killed. I may be way off base here, Mr. Glenn. But I think the victim mentioned your son before she died."

The other man in the group was tall, slender, with deep-set eyes. Two Band-Aids had been placed side by side just to the left of his forehead to make one large bandage. As for the women, one seemed to be close to Glenn in age, the other just out of her teens. Both brunettes, the older woman's eyes reddened from crying.

"Very interesting, Mr., er . . ." He had my card in his hand and glanced at it. "Mr. Oaks. But you're right. You are off base. That matter has nothing to do with us."

"Then everything's okay with your son?"

"Yes, of course. Erik took him to school this morning as always."

The guy with the Band-Aids nodded, tried a smile.

They were working hard at presenting a normal family atmosphere, but the maid had blown that when she ran from me screaming. If you could add two and two, you could figure out what had gone down.

"The hit-and-run was deliberate," I said. "Whoever was driving meant to run the woman down. Almost got me too. I only came by because I thought I might be able to prevent something bad from happening. Guess I made a mistake coming here. She must've been trying to tell me about someone else. I should've gone to the police in the first place. Sorry for the bother, folks."

"No, wait," the older woman gasped. "Mackey, stop him."

The little automatic appeared in his hand as if by magic. I didn't see him go in his pocket or waistband; the shiny little gun was just there. He was holding it so tight, the veins showed vividly on the back of his hand.

I could tell he wasn't comfortable holding the gun on me, which made me even more uncomfortable. I've had guns pointed at me before. I'd rather have a pro get me in his sights than an amateur any day—less chance of the thing going off accidentally.

"I . . . I think you'd better come inside," he said.

Four

I got directed to the study, where Erik patted me down for any weapons of my own. Finding none, I was told to sit on one of the two sofas in the room. It was then, to my relief and I'm sure to Glenn's also, he slipped the automatic back into his pocket.

"Forgive me, Mr. Oaks, but I just can't let you go to the police."

"Asking would've saved us a whole lot of heartbeats."

"Yes. I suppose you're right. But I . . ."

"What are the kidnappers demanding?" As I said, adding two and two is easy.

For just a split second he started to go for his pocket again, but then he stopped. I guess he figured he'd been down that route before. "Three hundred thousand, by noon."

"Can you get that much together?"

"Sure," he nodded. "I've got my bankers working on it."

Mackey Jr. had been snatched this morning as Erik was driving him to school. He said he'd been stopped by a policeman as he drove out the front gate, or at least by a man in a policeman's uniform. He tried to resist when he realized what was going on, but got a bump on his head for his efforts. The kidnapper left a note, done with a black marker in block letters, ordering them to have the money ready by noon, when he would call with further instructions.

The older woman was Glenn's wife, Jessica. The younger one was his niece, Karen, an upstate New York college student here to spend the summer with her uncle.

"We can't have the police involved," Mrs. Glenn said. "We just can't." Her eyes had begun to swell with tears again.

"They're trained to handle these things," I said. "They're the best chance your son has to come out of this all right."

"No, no. We'll pay them and they'll let him go. Tell me I'm right, Mackey."

They were sitting on the sofa across from me, while Karen was in a corner by a small desk and Erik was standing by the study door. I'm not sure where the maid had gotten to.

"Mr. Oaks is speaking in generalities," Glenn said, holding his wife's hands. "Tell her, Oaks. Tell her she has nothing to worry about."

"I can't say that. The kidnapper may keep his word or he may not. Strictly playing it his way gives him all the control."

She started crying in earnest again. Glenn shot me a

frown that could've shattered the windshields of a dozen cars.

I stood up. "I'll say it again. The cops are the best way to go with this. But it won't do any good for me to go to them if you're not going to cooperate—it might even be worse. So I'm leaving now, Mr. Glenn. I won't go to the cops. I hope everything turns out all right, but honestly, I have my doubts."

Glenn didn't try his trick with the automatic again, and Erik didn't try blocking my way. I made it to my car and sat there for a moment wondering if I should go back and have another try at them. I decided it wouldn't do any good. They were too scared for the safety of Mackey Jr. to try anything. Which, of course, was exactly what the kidnapper was counting on.

Five

It was a quarter to ten when I got back to the Game Room. There were a half-dozen or so people in the joint challenging the arcade games. Holly was behind the glass counter, perched on a stool reading an *Essence* magazine.

She glanced up at the clock on the wall behind her. "You made it back early."

"Ran out of things to do."

She's seven years older than I am, with a body that can match any of the showgirls on the Strip. I would've tried jumping her bones long ago, if it wasn't for the fact that she was married, happily so, and didn't fool around.

"Any messages?"

"Joe called. You neglected to tell me about last night."

"Nothing to it really. Just part of the glamorous life of a private eye."

"Sure." She nodded, her thin braided dreads bouncing as she did. "Just be sure to leave the place to me in your will."

I got a Coke out of the vending machine and took it back to my office. It's not much for space. There's room for a desk, couple of chairs in front, one behind, and a file cabinet. A number of the pictures on the wall are from my UNLV days. One in particular shows Joe Grover and myself in our football gear warming the bench.

He was Sergeant Joe Grover now, of the Las Vegas Metropolitan Police Department, and just about the best friend I've got. When I messed my knee up and felt like blowing up the world, Joe hung in there with me. He hadn't been able to make me stay in school, but he kept me from going totally off the deep end.

"Tree, I guess Holly told you I called."

I'd picked up the handle playing high school ball in Chicago. Trevor "Oak Tree" Oaks. It had stayed with me at UNLV. Joe was about the only one who still used it nowadays.

"Heard what happened last night," Joe continued. "Thought I'd get your end direct. You're always more colorful than a police report."

"I'll do my best," I said, and rattled off what had gone down last night, leaving off the part about Mackey Glenn.

"I take it back," Joe said, "you're as dull as the police report."

"Thanks."

"Don't mention it. We located the hit-and-run vehicle. It was dumped in the Hilton parking lot. It had been hot-wired. Owner's a Westley Blake. He says he was at Wicked Babes last night, but he got loaded and took a cab home. He didn't even know his car wasn't in the club's parking lot."

"You believe him?"

"Got to. We tracked down the cabby. His trip sheet says he picked up Blake forty minutes before the hit-and-run occurred."

The Hilton's on Paradise, the next street east of the Strip behind the Riviera Hotel. It was maybe six blocks from the scene of the hit-and-run. It would've been fairly easy to ditch the car there, then make it back to the club to catch a cab home. But the cab taking Blake home before the hit-and-run happened took him out of the picture altogether.

"What about the victim?"

I could hear Joe shifting papers at the other end. "Let's see. Miss Masachowski was picked up two years ago for solicitation. Never did any time. Lived alone. Working at Wicked Babes for the past year. Otherwise that's it. You got anything to add?"

The temptation to tell him about the Glenns boiled up again, but I said, "No, nothing. Just curious."

"You didn't know her? She wasn't involved in a case you're working on? Just an absolute stranger?"

"You got it."

It took him a while to respond. "Okay, Tree. Just wanted to hear it for myself. Continue being a good, law-abiding citizen and stay out of it. We'll handle it from here."

"Don't worry, Joe. I've got too many other things to take care of than to bother about some ex-hooker-dash-stripper who got herself run over. Even though the driver almost made it a doubleheader."

"Because the driver almost made it a doubleheader, Tree, I don't want you digging into this."

"Sure," I said, without making any further commitment. But I knew I had to stay out of it. I was sure I couldn't look into Jill Masachowski's death without butting heads with the kidnappers. The two were tied together somehow, but all I could do was speculate and wait. There was nothing I dared do until Mackey Jr. was safely home.

Six

I hadn't fully withdrawn my hand when the phone rang again.

"Mr. Oaks?" The voice was low, near a whisper. "This is Karen Thornbush, Mackey Glenn's niece. I retrieved your business card from the trash where my uncle threw it after you left."

"Yes, Miss Thornbush?"

"Mr. Oaks, I think my uncle is making a big mistake. I just don't feel he should trust this kidnapper."

"I'm with you there, Miss Thornbush. But there's not much can be done without your uncle's cooperation."

"What if you had my cooperation?"

"What do you mean?"

"My uncle's banker just brought the money to my uncle to pay the kidnapper. I could call you when my uncle leaves to pay the ransom. Couldn't you tail him or something? Then follow whoever he pays the ransom to?"

"I suppose so," I said. Although her uncle would probably be given a drop-off point, and the pick-up man would certainly be on the lookout for tails.

"Then it's all set—you'll do it?"

I didn't answer right away. The kidnapper was supposed to call at twelve. It was just barely eleven. I had plenty of time to get back close to the Glenns' estate and get in the position to tail him. It was a simple, straightforward plan.

"It just might work," I said. "But if it looks like I'm putting Mackey Jr. in any jeopardy, I'm backing off right away."

I gave her my cell-phone number, told her I'd need to know the color, make, and license number of her uncle's car. She thanked me, said she'd have the information about the car for me when she called next, and then we hung up.

I finished off the can of soda I'd brought into the office with me as I worked on the small safe that squatted on the floor behind my desk. Once I had it opened, I took out my Glock and an extra clip. I kept up my familiarity with the weapon at least once a month at one of the local ranges on Arville. But every time I stuck the thing in my belt I hoped I wouldn't have to use it. So far, I'd only had to fire it once, and that had been a warning shot.

I made good time. It was 11:44 when I pulled into a strip mall that had a Sav-On drug store on one end and a Von's grocery store on the other. It was the best strategic location I could come up with. The entrance to Glenn's golf course property was about a block south. I parked where I was facing the street. If he was going back into the more populated areas of Henderson, Las Vegas, or North Las Vegas, he would have to come this way. Otherwise, if he drove out and headed south, with enough notice from his niece I should be able to catch up.

I let the front windows down, cut the engine, and waited. The temperature was somewhere in the high nineties, due to pass a hundred by late afternoon. A typical Vegas summer day. It's something you get used to. The cross ventilation from the open windows made it comfortable enough.

I'm not sure how many times I asked myself if I was doing the right thing. I'd no sooner ask it and try to think of something else, than I'd wind up right back to the same question again. There was a lot that could go wrong, with Mackey Jr. coming out of this alive the only one thing that could go right. I was going to have to be really careful on this one.

I have my cell phone set to simply ring, instead of piping the *William Tell* Overture, or a selection from *Madame Butterfly*. I had it on the seat next to me, and it only got a chance to ring once before I answered it.

"Mr. Oaks. Erik just left with the money."

"Erik?"

"Yes. The kidnapper insisted. Said something about Erik knows firsthand what will happen if he doesn't follow orders."

The image of Erik and his double Band-Aids popped into my mind. If you're pistol-whipped once, it could make you prone to follow orders quicker.

"He's driving the same car he was driving taking Mackey Jr. to school this morning. Four-door dark-green Mercedes, license number MGLENN 1. The instructions were for him to take Lake Mead to I-15 and go north. The kidnapper says somewhere along the way he'll pull up behind Erik, flash his lights three times, pull in front, and hit his brake lights three times. He says from then on, Erik is to follow him. Once he gets the money and is safely away, he says he'll call back and tell us where Mackey Jr. is."

I got the car started. Erik would be heading in the opposite direction from where I was stationed.

"Okay, Miss Thornbush, I'll get back to you as soon as I have something."

"Good luck, Mr. Oaks."

"Yeah, thanks. Maybe a prayer or two wouldn't hurt either."

A Chevy minivan was blocking the parking lot exit closest to me. I pulled in behind it, wondering if I'd actually be able to catch up with Erik. The minivan finally drove out onto the street and I moved up, hitting my left-turn signal.

Erik and the green Mercedes passed by heading north.

Seven

I wasn't sure if I'd heard Karen correctly, or if she'd gotten confused on the kidnapper's instructions. At any rate, there was Erik and the Mercedes. I flipped my turn signal to the right and followed.

I've never had any concerns about using a Towncar to tail someone. In Vegas, a Towncar, or a Mercedes for that matter, is just as common on the streets as an '85 Dodge. I kept two to three car lengths back, trying to see if I could spot any other car tailing the Mercedes. I didn't. Other cars, vans, trucks pulled in, out and around, but there was no one vehicle following Erik other than mine. We went west on Warm Springs, eventually hooking up with I-15, and continued north. Still, there was no other car I could latch onto, and Erik didn't seem to be looking for someone to rendezvous with him. He'd been at the speed limit or above it all the way, occasionally darting in and out of traffic.

When he turned off on Spring Mountain, the brick wall finally fell on me. There had been no car signaling him to follow. Erik was in on the kidnapping, the bump on his head a small price to pay for his share of three hundred thousand dollars.

I lingered back even farther as he moved into the turning lane and started making the turn onto Industrial. There were five or six of us making the same turn. I stayed to the right, and kept going as he pulled onto the median and drove into the Wicked Babe's parking lot.

I pulled in a half block down at an adult book store, parked, and walked back. Wicked Babes hadn't opened yet. The sign on the door gave their hours as five to five. I took my time turning the corner, as I didn't want to just bust out in plain view. But the Mercedes wasn't in the parking lot.

Had Erik spotted me after all? Had he kept going once he turned into the lot? What of Mackey Jr.? The questions and doubt built rapidly. Maybe I should've told Joe.

The Mercedes and a red RV were parked at the back of the building. I pulled the Glock, slid between them to make sure they were both empty, then went back to the building next to the rear entrance.

Now what? The RV meant Erik had at least one accomplice, maybe more. For him to come here, odds would have it that Mackey Jr. was here also, but that wasn't a certainty. I tried the doorknob; it was unlocked. I had no idea of the layout of the place, where to look if I got inside. For that matter, someone could be on the other side of the door with a shotgun, waiting for some fool to stick his head in.

The one thing I felt sure about was if Mackey Jr. was still alive, he wouldn't be for long. One of the keys for a kidnapped victim to return unharmed is that they don't know their kidnappers. I couldn't think of any way Mackey Jr. wouldn't know Erik was involved. Which meant if Erik planned on getting in the clear, Mackey Jr. was history.

I went in. I had to; there wasn't anything else I could do.

The place was dimly lit, every third row of fluorescent bulbs providing what light there was. It was stuffy too, old cigarette smoke and stale beer. There was a time clock on one wall, next to a staging chart. A wrought-iron spiral staircase on my right led up to a second floor. Voices filtered down mixed with laughter.

"Told you we could still make it work."

"Got to hand it to you, Erik. After last night, I thought the deal was a wash."

I started up the stairs slowly.

"I couldn't let that bitch stop things."

"Hundred fifty apiece, just like that. Damn. I can't tell you how much petty shit I've gone through over the years."

"You and me both, Bobby."

"Hey, but that's over now."

"Right. As soon as we get rid of the kid, we're home free."

I stopped before I reached the top, stretching to peer onto the second floor. It was much brighter, a partitioned room to my left, its door opened inward. I could see Erik with his back to me.

"I did Jill," Erik said. "This one's yours."

"Hold it!" I yelled as loud as I could, rushing the open door. My old football training continually comes in handy. I caught Erik with an elbow as he spun around. He went down and off to my left. Mackey Jr. was lying on a sofa, hands and feet tied, a wide patch of tape over his mouth. Bobby, the block of granite with sideburns, was leaning over him. He straightened, ignored the gun I was holding, and charged me.

He must have played some ball too. His shoulder caught me just below my rib cage. I coughed up air and part of my breakfast from the hit. We crashed onto the floor, and the Glock went off.

"Ho," Bobby said, not quite a moan. I rolled him off me, getting to my feet as I heard Erik scrambling down the stairs.

I took the stairs two at a time, my knee reminding me I wasn't supposed to be doing things like that. I expected Erik to try for the Mercedes. Shooting at him or the car tires see-sawed in my head.

I left the back of the club in a crouch, gun ready, but he wasn't at the car. I wasn't sure if I was relieved at not having to shoot, or disappointed. I hobbled around to the parking lot just as he was crossing the street, carrying a canvas gym bag. He made it through the traffic flowing south, but a north-bound panel truck caught him square. It separated him and the gym bag, kicking them both high into the air. Erik came down first, smacking the asphalt hard, fittingly so, at about the same place Jill had landed. The gym bag spilled opened, raining the ransom money over his crumpled remains.

Eight

The shower of hundred dollar bills caused a mild panic. Motorists and pedestrians alike grabbed them as if they were in a game show. Mackey Glenn didn't quite get half his money back, but he didn't care. Mackey Jr. was returned, a little frightened but otherwise unharmed and considerably better off than his kidnappers.

The Glock at close range had made a shambles out of the bone in Bobby's left leg and torn away a lot of muscle. He'd come close to losing it. Erik hadn't survived his encounter with the truck. When the paramedics arrived, they took one look and threw a sheet over him. Industrial had claimed another one.

Metro got the full story from Bobby two days later, in the hospital when he was strong enough to talk. Erik had hatched the kidnapping plan. He was to turn Mackey Jr. over to Bobby, and Bobby was to take the kid to Jill. She lived in a part of town where the neighbors didn't pay too much attention to one another. Jill was to keep him at her place until the ransom was paid. The plans had been made weeks in advance, and everything seemed fine until Erik told them Mackey Jr. had to be killed. He'd informed them that night at the club. Jill balked at the idea and Erik told her two could be killed as easily as one. She'd run then. Erik and Bobby had followed.

They'd both watched my encounter with her from the darkened parking lot. Erik had to stop her before she told someone of their plan. Westley Blake was a regular at the club, and he always drank too much. He'd even left his keys in the ignition. They knew his car wouldn't be missed for some time. Erik had taken it, run Jill down, then left the car in the Hilton parking lot, pulling the wires to make it look like it had been rigged.

Not giving up on the kidnapping, they'd modified their plan. Bobby was one of the club's assistant managers. He had the keys and the club would be empty at least until four, when the dancers started filtering in. It had almost worked.

Joe called me into his office and ragged on me for about a half hour. It had been my duty to inform him of the kidnapping. I'd been extremely irresponsible. I'd put a strain on our friendship. Mackey Glenn saw it a little different, thanking me with a fat check. And Karen—well, she'd made it all happen and I definitely believe in giving praise where praise is due. She opted for dinner at Top of the World, the eight-hundred-foot-high revolving restaurant in the Stratosphere. We're set for this Saturday.

EYES ON THE ROAD
A LAMBERT ROWLAND STORY

by *Marcus Pelegrimas*

**The Street: Dodge Street,
Omaha, Nebraska**

Marcus Pelegrimas is a talented newcomer who has published several short stories in different genres—horror, western, and mystery—and appears equally adept in all. Here he turns his talent to the private-eye story with positive results. He presently lives in St. Louis but grew up in Omaha and manages to visit some of his old haunts in the telling of this tale, taking us along with him.

"This is Catherine Nelson with the News Center 3 traffic report, coming to you live and in the skies. Traffic on Interstate 680 is slow but steady this morning, getting slower as you approach I-80. Downtown is crowded, but moving steadily as well. Looks like we've got a stalled vehicle at the corner of 72nd and Dodge, which seems to be slowing things up considerably in that area, so you might want to take an alternate route—"

I leaned forward in the cramped confines of my '94 Hyundai hatchback and twisted the radio knob so hard I almost expected to rip the damn thing off. Looked like I was finally getting my fifteen minutes. Too bad my car had to die for me to get a mention in a news report. Then again, it didn't take much to show up on the news in Omaha, Nebraska. Hell, even scores for high school football games found their way onto television.

It was hot. Real hot. And of course my beat-up green economy ride wasn't air conditioned. With my windows rolled down, I could hear the line of cars creeping past me, honking occasionally as if I didn't already know my damn car was a piece of shit. Thanks for the tip.

I also heard the news chopper flying overhead, making its way downtown to take another peek at the morning rush hour. On a hunch, I reached down to the panel next to my left leg and pulled out the fuse for the ignition to find the little metal piece inside was snapped right down the middle. Great. Now, *that's* something I can fix.

Some college kid on his way to the University campus down the street honked, but I could hardly hear it over the rattling thump of bass and some barely audible rap lyrics. I couldn't see the kid since I was leaning toward my glove compartment, but I could just picture the baseball cap turned backward over glassy, incoherent eyes and the bony frame beneath a Cornhuskers T-shirt.

As much as I wanted to yell a few choice words at the kid, I kept my mouth shut until I found the spare fuses and clumsily fit one into the panel. The damn thing was still in my hand when it popped and started to smoke.

I knew enough about cars to figure that smoke from anywhere but the pipe in back wasn't good.

Leaning back in the uncomfortable seat, I tried to keep my cool as a hot August breeze, heavy with exhaust fumes and bad music, blew through my window. Actually, I managed to keep it together longer than I thought . . . all of three seconds.

"Shit! Shit! Shit! Shit!" I ranted while pounding my fists

on the hot plastic steering wheel with every syllable. And just in case my car didn't understand me, I added another "SHIT!" to get my feelings across.

Ignoring the perfectly functioning Firebird in the lane next to me, I dug out my cellular phone and dialed Triple A.

My car was on the side of the road next to one of those huge bookstores that had everything from CD's to videos to frothy West-Coast coffees inside. Across the street was Crossroads Mall and a few blocks ahead of where my car was stalled was the University of Nebraska at Omaha campus. I was trying to decide which of those places I should hike to while I waited for my tow truck when I heard the footsteps coming up behind me.

Now, I've been a private detective for close to six years, and I've never been attacked by anything bigger than an English Terrier. I've taken a few martial arts classes, but nothing that would make me feel confident walking through back alleys or anything. Normally, the cheating spouses I spied on were intimidated enough by my natural bulk. The thinning light brown hair didn't add much to my intimidation factor, but I had my cold stare down real good.

Unfortunately, whoever was grabbing me around my throat didn't seem to care about any of that. And since I couldn't reach the .38 I kept next to the fuses in the glove compartment, I found myself being yanked from my car as though my Adam's apple had a handle on it.

The sounds of the street started to fade beneath the roar of blood rushing through my ears. I still heard some honking and voices, but they seemed so far away. Instinctively, I grabbed for the forearms that were locked beneath my jaw while I felt myself being pulled into the street.

I managed to twist myself around to get a look at the guy's face just as a sharp pain lanced through my shoulder

and my left arm went numb. Heart attack? That'd be an un-
expected end to what should have been an easy stalker case.

My name's Lambert Rowland. I've been going by Lam
after years of all the kids saying my name in that goddamn
sing-song voice (LAAAAmmmBEEERRRRttt). I studied
Criminal Justice at the University of Nebraska at Omaha
when the idea of being a cop seemed like a suitable life's
goal. Too much TV, I guess.

My big mistake was burying my nose in those books and
listening to all the ex-cop professors who taught me about the
wonderful world of law enforcement. The more I heard, the
less I wanted to be a cop. So what does a guy do with a degree that's BS in name as well as value? Chuck everything
and become an artist? Nah. Once again, I blamed the media
for convincing me to set up my own agency with an office in
a renovated building in the Old Market area downtown
known for cobblestone streets and funky restaurants.

Thanks to my lack of marketing skills, I named my en-
terprise Rowland Investigations, which buried it so far inside the Yellow Pages that all I ever got were snoop jobs on
spouses and cheating lovers. Occasionally, I'd get the big
murder case brought to me by some beautiful brunette with
the body of a stripper and Ivana Trump's bank account. But
then I'd wake up in my garden-level apartment to the sound
of some guy getting lucky in the room upstairs, leaving me
with nothing but my fantasies and a hard-on to remember
her by.

Three days ago, when I thought my car would run fine
for a few more years, I got a message on my voicemail that
damn near almost wound up in the same digital wasteland as
the others I'd accidentally erased since I'd started paying the
extra ten bucks a month. I heard the clicks when I picked up

the receiver, managed to dial the right code, and heard a young woman's message that had been left while I was getting a sandwich at the place down the street.

After flicking some shriveled lettuce off my pit-stained, white button-down shirt, I dialed the number she'd left and asked for Vickie. Some peppy girl with the voice of a Telletubby who answered the phone screamed the name of her roommate loud enough to rattle my eardrums, even with her hand clamped over the receiver.

"Hello?" said the voice that I recognized from the message. She sounded scared and young. A little too young.

"This is Lam Rowland. Are you Vickie Dayton?"

There were a few seconds of silence, which gave me just enough time to picture her confused eyes rolling around in their sockets before she finally replied. "Oh! The detective."

I loved it when people called me that. Just like on TV.

"Yeah," I said. "The detective. You left me a message?"

"That's right, but . . . I'd rather not talk about it on the phone. Can you give me directions to your office?"

Now this was just the sort of thing I'd signed up for. I gave her the directions and tried to get some more info out of her, but Vickie wasn't ready to give up much. I whipped up my own little profile of Vickie Dayton based on the sound of her voice: cute, stupid, and paranoid. If not for the "too young" part, she'd be perfect.

I'd be testing that theory when I met her at my office the following day, bright and early, at noon. My kind of girl.

Vickie Dayton was dressed the way twenty-one-year-old girls dressed when they wanted to torture older men. Especially thirty-three-year-old private detectives. Short, muscular legs extended down into leather sandals from a pair of tight walking shorts. Thick blond hair was tied back and held in place by a pair of white plastic sunglasses. Her skin was fake-tanned, even in the dead of summer, giving it a dark, creamy texture that would turn to leather once she got a few wrinkles on her high cheekbones. She wore one of those shirts that was short enough to showcase a shiny new navel ring and tight enough for me to appreciate the air conditioning in my office. The kicker had to be the energetic bounce in her step, which sent every curve into motion.

"Mr. Rowland," she said while extending her hand. "We talked on the phone yesterday. I had an appointment."

"You still do. Why don't you have a seat and fill me in on your problem?"

Plopping myself down into the new chair that took nearly an entire day last week for me to put together, I enjoyed the feel of fine support and comfort while rolling to a stop behind a desk that looked like it was built in a shop class. She perched on the edge of one of the metal-and-leather chairs in front of my desk, not seeming to appreciate the fact that I usually tried to make my customers more comfortable than me.

Vickie took off her sunglasses and clutched them in nervous hands. "It's about one of my ex-boyfriends. At least, I think it is."

"He still thinks you two are an item?"

"That's right!" she said as though I'd just correctly guessed her weight.

"And he's probably following you," I added with my eyes closed and my fingers pressed to my temples.

Her amazement quickly gave way to an embarrassed smile. "You probably get a lot of these cases, huh?"

"Sure, but practice makes perfect. Did he threaten you or hurt you in any way?"

"He did threaten me. It's been going on for months now,

and at first I thought he just needed some time to get over me."

I tried to imagine getting suddenly deprived of a steady diet of sweet little Vickie and found myself feeling sorry for this ex-boyfriend of hers.

"At first he would just call me all the time," she continued. "I'd tell him to leave me alone and move on with his life, but he just couldn't take a hint, you know? The calls stopped, but then the letters started coming. Sometimes two a day. A few weeks ago, the letters started getting . . . mean."

"Did you bring any of these letters?"

Her eyes lit up as though she'd forgotten about them herself "Actually, yes I did." While digging through a small purse made of pink vinyl, she shook her head and gave me another nervous laugh. "I'm so nervous," she said, still sounding cute. "This is all getting me tired. I'm taking summer classes, finals are coming up, and I've never done anything like this before."

Sure. That's what they all said.

She pulled out a bundle of folded papers that seemed to be half the size of her little bag and handed them over. I removed the rubber band holding them all together and unfolded them. Each note was handwritten in pencil on sheets of lined paper that were smaller than a spiral notebook, but bigger than a pocket pad.

I started reading through them, and the first thing I noticed was the violence implied just by the sharp-edged lettering and the darkness of the markings, as through the person writing them was pressing down on that pencil hard enough to rip though the paper. Actually, after flipping some of the pages over a few times and holding them up to the light, I was surprised that the pencil hadn't done any damage.

When I started reading them, all the alarms in my head started going off at once. While psychology hadn't been my main field of study, it didn't take a shrink to tell you this guy was serious.

"Are these in order?" I asked.

"Oh . . . yes. I wrote the dates I got them on the backs."

In the upper left corner on the back of every note was a date written in red pen with flowing, cutesy letters. The earlier ones were your standard ex-boyfriend crap. I still need you. I still love you. Come back to me. Blah, blah, blah. After a bit of that, they started getting interesting. Same sentiment, but with sweet little things tagged on to the end like "more than both our lives combined" and "or else."

The last ones were strange. Instead of begging and pleading, there were threats and page-long descriptions . . . of her. "Do you know what this is all about?" I asked, holding up one of the more descriptive notes.

She glanced it over and quickly looked away. "Those are . . . that's exactly what I was wearing the day before I got the letter."

"So that means he's mailing them from the city. Do you still have his address?"

"I tried to call him and even visit him when this all started, but he wasn't at his old place. Changed his phone number, too."

Something else struck my nerves. Something that I couldn't quite figure out why it bothered me so much. "These are dirty," I said.

Vickie's face turned away from the window behind me and snapped back to the letters in my hand. After she was sure I was looking at the right thing, she furrowed her brow and tilted her head like a confused puppy. "I don't remember any sex stuff in there."

"No, not that. I mean the letters themselves. They're dirty." To illustrate my point, I held up one of them dated two weeks ago. The paper was creased neatly down the middle where she'd folded it, but was also crumpled and wrinkled with streaks of black grime embedded in most of the crisscrossing folds. "Did they come to you like this?"

Reaching out for the paper, she pinched a lower corner between bright orange nails and quickly let it go. "Yeah, they did. He was a slob."

"Slob's one thing. This," I stressed while looking over the filth that seemed soaked into the paper, "could mean something else." I read on for another few minutes until I got to the last one, which was dated two days ago. That and the one before it included a description, not only of the bikini top and necklace she'd worn last Friday, but of the outfit he wanted her buried in.

Dropping the letters onto a blotter that still had doodles of the first President Bush on it, I got up and went to the thermostat on the wall, which was one of those small rounded jobs that made me think I was copping a feel on a robot. When the cold air shut off, the sounds of a passing bus drifted up from the street.

"You need to take this to the cops," I said. "With what he said in those letters, there's more than enough to at least get a restraining order."

"I already talked to the police and they said I could get a court order, but that they couldn't do much until Kyle actually did something to me." Vickie straightened her shoulders and seemed to turn on a certain strength that filled her arms and clenched her fists into hard little balls. "I won't wait until he hurts me before I do something about it. I asked one of my professors about what I should do, and he said I could hire my own investigator. He recommended you."

That caught my attention. "Who recommended me?"

"Professor Hinton."

Funny, but I always thought he'd be disappointed to find out what I'd become after graduation. He still might be, and this could have been his way of throwing a wayward student a bone. Rather than take the chance of finding out for sure, I let it drop. "So what is it you want me to do? Keep him from following you?"

"That's the weird part. I know he's not following me."

"How?"

"Because I've had friends follow me and even security guys at the University, and nobody's seen him. I've never once thought I was being followed."

"Just because you don't see him doesn't mean he's not there."

"Well, that's what I want from you. Find out how he's watching me and how he gets so much information about me on a daily basis. Also, I want you to fill me in a few times a day. Here's my pager and cellular numbers. If he is following me, I want proof that I can take to the cops. If not, I want him to stop whatever it is he is doing."

"I'm not hired muscle, Vickie."

"I can tell."

Ouch. "I'll do what I can," I said while sucking in my gut.

She gave me a retainer check and enough to cover a few days' expenses. Standard deal. Maybe someday I could get my practice up a few more notches so that my services couldn't be so easily paid for by a college student. Then again, her daddy's money would spend just as good as everyone else's.

She was missing some of the spring in her step when she left my office, but not enough to keep me from admiring what was left.

* * *

Since I'm usually the one doing the following in my cases, I figured the best way for me to help Vickie would be to tail her and keep an eye out for anyone else doing the same thing. I started as soon as I cashed her check. There was a branch of my bank further back on Dodge, next to another mall called Westroads, which wasn't more than a few miles away from Crossroads.

With some cash in my pocket and a corn dog in hand, I left the Westroads food court and went to a wall of pay phones. A quick call to Vickie's cell phone was all I needed to find out she was in the middle of a lecture in her Marketing class at one of the newer buildings at UNO. Well, new to me anyway.

The campus felt like tuning in to a favorite soap opera after spacing it off for a few years. While some of the details and faces had changed, the basic structure was still there and I couldn't help but feel welcomed by it all. Even if I did have to work a little harder to keep myself from sticking out in the crowd of late teens and early twenties.

Vickie went about her day. She ate lunch. She talked to friends. Went to class, talked to friends, talked on her cell phone, took a nap in the library, and then called up some more friends. I, for the most part, went unnoticed. After changing into some jeans and a baggy T-shirt and slinging a pack over my shoulder, I chugged along within the University crowd, which was more concerned with their own business. Besides, I wasn't even the oldest one there. Just the one who seemed the most bothered by all the walking.

After her classes were over, Vickie got into her car and headed back down Dodge toward the Crossroads Mall and a huge, two-story arcade called the Family Fun Center. As much as I hoped for her to go in there, she kept driving south. Now, this was more like the tails I was used to and I slipped easily into my tried-and-true routine of following her car the way I would any other.

Dodge Street was known as the cruising strip of Omaha, even after the city put up signs making driving past a certain point too many times a crime. I guess my roguish good looks were all that saved me from getting pulled over by one of the cops who'd been busted down to cruising detail. That, and the fact that even a kid in his prime wouldn't be caught dead trying to cruise in a Hyundai.

Her apartment was on West Center near yet another mall called Oakview. The rest of her night consisted of more driving, which took her to some other apartments and a movie. Not once during this entire time did I spot anyone who seemed even remotely interested in the comings and goings of Vickie Dayton. In fact, after a while, I felt as though I was the one stalking her.

That feeling stuck with me through the next afternoon when I watched as she drove down Dodge Street and pulled off into a strip mall situated between Crossroads and Westroads. There used to be a decent local music store there, which had been bought out by a copy place. Thank God that same company didn't set their sights on Babba's Gyros next door. Seeing as it was lunchtime, I headed in there myself once she'd led me in that direction.

In the parking lot next to the strip mall was a giant A-frame topped with a blue roof. It was the only sushi restaurant I could think of in Omaha, and the main reason it stuck in my head was that whoever had bought the place from International House of Pancakes didn't think it strange to keep the same exterior decoration. All I could think of when I saw it was cold fish covered in maple syrup. Even though Vickie was parked outside the A-frame, I couldn't get myself to follow her in. So I let her have lunch in peace while I got a nice hot gyro.

On my way out, I called her from my cell phone. When she answered, I could hear the plinking and plunking of piped-in oriental music.

"It's Lam Rowland," I announced after she answered. "Can you talk?"

"Sure. I'm between classes at a sushi place on Dodge. My food's not up yet. Can you be here in a few minutes?"

I was hoping to avoid having to go in there, but the service was even slower than I'd thought. "Sure. I'm in the area."

A few minutes later, I was sitting in a booth across from Vickie. She had her books set up on the table and a plate of California rolls off to the side. Although she probably wore the baggy sweats and loose T-shirt to discourage guys' attention, she still managed to fill out the outfit rather nicely. I couldn't help but think that she wasn't wearing anything underneath.

"You're not being followed," I said. "At least you weren't yesterday."

She shook her head, a troubled look clouding over her features. "Well, then you might want to read this," Vickie said while pulling an envelope from a backpack under the table.

Just as I'd feared, it was another letter. Dated yesterday. Same dirty paper. Same dark writing. Only this time, the sheet was torn several times by the guy's pencil. First, there was the normal appreciative description of the clothes she was wearing. Then, he wrote: *I'll be waiting for you. My hands will feel so good on your body. I know you want it just as much as I do.*

"Waiting where?" I asked. "Did you two have a special place or favorite restaurant or something?"

"We went out for two years. We had a lot of places."

"Well, I don't think this guy is high-tech, but just to be sure I'd like to look over your car for bugs or tracers. Maybe a camera. I was with you all day yesterday and today and didn't catch sight of anyone following you. He might be tailing you in the morning, but I was with you since you left your apartment today."

"You were?" Her voice sounded more scared than suspicious.

"Don't worry. I would have told you, but I didn't want you acting any differently and scaring this guy off. There's still something about these letters . . ." Letting my voice trail off, I started looking at the paper in my hand, feeling the gritty texture of it as I held it between my fingers.

Almost without thinking about it, I lifted the page to my nose and took a deep sniff. It smelled like car exhaust fumes, which was a definite improvement over the way this place smelled on its own.

"Did your ex spend a lot of time outside?"

She considered that for a moment while holding a piece of her lunch at the end of a fork. Holding her food in front of her mouth for a few seconds, she parted her thin, pink lips and popped the bite into her mouth. Damn, this girl could make even cold fish look hot.

"Sometimes he worked outside," she said finally. "He took construction jobs when he could and spent a lot of his days pouring cement."

"Well, now I might be getting somewhere."

"So what about the letter? Where's he gonna meet me?"

"Unless you can tell me somewhere you think he's talking about, I wouldn't know where he was going to meet you," I said. "But since he didn't mention it in the letter, my bet is that he's planning on surprising you."

She stuck her lip out in a pout that had probably paid for her car and cellular phone. "I don't like those kinds of surprises."

"How much longer are you going to be here?"

"My next class is at two."

I looked at my watch. It was ten after one. More than anything, I wanted to get out of there and do some cruising on my own. Mainly to look for construction sites with a good view of Vickie's route to and from the UNO campus.

"I'll be back here in half an hour. Will you be able to wait that long for me to get back?"

"Oh, yeah. If I'm late, it's only Calculus."

I was more than happy to get the hell out of there and into the blazing heat. I did a quick check on her car and came up empty. Not that I really expected some college kid to plant bugs or tracers, but I needed to cover my bases. Once inside my car, I instantly felt like an abused mutt left in a grocery-store parking lot. Even rolling down both my windows couldn't relieve the fact that I'd been too cheap to spring for air conditioning.

Normally, Dodge Street was always under construction of some kind or another. Of course, when I was actually looking for it, hoping for it, I couldn't find a set of those bright orange cones to save my life. At one point I thought I'd hit pay dirt, but it was only a city van parked next to a median. The crew was nowhere to be seen and there wasn't so much as a pothole being repaired. Just an empty tripod standing on the concrete divider.

So much for that brilliant plan.

I was back with a few minutes to spare and found Vickie packing up her things. Luckily, I caught her right as she was bending over to get a pencil that had fallen from behind her ear. Resisting the urge to make a fish joke even though we were in a sushi restaurant, I waited until she straightened up before I approached her.

We didn't say a word as she paid her bill and headed out the door. She got into a red Camaro a few minutes later, and I followed her out into traffic in my little economy special. Rush hour wouldn't be for a few more hours yet, but there were still enough cars around to keep us from getting too close together. We got separated by a few poorly timed red lights and were within a mile of the campus when I heard car horns blaring at the next intersection. Something told me that couldn't be good.

My first reaction was to try to weave my way up to the next light, which was a side street leading to a few office buildings just past the huge Indian Hills Theater. It looked like a stalled car was causing the commotion and when I inched forward a little further, I could just make out the red Camaro's trunk and open passenger door.

Mashing my foot onto the gas pedal, I could almost see the words *"I'll be waiting for you"* superimposed over my view of the street.

I was able to cover most of the distance in my car, but when I got closer, there were enough other vehicles in my way to make me throw open my door and take off on foot. Just like on TV.

Feeling like that frog on the old video game, I ran between slowly moving cars and tried not to think about the ones in the next lane that were moving right along at faster-than-normal speed to make up for the stalled lane. Clipping my knee on the high bumper of a truck that looked like an escapee from a tractor pull, I raced up to Vickie's car just in time to see her getting pulled from behind the wheel and over the seat next to her by some guy leaning in through the passenger door.

In all the time I've been a private eye, I never got to chase anyone or even had a reason to pack the pistol I'd bought. Now, when my big day finally arrived, I found myself wanting to go buy a shotgun just so I didn't have to rely on my crappy marksmanship skills. My hand went to the little holster that fit inside the waistband of my jeans, only to remember that I hadn't been able to wear the damn thing since putting on those extra few pounds.

With no gun, no black belt, and no sidekick, I relied on the only weapon I had.

"HEY, YOU!" I screamed in my toughest voice. "Get the hell AWAY from her!"

I was about ten feet from the rear bumper when I saw the sunburned face of a guy roughly the same age as Vickie, with short-cropped bleach-blond hair and a mustache that would look more at home at the end of an old toothbrush. It must have been the sight of me charging toward him that got him to jerk away from the car. Or maybe what made the guy pay such close attention was the fact that, fat or not, I had roughly thirty pounds on him.

The kid seemed terrified, but I could tell that he still had hold of Vickie's hair and was pulling her, caveman-style, from the car. She was just about to fall out onto the curb when I jumped over the rear tire well with my hands grabbing for any part of the kid that I could get a grip on.

Like a goddamned ferret, the guy let Vickie go and started into a dead run across the street and into traffic. With her feet caught between the pedals, Vickie had her hands outstretched to keep her face from slamming against the bottom edge of the car door and her body was twisted painfully over the gear shift. I started to help her, but once she had adjusted herself so that she was able to sit up, she pushed me away.

"Don't worry about me," she said through the tears that covered her face. "I'm all right."

I tore off after the guy, but didn't catch any more than a fleeting glimpse of him as he darted between a set of buildings on the other side of Dodge. Sure, I made it to those buildings after almost getting turned into a grease spot by a speeding Buick, but by the time I arrived, he was long gone.

That didn't matter, however, since I had seen all I needed to track the kid down. He'd been wearing faded jeans and had something roughly the size of a hardcover book strapped to his right leg. It would have taken a blind man to miss that bright orange vest with strips of reflecting tape running down the sides that was worn by employees of the Public Works Department.

T.J. Hooker would be proud.

My first high-speed pursuit was in the books, and besides a lot of scrapes on my shins from where I'd bounced off a few bumpers, I didn't have much else to show for it. What I did have, on the other hand, was enough for me to think I was close to where Vickie's ex could be found and how he was able to see so much without following her.

All that had happened yesterday, and when I drove back to that city van parked on a median at the intersection of 72nd and Dodge, I thought the direct approach would be best. That van had been in the back of my mind all day long.

That van and that tripod.

A survey crew.

Those guys stood out in the middle of traffic long enough to smell like exhaust fumes at the end of every day. They wrote down whatever it was they needed to write on pads that strapped to their legs like little portable desks and their job was to stare through a tripod-mounted telescope all day long. I'd driven past those guys a thousand times at a thousand intersections, and my paranoid little brain always wondered if they ever turned their scopes on the nearby cars for a laugh to watch someone singing to the radio.

Guess I wasn't so paranoid after all, huh?

Pulling up alongside that van, I saw the SURVEY CREW sign posted behind the hunched-over figure of the kid who'd tried to strangle my newest client the day before and gave him one of my patented "bad looks." I then drove up to the stoplight just as it turned red and listened to my engine sputter to a stop. I would've called the cops on my car phone, but the forearm crushing my windpipe made that a little difficult. Which brings me back to my most recent pain in the neck.

For such a scrawny kid, Vickie's ex nearly managed to drag my ass all the way out into the street. I felt my body being lifted from my car's uncomfortable upholstery, and then came the sharp pain that set my left shoulder on fire. If I wasn't so busy trying to grab hold of the little bastard, I would have thought more about that pain. As it was, each time he tugged on my throat and lifted me up, that pain in my shoulder got worse and worse until finally my whole arm started going numb.

Then I saw where the pain was coming from. Turns out, the only thing keeping me from landing in a heap on the concrete was also the source of that fiery agony. Thank the lord for seat belts.

I was trying to say something to my attacker, but all I got out was unintelligible coughs and grunts. I'd also been trying to go for the gun in my glove compartment, but my vision was starting to blur and I didn't have enough time to root through a year's worth of traffic tickets. Another jarring pull, and suddenly I could hear something else besides the blood rushing through my head.

"You won't keep me from her!" the skinny kid in the orange vest growled into my ear as he kept trying to drag me out of the car. He still didn't seem to notice the fact that I was strapped into my seat as he cinched his stranglehold even tighter with every word he spoke. "You . . . won't . . . keep . . . me . . . from . . . her!"

That last one brought dancing blobs over my field of vision, which let me know I had less than a minute before this crazy punk killed me. Twisting my body around, I managed to grab hold of the skinny guy's vest with my right hand. After gathering all my strength, I pulled him straight toward me, slamming his face against the top edge of my car.

If anything, that just seemed to piss him off even more. So I pulled back hard on his vest until I heard that wonderful collision of flesh against metal. His arm was still locked around my throat, so I pulled again and again, harder and harder, until a thick string of blood and spit dangled down from his mangled face.

He was easing up on my throat, but not quite enough for me to get in a full breath. Some of the feeling was coming back to my left side. I grabbed hold of him with that arm, pulled him down toward me, and pushed the release button to my seat belt with my other hand. Free from the thick nylon belt, I pulled the kid's head until it was resting on my shoulder, braced both feet against the floor, and pushed myself up as hard and fast as I could. When his head and shoulder slammed against the inside of my door frame, I heard the wet snap of breaking bone, and for a second, I thought I'd killed the little pecker.

He slumped down to the ground, clutching a dislocated

shoulder like it was a wounded kitten. His eyes rolled up and he dropped into unconsciousness, but he was still breathing. Luckily, both our necks were still intact.

I felt a surge of pride as I sat back in my seat and rubbed the feeling back into my shoulder. Stepping outside the car, I looked down at the skinny blond guy sleeping at my feet and yelled loud enough for all the passing cars to hear, "That's for blasting that damn radio!"

Reaching down with my good arm, I ripped off the top sheet of paper from the notebook strapped to his leg. It read like all the other letters, listing what Vickie had been wearing on the drive to work. After a quick jog back to the tripod, I was able to pick out Vickie's Camaro and use the telescope to focus in on the back of her head. Sure enough, from all the way back here, I could make out her hairstyle, some jewelry, and the loose-fitting blouse she wore. Maybe a better detective would have noticed the fact that all his letters only noted what she'd looked like from the shoulders up, but not me. That would have been too easy.

The sound of a police siren was getting closer, so I waddled back to my car, leaned into the backseat, and dug out my cell phone from beneath a pile of pizza boxes. I wanted to call Vickie and tell her I'd found her man, but at the moment I couldn't remember her number. Probably lost it when my head hit the inside of my car door for the fourth or fifth time.

Not quite like Beretta would have handled this case, but what the hell. It got closed one way or another.

All I want to know is how come this didn't wind up on the radio?

DOUBLE-CROSSING DELANCEY
A Lydia Chin story

by S.J. Rozan

**The Street: Delancey Street,
Manhattan, New York**

S.J. Rozan's place in this business is secure. She has been nominated for many awards and has won several, including a Shamus Award for Best Novel several years ago. She regularly turns out short stories about her private eyes, Lydia Chin and Bill Smith, and one would expect a collection very soon. Her ability to tell her stories in the alternating voices of her characters is amazing. Here she manages to fashion a fascinating and entertaining tale centered around lychee nuts and con men told from the point of view of Lydia. There's no murder here—a rarity in crime short stories, these days—and the title is much more than a clever *double entendre*. The newest S.J. Rozan novel is *Reflecting the Sky* (St. Martin's Press, 2001).

I never trusted Joe Delancey, and I never wanted to get involved with him, and I wouldn't have except, like most people where Joe's concerned, I was drawn into something irresistible.

It began on a bright June morning. I was ambling through Chinatown with Charlie Chung, an FOB—Fresh Off the Boat—immigrant from Hong Kong. We had just left the dojo after an early-morning workout. The air was clear, my blood was flowing, and I was ready for action.

"Good work this morning," I told Charlie. I stopped to buy a couple of hot dough sticks from the lady on the corner, who was even fresher off the boat than Charlie. "You keep up that kind of thing, you'll be a rank higher by next year." I handed him a dough stick. "My treat."

Charlie bowed his head to acknowledge the compliment and the gift; then he grinned.

"Got big plans, next year, *gaje*," he declared. "Going to college." In Cantonese, "gaje" means "big sister." I'm not related to Charlie; this was his Chinese way of acknowledging my role as his wise advisor, his guide on the path of life. I tried to straighten up and walk taller.

"Really?" I asked.

Charlie nodded. "By next year," he told me with complete confidence, "my English gets better, also my pockets fills up."

In the dojo, Charlie and I practice kicks and punches on each other. Outside, Charlie practices his English on me.

Sometimes it feels the same.

Nevertheless, I said, "Your English is coming along, Charlie."

"Practice make perfect," he grinned, confiding, "English saying." His eyes took on a distant look. "Maybe can put English saying in fortune cookie, sell to China. Make big money."

Fortune cookies are unknown in China; they were invented by a Japanese man in New Jersey. "Not likely, Charlie. Chinese people are too serious about food."

"You think this, *gaje?*" A bus full of tourists pulled around the corner. Heads hung out windows and cameras pressed against faces. Charlie smiled and waved. "Probably right," Charlie went on. "I go look for one other way, make big money. Maybe import lychee nuts."

I munched on my dough stick. "Lychee nuts?"

He nodded. "In U.S.A., too much canned lychees. Too sweet, no taste, pah!"

"You can get fresh lychees here."

"Saying fresh, but all old, dry, sour. Best lychees, can't find. Import best fresh lychees, sell like crazy."

"You know, Charlie, that's not a bad idea."

"Most idea of Charlie not bad idea! Plan also, import water buffalo. Pet for American children, better than dog."

Sometimes Charlie worries me. I mean, if I'm going to be the guy's *gaje,* I have responsibilities. "The lychees may be a good idea, Charlie. The water buffalo is not."

Charlie, his mouth full of warm, sweet dough, mumbled, "Not?"

"Not."

Charlie hasn't learned to shrug yet. He did what Chinese people have always done: he jutted his chin forward. "If you say, *gaje.* Before invest big money, asking you."

"That's smart."

"Maybe," Charlie grinned wickedly, "brother-in-law also come asking you, now."

"Your sister's husband? He needs advice?"

"Too late, advice. Brother-in-law one stupid shit."

I winced. "Remember I told you there are some words you can learn but not say?"

Charlie's brow furrowed. "Stupid?"

I shook my head.

"Oh." He grinned again, and blushed. "Okay. Brother-in-law one stupid jackass."

I guessed that was better. "What did he do that was stupid?"

"Brother-in-law buying two big crates, cigarettes lighters

from China. Red, picture both sides of Chairman Mao."
Charlie stopped on the sidewalk to bow elaborately. I wondered what both sides of Chairman Mao looked like. "Light
cigarette, play 'East is Red' same time."

"Sounds great."

"Cost brother-in-law twelve hundreds of dollars. Thinks,
sell to tourists on street, make big bucks. When crates
come, all lighters don't have fluid, don't have wick."

"Oh, no."

"Brother-in-law complain to guy sold him. Guy saying,
'Why you thinking so cheap? Come on, brother-in-law, I
have fluid, I have wicks sell you.' Now brother-in-law sitting home filling lighters all night after job, sticking wicks
in. Don't know how, so half doesn't work. Now, sell cheap,
lose money. Sell expensive, tourist don't want. Also,
brother-in-law lazy jackass. By tomorrow, next day, give up.
Many lighters, no wick, no fluid, no bucks for brother-in-
law."

My eyes narrowed as I heard this story. Leaving aside
Charlie's clear sense that no bucks was about what his
brother-in-law deserved, I asked, "Who was the guy your
brother-in-law bought these things from, do you know? Was
he Chinese?"

"Not Chinese. Some *lo faan*, meet on Delancey Street.
Say, have lighters, need cash, sell cheap. I tell brother-in-
law, you stupid sh—" Charlie swallowed the word. "—Stupid jackass, how you trust *lo faan* guy with ruby in tooth?"

"Lo faan" means, roughly, "barbarian"; more broadly, it
means anyone not Chinese. For emphasis Charlie tapped the
tooth at the center of his own grin.

"Charlie," I said, "I have to go. So do you, or you'll be
late." Charlie works the eight-to-four shift in a Baxter Street
noodle factory. "See you tomorrow morning."

"Sure, *gaje*. See you."

With another grin and a wave, Charlie was off to work. With shoulders set and purposeful stride, so was I.

These clear June mornings in New York wilt fast. It wasn't quite so bright or early, I had accomplished a number of things, and I was sweaty and flagging a little by the time I finally spotted Joe Delancey on Delancey Street.

Delancey Street is the delta of New York, the place where the flood of new immigrants from Asia meets the river of them from the Caribbean and the tide from Latin America, and they all flow into the ocean of old-time New Yorkers, whose parents and grandparents were the last generation's floods and rivers and tides. Joe Delancey could often be found cruising here, looking for money-making opportunities, and I had been cruising for a while myself, looking for Joe.

I stepped out in front of him, blocking his path on the wide sidewalk. "Joe," I said. "We have to talk."

Joe rocked to a halt. His freckled face lit up and his green eyes glowed with delight, as though finding me standing in his way was a pleasure, and being summoned to talk with me was a joy he'd long wished for but never dared hope to have.

"Lydia! Oh, exquisite pearl of the Orient, where have you been these lonely months?"

"Joe—"

"No, wait! Do not speak." He held up a hand for silence and tilted his head to look at me. "You only grow more beautiful. If we could bottle the secret of you, what a fortune we could make." I laughed; with Joe, though I know him, I often find myself laughing.

"Do not vanish, I beg you," he said, as though I were already shimmering and fading. "Now that I have at long last found you again."

"*I* was looking for *you*, Joe."

He smiled gently. "Because Fate was impatient for us to be together, and I too much of a fool to understand." He slipped my arm through his and steered me along the sidewalk. "Come. We shall have tea, and sit a while, and talk of many things." We reached a coffee shop. Joe gallantly pulled open the door. As I walked in past him he grinned, and when he did the ruby in his front tooth glittered in the sun.

I'd once asked him what the story was on the ruby in his tooth.

His answer started with a mundane cavity, the kind all of us get. Because it was in the front, Joe's dentist had suggested filling it and crowning it. "In those days, I was seeing an Indian girl," Joe had said, making it sound like sometime last century. "A Punjabi princess, a sultry beauty with a ruby in her forehead. She gave me one that matched it, as a love token. When the embers of our burning affair had faded and cooled—"

"You mean, when you'd scammed her out of all you could get?"

"—I had Dr. Painless insert my beloved's gift in my tooth, where it would ever, in my lonely moments, remind me of her."

I hadn't fully believed either the ruby or the story, and I thought Joe Delancey's idea of what to do with a love token was positively perverse. But though I'm a licensed private investigator, I'm also a well-brought-up Chinese girl, and I hadn't known the Punjabi princess. I'd just looked at my watch and had some place to be.

Now, on this June morning, Joe waved a waiter over and

ordered tea and Danishes. "Tea in a *pot*," he commanded, "for the Empress scorns your pinched and miserly cups." He turned to me with a thousand-watt smile. "Anything your heart desires, oh beauteous one, within the limited powers of this miserable establishment, I will provide. Your money is no good with Joe. A small price to pay for the pleasure of your company."

I wasn't surprised that Joe was buying. That was part of his system, he'd once confided cheerfully. Always pay for the small things. You get a great reputation as a generous guy, cheap.

In Joe's business that was a good investment.

"Joe," I began when the tea had come, along with six different Danishes, in case I had trouble deciding which kind I wanted, "Joe, I heard about the lighters."

"Ah," Joe said, nodding. "You must mean Mr. Yee. An unfortunate misunderstanding, but now made whole, I believe."

"You believe no such thing. The guy's stuck with a garage full of garbage and no way to make up his investment. You've got to lay off the new immigrants, Joe."

"Lydia. My sweet. Where you see new immigrants, I see walking gold mines. And remember, darling, never was honest man unhorsed by me."

"Aha. So you're known around here as 'Double-crossing Delancey' for no reason."

"Sticks and stones." He sighed.

"Oh, Joe. These people are desperate. It's not fair for you to take advantage of them."

"Taking advantage of people is inherently unfair," he reflected, lifting a prune Danish from the pile. "And you can be sure each recently come representative of the huddled masses with whom I have dealings believes *himself,* at first, to be taking advantage of *me.*"

"Still," I tried again. "You took twelve hundred dollars from this guy Yee. It's a lot of money."

"Fifteen hundred, with the fluid and the wicks," Joe corrected me. "He stands to make quite a lot more than that, with the right marketing plan."

"Marketing plan? Joe, the guy's a waiter!"

"And looking to better himself. An ambition to be commended."

I sighed. "Come on, Joe. Why don't you pick on someone your own size?"

Joe bit into his pastry. "My ancestors would spin in their graves. Surely you, a daughter of a culture famous for venerating the honorable ancestors, can understand that. This street, you know, is named for my family." I suspected the reverse was closer to the truth, but held my tongue. "It is peopled, now as ever, with newly minted Americans seeking opportunity. For a Delancey, they are gift-wrapped presents, Christmas trinkets needing only to be opened."

"You're a rat, Joe."

"Not so. In fact, I detect in you a deep appreciation of my subtle art."

"You're reading me wrong."

"If so, why are you smiling? My glossy-haired beauty, I make my living reading people. I'm rarely wrong. It's you who're in the wrong profession. You have a great future elsewhere."

"You mean, doing the kind of work you do?"

"I do. With me beside you singing in the wilderness."

I sliced off a forkful of cherry Danish. Joe, by contrast, had his entire pastry in his hand and was gouging half-moon bites from it. "Not my calling, Joe," I said.

"I disagree. You have all the instincts. You could have been one of the greats—and owed it all to me. I'd have been famous, mentor to the reknowned Lydia Chin." He sighed, then brightened. "The offer's still open."

"I don't like cheating people."

A gulp of tea, a shake of the head, and the retort: "Thinning the herd, darling. I only take from beggars: people who beg me to."

An old line of Joe's I'd heard before. "I know, Joe. 'You can't catch a pigeon unless he sits still.'"

"Damn correct."

"That doesn't mean he wants to be caught."

"Wrong, oh glorious one. None of the people from whom I earn my bread will ever be rich, the brains to keep away from the likes of me being the minimal criteria for financial success. I at least offer them, though for but a fleeting moment, the warm and fuzzy sense that they might someday reach that dream."

"And you're doing them a favor?"

"Oh, I am, I am. Deep down, they know that fleeting moment is all they'll ever have, and they beg me to give them that. At least that. At most that. Joe, they say in their hearts—"

"Oh, stop it, Joe," I said in my mouth. "I've heard it before. And what about your Punjabi princess? Wasn't she rich?"

"You shock me, my sweet. Surely you cannot favor the grasping retention of unearned, inherited, caste-based wealth?"

"When the other choice is having it conned out of people by someone like you, I might."

"You cut me to the quick, my gorgeous friend. It pains me to feel your lack of respect for my ecological niche. Therefore let's cease talking about me and discuss you. How goes it with you? The detecting business treating you well?"

Joe winked and attacked his Danish. I sipped my tea. Around us bustled people making a living and people taking time out from making a living. I watched them and I watched Joe and finally I spoke. "Well, I have to admit that whoever told me this was no way to get rich was right."

"Wasn't that me?"

"Among others, maybe."

"I know I did. I thought, and think, you had, and have, chosen the wrong path. But enough of that. If the detecting of crime doesn't pay, what ecological niche do you propose to fill?"

I cut more Danish. "Oh, I'm not giving up the investigating business. But I do have to supplement it from time to time."

"And with what?"

"This and that. Nothing fun. A friend of mine came up with an idea this morning that sounded good, but then I thought about it. I don't know."

"And that would be what?"

"Lychee nuts."

"Lychee nuts? You intend to build your fortune on, excuse me, lychee nuts?"

"Well, exactly. He thinks it's a great idea, but I'm not sure. On the one hand, the best fresh lychees are hard to find in the U.S., and very big among Chinese people. You can get them canned, but they don't taste anything like the real thing. The fresh ones they import are third-rate. Premium fresh lychees, the best China has to offer, are very scarce and valuable."

"Really?" Joe sounded thoughtful. "How valuable is valuable?"

"Oh, not worth *your* time, Joe, not in your league. People would pay a lot, but they're expensive to import. You couldn't sell them down here. Just uptown, in the really fancy food shops." The waiter, to my surprise, had not only actually brought us our tea in a pot, but now replaced it with a fresh one. It's sometimes amazing what Joe can convince people to do. I filled both our cups. "You know, all those up-town Chinese doctors and investment bankers, the ones who buy raspberries in January and asparagus in November. They'd pay a fortune, if the lychees were really good. But the import business, I don't think I'm cut out for it."

Lifting his freshly filled cup, Joe asked, "Is there none of this fabulous commodity on offer as we speak in New York, food capital of the world?"

"There's only one shop, actually just down Delancey about a block, that sells the big, premium ones. Really fresh and sweet, perfumey-tasting. Go ahead, make a face. Chinese people think of this stuff like caviar."

"Do they really? Then why not go for it?"

"Oh, I don't know. If I could get my hands on lychees from India, it might be worth it."

"They are thought to be special, Indian lychees?"

"I've actually never had one. They don't export them at all."

"Why not?"

"Some government restrictions, I don't know. But if I could sell those . . . on the other hand, this whole import thing probably isn't right for me."

I finished off my Danish, drained my tea. "You sure you won't reconsider your marks, Joe?"

Flashing the ruby again, Joe said, "Perhaps if you, oh stunning one, reconsider my offer."

I smiled too. "Not in this lifetime. Well, I tried. Thanks for the snack, Joe. I have to go."

"There are Danishes yet untouched." Joe pointed to the pile of pastries still on the plate.

"I've had enough," I said. "More would be greedy. And I know what happens to greedy people when they get around you."

Joe bowed his head, as Charlie had, to acknowledge the compliment. He stood when I did, and remained standing as I worked my way to the door, but then he sat again. As I left he was ordering more tea and reaching for a blueberry Danish. From the distant, dreamy look in his eyes I could tell he was searching for an angle on the lychee nut situation. I wondered if he'd find it.

Four days later, on the phone, I heard from Joe again.

"I must see you," he said. "I yearn."

"Oh, please, Joe."

"No, in truth. Actually I can help you."

"Do I need help?"

"You do. Let me provide it."

"Why don't I trust you? Oh, I remember—you're a con man."

"Lydia! This is your Joe! My motives in this instance are nefarious, it's true, but not in the way you think. One: I can be with you, motive enough for any man. Two: We can both make money, motive enough for any man or woman. And three: You can see how smart your Joe is, and perhaps be moved to reconsider my previous offer. Motive enough, by itself, for Joe."

"That one's not likely."

"Let me buy you a refreshing beverage and we can discuss the issue."

It was a soggy afternoon, and I was, as we delicately say in the detecting business, between cases. My office air conditioner thinks if it makes enough noise I won't notice it actually does nothing useful, but I'd noticed. I'd finished paying my bills and had been reduced to filing.

I gave up, locked up, and went out to meet Joe.

Joe's meeting place of choice was a bench in Sara Roosevelt Park just north of Delancey Street. The refreshing beverage was a seltzer for me and an orange soda for him from the cart with the big beach umbrella. Joe's Cheshire-cat smile was not explained until we sat side by side, and with a flourish, he poured into my lap the contents of the paper bag he'd been carrying. The ruby flashed as I picked up one of a pair of the biggest, most flawless, most perfect fresh lychees I'd ever seen.

"Where did these come from?" I marvelled.

"Are you pleased, oh spectacular one? Has not your Joe done grandly?"

"Where did you get them?" I asked again. They were the size of tennis balls, which for a lychee is enormous.

"Sample one, my queen," said Joe.

"May I really?"

"They are for you, to lay at your feet. In the spirit of full disclosure, I admit there were originally three. I tried one myself and am left to conclude only that Chinese tastebuds and Irish tastebuds must have been created with irreconcilable differences."

"You didn't like it?" I bit into the lychee. It was firm and juicy, sweet and spicy, good beyond my wildest lychee dreams. As I dabbed a trickle of juice from my chin, I wondered if Charlie had ever had one like it.

"Your verdict, please," Joe demanded. "Is this the lychee that will make us rich?"

"This is a great lychee, Joe," I said warily. "Totally top-notch, super-duper, one of the best. Where are they from?"

Joe had been leaning forward watching me as though I were a race in which he had bet the rent on a horse. Now he leaned back, laced his fingers behind his head, and stretched his legs. He grinned through the leafy canopy at the blue June sky.

"The Raj," he said. "The star of Empire, the jewel in the crown. These are lychees from India, oh joy of my heart."

I stared. "You're kidding."

He spoke modestly, as befitted a man who had performed a miracle. "Procuring them was not a simple matter, even for your Joe. As you yourself stated so accurately, India does not as a matter of course export its lychees. But having been nearly engaged to a Punjabi princess does have its uses."

"You're not telling me her family still even speaks to you? They're willing to do business with you?"

Joe shuddered. "Heavens, no. Her male relatives would long since have sliced my throat, or other even more valuable parts of my person, had not my princess retained a soft spot for old Joe in her heart of hearts. But not all Indians of my acquaintance bear my former beloved's family good will, and the enemy of my enemy is, after all, my friend."

This was baroque enough to be pure Joe. "So you talked some other, what, Indian of your acquaintance into smuggling these for you? As a way to get back at your princess's family for whatever they were mad at them for?"

"Something like that. More important than those inconsequential details is the fact that there are, apparently, many more lychees where these came from."

"Is that a fact?"

"It is. And the fate of those lychees was quite a topic of conversation between myself and my South Asian acquaintances. We have, I am pleased to say, come close to a meeting of the minds. Of course," Joe paused significantly, "we also discussed remuneration, some serious compensation for their trouble, which will apparently include a certain amount of *baksheesh* to establish a home for blind customs officials."

"Really?" I asked. "How much did you promise them?"

Joe sent me a sideways glance. "I haven't, yet. That's why I needed to speak to you."

"Me? Why?"

"Well, putting aside my need for your mere nearness—"

"Say that again."

"What? My need for your mere nearness?"

"A great phrase, Joe. I just wanted to hear it twice. Go on."

He gave me an indulgent smile. "In any case: It is you and you alone who can set a price on these beauties. One beauty knowing another. What will your uptown Chinese pay? What shall I say we, therefore, will pay?"

"We?"

"We, oh shining vision! You and I! Your dream of riches! We shall reach the golden shore together. Whatever you say they're worth, I shall put up half. No questions asked. If you tell me these things will make us wealthy, then wealthy they will make us." He lifted the remaining lychee from my lap, flipped it high in the air, leaned forward and caught it behind his back. Tossing it again he listed like a sailboat in the wind, then looked around wildly for the lychee as though he'd lost it. Just before it beaned him, he reached up, caught it, and produced it with a flourish. I burst out laughing.

"Do I entertain you?" Joe's eyes shone like the eyes of a puppy thrilled that its new trick had gone over well.

"You do. But what really makes me laugh is the idea of going into business with you."

"But Lydia! This is nearly legit! There's the small matter of Indian export regulations, to be sure, but that aside, just look how far I've compromised my principles. I'm proposing to involve the Delancey name in a venture almost honest, for the sake of this dream, *your* dream. Oh, the ancestors! Surely you can bend your principles too?"

"Joe," I said sweetly, "read my lips. I will not do business with you. Legit or shady, risky or insured by Lloyd's of London. I'm more amazed than I can tell you that you found a source for Indian lychees, but I will not invest in any scheme that comes attached to you."

Joe looked at the lychee in his hand. He flipped it in the air, not nearly as high as before. "Time," he said to it. "She needs time to consider." He caught it, tossed it again. "The idea is new, that's all. Once she's sat with it for a day, the rightness of it will become clear to her. The inevitability. The *kismet*—"

He stopped short as I leaned over and snatched the lychee in mid-descent. "Thanks, Joe. I have a friend who'll enjoy this." I gave him my brightest smile, not quite a thousand watts but as many as I had. "Good luck with Indian customs." I stood and walked away, leaving Joe looking puzzled and forlorn on a bench in Sara Roosevelt Park.

I had told Joe I wouldn't do business with him. This did not mean, however, that nothing he did was of interest to me. In dark glasses and big floppy hat, I was up and out early the next morning, plying my own trade on Delancey Street.

One thing you could say for Joe: He did not, as did many people in his line of work, yield to the temptation to indulge in layabout ways. Joe's work was despicable, but he worked hard. I picked him up just after nine a.m. and tailed him for nearly three hours, waiting in doorways and down the block while he went in and out of stores, sat in coffee shops, met people on park benches. Finally, at a hole-in-the-wall called Curry in a Hurry, he was joined at a sidewalk table by a turbaned, bearded fellow who drank a *lassi* while Joe wolfed down something over rice. They spoke. Joe shrugged. The other man asked a question. Joe shook his head. Watching them from across the street, I was reminded that I was hungry. Luckily, their meeting was brief. When the turbaned gentleman left while Joe was still wolfing, I abandoned my pursuit of Joe and followed.

After a bit of wandering and some miscellaneous shopping, the turbaned gentleman entered a four-story building on the corner of Hester and Delancey. An aluminum facade had been applied to the building's brick front sometime in the 60's to spiff the place up. Maybe it had worked, but the 60's were a long time ago.

I gave the gentleman a decent interval, then crossed to the doorway and scanned the names on the buzzers. They were many and varied: Wong Enterprises; La Vida Comida; Yo Mama Lingerie. The one that caught my eye, though, was Ganges, Ltd.

That was it for a while. Now I had to wait until Charlie got off work at four. I hoped the staff of Ganges, Ltd., was as assiduous as most immigrants, putting in long hours in the hope of making their fortunes. Right now, having put in some fairly long hours myself, I headed off down Delancey Street in the hope of lunch.

At twenty past four, with Charlie at my side, I was back on the corner of Hester and Delancey, pressing the button for Ganges, Ltd. After the back-and-forth of who and what, the buzzer buzzed and we were in.

Ganges, Ltd., occupied a suite on the second floor in the front, from which the swirling currents of life in the delta could be followed. A sari-wrapped woman in the outer office rose from her desk and led us into the private lair of the turbaned gentleman I had had in my sights. The nameplate on his desk made him out to be one Mr. Rajesh Shah.

"Thank you for seeing us without an appointment, Mr. Shah," I said. I sat in one of the chairs on the customer's side of the desk and Charlie took the other. Rajesh Shah had stood to shake our hands when we came in; now he sat again, eyebrows raised expectantly. His white turban and short-sleeved white shirt gleamed against his dark skin. "I'm sure you're a very busy man and I don't mean to be impolite, popping in like this," I went on, "but we have some business to discuss with you. I'm Lydia Chin; perhaps you've heard of me."

Shah's bearded face formed into an expression of regret. "It is I who find, to my despair, that I am in a position to be impolite. Your name is not, alas, familiar. A fault of mine, I am quite sure. Please enlighten me."

Well, that would be like Joe: giving away as little as possible, even to his business partner. Controlling the information minimizes the chance of error, misstep, or deliberate double-cross. As, for example, what Charlie and I were up to right now.

On a similar principle, I introduced Charlie by his first name only. Then I launched right into the piece I had come to say. "I believe you're acquainted with Joe Delancey."

Shah smiled. "It is impossible to be doing business in this neighborhood and not make the acquaintance of Mr. Delancey."

"It's also impossible to actually do business with Mr. Delancey and come out ahead."

"This may be true," Shah acknowledged, noncommittal.

"Believe me, it is." I reorganized myself in the chair. "Mr. Delancey recently offered me a business proposition which was attractive," I said. "Except that he's involved in it. I won't do business with him. But if you yourself are interested in discussing importing Indian lychee nuts, I'm prepared to listen."

Rajesh Shah's eyebrows went up once again. He looked from me to Charlie. "The Indian government is forbidding the export of lychee nuts to the U.S.A. This is until certain import restrictions involving Indian goods have been reevaluated by your government."

"I know the U.S. doesn't get Indian lychees," I said. "Like most Chinese people, Indian lychees have only been a legend to me. But Joe gave me a couple yesterday. They were every bit as good as I'd heard." I glanced at Charlie, who smiled and nodded vigorously. "Joe also gave me to understand you had found a way around the trade restrictions."

"You are a very blunt speaker, Miss Chin."

"I'm a believer in free speech, Mr. Shah, and also in free trade. It's ridiculous to me that lychees as good as this should be kept from people who would enjoy them—and would be willing to pay for them—while two governments who claim to be friendly to each other carry on like children."

Shah smiled. "I myself have seven children, Miss Chin. I find there is a wisdom in children that is often lacking in governments. What do you propose?"

"I propose whatever Joe proposed, but without Joe."

"This will not please Mr. Delancey."

"Pleasing Mr. Delancey is low on my list of things to do.

You have to decide for yourself, of course, whether the money we stand to make is worth getting on Joe's bad side for."

"As to that, Mr. Delancey may be ubiquitous in this neighborhood, but he is in no way omnipotent."

Charlie had been following our English with a frown of intense concentration. Now his eyes flew wide. I smothered my smile so as not to embarrass him, and made a mental note to teach him those words later.

"Charlie here," I said to Shah, "has some money he's saved. Not a lot of money, I have to warn you, just a few thousand. Joe talked about putting up half: I think you'll have to assume more of the responsibility than that."

Shah gave a thoughtful nod, as though this were not outside the realm of possibility.

I went on, "What we can really bring to the deal is a distribution network. Well," I reflected, "that's probably a little fancy. What I mean is, I assume the cost of bringing these lychees in would be high, and so the sale price would have to be high for us to make a profit."

Rajesh Shah nodded, so I went on.

"Then you couldn't sell them on the street in Chinatown. People down here don't have that kind of money. But in the last few days—since Charlie first proposed this lychee idea, and before I knew about the Indian ones—I've done some looking around. There are a number of stores in fancy neighborhoods that are interested. Because I'm Chinese, they'll assume our lychees are from China. I'm sure you and Joe had already figured out a way to fake the paperwork."

Shah had the grace to blush. Then he smiled. "Of course."

"Well, then," I said. "What do you think?"

"Let me be sure I am understanding you," Shah said.

"What you are proposing is that your associate"—a nod to Charlie—"invest his modest sum and receive a return commensurate with that investment. You yourself would act as, I believe the expression is, 'front woman'?"

"I guess it is."

"And you would be receiving, in effect, a salary for this service."

"Sounds right."

"And Mr. Delancey would have no part in any of this."

"That's not only right, it's a condition."

Rajesh Shah nodded a few times, his gaze on his desk blotter as though he was working something out. "I think," he said finally, "that this could be a successful proposition. Mr. Charlie," he asked, "how much of an investment are you prepared to make?"

Since the talk of money had begun, Charlie had looked increasingly fidgety and anxious. This could have been fatigue from the strain of focusing on all this English; it turned out, though, to be something else.

Something much worse.

"Money," he mumbled, in an almost-inaudible, un-Charlie-like way. "Really, don't have money."

Shah looked at me. I looked at Charlie. "The money you saved," I said. "You have money put away for college. We talked about using some of that."

Charlie's face was that of a puppy that hadn't meant to get into the garbage and was very, very sorry. I wondered in passing why all the men I knew thought dog-like looks would melt my heart. His beseeching eyes on mine, Charlie said, "You remember jackass brother-in-law?"

I nodded.

"Brother-in-law takes money for next great idea."

"Charlie. You let you brother-in-law have your money?"

Charlie's chin jutted forward. "In family account."

This was a very Chinese method of keeping money: in a joint account that could be accessed by a number of different family members. I wasn't surprised to hear that Charlie's brother-in-law was able to help himself. But: "He had the nerve? To take the joint money? After the disaster with the lighters?"

Rajesh Shah looked confused. Joe must not have shared the story of his triumphant swindle of jackass brother-in-law. But that wasn't my problem at the moment.

Charlie was nodding. "Brother-in-law have big money-making idea. Need cash, give to cousin."

"And what did your cousin do with it?"

"Cousin not mine. Cousin his," Charlie rushed to assure me. This was a distinction Charlie had learned in America. In a Chinese family the difference is nonexistent: Relations are relations, at whatever distance.

"*His* cousin," I said, my tone reflecting growing impatience. "What did *his* cousin do with your money?"

"Comes from China," he said. "Comes from China, brings . . ."

Charlie petered out. I finally had to demand, "Brings what?" *Brought* what, Lydia, I silently corrected myself. Or, *bringing* what. Even in the face of stress and strain, standards must be maintained. "What, Charlie?"

In a voice as apologetic as his face, Charlie answered, "Bear gall."

I counted to ten. When I spoke, my tone was ice. "Your cousin—no, all right, *his* cousin—brought bear gall from China into the U.S.?"

Charlie nodded miserably.

Rajesh Shah spoke. "Excuse me, I am sorry, please: What is bear gall?"

My eyes still on Charlie, I answered, "It's gooey brown stuff from the gall bladders of bears. Certain uneducated, foolish, ignorant Chinese people think it has medicinal properties. It doesn't, and besides that it's very painful to the bears to have it collected, and besides *that,* it's illegal to bring it into this country."

Charlie stared at the floor and said nothing.

"How much, Charlie?" I asked. "How much did he bring?"

Charlie mumbled something I couldn't hear. Rajesh Shah also leaned forward as I demanded again, "How much?"

Just barely louder, Charlie said, "Four pounds."

"Four pounds!" I exploded. "That could get him put away for twenty years! *And* your jackass brother-in-law. And *you,* Charlie!"

"Me?" Charlie looked up quickly. "I don't know they doing this! Just brother-in-law, his cousin!"

"Tell that to the judge," I said disgustedly.

"Judge?" Charlie's eyes were wide. I didn't bother to explain.

"I say this," Charlie said, shaking his head slowly. "I say, stupid guys, now what you think? Selling bear gall on street? Sign, big characters, 'Bear gall here'? But brother-in-law say, so much bear gall, make twenty thousand of bucks, send Charlie to college. Someone in family get to be smart, then everyone listen smart guy."

"Sounds to me like in your family it's too late for that."

"Excuse me." This was Rajesh Shah again. I frowned and Charlie blushed, but we both turned to him. It was, after all, his office. "I must admit surprise on hearing these numbers. Four pounds of this bear gall can bring twenty thousand dollars, actually?"

"Probably more," I grumbled. "If it's a well-known

brand, people will pay close to five hundred dollars an ounce in this country because it's so hard to get. Because it's *illegal*," I snarled in Charlie's direction. "Because you can get *arrested* and put in *jail* for selling it. Or *deported*. Does your brother-in-law know that?"

"Brother-in-law know very little, I think. But say, know guy, going buy. Then brother-in-law, cousin, don't have bear gall, don't get arrested. Jeff Yang, on Mott Street?"

"Jeff Yang?" The words came slowly from my mouth. "Your brother-in-law is dealing with Jeff Yang?"

"Not dealing yet. Doesn't really know guy," he admitted. "Just hear guy buys bear gall."

"Jeff Yang," I said, emphasizing each word, as though I'd just discovered Charlie was a slow learner, "is the scum of the earth. I went to grade school with him, Charlie. I've known him forever. He used to steal other kids' lunch money. He'd sell you his grandmother if he could get a good price. Charlie, listen to me. You will not do business with Jeff Yang. Your brother-in-law, your cousin, *his* cousin, your kitchen god, *nobody* will do business with Jeff Yang. You will go home and flush this disgusting stuff down the toilet immediately."

Charlie looked stricken. I stood. "Well, so much for our plan, Charlie," I said. "Come on. Mr. Shah, I'm sorry we wasted your time."

Shah stood also. Reluctantly, so did Charlie.

"It is unfortunate we cannot do business," Shah said. He smiled in a kindly way at Charlie, then returned his gaze to me. "I must tell you, though, Miss Chin, that my door will continue to be open, if other possibilities occur to you."

"I don't think so," I said. "No offense, Mr. Shah, but I should have known better than to get involved in anything

Joe Delancey had any part of. It can only lead to things like this, and worse."

Without a look at Charlie, I swept to the door and yanked it open. I nodded to the woman in the sari, crossed her office, and stomped down the stairs. Charlie, with the look of a beaten pup, followed after.

The dog thing got him nowhere.

I was in my office early the next morning, stuffing papers in files and thinking I should sell my air conditioner to Joe Delancey because it was a con artist, too—or maybe I could palm it off on Charlie's brother-in-law—when the phone rang.

Picking it up, I snapped, "Lydia Chin Investigations," in two languages. Then, because whoever this was might not deserve to be snapped at, I added more politely, "Lydia Chin speaking. Can I help you?"

"I think you can," said a male voice from the other end. "How're you doing, Lydia? This is Jeff Yang."

Maybe the snapping hadn't been such a bad idea.

"Jeff," I said. "Good-bye."

"No," came the instant response. "Not until you hear the proposition."

"I can imagine," I said, because I could. "No."

"You can make money and keep your friends out of trouble," Jeff said. "Or you can not make money, and they can get in trouble. What'll it be?"

An echo in Jeff's voice told me I was on the speakerphone in his so-called office, really a tiny room behind a Mott Street restaurant, and not a very good restaurant at that. Well, two could play that game. I punched my own speakerphone button and dropped into my desk chair.

"Go to hell, Jeff."

"You know you don't mean that."

"I mean so much more than that."

"I'll buy it, Lydia. The whole four pounds."

"I have nothing to sell, especially to you."

"Well, you can stay out of it. Just tell me where to find this guy Charlie and his relations."

"Jeff," I said, "I wouldn't tell you where to find a bucket of water if you were on fire."

"I always liked you, too. Holding your teddy bear hostage until you kissed me was just my way of showing that. Let's do business, Lydia."

"Even if I were inclined to do business with you, Jeff, which would be about two weeks after hell froze over, I wouldn't risk my reputation for whatever piddly sum you're about to offer and then cheat me out of."

"It'll be a good price. In cash. You'll have it at the same time as you turn over the goods."

"No cash, no goods, no thanks. If Chinatown found out I was dealing with you, I'd never have a legit client again."

"I'll send someone else. No one will know it's me."

"Who, Rajesh Shah? Is that who's in your office right now, Jeff? Is that why you have me on the damn speakerphone?"

Jeff ignored my question, a sure way of answering it. "Lydia," he said, "if you do a deal with me, we can keep it quiet. If you don't, I'll do two things. One: I'll spread the word in Chinatown that you *did* do a deal with me, and you can kiss your legit clients good-bye. But that'll be the least of your problems, because two, I'll drop a dime on you, and you'll have to give the Customs people your friend Charlie and his brother-in-law to keep your own ass out of jail."

I was speechless. Then: "What?" I heard my voice, low and shocked. "Jeff, you—"

"Don't tell me I wouldn't, because you know I would. Lychee nuts are about your speed, Lydia. Bear gall is out of your league. Five thousand dollars, by noon."

"*Five thousand dollars?* For four pounds?"

"You're not in a great negotiating position."

"Neither are you. I told Charlie yesterday to flush the stuff down the toilet."

"And you *know*," Jeff said, "that you just *know* that he didn't. Five thousand, in the park, noon. Or your reputation is what goes down the toilet. And your friend Charlie goes to jail. Sent there by you."

Charlie in jail, sent there by me. That was an ugly picture, and I wiped it from my mind, replacing it with a vision of Jeff Yang in his back-room office. With Rajesh Shah.

"Ten," I said.

"Five."

"It's Golden Venture brand."

"Wrapped and labeled?"

"One-ounce packages."

The briefest of pauses, then, "Seven-five."

"I hope," I said, "that every ounce you sell takes a year off your life."

"The same to you," Jeff said. "See you in the park at noon."

"You must have missed it: I won't be seen with you, Jeff. Charlie will be there."

"How will I know him?"

"He'll find you. By your smell," I added, and hung up.

I called Charlie at the noodle factory. "I need you to be in the park at noon. With your brother-in-law's package."

Of course Jeff had been right: The package had not gone

down the toilet. "Only get half-hour lunch," Charlie said apologetically.

"This shouldn't take long." I hung up.

At noon, of course, I was in Sara Roosevelt Park too. I sat far away from the bench I had stationed Charlie at, half-screened by a hot-dog vendor's cart. I just wanted to make sure everything went all right: I felt responsible for this.

It went without incident. I had shown Charlie a picture of Jeff Yang and he spotted him, followed him until he sat, and then, in a burst of creativity, ignored him, walked to a soda stand, bought himself a Coke, and meandered back to Jeff's bench. He put down the brown-paper bag he was carrying and popped the can open. Charlie and Jeff exchanged a few words of casual conversation, two strangers enjoying a sunny June day. Charlie asked to glance at Jeff's newspaper, and Jeff obliged. Charlie opened the pages of the front section, slipping the back section unopened beneath him on the bench. When he was hidden behind the paper Jeff rose, told Charlie in a friendly way to keep the paper, and then set off down the path, the bag Charlie had arrived with under his arm.

In the early evening of the next day, the light was honey-colored, the sky was cobalt, and the trees were a glorious emerald green as I strolled through the same park, Charlie at my side.

"Rajesh Shah, that man, I see him yesterday night, on Delancey Street," Charlie said.

"Really?"

"Yes. He say, hear you have money now, Charlie. Asking if I want invest in lychees, still. From India."

"What did you do?" I asked, though I was pretty sure of the answer.

"I tell him, have to speak to *gaje*. Say Charlie not investing on own anymore."

"Very good, Charlie. Very, very good."

I had bought us pretzels from a cart and was explaining to Charlie the difference between Kosher salt and the regular kind when a trio of men rose from a bench and stepped into our path.

"Lydia," said Joe, with his thousand-watt smile. Rajesh Shah, in turban and short-sleeved shirt, was on his left, and Jeff Yang, bulging shoulders straining his black muscle tee, was on his right. The dark expressions on their faces wouldn't have powered a nightlight.

"Lydia," Joe said again, holding on his palm a paper-wrapped rectangle the size of a mah-jongg tile. "Oh shining star of the east, what is this?"

I peered at the label around its middle. "You don't read Chinese, Joe? It says, 'Golden Venture Brand Bear Gall, Finest In All China.'"

"Yes, exquisite one," Joe agreed. "But what is it?"

"Prune paste, Joe. The stuff they put in Danishes." I gave him a big smile, too, and this time I was sure I hit a thousand watts.

Charlie, beside me, was also grinning. Shah and Yang frowned yet more deeply. Joe just looked sad.

"Did you try to sell it?" I asked sympathetically.

"Indeed I did. And for my trouble was chased from the back alleys of Chinatown by dangerous men with meat cleavers. The damage to my reputation for veracity in those precincts is incalculable."

"No kidding? Nice side benefit," I said.

"Lydia." Joe shook his head, as though the depth of his disappointment was bottomless. "You have cheated your Joe?"

"Well, I was hoping you were behind Jeff's offer," I admitted, "but I was prepared to cheat Mr. Shah if he was all I could get."

"All the packages are prune paste? There is no bear gall?"

"There isn't, and there never was."

"You set us up?"

"I did."

"Lydia," Joe repeated, in a voice of deep grief. "You set up your Joe?"

"My Joe, my foot. Show some respect. You were setting me up, and I out-set you."

"I?" Bewildered innocence. "But—"

"Oh, Joe. Indian lychees. You know, you keep saying I have all the instincts. I don't, but I figured if I thought like *you,* everything would work out."

"How so, my duplicitous darling?"

"When I turned down your offer, right on that bench over there—which you *knew* I would—I asked myself, what would Joe do if he were turning down an offer from a middleman he didn't trust?" Joe wrinkled his nose at "middleman" but didn't protest. "Joe would try to cut the middleman out," I said. "So let's see how easy Joe makes it for me to cut *him* out. You led me around for a while the next morning, and finally you let me see you with Mr. Shah."

"I did notice you following me," Joe conceded.

"I should hope so. I couldn't have been more obvious except by waving to you. You really think that's the best I can do? Joe, you show very little appreciation for my ecological niche."

"Touché, fair one. And then?"

"Well, you clearly wanted me to go to Mr. Shah and do a deal, leaving you behind. Then you and he would split whatever cash Mr. Shah was able to con us out of, right? Of course there were never any Indian lychees any more than there was bear gall. But when Charlie and I figured that out, who were we going to complain to? I was the one who'd said importing them was illegal in the first place."

Joe sighed. "So, knowing the sting was on, you stung first?"

"Wouldn't you have?"

"I would indeed. And Mr. Yang, so reviled by you when suggested by Charlie as a purchaser for the nonexistent bear gall, had in fact been suggested *by* you *to* Charlie as a name to bring up at the appropriate moment, in order to draw in Mr. Shah?"

Jeff Yang was glowering at Joe's side. I said, "Well, Jeff was perfect for the spot. In a million years Jeff would never risk a nickel of his own on a deal like this. If he did a deal, someone would have to be financing it. I hope," I said to Jeff, "you charged a commission. Something for your trouble."

Jeff Yang's frown became fiercer, and his hands curled into fists. I could feel Charlie next to me watching him, tensing.

Joe sighed. "We're all so very, very disappointed."

"No, you're not, Joe. You're impressed."

"Well," Joe conceded, "perhaps I am. But now, my unequaled Asian mistress of mystery, the game is over. Yes, you have won, and I will proclaim that truth to all who ask. Now is the time to return your cleverly gotten gains so that we can go our separate ways, with no hard feelings."

Charlie's face fell at this prospect.

"You have to be kidding, Joe," I said. "When was the last time you gave back money you'd conned somebody out of fair and square?"

"An," Joe said, "but I would not—especially in my amateur days, which status I fear you have not yet left behind—have worked a con on such a one as Mr. Yang." He indicated Jeff Yang, whose fists were clenched, angry frown fixed in place. To emphasize the danger, Joe stepped away a little, Rajesh Shah with him, leaving Charlie and me marooned with Jeff Yang in the center of the pathway. "I fear I will not be able to restrain the good Mr. Yang from putting into play his threatened destruction of your professional reputation, unless we are all satisfied. Not to mention what look like fairly dire designs on your person."

This was, finally, too much for Jeff Yang. The frown exploded into a great bellowing laugh.

Whatever else you want to say about Jeff Yang, his laugh has always been infectious. I cracked up too.

So did Charlie.

Jeff, wheezing from laughter, turned to Joe. "I do have designs on Lydia's person, but not that kind. I've spent my whole life trying to make up for the teddy bear kidnapping incident. I'll do anything she asks. I'm putty in her hands. I'll even pretend to be a big-time Chinatown gangster if Lydia wants me to." He pulled a fan of bills from his pocket and waved them in the air. "I charged ten percent," he said to me. "If I buy you dinner, will you finally forgive me?"

"I'll never forgive you," I said. "But you might as well buy me dinner." I slipped my arm into his. Just before Jeff, Charlie, and I walked off in the golden evening I spoke once more to Joe, who stood openmouthed on the path.

"Oh, and thanks for the lychees, Joe. They were China's finest. From that place on Delancey, right? And do keep in touch with your friend Mr. Shah. When they start growing lychees in India, if they ever do, I'm sure he'll let you know."

Mr. Shah blushed and frowned. But Joe, with a wide smile breaking over his face like sun through clouds, swept forward into a low, graceful bow. He came up with a flourish and a grin. I bowed my head to acknowledge the compliment. The ruby in Joe's tooth flashed in a final ray of light as, with Jeff and Charlie, I turned and walked away.

NORTH WEST 33ᴿᴰ COURT
A JOE STANDARD STORY

by Dan A. Sproul

**The Street: North West 33rd Court,
Miami, Florida**

Dan Sproul is a regular contributor to the digest mystery magazines *Ellery Queen* and *Alfred Hitchcock*. In 1999 he was nominated for a Shamus Award for Best Short Story. When he responded to my call for short stories with this little gem, I was immediately attracted to Joe Standard's story of how he founded his agency. You see, Joe shares a passion with both his author and me—horse racing. Aside from that, this is an interesting tale of a series of interconnected and somewhat confusing streets. I expect Dan and Joe to appear again in some future anthologies of mine. Also, Dan and I may go to the track together one day. Who knows?

She transported a large purse in one hand, a fat file folder in the other. She moved to stand in front of my client chair. "Is it all right if I sit here?" she asked.

"What magazine did you say?"

"*The Detective Digest*," she replied.

Even though she wasn't a client, I could hardly deny her the chair since the alternative was my cot. She plopped down, put her purse on the floor, and opened her folder.

"You mentioned an interview on the phone," I said.

"What makes you think anybody would be interested in reading an interview with me? I mean, it's not like I'm a celebrity, you know."

"I realize that, Mr. Standard. You'll be just one of four or five private investigators in the article. I'll need some personal background information. But mainly what I'd like is for you to recount to me your most bizarre case."

"Look, Charlotte . . ."

"Charlene—my name is Charlene Ames."

"Oh, sorry, Charlene . . . practically all my cases are a little nutty. I wouldn't know where to start." The thought of tossing her out came and went fleetingly. I had nothing better to do, and it was more than two hours to first post. Besides, she wasn't hard to look at. She flashed me a crinkly smile, the kind that made a batch of little curls at the corners of her mouth. Encountering the dimple on her chin, her long, rich auburn hair, and that fetching smile . . . well, let's just say the memory would linger.

"I'm sure you'll do fine," she said sweetly. She paused to shuffle some papers around. "Tell me a little about yourself. How did you happen to become a private detective? Were you in the service?"

"I served in the Marines."

"Military Intelligence?"

"I was just a grunt. Can't say that I ran across much intelligence in there, military or otherwise."

She didn't write that down, but persevered with obviously limited expectations. "What about law enforcement?"

"What about it?"

"Any experience in law enforcement?"

"Military Police. Did a lot of shore patrol duty in the service, manhandling drunks mostly. Oh, yeah, I was a deputy sheriff in Defiance County, Ohio, for about a year. When I came to Florida back in the 70's, I went to work as an operative for the Baldwin Detective Agency in Miami—just for a year or so before I started my own agency."

"What about education?"

"Went to college on the VA Bill. Got a Bachelor of Arts degree."

She was rapidly taking notes. "Then you had a major in some form of law enforcement?"

"No, actually I was an English major. It was the only thing I was good at."

She gave me her special smile. "I see," she said. "What about your family? Are you married? Any children?"

"Had a wife once. Didn't work out."

She wrote that down and paused as her eyes traveled around the tiny office. Her attention fastened on the enormous photograph above my cot of the invincible Seattle Slew putting daylight between himself and Cormorant in the 1977 Preakness Stakes. She turned to face me. "I already know that much of your work is connected with the horseracing industry in Miami."

"I like to play the horses," I admitted. "One of the reasons I left Ohio, the racetracks were a long way away in Cleveland or Detroit. Also, back then, those tracks were only open two or three months out of the year. Here in Miami there's a track open year-round."

She pointed to my photo of Slew. "The large photograph of those horses—is there some special significance to the picture?"

I leaned elbows forward on my desk. She watched me quizzically. "Funny you should ask," I said. "Been a lot of people in this office over the years. Nobody's ever asked that before. Yes, as a matter of fact, Seattle Slew is pretty special to me. If not for him, I'd probably still be working in the Baldwin Agency."

She leaned back in her chair and allowed her hands to fold on top of her papers. "Tell me," she said. I was really beginning to like her a lot.

So I told her. Kenny Baldwin, owner of the Baldwin Detective Agency, was a chiseler of the first order. He was tighter than a Chihuahua pooping peach pits. I could see no future there. But, between him and the horses, I stayed broke. In the spring of 1977 at Hialeah, I stood at the rail and watched the undefeated colt, Seattle Slew, break the track record at seven furlongs in his first start of his three-year-old career coming back after a near-fatal illness. He used the race to work out a mile in preparation for the Flamingo Stakes a few weeks away. I knew then, if he stayed sound and fit, that no horse alive or dead was going to beat him at any distance. I took my savings—a hundred dollars—and gave it to Sid Perdue, who was booking bets in his feed store up in Davie. It was a chump's bet, Sid told me. And it probably was. I bet a five-horse win parley. I told Sid to put it all on Slew in the Flamingo. Take the winnings, if any, and bet it all on Slew in the Wood Memorial; bet those winnings on Slew in the Kentucky Derby; take those winning and bet everything on Slew in the Preakness. And then, if he gets that far, let it all ride on Slew to win the Belmont Stakes. I don't need to tell you that Sid was sweating beavers after the Preakness. Slew won them all—the only horse in history to go into and out of the Triple Crown undefeated. Was he the best that ever was? He gets my vote.

"That's how Standard Investigations got started," I finished.

She studied the photo once more. "Which one is Seattle Slew?" she asked.

"The one in front," I said. "Always the one in front."

She nodded, dismissing the matter as not pertinent. "Okay, you must have had some unusual cases during your twenty-odd years in the business. Which cases stand out for you as the most unusual—the most bizarre?"

She had stirred old memories asking about the Slew photo. "Well, since you've brought it up, I didn't just start out with that enlarged photograph. I had only a small, two-inch-by-three-inch photo clipped from a magazine. I kept it in a little frame on my desk. How I came to have the big picture of Slew involved a strange case: a very strange case."

"So let's hear it," she said. She turned to a fresh page in her notebook, then looked at me expectantly, pencil poised.

I told her the story of Abel Dexter, one of my very early clients. It was a time when I was still working now and again as an assistant trainer to Buddy Wayne when he happened to ship horses to Florida.

Abel was a manure hauler's helper. That is to say, he worked as a driver for the guy who was entrusted with removing the horse manure from the racetrack. When I asked Abel where he got my name, he brought his occupation to my attention and mentioned that one of the people in the backstretch at Calder Racecourse had told him about me.

Abel was on the thin side and bony. His teeth were corrupt. He didn't have a lot of hair on him, just a Bozo-the-Clown fringe circling above his ears and dangling down about three inches. There was also a sparse spattering atop his lip. Even with this extreme lack of hair, he immediately reminded me of a wet rodent. On the plus side, what Abel did have was a story and a $120 retainer.

As he told me his tale, I had a hard time grasping the essence of his situation. For one thing, Abel was very nervous. He appeared to be in a state of repressed panic if such a condition is possible. What he finally managed to convey was that his wife was missing under mysterious circumstances. Further interrogation revealed that she had turned up missing the night before so had only been gone for about thirteen hours. I mentioned to him that the facts so far didn't warrant his apparent extreme concern.

"But my car's gone too. I had to rent one so's I can get to work," Abel explained.

"Let me get this straight," I said to him. "About ten o'clock last night, your wife took off in your car and you didn't know about it. Were you home?"

"I went into our bedroom for a few minutes to use the phone. To see if I had to work the next day. When I came out into the living room, she was gone and so was the car."

"Did you have a fight?" I asked.

"*No* . . . no fight!" He fairly shouted this denial as he wrung his hands.

I suggested that he wait and go to the police, that she might come home at any time. Nope . . . he insisted that I take his hundred-and-twenty bucks and look for her.

"I got a feelin' she ain't coming back," he said. "She didn't even take no clothes with her. I think she mighta' been kidnapped."

"Kidnapped! Well, I'm not sure exactly what I can do. Maybe if I could check out her belongings, question the neighbors . . . try to get an idea what happened."

"I don't know about that," said Abel. "Can't you just look for the car?"

"Why don't you just report the car stolen?" I suggested.

"*No!* I can't do that . . . I mean, I don't want to get her arrested—you know, in case she wasn't kidnapped."

"Then I have to check out the house," I insisted. I was beginning to suspect that Abel was either a manure load short or he was embellishing the story as he went along. In any case he reluctantly agreed.

I followed Abel's rental car into West Miami toward Hialeah, home of the famous Hialeah Race Track. The drug stores were changing to *farmacias,* the restaurants to *restaurantes.* Spanish was definitely spoken here. We didn't make it all the way to the track. Abel veered sharply onto North West 36th Street and almost lost me. He took another right on North West 89th, then a quick left on North West 35th Street, made a sharp turn on North West 33rd Avenue, then a hard right onto North West 33rd Court. I had lived in Miami for twenty years, but I wasn't sure I could find my way back. Abel's place was a two-bedroom, no pool, with a one-car garage full of junk and no toys in the yard. The roof was shot. The grass needed cutting, and the mailbox was leaning about fifteen degrees off plumb. Abel's missing car was a 1982 Ford LTD, dark blue in color. It wasn't anywhere around. He pulled a key from under a flowerpot on the porch and unlocked the door.

I started in the kitchen. Abel followed close behind me, his chin almost resting on my shoulder.

"I don't know what you expect to find," said Abel.

One side of the double stainless-steel sink contained clean, washed dishes, cups and silverware. Several dinnerware items poked up out of the murky sudsless water on the other side of the sink. A few pots, pans, and bowls remained on the counter waiting to be washed. A toaster at one end of the counter sat askew, with the unplugged cord dangling down to the floor.

"Hmm . . . maybe nothing," I said. At the other end of the cluttered counter, past the unwashed pots and pans, lay a dish towel and half loaf of bread. The bread wrapper lay carelessly open. I moved the bread wrapper aside to dis-

cover a small ceramic ashtray hidden behind. The key ring
that lay in the ashtray contained four or five keys with an
embossed metal tag that said *Janie*. One of the keys was
square at the top with the FORD stamped on it. I dangled the
keys for Abel to eyeball. "These keys belong to Janie, your
wife?"

"Eh . . . yeah."

"How could she leave in the car if her keys are still
here?"

He fumbled with the question a bit before he answered.
"She ah . . . she took my keys off the dining room table. I
mean, she musta took my keys off the dining room table."

"Then you don't think she was kidnapped?" I asked.

"No . . . I don't know . . . she might have been kidnapped. You know, maybe the kidnapper got her. Then he
took my keys and my car."

I went into the bedroom next. Abel was right, all her
clothes seemed to be in the closet. In the back of the closet
were a large and small suitcase along with a travel bag—all
empty.

"Do you know if she took anything at all?" I asked.

"She took her purse," said Abel. He seemed sure about
that.

"How do you know she took her purse?"

"It's gone," he said. He then pointed to a small table by
one of the twin beds. "She kept it there on that table."

"So, she decides to leave you halfway through washing
the dishes," I said, thinking out loud, "grabs her purse, but
no luggage, no underwear, no change of clothes. Yet, you
say you two didn't have a fight."

"Or else she was kidnapped," Abel contributed.

"I see. The kidnapper was quiet enough to enter without

your wife making a fuss that you could hear in the next room and was considerate enough to allow her to take her purse."

Left unsaid was the fact that if Abel was in the bedroom using the phone when his wife took off, as he had told me earlier, how come he didn't see her come in and get her purse if she kept it there? Of course, there was another bedroom.

"Let's see the rest of the house," I requested.

The other bedroom was full of boxes and assorted junk. There was a phone jack, but no phone and no place to put one. The living room held no curiosities and the garage, piled high with more junk, held not even space to swing a crooked midget lawyer. I told Abel to stay put. Told him I'd be back shortly.

Abel's story had more twists and turns than a mile-and-a-half race at Tampa Bay Downs. He was lying to me. There had to be a reason. I walked next door to a well-kept stone-and-brick home similar in design to Abel's house, but much more elegant in every other way. The middle-aged woman who answered my knock became very animated when I introduced myself as a private investigator.

"I never met a private eye before," she disclosed. "Did you ever shoot anybody?"

I told her that Janie Dexter was missing. Once past the preliminaries, Mrs. Oberon was quite willing, even eager, to talk about her neighbors, the Dexters.

"Her family had the money, you know. I don't know why she even stayed with that bum as long as she did. All he did was haul manure and play the horses. She always complained to me that they couldn't save no money 'cause he would lose it at the racetrack. The poor thing, I think she was goin' to leave him. She talked about it a lot. I guess she finally decided to go."

I asked about Janie' s family, thinking maybe she went to them.

"They live in Europe, somewhere in the Netherlands, I think."

"I guess she couldn't drive there then," I commented.

"Oh, Janie didn't much like to drive," she remarked. "She wasn't very good at it, and the traffic made her nervous. The bum she married took their car to work most of the time anyway. I always took Janie to town with me to go grocery shopping."

I ended up asking Mrs. Oberon if she saw or heard anything at the Dexters' the previous night. She told me she had been visiting her sister the last several days and hadn't been home.

I said good-bye to Mrs. Oberon, crossed back over Abel's lawn, then squeezed between the hedge along the driveway to his neighbor on the other side. I caught the curtains moving in Abel's front window as he followed my travels across his front yard.

"Well, what are you lookin' at?" asked the old geezer who answered my knock. He continued before I could comment. "You'd look just as bad as me if you had to sell men's socks for forty years. What do you want, anyway?"

I explained who I was. He was instantly unimpressed. His name was Fred Frunkmueller.

"Look, Mr. Funkmueller . . ."

"That's Frunkmueller with an 'r'," he corrected me. "You can't be much of a detective if you can't even remember a name for fifteen seconds."

"Eh . . . yeah. Well maybe you could tell me if you noticed anything out of place next door at the Dexters' last night—or anytime recently." At that point an old lady in a wheelchair propelled herself into the living room. "Or maybe your wife heard something," I added.

"She's not my wife," Frunkmueller said. "And she can't hear nothin'—deaf as a stump. Dumb as one too."

"I heard that," said the old lady.

"No you didn't," said Frunkmueller.

"Tell him we don't want any," said the old lady. Turning the chair, she rolled out of the conversation as quickly as she came into it.

Frunkmueller more or less explained: "My brother's wife. He's dead."

After ten minutes or so, Frunkmueller sort of warmed up to me, if you could call it that. He told me that most of the homeowners on North West 33rd Court had lived on the street for some time. Everybody knew everybody else. He assured me that anybody I talked to on the street would agree: Janie Dexter was a saint, and Abel Dexter was not.

Finally he said: "She left him last night, all right. Heard the whole thing. Me and my brother's wife was watching TV. Course, she didn't hear nothin' 'cause she's deaf. Got special earphones so's she can hear the TV—cost me eighty-five dollars."

"Okay, so what exactly did you hear?" I prompted.

"Well, I was sittin' there by that window." He nodded to a chair across the room. "All of a sudden, I hear a car door slam. Then the tires start to screechin'."

"The tires were screeching?"

"Oh, yeah. I looked out the window. The tires was smokin'. She musta been madder 'n hell. She took off down the street, did a U-turn for some reason, slid sideways, tires still spinnin', then she come a roarin' down past the house and out toward North West Eighty-Seventh."

"How do you know it was Janie and not Dexter or somebody else driving?"

"Well it was Dexter's Ford all right . . . sittin' right out there under a street light. But it wasn't Dexter drivin'."

"You're sure of that?"

"Oh, yeah, Dexter was standin' out in the yard. Headlights caught him big as day when she roared past."

"What was he doing—I mean, was he yelling at her to stop or waving his arms or anything like that?"

Frunkmueller rubbed his chin and thought for a minute. "Nope, he wasn't doin' none of those things. He was just standin' there, holdin' somethin'—only caught a glimpse— looked like a cement block."

After leaving Frunkmueller, I talked to several other neighbors across the street. Most spoke limited English. It was clear enough, though. Frunkmueller was the only one who saw Abel's car depart, but everybody I talked to heard the commotion. I said good-bye to Dexter with the promise that I would continue on the case the rest of the day until I used up his $120. I turned the wrong way leaving North West 33rd Court and ended up on North West 33rd Avenue. I circled the surrounding streets, passing North West 34th Avenue at least twice before I finally ended up on North West 87th Street, which led back out to North West 36th Street.

Nothing added up. If Janie Dexter was not a confident or even a very good driver, it wasn't likely that she laid rubber for twenty feet and did a slide turn in the middle of the street. I didn't believe it. And Abel Dexter, what a help he was. The only thing you could trust about him was that he would rather lie to me than breathe. So, I ask myself why. And who was driving Abel's car if it wasn't Janie Dexter? And if it wasn't Janie Dexter, where could she be? And what the hell was Abel doing with a cement block?

I paused in my tale to collect my thoughts.

"I've got a question," Charlene said. "Didn't you think to ask Mr. Frunkmueller why he was living with his dead brother's wife? I mean, it seems strange, doesn't it?"

I shrugged. "Didn't figure it was any of my business. Anyway, it didn't seem as strange as somebody selling men's socks for forty years. Before he let me out of there, Frunkmueller insisted on proving that he could name off every major department store in the Midwest."

"Okay," she said, offering up another crinkly smile. "Did you find out what happened to Mrs. Dexter?"

"Not right away," I confessed. "I took the problem with me that night to the Surfer Bar and Grill, that gin joint just around the corner that you probably saw coming in."

She leaned back to take notes. I thought back and attempted to put the sequence of events in order. At this time in my life, I was inclined to take a few belts on a given night. Sometimes it helped me think. And sometimes not.

It was not my custom to drink alone. Two of the regulars there that evening were Buddy Skylar and Irving Berg. Buddy was a photographer by trade. He worked for the *Miami Tribune* as a stringer and aspired to land a permanent job as photographer. In the meantime he squeaked out a living with what he called nude art studies, sleaze photography that he freelanced to the girly magazines.

In the ex-con mainstream populace, Irving Berg was more widely known as the Heistmeister. He had recently been released after serving eighteen years for armed robbery, the second offense. Irv had retired to a life of part-time bag man for the local Cuban Bolita. The Bolita was sort of like the numbers game, but the numbers are poked off a piece of cardboard. His claim to fame was that as a young boy in the 30's he once met Willie Sutton just after the famous bank robber escaped from Sing Sing prison.

Avid horseplayers all, we were prone to discuss the great horses and pick apart the next day's races. But as the night wore on and the liquor gushed, the conversation stumbled on to the weird circumstances in the Abel Dexter case.

"It seems pretty simple to me," Irv contributed, slurring his words the slightest bit. "If the wife didn't take the car and Dexter didn't take the car—then somebody stole it."

"Yeah, that fits," said Buddy, sloshing his beer on his sleeve. "Damn, it's running down the inside of my arm," he felt it necessary to announce before continuing. "I mean, they was sure in a hurry to get away, you know?" He patted the length of his sleeve several times.

"I might believe that if it was a Mercedes or a Corvette," I chimed in. "But why would anybody steal an LTD . . . I mean, what's the street value?"

Irv made the comment "Oh, I don't know, if somebody needed a car that blended in . . . you know, if they was pullin' a job . . ."

"Okay, let's suppose you're right," I said. "What do you think I ought to do about it?"

"Well," said Irv, "if you find out who took the car, maybe they can tell you what they know about the wife. Personally, I think she ran off with her boyfriend and he swiped Dexter's car. But if you think somebody else stole it . . . well now, if you want to know how to run down a hot car, I can help you out there."

"Oh, really," I said. "And how would you do that?"

"Easy," said Irv. "I'll introduce you to Noodle Stoner over at Wiedimeyer's Garage. If there's a car stolen in Miami, he's either behind it or knows about it. I used to use him all the time for getaway cars. He chops some up for parts and exports others. He's the biggest operator in town."

By this time we were at that stage of inebriation where Irv's suggestion sounded like a perfectly logical, super undertaking. At any other more sober moment, perhaps the whole idea would have been dismissed, but those who drink do strange things. We collectively decided to visit Wiedimeyer's Garage and talk to Noodle Stoner. Even though it was nearing eleven p.m., Irv assured us that Noodle did most of his work in the wee hours. We all piled into my Mustang and were off.

It took a profuse amount of yelling and banging on the metal door to gain entrance. Then the door opened. If Abel Dexter reminded one of a wet rodent, Noodle Stoner made you think immediately of a beached walrus wearing suspenders and puffing a cigar.

"What the hell you guys want?" he asked, somewhat uncivilly. "If you're cops, you better have a warrant. If not, get the hell out."

"Noodle," said Irv. "Don't you recognize me? . . . Irv Berg."

Noodle squinted at him through the wafting cigar smoke. "Oh yeah, the guy that met Willie Sutton. I thought you was in the can."

Irv told Noodle that we were looking for a 1982 blue LTD that was stolen the night before. Noodle's face went ashen.

"Who is these guys with yeah?" he asked, backing slightly away.

"These are my friends," Irv told him. He introduced me as a private detective and told him that I was looking for a specific blue LTD that was stolen the night before in Hialeah. "What was that street again?" Irv asked me.

"North West Thirty-Third Court," I said.

"Jeezus, that dumb bastard," Noodle muttered. "How did you know to come here? It was that goddamn kid shootin' his mouth off, wasn't it?"

It took a while to draw the story from him. He still had the blue LTD. Noodle claimed he wanted to dump the car in an alley someplace, but nobody had the balls to drive it out of the garage. So there it sat.

"I been tryin' to get ahold of that kid to take it out in the boonies and dump it."

"What kid is that?" I asked.

"His name is Lawrence Bilsi," Noodle told us. "They call him Larry Bullseye. He's the one got me into this goddamn mess."

"What mess?" I asked. "You deal in stolen cars all the time."

"Yeah," said Noodle, "but this one had a body in the trunk."

The body in the trunk was a woman. Things began to finally make a little sense. Noodle related the story of how he had sent Larry Bullseye and his girlfriend, Hilda, to North West 33rd Avenue to steal a Volvo that was on order for export to Guatemala. Somehow they got lost in the maze of streets. Larry said that while they were wandering around they chanced upon the LTD parked at the curb with the motor running and the door open. It was too good to pass up.

Noodle claimed that the body in the trunk wasn't discovered until late the next day. Just a few hours before we got there. Larry Bullseye never knew about the body in the trunk. Noodle, however, was anxious to tell him.

I took a look in the trunk. It had to be Dexter's wife. She had been bashed in the head. Her purse lay alongside her. I ran the scenario in my mind. Dexter hits his wife in the head with something. I remembered the toaster with the cord dangling down. Maybe he used that. Now he's got a dead wife on his hands. He backs the LTD up to the garage door. When the coast is clear he dumps his wife in the trunk along with her purse. He gets in the car and starts to take off. But he remembers that he doesn't have everything he needs. He stops at the curb. He decides that if he is going to dump his wife in a canal he will need something to weigh her down. He leaves the car idling with the door open and goes back inside for a cement block. Along comes Larry Bullseye.

Abel gets the cement block and starts back across the lawn. Too late. Imagine his dismay as his car speeds away with his dead wife in the trunk.

It's little wonder that Abel was nervous. And it became clear why he came to me to find his wife. What he hoped to accomplish was obvious. Abel couldn't report his wife missing to the police for at least forty-eight hours. If the cops found his stolen car or his dead wife in the meantime, he was finished. But if he could establish that his wife left with the car alone or that she was kidnapped, he had a chance. Having me on the case could help to verify that argument and was the next best thing to reporting his wife or car missing. Obviously, he couldn't tell me the truth about what happened.

Charlene stopped taking notes. "I have to admit, it's the strangest case I've heard so far."

"You haven't heard it all yet," I said. "The question arose: What was I going to do about the murder?"

"What did you do?" she asked.

Before answering, I checked my watch. It was getting close to post time for the first race at Calder. I took the *Racing Form* from a drawer and laid it on the desk before me. It would be a tragedy to forget the *Form* after working all the races out. That task completed, I told Charlene the rest of the story.

My course was clear. Abel had paid me a $120 to get his wife and car back. I could not shirk my duty.

Irv donned his gangster gloves and drove the LTD. I assured him that the car had not been reported stolen and that he really didn't have anything to worry about as long as he didn't have an accident. We had to stop by Buddy's place for his camera equipment, at which time we opened the trunk and allowed him a few close-ups of the body.

Irv followed my Mustang back to Hialeah, to North West 33rd Court. Still, it took me the better part of an hour twisting thorough the maze of streets to find Abel's house. Irv pulled the LTD into Abel's driveway just after five a.m. He unlocked the trunk and threw the keys inside with Mrs. Dexter. He closed the trunk and locked the doors, then quietly shut the passenger-side door. I had parked the Mustang on North West 33rd Avenue, the next street over. The course of events had pretty well sobered us up by the time we stood on Frunkmueller's porch and knocked on the door.

Frunkmueller answered the door with a .45 automatic in his hand. It took a while to calm him down. His dead brother's wife wheeled into the room and immediately upon seeing Buddy's camera demanded that he take her picture. Frunkmueller rolled her into another room. During the introductions, Buddy explained to Frunkmueller that Irv had once met Willie Sutton. Frunkmueller topped that by claiming to have once taken a leak alongside Will Rogers in the toilet at the Copacabana.

I hastily explained to Frunkmueller that Dexter had knocked off his wife and her body was in the trunk of the LTD, and that we needed to use his phone to make an anonymous call to the police.

After Buddy made an anonymous call to the cops telling them he saw Abel put a body in the trunk of the LTD, he gave them the address on North West 33rd Court. We waited ten minutes before I disguised my voice and called Abel to tell him his LTD was back in his driveway.

It was just getting light out. We watched Abel come out of the house and jerk on the door handle of his car without result. He stood looking at it a minute then went back inside.

"What's he doing? He went back into the house," said Buddy, snapping away with his 35-millimeter camera.

"He's looking for these," I submitted, holding up Janie Dexter's car keys for all to see.

We watched a Miami Metro police car drive by on the next street over; then it turned and circled onto North West 92nd Street going directly away from North West 33rd Court. The cop was obviously lost. Buddy took a picture of the police car.

It wasn't long before Abel came back outside with a hammer. He smashed in the driver's side window. He looked in the visors, in the glove box and under the seats, but he didn't find any keys. By this time Buddy had to change rolls of film.

Abel went back into the house and came out with a pry bar. Just after he popped the trunk with the bar, a Hialeah police cruiser nosed its way down North West 33rd Court followed by the lost Miami Metro cops. They all stopped at Abel's driveway.

Buddy went out onto Frunkmueller's lawn to get better shots of Abel when the cops handcuffed him. The story, complete with pictures that Buddy turned into the *Tribune* got him a permanent job as photographer.

"But you framed your client," Charlene pointed out.

"Yeah, pretty bizarre, huh? It was my obligation to inform the police of any known criminal conduct. I just waited for the most opportune moment. Buddy was so grateful to me that he dug around and found the guy that took that picture of Seattle Slew and Cormorant. He bought the negative and made that big enlarged photo you see on the wall there."

"But didn't you have to testify . . . I mean . . ."

"Abel confessed when they caught him with the body. He pleaded guilty. They let him out about three years ago."

"What about the others in the case? Can I verify any of this with them?"

"Hmm . . . Well, Buddy died of cancer in 1989. Irv had a stroke and died in '92. Noodle Stoner was shot and killed in 1983 not long after the Abel Dexter case. Larry Bullseye evolved into one of the best car thieves in South Florida. He's around, but I doubt if he'll talk to you. 'Course there's Frunkmueller. He'd be in his nineties. But you have a problem there. I doubt if you'll be able to find North West 33rd Court."

"I really would like to use this story," she said enticingly.

I noticed that she wore no wedding rings. "How about if you go to the track with me? I'd be more than happy to run you over to Frunkmueller's later."

LAST KISS

by *Tom Sweeney*

The Street: Bourbon Street,
New Orleans, Lousiana

Part of the fun of editing anthologies is finding promising new writers. It's my pleasure to introduce another newcomer—along with Jack Bludis and Marcus Pelegrimas. Tom Sweeney impressed me enough in the span of thirteen pages that I had to have this story in the collection. It's perhaps the story in the book that most departs from the traditional P.I. form. It's probably also the darkest. A fitting story to close this anthology with.

Another porn shop in another cinderblock former service station in some dick town in east Texas. Two years to the day, and he was back within four hundred miles of New Orleans. Some fucking detective.

Jerry walked around the room once before approaching the waist-high counter by the reinforced entry door.

"Got anything with redheaded boys?"

The scattered customers in the store shuffled their feet, but the tattooed greaseball standing behind the counter lifted his head and glared.

"How the hell do I know? You think I look at everything I sell?" He leaned forward, hands on the counter, muscles tensed as though he was about to vault over it.

Jerry snorted. At one time, that might have scared him

shitless. Not now. Too many porn shops, too many losers trying too hard to be scary. Now only the quiet ones frightened him.

"I only want boys, and only redheaded ones. Nine or ten years old. You got it or not?"

"You're talking illegal shit, and you smell like a cop."

Jerry blew out his breath. No matter what he did, no matter how he dressed, he still did look like a cop. "How about this?" He raised his voice and spoke to the room. "I want to pay you for some child porn. Something with a little redheaded boy around nine or ten years old."

"The hell you doin'?"

"Entrapment. If I was undercover, I couldn't arrest you. It'd be entrapment." This place had shit.

"Get your ass outta my store, dickweed, before I bounce you out."

What a waste of time. Who the hell was it who had pointed him to this dump? He should've followed his instincts and gone east. Or tried the Internet again, taken his chances with the FBI cyber-cops. There was no reason to stay anywhere near New Orleans.

The other customers had moved away from him and a puffy-faced, redheaded hooker, looking middle-aged but probably in her twenties, stared at him from across the store. Jesus, he was tired of this shit.

Outside a cold rain had begun to fall, just drizzling now but with a promise of more to come.

The fear that he might be leaving behind the one photograph he'd been looking for pulled at him, but he'd learned to ignore that feeling. He flipped up the hood of his windbreaker.

He turned to walk the two blocks to the center of town, where he had left his car. Head down against the chilly early-winter rain, he looked into each doorway he passed, and when the light was right and the angle was there, he caught the reflection of the redhead walking behind him.

She caught up to him at the next corner and nudged his elbow. "You say you're looking for a redhead, mister?" Her voice was a harsh whisper, scraping low and raw.

"Sorry. Too old, wrong sex."

She smiled, showing teeth clothed with a slimy film. "I don't mean me." She smiled at him again, this time in an obvious attempt to be coy. "You don't need a magazine to see me—you can see the real thing."

The real thing. Jerry looked across the street, toward the Hygenic Restaurant in whose lot he'd parked his car, then back to the redhead. He saw neither restaurant nor redhead.

He saw instead the eyes of the little redheaded boys in the magazines. There were two kinds of eyes—normal eyes and hollow ones. That was how he learned to tell the staged photos from the ones using captive boys. It was the eyes of the captive boys that registered fear and shock, and most of all, disbelief. When Jerry scanned a magazine, he didn't bother with the staged pictures—only the photo spreads with real lost boys drew his attention.

She nudged him again. "I've got photos. Little-boy photos. Little redhead boys."

"How old?"

"How old you want?"

Jerry snorted and started across the street. The woman hurried after him. "Christ. What the hell's wrong with you? You want to buy some pictures or not?"

Jerry spun around in the street. "How old are the kids?"

A pickup honked and slid past them, the driver yelling something unintelligible through the closed window. The woman moved next to Jerry. "All ages. Whatever age you want."

Jerry took her elbow and led her to the sidewalk. "Where?"

"New Orleans."

Christ. New Orleans. It always came back to New Orleans, didn't it?

She evidently mistook the expression on his face as disbelief. "No, really. My friend George has 'em. He's got everything. We even did movies."

"Movies? You ever hear of Robeson Cinema?"

"Weren't they the Cajun company tried to make bayou movies and went bust?"

"They were a cover for a porno operation. They got shut down three years ago."

"Yeah, that's right. George told me about it. Some of the workers bought up all the equipment and started making snuff movies."

Jerry grabbed her by both arms and shook her. "Not snuff. I said *porno*. They made porno movies and they did stills. Lots of stills. No snuff films, you understand?"

The woman squirmed in his grip. "Yeah, sure. Whatever you say. You wanna meet George or not?"

"Where in New Orleans is he?"

"Right downtown." The sickening pseudo-sexy look crept back into her face. "I'm going down there now. I can show you, but I need a ride."

Movie connections, huh? Jerry released her arms. "You sure he's got shots of little boys?"

"Positive. George has got everything."

The woman—she said her name was Janice—had been mercifully quiet after he ignored her come-ons in the car.

Now she said, "George don't sell his stuff at night. He tends bar."

Jerry grunted, eyes on the road. Janice continued, "I'll show you where to drop me off, but you come to this address around noon, okay?" She pushed a piece of paper across the dashboard at him.

"Whatever."

"I'll draw you a map. You can't miss it. George's place is called the Iron Hammer. It's right between an old bookstore and a sub shop."

Janice watched the road for a while, then said, "You can stay with me if you want. I'll be with my sister. She's got lots of room."

"I'll find something open." *As long as it isn't the Merrill Hotel, who gives a shit?*

"You gay? Not that I care."

"No."

"Just like little boys, huh?"

Jerry sped up, giving no indication of having heard her. After a short silence, she asked, "You married, or what?"

"Divorced." Jerry drove faster now, the speedometer flickering its way up through the eighties.

Janice looked uncertainly at the road. "Kids?"

Jerry turned and stared. The car drifted into the right-hand lane, moving toward the breakdown lane.

"You see a fucking kid here? What do you think? I keep him in the trunk?" Jerry turned back to face front, but made no effort to correct the car, which was now driving half in the breakdown lane. Ninety. Ninety-one.

"No." Her voice caught, uncertain. "I mean, I saw the dinosaur towel in the back seat and I thought—There's a bridge!"

Jerry's jaw spasmed and both hands tightened on the

wheel. If he could just hold on for half a minute, just thirty seconds, it'd all be over. Just flick the wheel to the right a fraction and let the car kiss the bridge abutment. Please.

He squeezed the steering wheel until his knuckles turned bloodless, pasty white. Janice screamed and twisted sideways as though that would save her, but she needn't have bothered—he chickened out again. Still didn't have the balls. He slumped back in the seat, lifted his foot off the accelerator and pulled the car back onto the highway.

Without taking his eyes from the road, he said, "Just shut the fuck up, okay?"

He could have gone anywhere, should have gone anywhere else. But like a moth drawn to the flame, he walked into the Merrill on Bourbon Street.

The lobby was unchanged—either that or it was like so many other lobbies he had seen over the past two years that he couldn't tell the difference.

They might be full—he half hoped they were. But even if they weren't, what were the odds they'd give him Room 327? And even if they did, he could just leave, go somewhere else.

"Single or double?" asked the woman with the tall hair and professional smile.

"Is Room 327 available?"

The woman blinked, but tapped on her keyboard.

She smiled, frowned, then smiled her desk-clerk smile. "It's available, sir, but not at the rate on the sign outside. It's—"

"I'll take it."

Her smile faltered, recovered itself into the frozen faux friendliness of a helplessly angry clerk. "—Available-at-the-

corporate-rate-of-two-hundred-twenty-dollars-a-night-how-
many-nights-sir."

The same room. "You still have a pool?"

"It's November."

"Same place? Around back?"

"It's November, sir. The pool is closed." Her smile disappeared and now her eyes faltered, sliding to a side door
and back.

Room 327. "Visa okay?"

In the elevator, he could barely breathe.

The room looked down on the pool, as he knew it would,
but the pool was covered and no loungers were out. Jerry
turned from the window and opened the pint.

Jerry pissed himself during the night, but at least he didn't
have the dream about the goddamn fortune teller again.

He showered and packed his bag. At the last minute he
went back and left ten dollars on the dresser for the chambermaid. The mattress was probably soaked with urine.

The Iron Hammer was supposed to be at the other end of
Bourbon Street, beyond the tourist bars and T-shirt shops.
Except that when he got to where Janice's directions said it
was, a fortune teller's shack stood between the bookstore
and the deli. No name or business sign showing, just a silhouette of a turbaned woman leaning over a ball, presumably glass. How many times had he seen this same silhouette
in dreams?

This was the end of the trail, then. Same hotel, same
room, same fucking fortune teller. No dream this time. And
all he had to do was walk in.

He sat in the car, tapping his thumbs on the steering
wheel. He watched as two girls, about ten years old—as old
as Andy would have been—came out of the deli, each car-

rying a bag of chips and a plastic bottle of soda. He checked his watch. Noon.

What the hell. He moved quickly up the unpainted stairs and opened the door without knocking. He stood in a long, dim hallway, familiar from his dreams. Dark wood paneling lined the walls, and a dirty maroon-and-cream Persian rug covered the floor. The only light came from a partially opened door halfway down the hall, where he knew she would be sitting.

He went in and sat at a small round table. Directly across, leaning over a glass ball, was a woman built to match the silhouette on the sign outside.

The room, already so dark that the walls weren't even discernible, darkened further.

Jerry waited, then heard his own voice. "Time, Andy. I'd like to go up to the room now."

Andy rolled over backward in the water as if he hadn't heard a word. He disappeared for a minute, then surfaced, flailing his arms and sending water splashing toward Jerry's loafers. His hair lay plastered to his skull, looking like a carrot-colored bathing cap.

"Time, Andy."

"Five minutes?"

"I already gave you five minutes. Let's go."

"The room's no fun. I can't even watch TV."

Jerry swirled the empty ice cubes in his glass. Any hint of whiskey was long gone. "Nope. Have to go, little buddy. Tell you what, though. You can stay a while longer."

Andy lit up and swam to the edge of the pool. "Thanks, Dad!"

"But I'm going back up."

Andy hung on the lip of the pool. "You mean I'll be alone?"

"No, I'll sit by the window." Jerry pointed vaguely toward the hotel. "I can see the pool from up there."

Andy looked doubtful. Jerry put Andy's dinosaur towel on the lounger. "Look, I'll be back in half an hour. If you want to come back up before then, just take this towel off the chair, okay? I'll see it and come get you right away. But don't leave the pool area without me. It's not safe to walk around by yourself." He smiled. "Got it, bud?"

"Okay. Can I have a kiss first?"

Jerry glanced around the pool. Two men in Bermuda shorts and T-shirts were lounging at the far end. They couldn't have heard, weren't even paying attention to what was going on, but still . . . "You're eight years old, Andy. A little old for that stuff, don't you think?" Jerry held out a hand. "Shake."

Andy ignored the hand, pushed back into the pool.

"I mean it, Andy. Don't leave this pool area unless I'm here."

"I said okay, didn't I?"

"See you in half an hour."

Jerry endured the long walk into the lobby, the wait for the elevator, the slow ride up. He unlocked the door, stepped across the room, and pulled aside the blinds. Looked down at an empty pool, at two men hustling a small redheaded boy into a dirty white van waiting in the parking lot. He could just make out the faded logo on the van: *Robeson Cinema.*

Staring, not believing. Turning to run downstairs.

And seeing Andy in the doorway.

A ten-year-old Andy. The age Andy would be today if . . . if . . .

"It's not your fault, Dad."

"I—"

"I'm all right now. I didn't hurt very much, and I'm not hurting now. I just can't see you anymore."

"Andy—"

"It's all right, Dad. You can stop looking for me. I'm not here anymore."

"No! Give me a kiss!" Jerry ran toward his son, tripped over his briefcase, and fell to the floor. His underwear was wet, Andy was gone, and he was back in Room 327. He pounded his fists on the floor. It was the damn dream again. It felt so real this time. How could it be a dream? It was so fucking real.

He lay there in his warm, wet underwear, unmoving, unable even to cry.

He'd dreamed it all. This time he almost got to kiss Andy good-bye, and it was only another dream.

He stood up, wiped his dry eyes. It won't fool him again. Let it try to make him stop searching. Try to trick him with a forgiving Andy. Andy would never forgive him for leaving him at the pool, for not kissing him before going away. Never. He's out there, somewhere, waiting for me to find him. Waiting for that last kiss.

But, just for a minute back there, it felt good to be forgiven. Andy sounded like he meant it. More this time than in the other dreams. Maybe because he was in New Orleans. Right on Bourbon Street. Maybe Andy never made it past this street. Maybe Jerry couldn't track Andy down, not because he was a shitty detective, but because there was no longer an Andy to find.

He showered and packed his bag. Just like in the dream, he went back and left ten dollars on the dresser for the chambermaid. The mattress probably *was* soaked with urine.

He drove down Bourbon Street, and this time the Iron Hammer was right where it was supposed to be, next to Moe's Deli. Jerry watched as two girls, about as old as Andy would have been, came out of the deli each carrying a bag of chips and a plastic bottle of soda. He checked his watch. Noon.

Jerry knocked on the front door of the Iron Hammer.

"We're closed." The voice inside was large, angry.

Jerry knocked again, louder. "Janice sent me," he said to the door. Another moment and it opened.

"You better not be a stinking cop, or you and Janice are both fucking dead. Stupid bitch." He spat on the porch. "What you want?"

"Got anything with redheaded boys?"